PRINCE OF DARKNESS

REALMS OF LORE: FAE

AMBER THOMA

The Fae
Master Upridge's Cave
Nocturia Mountains
Nightfell
Borderlands
The Falls
Lunarmist
Ebonmere
Night Court
Cresctaria

Realm
Solarath
Falling Star Coven
Crystal Coven
Owed Crescent Coven
Daybreak
Day Court
Flarimmar
Silver Moon Coven
Mystic Fate Coven
Coven of Remembrance
Anini's Village
Temple
Cauldron Coven
Southern Day Court

For my sister friend
From the window—to the wall.
Skeet, skeet.

Dear reader,
If you're reading this it means you are about to read my book, Prince of Darkness. Thank you so much for picking it up and traveling to the Fae Realm with me! I hope you enjoy your adventure! While this story is a work of complete fiction Please read the trigger warning below to make sure this book is right for you!
Happy reading!

Amber Thoma

PRINCE
OF
DARKNESS

CONTENTS

Also by Amber Thoma:

One
ETAIN

Etain checked her satchel one last time and sighed deeply. This is not what she wanted to be doing tonight. Grabbing her bag, she went to the front door of her two-room home and glanced up at the sky. She was hoping her calculations had been wrong. Another deep sigh escaped her as she watched the red creep across the full moon, slowly becoming a blood moon in front of her eyes. Her calculations were, as usual, correct.

On one hand this was good. She needed to collect multiple potent herbs, plants, and fungi that were only harvestable under a blood moon. When it rose in early fall, like now, their medicinal properties were at their strongest. On the other hand, the veil was the thinnest and that meant the magical folk were going to be out, and they would delight in her torment. She would need to be extra vigilant, looking for traps and the creatures that hide themselves in the shadows. She grabbed her long, dark green cloak hanging next to the door and draped it around herself. She hoped it would help her blend in with the shadows and help her survive the night unscathed.

As she began her trek to the edge of the woods, she chided herself for being a fool. Going out alone on a night as dangerous as this one to forage in the woods was not her best idea. She was sure to make noise and draw unwanted attention. There was nothing to be done for it; she needed the medicinal ingredients. The people of Havenston never truly cared for her, and lately they have been growing "suspicious" of her "activities".

The new religion showed up several years ago and bit by bit sunk its claws into the people of Havenston. The town's people have always been wary of her and her mother. However, over the last couple of years it started making the townspeople fear witches, or more precisely, Etain.

It did not matter that she grew up with a good portion of the townsfolk. Just like it did not matter that her mother had delivered most of them when they made their way into the world. She herself helped Nessa deliver her third baby not even two nights ago. Nessa had once been a friend, and the two had played together for most of their early childhoods. Until one day, even Nessa looked at Etain with fear and wariness in her eyes. It pained Etain to have been asked to leave their home immediately after the baby was born. She was not permitted to hold the sweet little girl she had just helped usher into the world.

A long line of Walsh women cared for this town as far back as it has existed. Where they were once celebrated, she was now a pariah and likely the last Walsh witch to exist. At two and twenty and still unwed, the prospect of children seemed out of the question, particularly when not a single man would come close enough to her. Well, she supposed that was not entirely true—there was Seamus after all. He was convinced he had been sent by the "God of Light" and needed to save her from her "devilish ways," whatever that meant.

Seamus was attractive enough, she supposed. Tall and wide with sandy blonde hair and brown eyes that used to be filled with warmth, but now held brutal coldness instead. He inherited his father's farm two years ago after his father fell off his horse. There had been nothing Etain could do to save him. Shortly after that, Seamus began calling on her again, if that's what you could even call it. He would show up at inappropriate times in the evenings to tell her how "wicked" she was. How she should fall to her knees and ask someone—*perhaps him*—for forgiveness of her sinful ways. It did not seem to matter how often she asked him to stop frequenting her door, he always came back. Lately, he had grown bolder and attempting to shove the door open and force his way in. His eyes had taken on a dangerous glint that made her wary.

They had grown up together. As children, she thought they would wed and start a family some day. Seamus even officially courted Etain for a few years before her mother's death. Not even a few months into their courtship, the Shepherd began to dig his claws into Seamus' mind. Little by little, he began to exude a wild fanaticism for the "one true God" and the "Beings of Light". From what he told her of his religion, she thought the Shepherd was a liar and wove these tales of doom and gloom to give himself power over the townsfolk. To what end, Etain had yet to figure out.

The Shepherd was the harbinger of the new religion, the one who claimed to speak for the "God of Light". He showed up swiftly one day, and not too long after that, the people of Havenston had begun to listen to his sermons about the "Beings of Light" and their God. He had worked quickly to win their hearts, though it was not too hard for him considering he went house to house and made everyone's gardens flourish. Since many were struggling to survive after the hard winter, it appeared to be an act of God. Etain was not impressed. It was obvious to her that he held some form of plant magic, which made her even more cautious when it came to the Shepherd.

She scoffed at the number of times she had tried to bring Seamus back to his old self. It usually ended in a rather public argument that left him in a rage for several days. He always claimed it was entirely due to her refusal to obey him as well as the embarrassment she caused him publicly. During the last argument of their courtship, Seamus declared they would be married the following week. Once married, he would make sure she followed the words of the Shepherd so they could both ascend to join the "Beings of Light". He did not take kindly to her bold and vehement denial of his proposal and his so-called "Beings of the Light" in front of the entire town. He changed dramatically over those couple of years, going from a kind, stoic young man to a hard, angry man who had become increasingly violent. No, Seamus was *not* an option. Even a witch had to have standards.

Etain's very public refusal to marry Seamus had not helped endear her to the people of Havenston. For now, the town depended on her expertise to deliver their babies and fix their ailments. In the few instances where she could do nothing to prevent death, she noticed the whispers around her becoming just a little louder, and the "suspicions" seemed to grow further. It was as if they thought she had done something to bring along death, not the illness or injury that happened before she arrived to help.

She never went to listen to their Shepherd preach about their God and the "Beings of the Light," but she heard some of the lies he spread about witches. She even heard about some witches being burned two towns over. And for what? Man's interpretations of a God? As if witches would ever harm another. It went against their very beliefs to uphold the balance the land demanded and celebrate the gifts of nature the Great Mother gave them. And who did these men think they were, daring to be the voice of a God? She thought it wildly presumptuous; she would never deign to speak for the Many Faced Goddess.

He should be reminding the town to be wary of the wild places, especially on nights like tonight. Instead, the Shepherd had been attempting to turn neighbors against neighbors and weaken the community by sowing distrust and jealousy. What good would that do for any of them? They relied on each other to stay safe and healthy, even more so during the hard months.

She knew the townsfolk wanted her to leave. Where was she supposed to go? It was not as if she could fold up her home and take it with her. Besides, her constant state of exhaustion was sign enough that they still needed her even if they did not want her. For now she knew she was safe. However, it was uncertain how long she would remain that way. She desperately missed the feeling of belonging.

Nearly two years ago her mother passed away. While she had been lying on her deathbed she told Etain to prepare herself, for in her lifetime Havenston would become unsafe for her.

"Where would I go, mother?" Etain asked. Her mother looked at her hard for a moment, and she thought that was going to be her only answer. Her mother often used silence as an answer, as if telling Etain to use her brain like the intelligent witch she raised. Finally, her mother spoke and said something completely unexpected.

"When the town feels like it has reached its tipping point, seek shelter with the fae. It will be a different and equally dangerous life, but at least there you will have access to your full power and magic, not the nothing we have on this side of the veil."

Etain looked at her mother as if she had lost her mind. "The fae? Mother, you cannot be serious! You have taught me my whole life to avoid the fae at all costs. I will be eaten alive there!"

This time, when she pointedly looked at her, silence was her answer. It was the last time they were able to talk about the future and how she was going to survive it. Her mother slipped away quickly after, and with her went Etain's sense of security and belonging. She spent many nights lying awake, considering her mother's words. Had her mother really thought the mortal realm would pose such a high risk to Etain that she would need to cross the veil and learn a whole new way of life? The idea of having actual magic in the Fae Realm filled her with a ball of nervous energy that fluttered fiercely within her stomach.

She was more than curious about the power she read about in the family grimoire. It was a book passed down generation after generation that detailed the lives of the witches that came before her. The earliest entries contained spells and recipes that required the use of magic—nothing Etain could even comprehend.

It also held the stories of long ago wars in the Fae Realm. Like her ancestors using their full magnitude of power to aid whichever side they had aligned with to preserve the balance the realm needed to survive. It was like something out of a fairytale. She believed all of it because the book itself was magical. No matter how many entries were made, the book only grew and never ran out of fresh pages. That alone was proof enough for her.

Standing at the edge of the dark forest, she could feel the magic bleeding from the veil. It felt raw and primal, with an unnatural stillness that had the little hairs on her body rising. Yes, she knew better, yet she also knew she needed to ingratiate herself with the townsfolk for a little while longer. At least until she figured out how to survive the upcoming societal shift. She was attempting to be seen as an apothecary instead of a witch. Plant medicine seemed to also be from their God, so maybe they would not get the idea of mounting her to a stake anytime soon. Unfortunately, it seemed being a woman who did not follow the popular religion, and ran a business was just as bad as being a witch.

Running to the other side of the veil would be a last ditch effort, no matter how tempting her magic might be. She was not sure what she feared more—the townspeople she knew well or the fae she had only ever read about. She felt as though she were stuck between two impossible choices and almost wished fate would intervene and choose for her. She let one final, exacerbated sigh out before she pulled her cloak's hood over her dark auburn hair and entered the woods.

She wished now more than ever that she had the power her ancestors once held. For now, the only thing she could do was send up a prayer to the Many Faced Goddess and ask her for protection.

Two

CIARAN

The Wooded Veil Tavern in Ebonmere was louder than usual, filled with wicked glee for the upcoming hunt. The veil thinned only near this one particular village in his court during the Blood Moon once per year. They did not have the pleasure of hunting across the veil without the prospect of running into one of the Day Court's pompous pricks, except this one wickedly wonderful time of year. Typically, the veil thinned in the Borderlands, making it fair game for all in the realm. When the Human Realm had its longest day of full sun, the veil thinned in the Day Court, making it the one time the Night Court could not cross. He assumed this was to ensure a balance of some kind.

This was promising to be a much needed and enjoyable night for Ciaran. He was still in a foul mood from yesternight's council meeting. Royad, one of Ciaran's council members, was beginning to gain support from the others in his quest to wed Ciaran to his daughter, Leona. Royad was using the current conflicts with the Day Court to pressure him into marriage, which would strengthen the Night Court and allow Ciaran to ascend the throne as king. Little did they know that unless

Ciaran found a way to break the curse he inherited, it would not strengthen the Night Court at all. He was unable to speak of his curse to any other soul besides Kes for some reason. Whenever he tried to discuss it with anyone else, his mouth would simply not open.

Leona was vicious enough, and Ciaran supposed she was beautiful in that dangerous kind of way many in the Night Court coveted. However, she did not fulfill the requirements of the ridiculous prophecy—the prophecy that would apparently lead him to end this curse. The Many Faced Goddess refused to tell him outright exactly how to break it, instead giving him a prophecy to fulfill in order to become the true King of the Night Court. Like a curse was not enough to deal with. This pissed him off to no end; he found the shifting woman to be incredibly difficult.

The council likely thought him mad, and not in a good way. To them, there was no reason Ciaran should not be doing everything possible to take the throne. If only they knew how hard he had been trying for hundreds of years to find a way to break the stupid fucking curse. He was not sure how long the curse had been plaguing his ancestors or even why they had been cursed in the first place. He held no doubts members of his council were making moves behind his back, thinking him unfit to rule. He was only waiting for them to show their hands.

The Night Court had been without a true king or queen for multiple generations, and it was beginning to take its toll by weakening the Night Court as a whole. It had been going on so long that the members of his court had forgotten what it was to have a true king. He wanted nothing more than to tell the council about this stupid fucking prophecy and this equally stupid fucking curse plaguing him. The only other soul who knew of it was Kes, and that was only because he had been there. He sat right next to Ciaran when she burdened him with the damn riddle of a prophecy.

"Care to make a wager, cousin?" Kes asked as he returned with their next round of drinks, pulling Ciaran from his thoughts.

"Careful, consider who you are wagering against," Ciaran said with a cruel smirk and more venom than was likely necessary. He could not help the foul mood he was in.

Kes laughed at him in that carefree way he seemed to go about everything. "Cousin, I would never forget who I am dealing with—you make that impossible. I was simply suggesting a little fun. You do remember fun, right?" He smirked at Ciaran, who glowered back.

"The wager?" he asked.

"Whoever returns with the most fascinating prey wins!" Kes exclaimed with more excitement than was necessary. He considered his cousin's wager.

Kes was possibly the most dramatic and theatrical member of the Night Court. It made him all the more ridiculous for he was also one of the most terrifying fae in appearance. His bird-like features were unsettling, with his inky black feathered wings, legs that ended in taloned bird like feet, and retractable talons in his fingers. He also boasted feathers for hair—not just on his head—his brows were downy with the tiniest of feathers, along with his arms and legs. If all that did not terrify enough, his teeth were sharp points, and his eyes were bright red orbs set against his burnished skin. To top it all off, he was equally deadly with a sword and magic as Ciaran.

"Sounds like a fun wager, I suppose. What does the winner get?" Ciaran asked, hoping for something wickedly delightful.

"Why bragging rights, of course! For there is nothing you loathe more than losing and nothing you love more than winning," Kes said with a wink.

Ciaran released a booming laugh. His cousin was entirely correct. He was always a sore loser, even if it only happened on rare occasions. He could always count on Kes to lighten his mood.

"Why cousin, I do believe you know me all too well. It's a deal then." He raised his drink to clink it with Kes's, solidifying their wager.

Lifting his drink to his lips Ciaran surveyed the inhabitants of the tavern; beings from all over the court had come to join in this year's hunt. They were laughing and carrying on in the way only the Night Court was capable of—filled with mayhem and debauchery. None seemed to notice how precariously out of balance their realm was becoming, and the only way it could continue to exist was by maintaining the natural balance.

There was an unnatural power surge coming from the Day Court, and they were continuing to permeate the Night Court's border. Ciaran even heard of them invading the Borderlands, creating conflict with the witches, who tended to remain neutral unless the balance was disrupted. If he did not find a way to claim his throne soon as a true King of the Night Court, there would undoubtedly be war between the two courts. He thought that might be the main goal. They were fools. Disrupting the balance would harm them as much as it would harm the Night Court.

If Ciaran was unable to claim his throne before war broke out, he would not have access to his full power, and the Night Court would be at its weakest. The Day Court Queen and King knew this, and Ciaran thought it was precisely the reason they continued to push their boundaries. If it came to war, Ciaran was not sure the Night Court could survive if the power continued to be skewed in favor of the Day Court.

They were fucking idiots if you asked him. Nothing but power hungry idiots. He was surprised the land of their court had not rejected them yet. Perhaps it had, and they were somehow generating more power to make it seem as if they still held the power of their land. Kes was watching him, and Ciaran's eyes slid back to his cousin's, feeling his scrutiny.

"I see the worry in your eyes, cousin," Kes said in a near silent whisper, so it was for Ciaran's ears only. "Let us release the worries of this realm for one night and enjoy our hunt. The problems of tonight will still be there tomorrow."

Ciaran glared at his cousin. What did he know about worries? He did not have the survival of the entire Night Court on his shoulders. Never mind the ridiculous prophecy the Many Faced Goddess gave him, with a curse on top of it all. Kes was lucky to be second in line for the throne. He would never know the weight of the crown as long as Ciaran lived.

There had been a time Kes tried to fight him for the throne, but once they realized they were of equal power and Ciaran had the birthright of the crown, Kes relented and even admitted he did not truly want it. He just wanted to see how their powers matched up. Apparently, he had been furious at Ciaran for disappearing for hundreds of years. They had been close as younglings; however, Ciaran had his reasons.

"Oh do cheer up, cousin. Perhaps you will find a mortal to unleash your wrath upon this evening. What fun that would be!" Kes declared.

Ciaran knew Kes was speaking of the prophecy. The prospect of finding the one human who could complete it filled him with a restless sort of energy that buzzed inside his chest. He was more than eager to break the curse and become the true King of the Night Court. Even though he had yet to claim the title, he was still the ruling monarch.

"Now that would bring a bit of warmth to my cold, wicked heart!" Ciaran said sarcastically, letting his smile stretch his face in pure, vicious joy. It had been many years since he last caught a mortal out on such a night when the veil was thinnest and the fae could cross into their realm. Humans seem to have forgotten about the things that go bump in the night. The assorted fae that filled the tavern were more than willing to be a reminder.

Humans used to be in steady supply for his realm's amusement. The stupid mortals thought the fae could gift them immortality, riches, or any of their other ridiculous desires. The only thing any of them, including the Day Court, have ever been interested in is their own schemes and desires. The Night Court makes no effort to hide their nature from any being, while the Day Court finds joy in tricking and weaving illusions to humiliate unsuspecting humans and the lesser fae of their own court. The smart humans knew the Night Court was terrifying and lethal, yet mostly honest. The Day Court is just as lethal.

However, it is also manipulative and filled with liars parading around as do-gooders. Maybe not exactly liars, for no fae could tell a true lie.

Over the past several decades, the stream of humans has slowed to a trickle. Recently, it has come to a near stop, making it that much harder for him to fulfill his prophetic task. A human of all things would help him save his kingdom? What a complete mockery it would make of him. How could a weak human help him take his throne? They spent their entire existence in the Night Court sputtering like fools and pissing their pants in fear. Ciaran could not help the scoff he released.

"Your thinking is so loud, cousin. I would imagine the entire tavern can hear your thoughts. Come, let's finish our drinks and get ready for our hunt. Remember, this is meant to be a night of fun and debauchery. For one night, forget about the prophecy and the curse. They can be problems for tomorrow." Kes drained his drink and then raised his brow at Ciaran.

He knew his cousin was right, and it had been a long time since he had a human to wet his knives. He did truly enjoy the way their blood ran vibrantly red before drying into an exquisite dark red. Ciaran sighed and downed his drink. He slammed his cup hard onto the table in a way that gathered attention.

He loudly declared to all the beings surrounding him, "THE VEIL THINS—LET THE WICKED HUNT BEGIN!"

The entire tavern erupted in shouts of agreement and menacing joy as they drained their drinks and made their way to the point where the veil had already thinned.

Three
Etain

Etain stood and pushed her hands into her lower back, stretching backwards to relieve the tightness that was starting to turn into a sharp pain from bending down repeatedly. The harvest was proving to be bountiful. She missed her mother most on nights like this. Harvesting this quantity on her own was laborious and tedious without a second set of hands. The extra set of eyes to watch the surrounding area did not hurt either.

The night had been mostly uneventful. She could have sworn she heard the sound of a far off other-worldly cheer, sending chills down her spine in fear. The horrible sound made her feel like prey being hunted and left her further on edge. She nearly screamed earlier when a little rabbit hopped out while she had been digging up a particularly fussy evening primrose. Even after it hopped away, she was still left with an unsettled feeling. It was as if something was coming for her, and she felt eyes watching her all night.

A loud snap of a twig, or perhaps a branch, had Etain's spine straightening as a tingling sensation began to pulse on the back of her neck. She was certain she was being watched now. She began to slowly reach for her bag, still lying on the floor next to the remnants of the midnight mushrooms she had just harvested. Before she was able to grab it and attempt escape, a hand clasped over her mouth and an arm locked around her waist, pinning her arms to her sides.

"What dark ritual are you attempting out here, evil woman?" said a voice far too loud, dripping in menace.

Only Seamus was foolish enough to be that bold.

"The Shepherd told me you would be out here doing the darkness's bidding." He released her mouth, likely expecting her to explain herself or, more likely, grovel at his feet.

"Seamus, you fool! Do you wish to draw the attention of what lurks in these woods on the night of the fall blood moon? Have you no sense?" Etain whisper-yelled at the idiotic man.

"I do not fear your devil worship you evil woman! How dare you speak to me in such a way! I am righteous in the *light*, and you would do well to remember it. I am a man and therefore your master!" Seamus boomed into the suddenly deathly silent woods.

She thought he must truly have gone mad. "Seamus, I do not worship any such devil, nor are you or any man my master, you pathetic little worm. Have you truly forgotten the old ways—the things that prey upon humans? You would happily announce our location on a night like tonight when the veil is so thin? You have likely called all manor of magical folk to our exact location. Can you not feel the eyes upon us? Unhand me this instant. We must flee. Now!" she said as quietly as her rage and panic would allow.

There were still many things she needed to harvest tonight, which Seamus had successfully ruined. The feeling that something was coming grew inside her chest, along with her panic and her intuition to flee. Something powerful and wicked was nearly upon them. She was certain of it. They needed to move now, and even then, it was likely too late. Etain opened her mouth to say this to Seamus as she tried to break free from his grasp.

"You are going nowhere you demon whore, and you will mind that vile tongue!" Seamus said as he roughly threw her to the forest floor, immediately kicking her hard in the stomach. "I have been patient with you, Etain. I have tried to bring you into the light of God and save you from your dark magic ways. I will now have to purge you of the devil and fill you with God's light," he said as he kicked her again and again.

Etain felt ribs crack. She never truly feared Seamus until this moment. She never thought the boy she knew could ever be this violent.

"I will beat the Devil out of you, then you will submit to be my wife, wicked woman!" He yelled as he climbed on top of her and grabbed her by the throat. His hand wrapped all but completely around her neck, being significantly larger than her. He began to apply pressure, and it became impossible to pull air into her battered lungs.

Etain kicked her legs and flailed her arms in an attempt to dislodge her attacker. Darkness began to creep into the sides of her vision. She felt her arms and legs begin to go limp while Seamus began to pull her dress up around her waist.

"You will submit, and I will fill you with my seed of light to cleanse the evil from your womb of darkness!" He released the pressure around her neck, and she gasped in a desperately needed breath.

She croaked out a soft scream as Seamus began to try to remove her undergarments.

No! Not this, never this.

He struck her hard across the face, and tears began to fall freely from her eyes.

"Seamus *please*, do not do this. Oh goddess, please!" Etain cried out in her shattered voice, her fear and desperation clearly evident.

No, no, no, no, no...

"There is but one God, you stupid whore," he said while striking her a few more times across her face. "If this does not purge the evil from you, I will have no choice but to tie you to a stake and burn you myself!"

Etain knew Seamus had become enthralled with the Shepherd, but she was shocked by how different he was compared to the boy he used to be. She thought that boy would be mortified by the older version of himself.

Seamus went to strike her again, but he was suddenly removed from atop her body. As the darkness began to take Etain, she could have sworn a prince of swirling darkness had come to her rescue. Seamus must have hit her head much harder than she thought, because that made no sense to her. This was her last coherent thought as the pain and darkness finally took her to sweet oblivion.

CIARAN

The hunt was turning out to be a complete waste of time for Ciaran and he could only hope Kes was having as little luck as he was. The last thing he wished to do was listen to the insufferable gloating of his cousin. At this point, any prey would be interesting compared to his complete lack thereof.

He had followed the pull in his chest that began immediately after crossing the veil to this exact location. He was beginning to think the Many Faced Goddess was playing a hateful trick on him once again. Ciaran was considering returning when he heard the bellowing of what he thought might be a madman doing some ridiculous human thing. A madman would be rather fascinating. He began to silently stalk his prey, finally having a true hunt.

As he closed in on the location, his excitement grew when he noticed his prey was now two humans! He casually leaned against a tree and crossed his arms as he settled in for a show. The violence humans enacted upon each other was something he was always happy to watch.

The second human looked to be either a small woman or possibly a child. Something inside of him began to unfurl, and that thing he had been feeling in his chest grew stronger as he heard the second human speak. The feeling made him shift uncomfortably against the tree.

"...can you not feel the eyes upon us? Unhand me this instant, we must flee now!" The woman, not a child after all, said in a much quieter voice.

At least one of them had the good sense not to draw unwanted attention from the fae roaming the woods. Unfortunately for them, yet lucky for him, his attention had already been garnered.

He contemplated the cause of the pull in his chest while shifting against the tree again, feeling restless. It had all but dragged him through the woods to find the two humans who fought in front of him. It was not something he had felt before, and it was mildly unsettling. He would have to think about it later, for now, he was enjoying the performance in front of him.

The small woman had a sharp tongue, making a mischievous grin cut across his face. He thought she might hold her own in his court. He could not help wondering if these humans would hold the key to fulfilling his prophecy. He knew it was likely a false hope.

He watched as the man roughly threw the woman to the ground and kicked her hard in the stomach. Normally, he would feel nothing watching a human show like this. If anything, he would typically feel excited by such a violent display. Something began to twist inside his chest as he watched the much larger man strike the small woman. When the man began to make it clear his intentions were to take what he wanted from the woman against her will, Ciaran had no choice but to step in. The thing in his chest demanded it. He did not seem to have any control over his deep desire to harm the man. Not even the fae would take without consent. The fae are known to trick and even manipulate to get what they want. Even they, at the very least, offer the illusion of consent.

He could not understand what this burning in his chest was, but he could not stomach the violence against this woman any longer. He thought it strange, for he was no hero, yet the need to protect this woman intensified. In a blink, he crossed the remaining distance between him and his prey. He picked the man up off the woman and tossed him several feet into the base of a tree.

"As much as I typically delight in a good show of wicked violence, that was rather crass, would you not agree?" Ciaran asked the man, who was slowly picking himself up. "You are a rather large man, and she is a particularly small woman—it seems hardly like a fair fight. Perhaps you would enjoy a match against someone closer to your own size?"

Truthfully, Ciaran was at least a head taller, plus the added advantage of being fae made it impossible for it to be a fair fight between the man and himself. Not that he was ever one to fight fair anyway.

"What dark magic is this?" the man said as he finally came fully to his feet and stood up.

Ciaran knew what was coming, and he could barely contain his excitement. When the man finally laid eyes on him, it took him a blink or two to truly understand he was not hallucinating. Ciaran let his grin stretch into a too-wide smile that clearly marked him as 'other,' showing off his particularly long, sharp incisors. He counted down from three in his head.

"Whaa..wh..." The man tried to form words, but appeared unable to make his mouth work accordingly.

Spluttering. Typical.

This next bit was Ciaran's favorite part. He stretched his bat-like wings out with an audible snap, and before the man could finish his next blink, Ciaran was standing before him mere inches apart. The man let out a piercing scream—the pitch surprised even Ciaran—then promptly pissed himself and fainted. Ciaran did, on occasion, have a flair for the dramatic. Not to the extent of Kes, but he did enjoy putting on a terrifying show for humans in particular. He threw his head back and laughed a deep belly laugh. He could not wait to tell Kes about this. His cousin would surely appreciate and maybe envy his hunt.

He reached down and tapped the man's forehead, instantly sending him to the cage he had spelled earlier that night in preparation for the hunt. Turning, he cautiously walked towards the woman, who was still passed out in the dirt. Something about the way she looked, battered and dirty with her clothing askew, made Ciaran furious. The sight made him want to make the caged madman hurt for a very long time.

He brushed back the hair from her face and saw the damage the man had inflicted on her. Even with the blood, swelling, and bruising already starting to show, she was exquisite. He picked up a length of hair that had escaped her hood and rubbed the silky texture between his fingers. The unique color reminded him of dried blood. Her skin was a beautiful milky light rose expanse, and she smelled of lavender and dried herbs. There was no question this woman was beautiful.

"Hello Pet, you are mine now," he said to the unconscious woman as he picked her up and righted her clothing. A bag not far from her caught his eye. He lingered for a moment, trying to decide if he should take it with them. He could not for the life of him figure out why he cared if it was hers or not or if she would miss it. He looked down at the woman again, wondering what spell she could have placed upon him.

Letting out an annoyed huff at himself, Ciaran made the choice to pick it up and take it with them. He was so confused by his reaction to this tiny little human. It made no sense. He knew for a fact he had never seen this woman before, yet he could not help the possessiveness he immediately felt for her. Looking down at her battered face one last time, he ported them to his bedchambers.

Laying the woman on his bed, he touched one of his hands to her forehead, the other to her belly, and closed his eyes. Immediately her injuries began to heal as Ciaran pushed his power into her. He cataloged each and every one of her wounds, storing them away in his mind for later when he went to visit the man responsible. Within moments, he healed her and sent her off into a deep, restful sleep. He walked over to the basin in the corner, wetting a cloth that had been hanging over the side, and brought it back over to her. He gently began to clean the blood and dirt from her face and hands.

He had never in his hundreds of years of life felt more like a simpering fool than he did cleaning this woman so she did not have to wake up covered in blood. Frustrated with himself, he threw the cloth on the floor, draped a blanket over her, and went to leave the room. He needed to find Kes. He looked towards her one last time as he pulled the door shut, locking her in. He stood just outside, hesitant to leave her, and cursed himself again for being such a fool. He could not help it; he opened the door one more time to gaze upon her sleeping form and shook his head at himself. He closed the door again, did not give himself the chance to change his mind, and ported away to find Kes.

FIVE

ANIN

Anin flew for as long as her wings could go. They were sheer, flimsy things she wore mostly tucked around her like a gown. They tired out a couple hours ago, and she still had not crossed from the Borderlands to the Night Court. Once she got there she would need to be on high alert. A member of the Day Court was never welcomed in the Night Court.

She did not have a choice though, the Day Court saw to that. They had been hunting her for a while, and at some point they discovered she was living out her life in the Borderlands. Now Anin's only option was to make it to the veil, which would open in mere hours. She wished desperately to be able to port, but she never learned how with no one around to teach her. She needed to pick up her pace if she were to make it in time to sneak across the veil *before* the hunt officially started.

She began to run and hoped by the time her legs tired, her wings would be rested enough. She tried to save as much of her power as she could, but it was already half depleted, and she knew she would have need of it once she neared the village of Ebonmere. It would be crawling with all kinds of fae from the Night Court to hunt the Human Realm.

Just as her legs began to tire, she saw the border where she would cross and enter the Night Court. Deciding it was a good time to slow down and use caution, she stopped just before the line separating her from the Night Court. She listened carefully, making sure nothing lurked nearby. It was her understanding most Night fae did not come too close to the border. This was not surprising since it was uncommon for the Day fae as well. This, of course, did not account for the particularly vile Night fae who patrolled their border. She had heard the stories, and yet she was still willing to risk it.

Not hearing or feeling any other creature nearby, she began to slowly walk across the border. She had never been to the Night Court before and was unsure if there was some spell meant to keep her kind out. As she came out on the other side completely unscathed, she took a deep breath and then another. She was certain she forgot to breathe the entire time she crossed. She was too consumed by the fear she would burst into flames or some other form of torture from this court.

Feeling safe—well, as safe as she could feel—she unwrapped her wings from the simple dress she had tucked them quickly into earlier. She stretched them out a few times, nearly groaning at the ache building within them, before taking off in flight. Flying was useful, allowing her to move quickly through the woods without being heard. It did, however, make her easier to spot, and she feared she was flying too fast to be able to see any danger and have enough time to hide.

There was no other choice—she was running out of time. If she did not cross the veil this blood moon, the Day Court could hunt and find her anywhere. There was no other place to hide besides the Human Realm. Perhaps if she were lucky, someone from the Night Court would find her before they did. That would be an easier death.

The Day Court did not like how Anin contained a more powerful well than most of them. Not when wood nymphs were considered lesser fae, and not when the high fae considered all lesser fae worthless. It was common practice for the high fae to enslave lesser fae by striking bargains they had no choice but to make, the other option was typically death. They would drag out her pain for as long as they could, and with the depth of her well of power, she could easily live on for hundreds—if not thousands—of years.

After flying for a few more hours, her wings were nearly exhausted. There was not much time left, which made her push them to their limits. Once they faltered, she reluctantly resumed running. Just when she thought she could go no further and would need to rest, she heard the bustling of a town near by. She slowed to a silent walk until she was near enough to a ridge to spy on the activity below.

This has to be Ebonmere.

Anin nearly cried with relief; she was going to make it in time. That was once she snuck past all the Night fae crowding the streets of the small town.

While looking for the best way in, she noticed many beings entering a tavern, leaving most of the streets clear. She waited a little longer, then crept her way down. She was nearing the location of the veil and had yet to run into anyone. She thought it might be easier than she expected to sneak across to the Human

Realm. That was until she saw the several creatures guarding the entrance.

At first glance, it would likely go unseen. Well, unless you knew what you were looking for. If you did not, you would easily miss how the air where the veil thinned rippled like water and shimmered ever so slightly. By the end of the night, the entrance would close, not to be seen again until the next blood moon. The idea of committing to a whole year in the Human Realm almost had her turning around. Taking a deep breath, she reminded herself the only thing for her on this side of the veil was the promise of pain and death. An unknown life was better than no life.

Anin still only had half of her power; her body was using up any it replenished trying to ease her painfully tired muscles. Being a wood nymph meant she could easily become a tree, a plant, or any woodland creature. However, none of these possibilities were helpful. There was no way they would not question why a creature, or even worse—a tree, was making a beeline for the veil. That would be absolutely ridiculous. She decided there was no way she was going to risk something so foolish. She also knew there was no other choice and she would have to use up a great deal of power. It was no small task to create a glamour, making her appear invisible to the guards. She had to be careful because if they looked close enough, she would be visible. They could still see movement around her, like a bubble going by. Using a bit more power, she created a barrier around herself that would keep any sound she made from being heard. Ever so slowly, she made her way towards the veil; her anxiety was a living creature inside her the entire time.

As soon as she was through, she dropped her glamour and the sound barrier, which left just enough power to keep her from bottoming out. Whenever that happened, her body would force her into a deep sleep until it regenerated enough power to release her from slumber. She might sleep forever in the Human Realm, where power did not regenerate and where magic was lost as soon as she stepped foot off the lands of the Fae Realm.

She knew she needed to get away from the veil as quickly as she could before the Night Court began crossing. She was loath to use any of her power since the little she had was all she would ever have in this realm. She tried to use her wings, but they were useless and refused to do anything besides hang limply off her back. She hoped they were just too tired to work and not lost to her forever. Anin was doing her best not to panic while she ran as fast as her tired legs would take her.

She had been running for nearly an hour when she heard a great cheer come up from behind; the Night Court was getting ready to hunt the Human Realm. She started running faster, needing to put as much distance between her and the veil as possible until her body gave up, and then she would hide as well as she could. It felt like a good plan at the time; it was really the only plan, but she really should have noticed how much her body had slowed while she kept running for two more hours. She realized—too late—she had not gotten far enough away when she was tackled to the ground by a giant bird.

"No!" she tried to scream, but between the air leaving her lungs from the impact with the ground and her lack of energy, it came out as nothing more than a whisper.

As soon as it flipped her over, she was prepared to fight as hard as her exhausted body would allow, until their eyes met. Something warmed inside Anin's chest, and she was strangely relieved to be in his presence. He seemed just as confused, with his downy brows furrowed while he reached out a finger and touched her forehead. She was no longer in the woods, instead she found herself in a small cage hanging in a dungeon of what she assumed was the Night Court. She closed her eyes and leaned her head against the bars. She had been so close to freedom, now she was close to certain death.

At least it's not the Day Court.

Six

Kes

She was crammed into the small cage he left hanging in the dungeon prior to leaving for the hunt. It forced her to sit while her legs dangled out between the bars and her arms rested across the one in front of her. Kes could tell she was doing her best to give off an air of indifference, but the smell of her fear gave her away. He had to admit she was braver than most in her position. At this point, the typical Day fae he brought back would be in hysterics, yet she calmly sat there looking down on him.

"How's it hangin' nymph?" he called up, highly amused by his own joke. The nymph, however, did not look amused in the slightest. Kes did not care for being looked down on, even if it was from a cage. He flew up and grabbed the bars just above her hands before bringing his face as close to hers as the cage would allow. He was surprised when she did not recoil, most beings were terrified of him at first sight. She did not even flinch, and he wondered if he was losing his flair.

The smell of her unique scent, pine and something floral, enveloped his senses; the aroma intriguing if not overwhelming. He was distracted; between that and the delicate beauty of her face, nothing else existed. Her eyes were fully black orbs with a depth to them he knew firsthand could only be achieved by a painful past. They were enthralling and, given the chance, he could get lost in them for an eternity.

"What?" He asked, realizing she said something.

"You are an insufferable ball of fluff!" she raged. "How I would love to pluck your feathers one by one, and then use them to stuff a bed!" she said through gritted teeth. Oh, she was mad. Not just mad, but mad mad, and Kes loved it.

"So what you are saying is you have been thinking about me?" he grinned when she growled at him. She actually growled—it was rather adorable. She appeared to be struggling to respond, like her mind was slow to produce the words she searched for. It reminded him how exhausted she had clearly been when he found her in the woods.

"Only about the ways I wish to kill you! I wonder if you would roast up nicely like a chicken. On second thought, I bet you're nothing but gristle," she said in her lilting voice that only made his enjoyment grow, among other things. He never met a female, or anyone really, who was not afraid to banter with him in this way. He could do this all night.

"Oh, I think you would find me full of long... thick... meat," he said as he cocked a feathered brow. She rolled her beautiful black eyes at him. He came close to pulling her from the cage to show her just how long and thick. Then he would give her something better to do with that sharp tongue. He managed to barely control himself, something about this nymph made him want to claim her—loudly, so the whole realm knew she was his. Which was insane, he was clearly losing his feathers. He needed answers from her, and he did not think she would be as forthcoming if he lost control.

She cocked her head to the side and dragged her eyes slowly up and down his body, taking his measure. He felt the burn of her gaze everywhere it touched him. "Hmmm. I do not know, I think you'd be a little fowl, honestly," she said, emphasizing the word little and looking far too proud of her little pun.

Kes released a deep, booming belly laugh. He liked her sharp tongue almost as much as he liked her eyes.

She snapped her fingers, with their long, sharp nails, in front of his face. "Now listen up, you big bird. I have information the prince would find valuable, and I will only divulge the information if the prince is willing to take a blood oath to protect me." At my skeptical look she added, "It's about the Day Court." She tried to look like a haughty high fae. Oddly, it suited her.

"And what is it you need protecting from, my darling nymph?" he asked, wondering what could be that dangerous for a wood nymph. He did notice her well of power was surprisingly deep, and not just for a nymph.

"Apparently the Day Court is no longer satisfied with allowing me to live out my existence in the Borderlands and now wants me dead," she said, wilting a little with her words.

He gripped the bars tighter, his knuckles turning white from the strain. The thought of anyone other than him hunting her enraged him. He had no idea why he felt anything for a Day fae, however, he did know two things that confused him even more. He had never met another being like her, and if any hands—besides his—dared to touch her, it would be the last thing they ever did. There was something wrong with him, more so than normal. "I will bring your proposal to the prince, but only if you answer another question for me."

She made an exasperated sound, as if he were annoying her to no end.

"Fine. What do you wish to ask?"

"Why were you in the Human Realm during the hunt? There is no way you got there without trespassing into the Night Court; do you have any idea what could have happened to you if any other fae had found you?" He wanted to take back those last words the second they left his lips; he did not even know he was going to say them until they tumbled out of his mouth.

She stared at him for so long in disbelief with a look that clearly said she thought he was the biggest idiot to ever live. "I would think it obvious, but apparently not. I was running to the Human Realm to escape the Day Court. I was going to live the rest of my days there," she said, as a flash of emotion crossed her face and was gone before Kes could read it. She would have never been able to blend in among the humans, and he did not like she thought it to be her only option.

"It did not matter if anyone else found me, not when the alternative was death—or worse," she said, anger seeping into her words he was sure had nothing to do with him. He needed to get away from her before he marched into the Day Court and eviscerated every single fae after her. Needing to take control of himself, he put on his normal smirk and backed up, giving him some much needed distance.

"I will bring your proposal to the prince, but", he said, dragging the "U" out. "I would not hold your breath. The prince is not known for his kindness." His smirk almost faltered when her face fell, the strength she had been wearing like a shield cracking with his words. He could tell she was counting on the prince giving in to her demands. He did not like seeing the fire in her reduced to mere embers; he would do what he could in regards to his cousin.

She locked eyes with him and released a shaky breath. "Would you..." her voice shook, and she cleared her throat. "Would you make it quick then? Please?" she asked quietly.

He furrowed his brows in confusion; he had no idea what she was asking. If it were to hurry up and speak to the prince, he doubted she would be remotely nervous and would likely demand it rather than ask. It dusked on him then, she was asking him to make her death quick. Her request angered him so viscerally, he vibrated with it.

"I will *not* be killing you," he growled at her.

For the first time, fear pooled in the depths of her black orbs, and something in his chest burned at the sight. Her mask of indifference finally cracked, and a single tear slid down her face. He reached through the bars and caught her tear in his hand as it dripped off her chin. She flinched away from him as he wrapped his fingers protectively around her tear. His words were meant to calm her fears, not ignite them further. It occurred to him she thought he meant to torture her for an eternity instead of giving her death. Assuming they were the only other options available to her—and they were, or at least should be.

He looked her in the eyes. "I promise, no harm will come to you by my hand."

She finally relaxed, knowing fae cannot outright lie, and his words seemed to ease the fear from her eyes.

He needed to leave before he made her any other promises, distance would clear his mind. His madness had to have something to do with her scent, and once he got away from it he would be able to think again. Before he could leave, she reached out one of her delicate hands and placed it softly on top of his—lighting ripped through his body. They both gasped in shock, staring down at their hands. Hers was small and slender, while his was large and forged from centuries of weapons training. For the barest of moments, everything else ceased, even the incessant shouting of the human Ciaran must have captured.

She cleared her throat, breaking the spell. "Please do not leave me down here in this cage," she begged him, without removing her hand from his. He slid his out from under hers and gave himself some distance again.

"I must for now, however, I can make it a bit more comfortable for you," he said cheerfully. He really had no choice, and what if he did? What would he do? Release her to the fate she claims awaits her? He needed to find Ciaran, he would know what to do. However, there was no chance in all of the realms he would ever mention the strange urges the nymph inspired in him. He expanded the cage so she could lay down and added some pillows and blankets. He made to leave again when she pleaded with him one last time.

"Please, please do not leave me here."

He held her dark gaze for a moment before giving her a tight smile. He turned away before he could give himself the opportunity to do something foolish. He ported directly to his chamber, unnerved by the entire exchange. He had no idea what came over him down there, he had not even recognized himself.

The burning sensation he felt earlier in his chest returned, another unknown plaguing him.

Whatever it was, one thing was certain—he was *fucked*.

Seven

CIARAN

Ciaran paced his cousin's quarters while waiting for him to arrive. If Kes was not here in the next few minutes, he had every intention of calling him back from his hunt early, their wager be damned.

A surprised Kes ported into his chambers before Ciaran could act on his thoughts. "Cousin! I saw your hunt was successful. However, I do believe I have wo…" his words dropped off as soon as he saw Ciaran's face. "What is it?" Kes asked once he had a chance to fully take in his cousin's demeanor.

Ciaran looked around. He never trusted anywhere but his tower, knowing the wards were strongest there. "Not here." He grabbed his cousin and ported them to his private study. It was two floors below his bedchamber where the human woman slumbered.

"Cousin, you could have just said, 'meet me in my study,' and I would have gotten myself here." Kes said, sounding mildly perturbed. Ciaran just waved him off and glared at him.

"Well then, let's have it. Why do you look like you are about to crawl out of your skin?" Kes asked. "I saw the human you captured in its cage down in the dungeon. While he does seem like a raving lunatic, and that is always *delightful*, I did manage to hunt a member of the *Day Court*."

Ciaran stopped short. "What was a member of the Day Court doing in the Human Realm? The veil only thins in our lands on the blood moon? The creature is lucky you found it; anyone else would have killed it in the Human Realm." Ciaran's rage was beginning to boil inside of him. He was completely done with the Day Court and their deliberate disregard for the Night Court and the customs of the realm. If he did not come into his powers soon, he would have to start looking at other possibilities to check the Day Court. Perhaps the witches would lend a hand.

"My thoughts exactly, so I asked her what she had been doing, and you will not believe her response!" Kes, ever the showman, enjoyed dragging out a story. He was gearing up to make the encounter far more entertaining than it likely was.

"Get on with it already, Kes. I have my own story to tell you about my hunt," he said, as his rage was nearing the surface. Kes smartly decided to deliver the important details.

"Fine, cousin... Have I ever told you what lousy fun you are? After such a successful hunt, one would think you would be far more jovial," he said before giving him a mock sad face.

Ciaran growled at him.

"Oh, hush. I caught a wood nymph. She says she was trying to escape our realm—the Day Court, particularly. She was going to attempt to live among the humans, silly creature. She also claims to have knowledge of how the Day Court's power keeps growing. However, she will only divulge it to you with a blood oath of protection."

Ciaran contemplated this, and for one moment, thoughts of the human two floors above ceased. "What do you make of this wood nymph?" he asked Kes.

"Honestly, she looked terrified while she was running through the woods. Then, once I caught her, all the fight drained from her immediately. It was as if she had been thoroughly exhausted before the hunt even began. The most outrageous part of the whole ordeal is when she realized who caught her—she was surprisingly looked relieved! Oh, the blow to my ferocious ego, cousin! Am I not terrifying after all?" Kes bemoaned.

Ciaran arched an eyebrow, indicating his patience for his cousin's antics was wearing thin.

"I do think there is some truth to what the nymph claims. How helpful her information will be is yet to be seen. I cannot imagine how it would hurt to find out. Though her power was fully exhausted when we met, I could feel the depth of her well. She is rather powerful—odd for a wood nymph."

"Perhaps we can use other means beyond a blood oath to get the information. I do not enjoy being beholden to anyone, especially a Day Court member," he spat.

It was indeed strange for a wood nymph to be as powerful as Kes led on. A small well of power and some earth magic to manipulate the woods they lived in were all they typically possessed. Who was this wood nymph, and why was she running from the Day Court?

Kes looked thoughtfully out the window into the night sky and the city below. He wore a faraway look, as if he had drifted off somewhere lost in thought. He quietly replied, "Yes, perhaps something could be worked out." He turned and faced his cousin, snapping himself out of wherever his mind had just gone before saying, "I will enjoy questioning her and figuring out the puzzle of the powerful wood nymph who deathly fears her court."

A devious smile split his face. "You should hear the absolute filth she spits from her wicked mouth. It is positively enchanting. Now, cousin, do tell me what has you on edge after such a successful hunt. I dare say while the look on your face is amusing to me, you seem to be troubled. Out with it."

Ciaran growled his frustration again, and Kes smirked. "It looked as though the hunt was going to be a complete waste of my time..."

While Ciaran told his cousin about the events of his hunt, he watched Kes's face go from outright amusement to complete confusion.

"You mean to tell me, my cousin, the Prince of Darkness intervened? You stopped the human you have down in a cage from exacting violence upon a human woman, something we have watched with outright wicked glee in the past?" Kes laughed, likely at how ridiculous Ciaran's behavior had been. "Where is this other human? I only saw one in your cage."

He stopped to scrutinize Ciaran. "Are you ill, cousin?" Kes asked. It appeared to be the only possibility for the dramatic shift in Ciaran's behavior.

"Yes, that is exactly what I have been trying to tell you. For some reason, I could not stomach the violence against this particular human. It caused a strange pain in my chest to watch her be abused. When the man began to make his intentions clear—he was going to take what was not his—my body took over. Suddenly the human man was thrown against the tree, and I was overcome with the need to bring him the pain he made her feel. Kes, she makes me feel. The only explanation is that she must be the human for whom I have been searching. I have never felt anything like this before; it's quite unsettling."

As Ciaran said this, he could feel the shock all over again. He gave his cousin an almost sheepish look when he said, "I did not know what to do with her, so I took her to my bedchamber, healed her, and sent her into a deep sleep."

Kes's jaw nearly hit the floor. "You did what?" And then, to Ciaran's utter annoyance, he began to cackle. "You... have... a human... woman... in your... bed? That you have healed and cared for," he said in between laughter. He took a deep breath, then said, "Cousin, have you found your mate in a human woman, of all things? Oh, I cannot wait until the council gets wind of this!"

Kes began laughing again, and Ciaran did the only thing he could think of; he punched his cousin as hard as he could in the face. This only made Kes howl with more mirth, while Ciaran wore a deep scowl.

Kes was obviously joking with the mate comment. Neither of them believed in such things for themselves. Ciaran had only ever seen one mated pair, and it was just once. He did not know what this was between him and the human. He hoped she was the human who would help him break the curse. He was willing to bet the Many Faced Goddess had her hand in this mess.

Ciaran sighed and glared at his cousin as he continued his dramatic mockery of Ciaran.

Eight

Kes

"Kes, enough of your antics. You act like finding your mate is commonplace, and she's human. Impossible! Humans do not have mates. I think this whole situation has been influenced by the Many Faced Goddess. Perhaps my search for that particular human is over. The entire time I was hunting, I followed a pull I felt from within my chest. It led me directly to where the two humans were… Well, let's just say the human in the cage will be regretting his choices in the very near future," Ciaran growled out, glaring at Kes with obvious annoyance and a rage that had nothing to do with his *antics*.

At the mention of an unseen pull, Kes's laughter quieted. "Hmm, perhaps this is the work of the Many Faced Goddess. Do you feel the pull towards her even now?" he asked, in all seriousness—for once.

Her prophecy had been vague, and she seemed to only speak in riddles. Kes was of the mind she did so on purpose, as if this curse were a game to her. She always had her hands in everything, weaving their fates together into a tapestry of her own design. Kes grimaced at the thought of the goddess and her meddling ways.

"Yes, but the urgency has left," Ciaran replied. "It's more of an awareness of her location now."

Kes considered this for a minute, his cousin had just described the exact feeling he had now, too—an awareness of the general location of the nymph at this very moment. The urgency he had felt all throughout the hunt vanished as soon as he placed her in the cage. The same one he had struggled to leave her in. It was not so much the cage as the location of it that bothered him. He would need to devise an excuse to bring her to his chambers where he could keep an eye on her. He left her next to that raving lunatic, and for some reason, the man's proximity to the nymph drove him insane.

"Well that's all fine and dandy, but it still does not explain your near revenant treatment of the human woman. Tenderness—that's what you were doing, Ciaran. You, the Prince of Darkness... *tender*." Kes threw his head back and laughed at his cousin. It really was comical to picture his cousin being tender to a being in any realm.

He hoped keeping the attention on his cousin's strange actions would distract him from noticing Kes' own unusual behaviors. He did not trust his own mind when it came to the nymph. Any other time, he would have delighted in the bloody torture and slow, inventive murder of any member of the Day Court he caught sneaking about. He had been doing just that for most of his life while patrolling the border. It was an understanding between courts that one was fair game if caught, unless royalty. Not that any of the royals on either side had any desire to spend even a moment in the opposite court.

Ciaran glared at Kes. "I hope I do not need to impart on you the importance of keeping all of this to yourself? The council will already be asking questions about the nymph living in our dungeons. The last thing I need is for them to know I have a human sleeping in my chambers. I can already hear the insufferable *opinions* flowing from each of their worthless mouths. I am already dealing with Royad shoving his daughter down my throat in his ambitious desire to see her become queen. The last thing I need is for Leona to see the human woman as a threat and cause her harm, not until I can figure out who and what she is to me. Perhaps I can convince them I have taken a human pet."

Kes could never understand why Ciaran put up with the council at all. He did not need them, nor was it a requirement for the rulers of any court to have one. They continued to exist out of some misplaced loyalty to tradition. That was a concept he never grasped; because it has always been done, it must continue to be done. What a load of boggart shit! He would love to shove tradition up its own ass; however, he would follow Ciaran's lead. After all, he is the crowned prince.

"I agree, especially if the human is the key. If only we could tell the council of your dealings with the Many Faced Goddess and of the curse. That bitch could not have been more vague with her mutterings if she tried," he said, his voice dripping with disgust.

He watched his cousin drag a hand down his face and sigh, sounding tired from just thinking about what was to come over the next few nights. Sometimes he felt sorry for his cousin; the crown was no light weight to bear. However, he was always quick to remind himself Ciaran chose to bear it.

Dumbass.

"I will call a meeting so we can try to get ahead of this. Talk to the nymph and find out what she knows. Use whatever means are necessary," he ordered. Kes had to fight to keep his usual expression of "something is always funny" in place when he thought about forcing the nymph to say anything through violent force.

"Okay," he nodded and tried to think as fast as he could for an excuse to not harm her and help her get what she was asking for. "Cousin, you know I am always a fan of violence, particularly when it comes to the Day fae. However, I think we might catch more pixies with nectar, if you know what I mean." he said, giving his cousin a devilish grin.

Ciaran studied him closely, and Kes wondered if he had unwittingly shown his hand. He did not know why he wanted to keep his own strange behaviors a secret, particularly after hearing he was not the only one experiencing them. He had meant to tell him, hoping he would have a solution to his nymph shaped problem. Yet here he was, keeping it locked up tight and hidden away with everything else he wished he could forget.

"Very well," he said, narrowing his eyes at Kes. "I do not have time to deal with her myself. I will let you decide on the best course of action when it comes to the Day fae. I need to know what she knows. The power imbalance between us and the Day Court is pissing me off. If she has any information that might help us even the odds, I want to hear it immediately." Kes held

Ciaran's gaze for what was likely a moment too long before shrugging and laughing.

"Of course! What do you take me for? A Day lover?" He laughed, and Ciaran gave him one of his extra wide grins. On the outside, he was laughing, but on the inside, he was terrified. Refusing to validate any of the ridiculous notions his mind was manufacturing, he buried each one in the dark recesses of his consciousness.

"You? Not in a lifetime." The words he said and the tone he used did not match. Ciaran was always too good at seeing what most could not. Kes hoped this next suggestion did not lead to a whole string of questions he had no intention of answering.

"I do think it's worth considering her offer. She has an unusually deep well of power, and if the few moments I spoke with her are any indication, she is stubborn as well. If she desired it enough, she could keep the information from us no matter what pain we subjected her to," he said, trying to sound logical and not desperate.

"I will think on it," Ciaran replied after a very long pause. Kes needed to get out of there to keep his cousin's scrutiny from looking any deeper into his actions.

"Well then, if you will excuse me, I shall begin unraveling the story the nymph claims to have. I shall move her cage temporarily to my quarters while I question her. This will prevent anything she says from traveling throughout the palace within a single breath. As soon as I gather any real information, I shall report back to you." He hoped his reason for moving her came across as practical and not possessive. At last, Ciaran nodded and Kes took his leave to collect his nymph.

"His...?" Yeah, he was definitely fucked.

He ported back to his own quarters again, snapped his fingers, and brought the nymph and her cage to his lounge.

She startled and sat up. It looked like his nymph had been taking a nap. She still looked exhausted, and she was probably hungry and thirsty by now. He passed her a meal and some herbal water through the bars, then told her to get some rest. First night was quickly approaching, and they would have much to do.

She did not say anything as she drank all of her water down in a few gulps. He refilled her cup, and internally kicked himself for not giving her water sooner. He had never needed to consider another's well being before.

He sat on a couch to keep an eye on her—at least that was what he told himself, watching as she finished her meager meal. He wanted to provide her with a feast, yet he refused to allow himself to be that kind to a Day fae. He had a reputation to maintain, and there was no realm in which the entire palace did not already know she was here. They probably knew he was the one who brought her here, and her sudden disappearance from the dungeons would not go unnoticed.

He wondered what god he pissed off to deserve such a curse as she stared angrily at him. Their stare-off only lasted a few moments before she looked away and curled back up in the nest she created in the cage. Kes watched her sleep for a while longer, attempting to figure out what spell she could have placed on him before he fell asleep.

Nine
ETAIN

Etain awoke slowly in a bed, and for a moment, thought the whole thing had been a dream. No, she knew her sheets were not made of the finest silk, nor did her bed smell of the darkest night just before the snow fell with a touch of hearth fire.

She stilled her movements and calmed her heart to listen to her surroundings. Her mother taught her never to trust a morning when you have no recollection of the night. Listening carefully, she could hear the very distant sounds of night creatures, suggesting she must have only been out for a short period of time.

She opened her eyes just wide enough to take a peek at her surroundings. The only light was from the moon sitting high and large in the night sky. It brightly illuminated most of the room. She was in a bed with high posts of dark, near black wood and bed linens of dark blues and blacks. From what she could tell, all the room linens were the same color, and the woods were of the darkest variety. It was hard to know for sure because the moon cast strong shadows as well.

It was those shadows she was inspecting when she noticed glowing golden irises. They were floating in a shadow across the room from where she was lying. She stared at the floating eyes, and they stared back at her. It felt like hours passed when, in reality, it was only a few seconds at best before the floating eyes stepped forward. A face materialized, followed by a body—an unnaturally *tall* body.

As the male stepped out from the shadow, the moon illuminated his dark blue skin and his long, dark, oil slick hair. Every time he moved, his hair shifted from black to blue, green, or purple. It was beautiful—he was beautiful, in a cruel and deadly way. She knew he was not human. If the blue skin and ever changing hair were not indicators enough, the pointed ears, elongated teeth, and bat-like wings were a dead giveaway. Etain had never seen a creature like the one standing across the room.

She must be in the Fae Realm.

Too late, Etain realized she had been thoroughly investigating the male—more like staring—and darted her eyes back up to his. The fae male smirked his lips into a toothy grin that was too wide and showed far too many teeth to be natural. It gave him an oddly seductive, if not menacing, appeal.

Her heart rate picked up as her situation began to sink in. She felt entirely unprepared and overwhelmed. She was on the other side of the veil in a strange room, in a strange bed, and there was an exceedingly tall, blue, winged fae male prowling towards her. She knew she must be in danger, even though she had an odd feeling she was safe with this male. All the stories her mother told her came crashing to the surface of her mind, and odd feelings or not, she was in danger.

Etain moved too fast for her brain to keep up. She scooted backwards out of the bed, limbs flailing and legs tangling in the bedding, before ungracefully dumping herself onto the floor. She landed hard on her rear and groaned while trying to untangle herself enough to stand. The fae moved so fast she could not be quite sure if she had blacked out or if he really moved at such an impossible speed. She had to remind herself she was now in the Fae Realm. She would need to get used to the impossible, or she would make a fool out of herself by gawking all the time.

"You move with the grace of a newborn fawn, Pet," the stranger said in a silky, low voice that seemed to reach into her very core as he bent down to help her remove herself from the tangled bedding.

Her skin tingled every time his touched hers, and she found herself gawking at him just like the fool she knew she would be.

She looked up into his eyes, and that feeling of time stopping happened again. It was the same as when their eyes locked as he stood in the shadows. Time rapidly started again when he quickly pulled her to her feet, causing a dizzy spell. He gently grabbed her shoulders to steady her.

"The bath and necessities are through that door," he said, pointing to the door directly behind her. "There will be a fresh set of clothes for you on the bed when you are finished. I will come and fetch you in an hour. Do not make me wait, little one." He said, clearly someone used to having every order followed without question.

In the next blink he was gone, and she was left reeling. She realized she had not said a single word to the male.

TEN

CIARAN

Ciaran shook from the thrill of the encounter with his tiny little human. He watched her sleep for a couple hours, knowing she would wake soon. He had never been captivated by the gentle rise and fall of a body's breathing before. When she turned on her side and pulled her top knee up, the curves of her body became apparent. She was small, even for a human woman, yet her curves were generous. He had to restrain himself from taking her as she slept. He had this intense possessive feeling when it came to her, as if she were already his. The feeling was so strong it took everything in him not to bellow the word "mine."

He had not been able to silence the thought, and it cycled over and over through his mind while he watched her sleep. There was no way he, Prince Ciaran of the Night Court, descendant of the Mórrigan herself, could possibly ever have a human mate. Humans were incredibly fragile, and Ciaran was not known for being gentle or taking good care of breakable things.

Yet, he could not deny this overwhelming urge to keep her safe and protected. Well, from everything but himself, because he very much wanted to see how beautiful she would look as he chased her through the woods. He wanted to taste her fear, but more than anything, he wished to taste her.

Still, a human mate? There was no way. He was sure after his conversation with Kes this was the work of the Many Faced Goddess. He pondered the prophecy she had given him.

"A human will come, one of balance. They are the key to unlocking the curse. Only then will you sit upon your throne, and your true wealth of power will be yours."

That was it. That was all the goddess had given him. He could never figure out what the hell a human would be balancing. Would they be a key or find a key? How would they unlock everything Ciaran had ever wanted? It was infuriating, and with the arrival of his little human, the questions were ever growing.

He knew the exact moment she woke because her whole body went still. He was impressed with her ability to stay calm and take in her surroundings. Had he not been watching her, he was not sure he would have known she had awakened. He moved himself into one of the deeper pockets of shadows across from the bed and then removed the glamour that was hiding him from her sight. The second her eyes connected with his, time stood still.

Her rich brown eyes, flecked with gold that sparkled in the moonlight, widened as he strode towards her. The scent of her fear began to permeate the room. He had never smelled a scent so alluring. It made him wonder what she would smell like if she had other strong *emotions*.

It took everything in him not to laugh hysterically at her chaotic exit from his bed. He liked that she seemed more unsettled than him. He could tell she knew what he was, which made him even more curious about the life she lived in the Human Realm. The humans that visited his court over the last several decades seemed to not remember the fae. He expected her to scream at his touch as he helped to disentangle her, feeling a mild buzzing under his skin each time they made contact. He was surprised and only mildly disappointed, as she merely stood there and looked way up into his face. He must be two or even three full heads taller than her, and his hands nearly wrapped the full width of her shoulders as he steadied her.

She was such a small human, yet she was obviously quite brave. Tiny yet fierce, Ciaran could feel a well of power growing within her that made him all the more curious. Even with that well of power, there was something about her small stature that made him feel protective. Yet he could tell she had never needed someone else to fight her battles, not until that moment in the woods. Her shock that the man had laid his hands on her was visible, as if it never crossed her mind that he would do such a thing.

He could feel her trembling under his touch and knew she must be feeling confused and overwhelmed. That's why he gave her instructions and swiftly left the room by porting to his study and messaging Kes. He wanted her to regain her balance and courage, though he mostly wanted the fire burning within her to make an appearance.

Again, he found himself making concessions for this human and her well being. This was the worst form of torture he had ever known; he didn't even recognize himself. Pulling out his spelled parchment, he wrote a message to Kes.

My study. One hour. Bring your wood nymph. I will bring my human.

He ordered a small feast to be sent to his study in an hour's time, thinking his tiny human must be hungry by now. With a little less than an hour until he went to retrieve his pet, he began pulling all the books he had on mates.

After several minutes, there were only two books to show for it. Most of his books were about war histories and strategies, torture techniques, spells, and the more modern histories of the two courts. He was looking for anything explaining how one knew if another was their mate. He also wanted to know if it were possible for magic to create this unrelenting need to protect another. He was skimming through the first book when Kes appeared.

"So, I get to meet your human?" Kes said, wearing a grin full of mischief and open mockery.

Ciaran glowered at his cousin. "Yes, but if you try to harm her in any way, I will not be held responsible for my actions."

Kes rolled his red eyes. "You wound me, cousin!" he said with his typical theatrical flair. "I would not dream of harming your precious," he said, pausing for his usual dramatic effect. "Mate." He snickered, making Ciaran even more agitated. His cousin knew all the ways to get him riled up.

"I do not understand, though, why you wish to bring the nymph to this so-called 'meeting'." Kes used air quotes when he said the word meeting, as if it were not in their best interest to figure out both of these females.

Ciaran checked his hourglass before responding to his cousin. "I am not convinced she is my mate. Perhaps she is just an infatuation that I will grow bored of soon enough. Or perhaps this pull toward her really is as simple as fate bringing me the human that would break the curse. As for the nymph, I need to be around her to see if I find her trustworthy enough to have her tied to our court in any way."

He noticed the way Kes stilled when he spoke of the nymph. His hands clenched as if he were either ready to be rid of her or if he were willing to fight to keep her. It would be interesting to find out which.

"Plus, I like the idea of bringing both females together to see what happens. Perhaps they will each give up information they would not have so readily. You know how much females enjoy gossiping. It might endear them to each other in a way we can use to gain information from both of them. If anything, it will be fun to watch."

Kes's body released its tension as he laughed and gave his cousin an approving grin. He vigorously batted his eyelashes at Ciaran in the way females do when they wish to garner attention. Ciaran found it horribly annoying.

Kes knew this and often used it against him when he was in one of his particularly dramatic moods. "As you say... my dear glorious Prince of Darkness," he said before pretending to swoon.

Ciaran was used to this behavior from his cousin. More often than not, he found it rather humorous. However, he would never let Kes know it. Before he could throw something at his cousin, Kes ported away.

Eleven

KES

"Hello, my darling nymph. Did you miss me?" he asked, winking at the beautiful creature raging from the cage.

He returned to his quarters moments ago and found her awake and now openly glaring at him. The complete contempt she regarded him with excited him. There was no containing the maniacal smile that spread across his face—her fire was back.

"Let me out of this cage, you overgrown turkey!" She spat at him with that deliciously wicked mouth of hers. Her eyes were wild and swarming with anger, making them all the more alluring. There was something else beneath all of that—fear of having no control over her situation.

He wondered what it would feel like if she freely gave her control to him. Could she trust him enough to bring her to unexplored heights of... His breathing became faster with all the possibilities invading his mind. He needed to stop that line of thought immediately before he required adjusting himself right in front of her. Her rage began to overtake her fear when he continued to give no response. He had not ignored her on purpose. He had been preoccupied with imagining the way her face would look when flushed with pleasure. It was an added bonus her mouth came out to play.

"Look here, you... *feather duster*. Let me out of this cage right this minute or I'll... I'll..."

"You'll what?" he asked her with mock worry.

Feather duster—that's a new one.

"Let. Me. *Out!*" she screamed, grasping the doors of the cage and shaking them with all of her might. Her efforts, while adorable, were futile. The cage was spelled, and the only way she was getting out was if he allowed it. She had only tired herself out further.

"I do not blame you for wanting to get out of there. It is rather small for such a," he said, letting his gaze travel the entire length of her. "Tall nymph." She rolled her eyes at him before returning to her attempts to set him on fire with her gaze alone.

It was just tall enough for her to be able to sit up straight. He had only elongated it enough to allow her to lay down, curled up. He knew a good part of her rage was likely from being in the cage itself. It might also have something to do with his taunts. He could not help himself, her venom was addictive.

The fae do not fear much; however, being caged in a small space was high on the list. It was made all the more so when left in one for an unknown period of time. Fae do not die easily; their power can sustain them without food or water for a very long time. The madness would set in before they finally faded away into the next life. A fate worse than death.

"I will make you a deal, my darling nymph. If you allow me to place a tracking and truth spell on you, I will let you out of the cage." There was no way she would capitulate to both demands.

He thought if he gave her two horrible options, he might be able to trick her into choosing one of them—likely the tracking spell. It's the one he would choose.

Truth spells make fae tell the entire truth without leaving any room for weaving their words in a way to mislead or give a non-answer. That sounded awful to Kes, not that the tracking spell sounded much better. If that were what she chose, he would be able to activate the spell on any map and find her exact location within the span of a breath. He thought even without the spell, given enough time, he might be able to find her anywhere in any realm.

"You must be mad! There's no way I am agreeing to a truth spell. I may as well give you full access to stroll around inside my mind. Not happening," she said indignantly.

Oh, how he would love to do just that.

"I will agree to the tracking spell, if I must, for as long as I am in this realm and as long as you are the only one able to access it." She dropped her forehead to the bars of her cage as if she could not believe what she had agreed to.

He wanted to fluff out his feathers and beat on his chest over her requirement he be the only one. It was likely a way to keep more than one being from having power over her, but a win was a win, and he was counting it. He was also actively ignoring the confusion it caused within him.

Push that directly into the "never to be looked at" box.

"Hmmm, my silly little nymph, that was not the deal," Kes said in a sing song voice. He would do whatever it took to get everything from her—and he did mean everything—but this would do for now. She glared at him, and he bet if he looked close enough, he could see flames raging in the black depths of her eyes.

"Fine," she sighed, and the fire in her flickered out completely. The sudden change was unsettling. She looked defeated, as though this was just another thing in a long line of events that, together, had broken her down entirely.

That had not been his intention; he liked her fire. If he were honest, he more than liked her fire. The idea of her fire going out because of him caused an ache in his chest he refused to name. He did not like it. When he first spotted her in the woods of the Human Realm, he could not tackle her the way he would have tackled any other Day Court fae. Something within him, even then, refused to harm her. It appeared Ciaran was not the only one with new feelings.

He could not figure out what was causing him to react to her in such a way. Nothing about any of this was natural. He was a Night fae and she a Day fae. He should feel nothing beyond a desire to cause her pain, yet instead he cared about things like keeping the fire in her eyes blazing. He was not in control of whatever this was. It had been a long time since he felt as though he were not the one directing his life.

What Kes could not understand was what was causing him to react to her in such a way. It wasn't natural; it was almost as if something else was in control entirely. Just like his nymph, he did not like not being in control of himself.

Avoidance, he decided, was best in a situation like this. If he refused to examine any of it, he could continue on with his wonderfully wicked existence, unbothered by emotions.

It does not exist if it is not acknowledged, right?

Twelve

Anin

Anin could not believe her misfortune, even if it was not the worst thing that could have happened. She still had yet to recover from the physical exhaustion her near escape had wrought on her. Her power was trying to refill itself and do what it could to ease her painfully aching muscles and wings. Which was not much.

She finally lifted her head back up to look at the male in front of her. He was asking far too much, and he knew it. Sighing, she said, "I will agree to five questions about the Day Court. I will be truthful in my answers in their entirety with no misleading, nor will I omit anything to the best of my knowledge. Is this good enough?"

The male regarded her for a moment before walking up to her cage. "I will agree to the deal if you give me four questions about the Day Court and one question about you. You must answer all questions truthfully, with no omissions or misleading. However, if you do not truly know the answer to the question, the question does not count."

Damn this male. He might as well gut her and get it over with. She was feeling rather defeated and felt her whole body slump as she sighed. She had lost her fight, and she wished for nothing more than to go back home to her adoptive sisters. She missed them fiercely.

"I will give you four questions about the Day Court and will answer them truthfully, with no omissions or misleading. If I do not know the answer, the question does not count. I will give you one question pertaining to myself." There was no way I was handing over personal information to this big, feathered brute. Blood oath be damned.

"Hmmm, what is the point of being owed a question if you do not have to answer it?" he asked, giving me a smirk full of razor sharp teeth.

"Fine, you get what you want. It's not as if I have a choice. Unfortunately, I seem to be completely at your mercy, and that is the last thing I could ever possibly want. I will answer your stupid question." She felt her bottom lip begin to wobble and turned her head away from him to hide the slip in her control.

"You have a deal," the big bird said, looking rather smug.

It irritated her that she found him so damn attractive. She never cared if a being was Day fae or Night fae; fae were fae to her. She knew it was a highly unpopular opinion, and she was likely the only fae in the realm to have it. Spending most of her life with the witches was bound to leave a mark on her beliefs. Witches did not discriminate between the courts, and neither did Anin.

After the death of her mother, she had nowhere to go. When the first of the golden Day Court guards showed up in her little village, she ran. She had no idea where to go and found herself in the Borderlands. She had been lucky enough to be taken in by a coven and treated no differently than any of the youngling witches. She planned to live there with her sisters forever. She should have known fate would never allow her a peaceful life.

Every time her life felt safe, fate had a way of disrupting that sense of security and turning her life upside down. Twice now, the life she loved has been ripped from her. Never in all of her hundreds of years had she felt this low. What was the point of living a miserable existence like hers? Her thoughts continued to spiral into the gaping, dark abyss within her until she thought of her sisters. They would be angry if they knew how dark her thoughts had gone. Though she was not sure she would ever see them again anyway.

The male had been watching her the whole time she allowed herself to drift, studying her. Something in his molten red eyes told her he knew exactly where in the dark her mind had gone. He reached a hand through the bars, and with a gentleness she had not expected from him, he gripped her chin and turned her face back to him. There was a brief moment when he allowed his eyes to emerge from whatever wall he had constructed to acknowledge her in a way only someone who knew pain could.

"My darling nymph, I told you I would not harm you. The tracking spell is for your protection. If you were taken I would be able to find you, or if you decided to run off I could find you before some other creature did. I promise you they would not be anywhere as kind as I have been."

Anin thought him oddly beautiful. He was dark and menacing, and yet something about him being different enraptured her. While he was extraordinarily birdlike, his body shape and face were those of a typical high fae male. He was obviously strong in his build, and his face was chiseled and ridiculously handsome.

How can one be that beautiful and so dense at the same time?

"There are other ways to do harm, you know," she said softly. This cage, no matter how comfortable he tried to make it, was still a cage. She needed to bathe, sleep in a real bed, and eat a meal. She had run herself to the brink, and she had yet to recover from it. She watched as he considered what she said; whether he understood or not, she was not certain. He had a furrow between his brows that formed when he was thinking that she wanted to reach out and smooth.

Whatever moment had been unfolding between them, he abruptly broke when he took a step back and held his hand out for her to take. He wanted to solidify their deal, a moment that would bring his victory and her damnation. For a while she just stared at his hand, and to his credit he did not once push her to hurry nor drop his hand. Sighing and mentally accepting her new conditions, she put her hand out to clasp his.

She felt a strange current wrap around her middle finger, leaving five black ink rings on it, one further from the other four. The exact same rings marked the male's middle finger, binding them to their deal. Anin swallowed hard. She had never needed to make such a bargain before. She had always been able to get by on her own without them. She had been forced to do many things she had never done before since the Day Court began their relentless hunt. She did not even know this male's name, and he did not know hers, yet he had not only demanded but won a debt from her. Five debts, to be exact.

"I'm going to place the tracking spell now, and then we have a date," he said, as if it were the most casual thing. He switched from almost genuine to indifferent so quickly, he nearly gave her whiplash.

She watched as he murmured under his breath what she was assuming was the tracking spell she had reluctantly agreed to. She had never seen a being like him before. His dark hair was not hair at all, but feathers matching his jet black feathered wings. She was willing to bet his red eyes unsettled most creatures, though she found them captivating.

What was wrong with her? She was romanticizing her captor.

She blamed her thoughts on being locked away in a small cage with no control over her own life. It was causing her to go mad. There was no other reasonable answer.

She felt a burning sensation on the inside of her left wrist, and a black mark appeared in the shape of a triangle with three small dots of equal size underneath it. The tracking spell, a mark she would wear until he released her.

"Ah, and now I'm off. I will see you in a few moments, my darling nymph. I do enjoy a dramatic entrance." He gave her a wide smile that did not meet his eyes, and she knew he was not letting her out. He tricked her.

"I agreed to your terms!" she cried. "Please do not leave me in this box any longer." Her voice dropped into a whisper. "Please."

His overdone smile faltered slightly when some of her anguish slipped into her words. He fought some internal battle with himself before hardening his features, and Anin knew he was not going to let her out. She had given much away and received nothing in return.

"You should have specified when I would let you out." He winked at her, and she screamed furiously as he disappeared again. Silent tears fell freely from her large, black eyes, and that strange pull in her chest burned again.

She would never again trust that feathered fae. He had broken not only the small amount she had been willing to give him, but he had also broken something deep within her. Trust was not something she gave freely, if ever. Even her sisters had taken decades to earn it. She curled up into her little nest and let her mind drift back into that dark space. Fate always made sure to remind her of the one thing she seemed to constantly forget.

She was alone.

Thirteen
Etain

Etain stood frozen alone in the room for several minutes, trying to figure out what the hell just happened. He terrified her, yet when he put his hands on her, Etain instinctively knew he would never harm her.

That's ridiculous.

She had never met this fae—or any fae, for that matter. From the stories her mother told from the grimoire, the fae were the ultimate tricksters. She needed to be on guard, no matter what her instincts said. What she really could not understand was that tingling feeling every time they touched. She thought he might be using magic on her. For what, she was not sure. Whatever the reason, it definitely made her nervous.

Once Etain gathered herself, she was not sure how much time she had left. She needed to prepare for what would likely turn out to be a battle of wits. Mostly, she hoped to keep her own when she actually spoke to the fae male. She just gaped at him when he spoke to her, and she was embarrassed by the encounter. He had not seemed phased at all, and there she was, unable to form a single word. She groaned just thinking about it.

Etain's mood went even further south when she realized no one would miss her from Havenston. She wondered how long they would wait until someone claimed her home and all of her belongings. She had not had much, yet her home was cozy and it held the last remnants of her mother. Her mother had been the one to dye and embroider the curtains with the various phases of the moon and stars all around them. She made Etain her finest dress, which still hung on the peg in her room. The table, well worn by the time Etain had been born, was made by one of her ancestors many generations ago. What would happen to all of her things? The thought of all the people from her village pillaging her home made tears brim in her eyes.

Etain sucked a breath in through her nose to clear the tears and realized she was likely running out of time. She wanted nothing more than to scrub her body. Cautiously, she made her way to the door he had indicated. She was greeted by a room that was made entirely of obsidian. The tub looked like it was carved out of a giant block of the stone with intricate carvings that gave it a whimsical appearance. A waterfall cascaded over the far wall, and rivulets ran off to create little streams ending in small basins. She had never seen anything this magical. The walls and ceiling were polished to such a shine that it was like having a dark mirror reflect back everywhere you looked. In a room made entirely of black stone, she was surprised it was still bright enough to see clearly. The dark walls and ceiling reflected plenty of light. The room had a relaxing presence, and as unusual as it was to her, she loved it.

Finding a stack of linens near the fall, she contemplated only washing her face and hands. Until she found the actual looking glass and realized what a mess she was. The previous night's events all came crashing back to her in an instant.

Seamus.

He had attacked her. He had been about to abuse her in a way she was not sure she could ever recover from. Broken bones and bruised skin would heal. However, the essence that made her who she was would not heal so easily, if it healed at all. Taking stock of her body, she could not feel any injury at all. She could not be sure if he succeeded or not, and the unknown made her feel dirty and fearful. What if the blue winged giant wanted that from her, too? He could take whatever he wanted, and she would be unable to do anything to stop it.

Either way, she felt like her skin was crawling, so she quickly undressed and stood under the waterfall. She was expecting it to be ice cold, but instead it was pleasantly warm. The little alcove in the wall next to the fall housed a dozen bottles. She started to pick them up and smell them. Finding what she assumed was a soap that smelled of lavender and a hair oil that smelled of jasmine, she used both. She was finding it hard to move quickly because it was such a luxurious experience.

Sighing, she remembered she had limited time, and the last thing she wanted was for the male to suddenly appear while she was dressing. She was surprised again when she did not feel the fear she expected. Instead, the idea made her excited in a way that convinced her she was likely broken. How could she feel something like that immediately following the encounter with Seamus?

She reluctantly stepped out of the fall of deliciously warm water and moved towards the small basins to inspect the pastes and sticks. She decided they must be for cleaning her teeth, and she was pleasantly surprised by the minty taste. Feeling far more relaxed and in control of herself, she exited the bathing chamber and saw new clothing laid out on the bed, just as he had told her there would be. The chemise was a silky black, lacy item, far shorter and far more risqué than anything she was used to wearing. It stopped just past her upper thighs. She could not help but think the male must possess an overinflated opinion of himself if this is what he expected her to wear.

The dress itself was dark green velvet. However, the bodice laced up her chest in a way that allowed anyone to view the lacy chemise below. At least the skirt fell to her feet, even if it was form fitting. However, when she walked, she noticed matching slits on either leg going up enough to catch a couple inches of the black lace that stopped high on her thighs. She sighed and shook her head at the ridiculousness of it.

She felt the heat of impropriety rise in her and was sure her chest and face had turned a deep crimson. She had never felt so bare. She was also sure she had never felt such fine fabrics caressing her body. There were no shoes anywhere that she could find. He would have her dress in such a way and forget to be decent enough to give her shoes? She went back into the bathing chamber to look for her old boots and was surprised to find all of her clothing had disappeared.

She looked around everywhere, sure she had misplaced them. She recalled her mother telling her stories about the brownies in the Fae Realm. They love to clean and run a household. They do it for free and are incredibly loyal, unless you smite them. Then they could make your life miserable. Not wanting to offend, she said, "Thank you," to the bathing chamber just in case they were still around and could hear her. She gasped when she reentered the bedchamber to find the blue giant had appeared again. "Talking to yourself now, Pet?" he asked her.

"My name is not Pet, nor am I a pet. I will kindly ask you not to refer to me as such. No, I was not talking to myself. I was talking to any brownies that might have been around. I assumed they were responsible for cleaning up the garments I left in the bathing chamber. I wish not to offend them. I have heard they can be rather spiteful when provoked," she replied indignantly.

The fae was obviously trying to hold back a smile as he took in her words. "Well, what is your name then, little human?"

She glared at him. She could not be sure, but she felt like he was being condescending. "My name is Etain." She paused, trying to give him her most unapproving scowl. "You blue oaf of a giant!"

The fae stared at her for a moment before he let out a loud bark of laughter. "Blue giant to you indeed, Etain. It is a lovely name for a lovely little human. However, I quite enjoy calling you Pet. Thus, I will have to rudely decline your request." He grinned at her, and his mouth grew wider the longer she glared at him.

She was not ready to admit how her stomach fluttered when he called her lovely. She huffed and glared at him some more. Which did nothing but amuse him further. "So what am I to call you? Or shall I stick with 'Blue Giant' and the many renditions I have been circulating through in my head?"

He laughed at her again, and Etain was starting to feel like some animal whose owner found them amusing when they did silly tricks.

"Oh, I like you Pet. I think I shall keep you. And 'Master' would be an acceptable name. However, something tells me you would never use it." He chuckled at the incredulous look she gave him. "So Ciaran it is—at your service, my lady."

He gave what she could only assume was a mocking bow. It was like everything he said or did made her the object of a joke. She was desperately trying to keep up, yet she consistently found herself several steps behind.

Well, *Ciaran*," she said his name with as much venom as she could muster, "perhaps you can tell me how it is that I have come to be in your keep? Last I recall, I was in the woods being beaten and... and..." She was not sure if she should even ask, afraid of him making a joke out of her pain. She softened her voice, fearing his answer in multiple ways and yet needing to know nonetheless.

She turned slightly away from him and wrung her hands together. "Did he... I mean, was he able to..."

Moving in the lightning fast way she was beginning to think was normal for him, Ciaran was suddenly standing toe to toe with her. He gently grabbed each of her hands and placed them softly in his much larger and oddly long blue ones. They were human-like, yet they had an extra joint at the tip of each finger that was topped with long black claws that he retracted once he saw her looking. As if he did not wish to frighten her.

"No," he said definitively.

She looked up into his glowing golden eyes.

"He was not able to take that from you. I threw him into a tree before he could," he said, sounding like he threw men into trees often. "He is at this moment suspended in a cage in the dungeons, awaiting his punishment."

Etain let out a breath of relief. He could not know how much her self worth had been riding on his answer. She smiled at him softly. "Thank you, Ciaran. I am sure your kindness has or will cost me, but I cannot find it within me to be upset, and I am only grateful at the moment."

He slowly reached a hand towards her face, like she were a skittish animal he did not wish to startle. Etain's breaths grew shallow as he gently tucked a damp strand of her dark auburn hair behind her ear and brushed his fingers across her jaw before pulling away.

"You owe me nothing, my Pet." He stepped back from her quickly, and whatever spell they had been under ended. "Come—we have a meeting in a few minutes," Ciaran said, and suddenly she was nervous again.

What could that possibly mean? She was already having a hard time keeping her wits about her around one fae. How could she ever handle more? Not only that, but she had been feeling something building inside her since she woke up. She had never felt something like it before, and yet it also felt entirely natural to her. She had so many odd new feelings in this realm.

"A meeting? What does that mean?" Etain asked fearfully. Was this when he took her to his court and made her do despicable things for their entertainment? Her anxiety was reaching new heights, and it was taking all of her self control not to completely lose her sanity.

"You have no one and nothing to fear here. Well, except me," he said menacingly as he walked up to her again and wrapped his arms around her.

She was startled by the sudden contact after such a declaration. As much as she hated to admit it, his arms around her made her feel safe. That was until he bent down and inhaled the top of her head.

"Your fear smells delightful, little human."

Etain was once again reminded that he was a fae, she was in the Fae realm, and she was very much in danger as Ciaran ported them out of the bedchamber.

Fourteen

Ciaran

He was going to murder his cousin. Kes was again putting on one of his theatrical performances, only this time it had gone too far.

Kes strolled up to Etain, bowed low, and said, "It is a pleasure to meet you, my lady." Upon standing, he grabbed her hand and kissed it.

Ciaran let out a deep rumble in warning. He needed to take his hands off Ciaran's little human immediately.

Of course, Kes being Kes, found this hilarious and chuckled. "Cousin, I am simply making the acquaintance of your human. You did not tell me she was so tiny. How delightfully fragile." He grinned at Etain, showing all of his sharply pointed teeth.

"While she is rather tiny, she is anything but fragile." Ciaran glanced down at Etain and noticed his words made her stand just a bit taller. Something warmed in his chest, knowing his words were the reason why. "And where is your nymph? Did I not request you to bring her in attendance?" He scowled at Kes, knowing full well he was about to make a scene.

"Oh! Yes, of course—how silly of me." Kes snapped his fingers, and a small cage containing the wood nymph appeared in his study.

Ciaran heard Etain gasp in shock as she quietly asked, "Why is she caged?"

Before Ciaran could decide what he wanted her to know, Kes answered while he poured himself a glass of wine.

"Well, you see little Etain, this wood nymph is of the Day Court, and I found her while on my hunt in your Human Realm. The same hunt in which Ciaran found you. I caught and jailed her, for no Day Court is to be across the veil during the hunt of the Night Court."

Ciaran rolled his eyes at his cousin, then turned his attention back to Etain. "You seem to have some knowledge of the fae if you know about brownies and the two courts. Are you well versed in our realm?"

Etain cleared her throat and looked back at the nymph in the cage. He could tell it bothered her.

"While I confess I know more than most humans, I do not know anything about the inner workings of your realm. I know stories about different types of fae that have been passed down through generations of Walsh witches."

The wood nymph let out a slight gasp, and Ciaran snapped his attention to her.

"You have heard of the Walsh witches?" Ciaran asked her.

Anin's fully black eyes widened as she took in Etain, as if recognizing her. "I see it. Particularly in your hair color."

Etain marveled at the nymph, no doubt wondering at the knowledge she might hold.

"Yes, it's the one trait that has always been passed down to the Walsh women. Apparently, our magic with it," his little human said.

Ciaran looked at Etain, stunned. Though he had no right to be surprised, he had felt her power growing ever since they returned to this realm. He had apparently underestimated her. "You have magic, Pet?"

She glared at him, obviously despising the use of that name. "According to my mother, we come from a long line of powerful witches. We were forced many generations ago to live in the Human Realm. Our power and numbers diminished, leaving only me. It's believed the child of the first Walsh witch to live in the Human Realm was born in the Fae Realm, and that was why she had power. After her, none of us had a drop without the connection to the Fae Realm. Mostly, we just have plant medicine, which can aid in healing minor illnesses and injuries. Now that I'm across the veil, I'm not sure what kind of power I may have, so I suggest you watch yourself, you big blue giant!" she seethed, letting him know he was on thin ice if he continued to use the name.

Kes happened to be taking a drink and nearly spit it out. It took Ciaran all of his willpower not to laugh hysterically at his tiny witch. Power or not, there was no way she would be a match for the prince of the Night Court, cursed as he was.

He stepped into her space, causing her to look way up at him. "Yes, I am big, in every way, little witch. If you keep speaking to me with that wicked mouth of yours, I will have no choice but to take you back to the bedchamber and show you what I would rather have your mouth doing. Then, I might see what you have under that delectable dress I keep seeing tempting peeks through. The black lace is incredibly enticing." He gently ran a black claw down the side of her face and down her neck to the laces holding up her dress. He tugged on them lightly enough not to cut them, but hard enough to let her know he could.

Etain sucked in a gasp, and Ciaran could hear her heart rate pick up. However, it was not fear he could smell on her. His eyes dilated when he took a deep breath and realized it was her desire he was scenting. There was no question in Ciaran's mind that his little witch was feeling the same pull as he did. They stared at each other longer than was likely comfortable for those around them, neither of them remembering there were others in the room.

He could not care less.

That was until Kes cleared his throat in an obvious attempt to break the spell they both looked to be under. The nymph cocked her head to the side with a grin, as if she knew something no one else did.

Etain blinked and took a step back from Ciaran, who was once again feeling rather murderous towards his cousin.

Fifteen
ETAIN

Etain glanced desperately around the room, looking for anything to help settle her nerves. She could not believe the effect she was allowing this insufferable giant to have on her. Every time he touched her or their eyes met, she felt warmth bloom in her body and a distinct pull in his direction. The only thing she could think of was he must have used his magic on her somehow. It was unsettling, to say the least. She glared at him, and he smirked back. He definitely placed some kind of spell on her.

The round room was filled with bookshelves that ran along the curved walls. For several stories up, you could see ladders and balconies, which could be shifted around the room to gain access to any book. One of the balconies moved to the other side of the room. The entire thing just floated over the room two stories up without being attached to anything.

She was speechless. This was now the most magical thing she had ever seen. She glanced up at Ciaran and found him watching her with a softness she had yet to see in him. She thought perhaps he was the one responsible for the show, and he had done it just to see her reaction. It was rather incredible, if she were to be honest, and she gave him a small smile.

The only section of wall free from books was the large obsidian fireplace. The dark black seemed to devour the color and light around it. The fireplace surround was ornately carved into a scrolling design that fit the aesthetic of the room well. She could see herself curling up in one of the extra large plush chairs that were in front of the giant hearth, which was several feet taller than her.

The center of the room closest to the fire held a stately, dark wooden desk covered in several books and scrolls. It looked as if someone had been working there and left in a hurry. Farthest from the fire was a round table of the same dark wood as the desk. It was covered with a veritable feast. The moment that Etain's eyes saw the table covered in food, her stomach let out a fierce rumble.

"I had a feeling you would be hungry and had a little bit of everything delivered. I hope you will find something to your liking," he whispered close to her ear from behind.

She jumped and let out a squeak. "Do not do that!" Etain swatted Ciaran. "You cannot just sneak up on someone. It's entirely terrifying, and you move so fast and silently, it's unsettling."

He grinned mischievously. "What makes you so sure I do not wish to give you a fright, little witch?"

Yet again, she was thinking he must have done something to her because she was finding it hard to be annoyed at his little nickname. Only then did she remember the last time someone snuck up on her.

"Well the last time someone snuck up on me, it did not go well," she said casually as she walked around the table, inspecting its offerings. She saw Ciaran flinch slightly at her words before he was standing directly beside her. She would never get used to the way he moved.

He lifted her chin, so she was forced to look up at him. "That man will never hurt you again."

Etain could tell he meant it, though she did not know how he could guarantee it. She knew Seamus was hanging in a cage in the dungeon. That did not mean he could not get loose, and Etain was not sure she was comfortable with the alternative option of dealing with him... *permanently.*

"Well, let's hope not, at the very least." He looked like he was slightly offended she did not completely trust his word. If there was anything Etain had learned throughout her years, it was that fate always got what fate wanted. It rarely aligned with what she desired, so she would remain skeptical. Not wanting to talk about Seamus any longer, she filled a plate with food. Even though she had no idea what several things were, she was determined to try everything.

"Am I to be the only one eating?" Etain asked the other beings in the room. She looked pointedly at the nymph, who was still in the cage. She did not like the idea of eating while they stood around watching her, particularly when one of them was in a cage.

Ciaran and Kes appeared to have a nonverbal discussion. Kes's gaze went to the nymph, and he said, "Right then, come along my darling nymph—best behavior."

Ciaran only stared the female down. "Try anything, and it will be the last thing you do."

She held her hands up and gave him a sharp nod. Etain was becoming furious with the way the two males spoke down to the nymph.

At least they let her out of that ridiculous box.

She felt a bit of a kindred spirit with her. They were both taken rather than invited, and both wore a look of deep exhaustion from life in general. The nymph also knew about her family, which was incredibly intriguing. Etain wondered at the possible stories she might have for her. Maybe she could even help her tap into the magic she should have in this realm.

Taking their seats, the nymph sat across from Etain. She was amazed when she noticed the nymph's dress was actually her wings wrapped around her body. The way she tucked and folded them into an intricately wrapped gown was impressive.

She suddenly blurted out, "What's your name? I confess, I am growing rather annoyed at referring to you as only 'the nymph.' I hope you do not mind me asking..."

The nymph gave Etain a warm smile, and she knew the two could become good friends. Maybe even great friends if given enough time. "My name is Anin. It is a pleasure to make the acquaintance of a Walsh witch."

"You truly know my family name?" Etain wanted to know everything about her ancestors, who lived on this side of the veil and were able to use their magic. She often wondered in her earlier years what it would have been like to grow up in this realm. Etain was about to get up to refill her plate until she looked down to see it was already covered with a few things she had not tried yet. Looking around, she did not see any little creatures. It is always better to be safe than sorry, her mother always said, and just in case, she whispered a thank you.

"Cousin, I think your human might be defective. She seems to be talking to the air. Does she have a friend we cannot see?" Kes asked, laughing at her.

Etain felt her cheeks heat with embarrassment. Her fair skin easily flushed, allowing others to quickly read her feelings.

"Well cousin, she thinks she will offend the brownies if she is not polite enough." Ciaran boomed out a laugh.

Etain's face was the reddest it had ever been. She was sure of it.

"Oh little witch, we only laugh because while brownies do work in the palace, I do not let them into my tower. I do not let anyone besides Kes into my tower," he said, and then looked around the table. "Usually. The brownies would never let me have a moment's peace. I would wrong them in their eyes nearly every day. When I was a youngling, I could never get on their good side. I grew tired of dealing with the creatures and created a spell that does exactly what a brownie would do without the nuisance."

"Well, that sounds like an awful lot of trouble to go through. You could have been respectful to the creatures and willing to do what they require in exchange for the hard work they likely do. Perhaps then I would not have been made to look like such a fool."

Ciaran gave her one of his wicked smirks that seemed to always set Etain's stomach fluttering. She turned back to her plate, deciding that was far more interesting than his handsome face. The food was delicious. She had to use all her willpower not to shovel the entire plate into her mouth in one breath, as she did with the first one. While she had not gone hungry in her village, her menu was bland at best. She tried to season her food with what she foraged. However, no amount of foraging could ever make anything taste this good.

"Anin, I am curious to hear what you know of my heritage. How did you come to know a Walsh witch?" Etain looked excitedly across the table at the other female.

She was beautiful. Her skin was the palest green-yellow with flowers growing up her left leg, while a vine grew out of her right arm, wrapping around the limb and linking around her little finger. She could tell Anin's hair had once been pinned perfectly up and away from her face. Now, several golden strands had fallen in long, curling tendrils down her back and around her face. It looked as though her night had not been much different than Etain's.

"It's a rather long story, and I would be happy to tell it, though perhaps when I am more... rested." She glanced at Ciaran. "I do believe we have a deal to work out, Prince of Darkness."

Etain's eyes nearly bugged out of her head. She was not sure why she was surprised. If she thought about it, his quarters were exceptionally fine, and he had a whole tower to himself. He even had a flying library, for goddess's sake. "Prince" was written all over him. She had just been too distracted to notice. She had the strangest feeling that somehow she had already known.

That meant he really could do anything he wished with her. What if he grew bored of her and locked her in the dungeon with Seamus? Or kicked her out of his palace? She had nowhere to go, and she did not know how to cross back to the Human Realm. It's not like she could go back there anyway. There would be nothing there for her as well. She was certain her neighbors had their sights on her place, and she likely only had a couple more days to get back before her home was gone.

Did she even want to go back?

Her mother told her to come here, suggesting she thought it was the better choice. Perhaps she could find the witches, and maybe they would have her. She wondered what it would be like to live with a bunch of witches—was it like a sisterhood of some kind? That meant she would have to figure out where in this land they resided, and she would have to survive the Night Court to get there.

Etain's heart began to beat rapidly. How did she manage to keep forgetting where she was, and how much danger she was in? A fae prince was her hunter, and she needed to remember that. He took her, and he could easily discard her. She did not find it difficult to imagine a prince's heart being rather fickle. She would need to come up with a contingency plan.

"Prince of Darkness," Ciaran scoffed. "I swear, you Day Court creatures are so dramatic." He turned to look at Etain. He must have noticed the panic and fear she no doubt wore pasted across her face. "Yes, I am the Prince of the Night Court. I promise you, Etain, you can trust me. At least for now."

Etain looked Ciaran in the eyes, searching for answers. She worried his words had just given her the proof she needed to know he would be done with her, likely in the near future.

"And later?" she asked, trying to keep the panic out of her voice.

"I guess we will both find out when later comes," he said while he continued to stare into her eyes. She did not know how it kept happening—that every time she felt like she was spiraling, it only took one touch or eye contact from him to calm her. It felt like their souls were having a conversation that Etain and Ciaran were not privy to.

"Would you tell me if I should no longer trust you?" she asked breathlessly.

Sixteen

CIARAN

"**Y**es. I promise it," Ciaran replied without hesitation. He could easily tell her if she could no longer trust him, though the problem was not in *telling* her. It was the feeling he got when he thought of her not trusting him. It made him feel oddly bereft, like he was mourning the loss of her trust. Something he did not even have yet. He had never felt something like this before and knew he *wanted* her trust—*craved* it. He had no idea what was happening to him. He should be disgusted with himself, though all he felt was curiosity.

He wanted to know what this bond was they were both obviously feeling. He wanted to know everything about her, what she desired most, and what it had been like for her to grow up in the Human Realm. He wanted to learn all the ways to stir up sounds of pleasure from her while learning every square inch of her body. He wanted to know her deeply, in such a way that neither of them knew where one stopped and the other began. He wanted *her*.

He was, without a doubt, fucked.

He looked over at Kes, who was already staring at him with his jaw hanging open. He knew Ciaran never made promises and never spoke so plainly. Fae cannot lie, although they often spoke in riddles to hide their deceptions and give themselves a way out. It was an art the Day Court had perfected, and it made them deceitful in every way. The Night Court was no stranger to deceit, yet they preferred to wear their wickedness with pride. Ciaran let his confusion show for a moment, letting his cousin see he had no idea what was happening to him. He also gave Kes a slight shrug, as if saying he did not really care.

Returning his gaze back to the nymph, Ciaran remarked, "Kes tells me you have information you wish to share with me in regards to the power surges the Day Court has been obtaining. For a fee, of course."

He had been thinking about the blood oath she requested ever since Kes had brought it up to him, and he found the perfect solution. He gazed at his cousin and smirked. "I have decided you will get your blood oath nymph, only it will not be with me. It will be with Kes."

He nearly laughed out loud when the nymph and his cousin said, "What?" at the same time; both of their mouths dropped wide open in shock. It brought no small amount of joy to Ciaran's wicked heart when the two fae looked at each other. Kes's face showed every ounce of terror at the prospect of being bound to the nymph. He could not be sure if it was because Kes loathed the idea of being bound to a Day fae, or if it was something entirely different.

"Cousin, you seem *terrified*. You cannot be that *scared* of a little wood nymph, can you?" He never missed an opportunity to get back at his cousin for all of the times he tormented Ciaran with his dramatics, just to get a reaction out of him. "You will swear to protect her from any threats inside and outside our court. So I suppose you better keep the nymph very close at *all times*."

Kes's face resumed its customary look of mischief and nonchalance. "Well cousin, that is the best idea you have had thus far. I think I would rather enjoy having a nymph *close* and... *available*." Kes said while giving Anin a salacious grin.

The innuendo was not lost on anyone.

The sudden sound of a hand connecting forcefully with the table coming from Etain's seat made all eyes snap to her.

"Her name is not nymph! Her name is Anin, and yet you both refuse to use it. Am I to believe males in all realms are absolute pigs when it comes to the treatment of females? You mock her and degrade her while making thinly veiled threats to abuse her body! No one deserves to fear the possibility of molestation! I will not sit by and continue to let you abuse her in this way while you both continue laughing at her expense. Are you so full of yourselves you cannot see you both have wronged us?" Etain's anger was becoming tangible.

The tableware began to shake and clatter together while the fire in the hearth suddenly shot up several feet. The flames of the candles around the room began to grow to unimaginable heights. Etain's hair began to float around her, making it look like she was under water. The three fae looked at her in wonder.

"You stole us away. You did not give us the choice. You took that from us. Of course, I am thankful for your intervention on my behalf, Ciaran. However, you could have found a way to give me a choice. And you," Etain seethed towards Kes, "Anin was obviously running from this realm if she needed to be protected within it. Yet, you take her salvation right from under her and say she has committed a crime? She was in my woods on the night of this hunt, not yours. Then you have the audacity to put her in a small cage? Do not think me naive. I saw what a spectacle you wished to make by presenting her to us like that!"

Things were beginning to float around the room. Everything circled around them, picking up speed as she fell fully into her rage. The recent events likely sent her over the edge and into the abyss of her power.

"No one has the right to take another being's body! You may play your games and spin your illusions," she said in a low, deathly voice as a knife jerked across the air to reside under Kes's jaw, "but that is too far! It's not right! Just as it was not right for you to steal us away as if we were some prized beasts!"

Ciaran had never seen anything as beautiful in his entire existence.

Anin gently called her name. "It's alright. The fae, while wicked, do not take that without consent. No Day or Night fae would ever. We enjoy the game of persuasion far too much. You are right. They had no right to steal us from where we wished to be. However, do not forget, fate gets what fate wants."

The knife dropped to the table as the flames returned to normal and the table stopped shaking. There was a loud shattering as the objects that had been spinning around them fell to the floor, many of them breaking. Etain's hair continued to float around her as the only indication that her rage had not quite left.

"Thank you, Etain. I will not forget your kindness."

"Little witch," Ciaran called. There was no question, she was a powerful witch. She might even match him in power.

Etain whipped her head to the side to meet his gaze and glowered at him.

Ciaran smirked. "You are truly magnificent. You should see how stunningly beautiful you looked, all full of rage and power. You are correct. I had never thought of the hunt in that way. We are used to playing games and using beings for our own amusement. We forget they, too, have a life. You must understand we are wicked creatures, it is our nature. It may not be right, as you have said, but we are what we are. Living such a long life and being raised to be as wicked as possible strips us of any empathy we might have once had. This does not mean we do not feel, we do. However, to do so publicly would give the appearance of being weak. Do not doubt me when I say that in my incredibly long life, I have never seen anything that has enraptured me the way your rage just did. I have never seen anyone as wickedly beautiful as you were just now." Slowly, the rage left Etain as her hair fell back down around her.

Ciaran could not pull his gaze away from Etain if he tried. The heat that seemed to always grow when they locked eyes was becoming a near inferno.

Etain's breathing became more rapid with her growing arousal Ciaran could smell and feel coming from her. He could also feel the pull between them becoming even stronger, along with the tightening in his pants. He nearly shifted in his seat to alleviate the pressure.

Ciaran noticed the exhaustion begin to sweep across his witch's face; the display of power had nearly drained her. The power in his little witch was indeed mighty. He broke the connection before he lost control and took her on the table in front of Kes and Anin. He was positive she would not appreciate that.

Ciaran looked at the two other fae in the room. "We will continue the discussion and find terms we can all agree upon. First, I believe my little witch needs to rest." Ciaran rose, and before Etain could say a word, he picked her up in his arms and ported them back to his bedchambers.

As he placed Etain on the bed and began to cover her up, his little witch drowsily looked out the window. "Is it still night?" she asked, confused.

"It is always night here. Just as it is always day in the Day Court."

She looked back at him, and their eyes locked once again. This time, all Ciaran could feel was adoration. "Ciaran?" she called softly.

"Yes, my little witch?"

"Have you spelled me?" she asked in a near whisper, sleep coming quickly for her.

"If I have spelled you, little witch, then you have spelled me as well."

Etain's eyes began to drift shut as he leaned over and gently kissed her forehead and whispered, "You are mine, Etain, as surely as I am yours." In that moment, Ciaran knew the little witch had defeated him, and he would never let her go.

He was terrified. To care for another was to have a weakness that could be exploited, but he knew without a doubt he would burn all the realms for this witch.

His little witch.

Seventeen

Kes

Kes stared at the chair the human witch had vacated. It had been a long time since he had seen such a wild display of power, made even more impressive by her lack of any formal training. Most fae and witches were taught how to use their power and magic by their parents or tutors as younglings. Growing up in the Human Realm meant her mother would have no need to teach her, nor know how.

Her untamed power was bound to cause trouble, and he could not wait to watch it unfold. His cousin needs order and control, or he's prone to fits of anger. It was why Kes made it his life mission to keep things as chaotic as possible. He found his cousin's anger hilarious and laughed hysterically while he destroyed any number of rooms—or unfortunate creatures—in the palace. He wondered if Ciaran's near reverent treatment of the witch was because he thought she was the key to his salvation, or was it something else? Either way, she would keep his hands full. She had a lot to learn, and none of them knew how to teach her.

Anin.

It was a beautiful name for the ethereal being. He found himself rolling her name around in his head over and over. She surprised him when she claimed to know about the Walsh witches. He should not have been surprised he knew next to nothing about her. It unsettled him how much he wanted to know everything there was to know.

Then he remembered he would be making the blood oath with her, and likely soon. He knew he should be enraged with his cousin for making him do such a task with a Day fae, and yet he was not. The thought both thrilled and terrified him. Something about making a blood oath with her felt final, as if there were no going back once it was done. Back from what he had no idea, it was a feeling he had in his gut. Something he still refused to examine too closely.

He cleared his throat and tried to return his face to his typical cocky and aloof smirk. "Well, that was incredibly dramatic. I am rather impressed. I think the witch has inspired me to step up my theatrics. I do hate to be upstaged."

Anin looked at him as if he had grown a second head. "What is wrong with you? Too many feathers short of a plume?" she said, as she cocked her head to the side and gave him a sly grin of her own.

He barked out a laugh he could not have contained had he tried. His nymph could play the game nearly as well as he could. There were not many things he loved more than wicked banter. He was going to have a good time with this nymph. He hoped to at least, although he thought he likely ruined that possibility.

He would do everything he could to insure she did not have another near breakdown like she had earlier. She had been vulnerable, and he watched her dip into a darkness he knew all too well. It might have been a long time ago, but that is not a feeling one forgets, no matter how hard they try. He would know. It made him an even bigger ass because he knew and still left her there, alone in the cage.

He should apologize; however, he could not recall a time he had ever apologized for anything. He was not sure he would even know where or how to begin. There were two versions of him fighting for control. The one who wanted to tuck her away under one of his wings and never let anything happen to her, and the other who could not come to terms with the fact she's a Day fae. The version he wanted to win changed with every breath he took. How could he feel so protective of one of the very beings he has sought to destroy for the majority of his life?

She looked uncomfortable around him, as if she were always on guard, waiting for him to do something cruel. He could not blame her; he deserved it. While the witch's display of power had been awe inspiring, her words had hit him harder than any physical blow. He did not like the idea of being the one responsible for placing Anin in danger again.

He wondered what her story was. What did the Day Court want with her? Where had she come from before sneaking into the Night Court to cross the veil? Did she have someone she longed for, wherever that had been? He had been staring at her while lost in his thoughts, and she looked warily back at him.

He should take her back to his quarters to allow her to clean up. It had been inconsiderate of him to not give her the minimal dignity of being clean when he took her to meet Ciaran and his human witch. Etain had looked clean, fresh, and rested.

He was not taking good care of Anin, not that he was used to caring for anyone but himself. He was having a very difficult time wrapping his mind around his desire to please her and his nature, which made him want to harm any being from the Day Court.

He was about to open his mouth to say something to her, likely the wrong thing when Ciaran reappeared, saving him from himself.

"Ah, good—you're both still here," he said, returning to his seat at the table. "The Blood Oath... What are your terms?" he asked Anin.

She looked at him warily, obviously exhausted and likely fearful of another deal after Kes's trick on her. She sat up straight in her chair, using the last dregs of energy she had. She then gave a small sniff and cleared her throat to gather her wits.

"I need protection if I am to remain in this realm and also remain alive." She looked back at Kes. "Someone strong enough to protect me against the Day Court, so surely it can be no one but yourself, Prince Ciaran. Even then, I am not certain it will be enough. The Human Realm was my last resort to save my life. I did not wish to go there, and I could never hope to blend in. I knew I was signing up for a lonely life. Any life is better than death, is it not?"

Kes held her gaze and then smirked at her. "You think I am unable to go toe to toe with anyone from the Day Court, and yet you think the blue giant here can? By the way, Ciaran," Kes shifted his eyes to his cousin, "I do adore your witch. She has such lovely names for you." He barely dodged the apple Ciaran chucked at his head while looking back at the nymph.

"My darling nymph, I must confess you wound me. I will have you know, the last time the prince and I got into a bit of an argument, we fought for six nights straight. I promise you, we were trying very hard to kill each other. Eventually, we became bored fighting with no clear winner and called it a draw."

Anin's mouth hung open, and Kes enjoyed being able to surprise her. It was common for those who did not know him to underestimate his abilities. His constant antics and lack of seriousness made others believe he was incompetent. They always regretted their assumptions in the end.

"I would hardly call it a mere argument," Ciaran mumbled under his breath. "My cousin is correct, nymph. The two of us are equal in power, and he is just as good a candidate to take the blood oath as I would be. Therefore, he will be the one to do it."

Kes realized too late that by singing his own praises, he had signed up to take the blood oath. Yet he found it impossible to be mad. The idea of anyone else making a blood oath with her made him feel rage deep inside and a desire to destroy anyone who would dare.

Eighteen

Anin

The two males sitting in front of Anin were really starting to piss her off. The giant bird tricked her into a deal she would never have made under any other circumstances, and now the giant bat was trying to do the same. The more she thought about Etain's words, the angrier she became. They would not look out for her unless it were in their best interest, and she needed to remember that.

Now the prince expected her to make her demands. She was exhausted. She had not had solid sleep in days and was nearly too tired to think clearly. Somehow, she had to make sure she did not fuck herself over again.

She was beginning to think that was the plan all along: keep her out of sorts and force her into making a bad deal. She knew it was the way of the fae, but she could not help but feel wronged. Could they not see she was already balanced precariously on the edge of sanity, and if she fell off, she would never come back from it? Probably not, since they appeared only to care for themselves. It might be the fae way, but that did not mean she had to like it.

"Okay, then," she said with a sigh. "Protection within the entirety of this realm, comfortable quarters, no more cages, access to all of your libraries, and one on one time with Etain."

She could see the prince visibly tense at the mention of Etain. "I promise, prince, I mean the witch no harm. I only wish to protect her privacy while I tell her what I know about her family. It seems like a courtesy she should be afforded, does it not?"

Ciaran held her eyes for a few moments. She could not quite read him, but thought she saw his internal battle to do what's best for Etain—not an action or thought process he was exactly comfortable with. It was interesting, if not shocking, to see how kind the prince was to Etain. A human had never been treated so well by any fae, let alone the Prince of Darkness.

Finally, he nodded at her and said, "I believe we can be agreeable to this. We will meet again tomorrow, and I will have my demands ready for you both."

Of course, he would give himself time to think up his terms. She should have known to require a counteroffer once she heard his demands. She knew she was going to fuck herself over again by making deals in her current mental state.

"Kes, do not be late for the council meeting." Before either of them could acknowledge his words, he was gone.

Anin looked at Kes. "I am rather tired, and I would very much love to bathe before I sleep."

She let the exhaustion seep into her voice, tinged with the anger she could not hide. She really did not know how much longer she could stay awake. The thought of being vulnerable in bed near him made her especially uncomfortable, and yet she did not truly fear him. She hated him almost as much as she wanted him. She seemed to have no control over her desires around him, and she hated him even more for that.

He simply stood, placed his hand on her shoulder, and then they were standing in a bedchamber. He knew how to port, and she found herself jealous, wanting to ask him to teach her how to do it. The idea of asking him for anything made her cringe. It would likely set her up for another cruel trick he could play on her. She had never been able to ask for help from anyone, with the exception of her sisters. She found it difficult to even ask them for help most of the time. She was used to fending for herself.

"Through that door over there, you will find your own personal bathing room, and these are your bedchambers. Feel free to do whatever you please with it. It's yours for however long you reside in the palace. My room is across the hall. You know... if you should find yourself in need of anything," he said suggestively.

He winked at her, and it took every ounce of willpower not to strike him across the face. She likely would have had she not been so damn tired. She did not want to pick a fight that she had no energy to finish. Sleep first, fight tomorrow.

She decided the best way to ruffle his feathers would be to not acknowledge his behavior at all. He appeared to live for the reactions his words and behavior often gave him. She turned without saying a single word to him and made her way to the door he had indicated for bathing, making sure to sway her hips excessively as she walked.

She shut the door behind her. Leaning against the back of the door, she took a deep breath and finally found some peace. She knew a simple door would not keep him out if he wished. Once she was fully rested and her power had recharged, she would place wards all around her new space. She jumped when there was a loud bang on the bathroom door.

There went her peace.

"Now, now, my darling nymph—be a good little girl while daddy is at work," he said heatedly.

She growled at him through the door, trying hard not to give him the reaction he clearly wanted from her. She could not keep up with his rapidly shifting treatment of her. He was hot, and then he would be cold. It was like he was mad at himself for being kind to her, and to make himself feel better, he would punish *her* for his actions.

She was sick of it.

That was it; she finally cracked and was going to give him a piece of her mind before slamming the door in his face. She threw open the door and planned to spew the vitriol bubbling inside her, but before she could get a single word out, Kes ported away, leaving the echo of his laughter to taunt her.

She hated him.

He infuriated her like none other, and he took pleasure in doing so. She needed to get the rest her body desperately demanded. Once she did, she would be ready to take him on. She decided she would kill him and then make extravagant hats from his feathers.

She groaned when a tightness in her chest told her she felt the complete opposite of hate for the overgrown peacock. He had wronged her and broken her fragile trust. She had no idea how she could ever feel anything but contempt for him. She was not an idiot. She knew who he was, but she refused to accept it. She would hate him until her dying breath, although deep down she knew that was a lie.

He would find a way to dig himself under her skin, where he would live the remainder of her existence. She would never be free of him, but that did not mean she needed to make it easy for the birdbrain. He did not deserve it. No, what he deserved was to walk his chicken feet over burning coals while begging her for forgiveness.

She smiled to herself as she stood under the fall of warm water in the corner of the black marbled bathing chamber. It felt good to have a plan. All she needed was sleep, and then she would be ready.

Hang on to your feathers, bird boy.

Nineteen

CIARAN

Ciaran was always the last one to enter the council chambers. He delayed entering until all council members were waiting on him. He liked to make them wait. He would randomly appear after the scheduled meeting time, sometimes making them wait for hours. He always had Kes walk in just before him, and then he would finally enter. He did not do it as a show of rank. He did it simply because he knew it pissed them off. He enjoyed watching their faces change color with rage. He always hoped it would make any of them step down. None of them had yet.

His council never actually got anything accomplished. It only served to give the fae in the room some kind of hierarchy with the rest of the high fae. The council was full of the most wicked fae, and Ciaran despised almost all of them. The only member of his council he trusted was Kes, and that trust had been hard earned and was not always given. However, there were still some things he could trust with no one, not even Kes. He thought about his little witch. Maybe she could be the one he trusted with anything. The ridiculous idea nearly made him scoff out loud.

He sat back in his chair at the head of the table, Kes to his right, and propped his feet up. He loathed council meetings. Since he could not tell them about his curse or the prophecy, he could not say much about the power imbalance the realm was facing. They would all push for a marriage to some being that would benefit their station.

He wondered what the councils of the Night fae long ago discussed. Did they sit around this table and gossip like his council, while all vying for a better position in court? He found it hard to believe it had always been this way. If it had, surely a king would have tired of their antics and dissolved the council long ago.

It's not a bad idea.

"What whining must I listen to today? Hurry up! I have things to do and a human to see," he said with a bawdy grin.

Council Member Royad cleared his throat to begin speaking, and Ciaran nearly groaned. He knew the ass wipe would speak first, as always, and he feigned shock while rolling his eyes at the male.

"My Prince, have you thought further on the betrothal to my daughter? She would make a strong queen, and most importantly, you would finally ascend the throne and become king."

It was a requirement for the king and queen to ascend the throne at the same time. It represented the balance the land required. His council no doubt thought it was all he needed. Royad was a constant pain in his ass with his desire to push Ciaran to take his daughter as queen. Ciaran glared at the being. He was a goblin, and one of the uglier ones Ciaran had ever seen. Honestly, it was a miracle Leona looked nothing like him.

"Royad, do you think me a fool? If I married your daughter, it would make you the father of the queen. We cannot have you meddling in my daily life anymore than you already do, now can we?" He gave the goblin a mocking smile. "Do not ask again. I have my reasons, which I cannot share with any of you." Ciaran did not know it was possible for a goblin to turn such a dark green in anger. It brought him immense joy.

"My Prince," council member Fiandra began. "I hear there is a human in the dungeons. Was he your catch during last night's hunt? What will you do with him?" she asked with a malicious gleam in her eye. She wanted to play with him, and as soon as Ciaran had gotten his revenge for his little witch, he would gladly give the man to his court to play with.

"Yes, he is quite mad—it's rather entertaining. I plan to spend a few days giving him a true Night Court welcome, and as soon as I have sufficiently imbued enough hospitality upon him, you are welcome to him."

The council members all chuckled darkly at his words.

"I hear that was not the only interesting prey of the hunt," Council Member Balric said, causing all laughter to cease. Everyone looked at him expectantly.

"Well, do enlighten us. What else did you hear, Balric?" Ciaran asked, well aware that it was either going to be his witch or the nymph. He was betting on the nymph since she spent some time in the dungeons. Although he would not put it past the male to have somehow heard whisperings about another human in the palace.

Balric grew up with Kes and Ciaran. His powers were weaker, and the male had it in his mind that somehow it was Kes and

Ciaran's fault he fell short. Perhaps it was their fault he was never able to forget it. As younglings they had made it their life's mission to constantly remind him of how he was lacking. While Balric's power may be less, he made up for it with cunning schemes. His mind was the only reason he had a seat at this table.

"I have heard a member of the Day Court is somehow still living in this very palace. How a Day fae could ever survive the Night Court is a mystery. If that were not vexing enough, I also heard of a mysterious human woman that the lunatic man in the dungeon has been raving about. Apparently, she was taken with him, and yet there is no sign of her. I wonder where she could be hiding, Prince," Balric said smugly, knowing he had just revealed information Ciaran did not wish to be shared.

Ciaran's fist clenched under the table. It was the only physical response he made until he let his face morph into his most common mask of wicked delight. He glanced around at all six of his council members and grinned his too wide grin.

"Ah, yes—my pet. She is quite entertaining to me. Did you not hear I was lucky enough to have caught two humans during the hunt?"

Most of the council members nodded in approval, though Balric seemed to study Ciaran. He would not doubt the male could read Ciaran's slightest tells. Balric would be a problem; Ciaran could feel it in his bones.

Twenty

Kes

He was annoyed the council knew of his nymph. He was not surprised, and truly, he was annoyed at himself. He was the fool who left her hanging in the dungeon after his return to the palace following the hunt.

The last thing he wanted was to find himself caring for anyone, and definitely not a Day fae at that. He wanted her and hated her at the same time. Except that was not exactly true. He wanted her, yes, but he did not hate her. He hated the way he felt out of control around her. He barely knew her and had barely spent any time with her. Yet when her fire came out to play, he felt happier than he had in a long time. Possibly even ever. That was what he hated most.

He was finding it difficult to stay away from her, even if that was all he wanted. He wished he never found her in the woods, but the thought of never hearing her smart mouth again caused him physical pain. He suspected it did not matter if she were near or not; he would never be rid of her because she had already taken up residence inside his mind.

"And what of the Day Court trash? Are we truly to allow it to live here? In our court?" Syndari sneered. They were one of the few members of the council who did not seem to have their own agenda. *They were just the embodiment of pure evil.*

They were a shifter who had the ability to become nearly anything. They preferred this lizard-like body and wore it most of the time. They could easily shift colors to blend into their surroundings and, for small periods of time, they could shift their entire being to identically resemble anyone. They could even change their voice. It gave him the creeps.

Balric's mouth opened, and Kes would rather set himself on fire than listen to that sniveling little cunt. If one thing came out of the conniving shit's mouth about Anin, it would be the last thing he ever said.

He looked at the shapeshifter before Balric could get a word out, and he cracked a devious grin before saying, "And why would we not? She is my prey. That should be reason enough. Since you all think yourselves entitled to more, she has information. That's all you need to know. If your prince wishes you to know more, that is for him to decide." It took everything in Kes not to fly across the table and wipe the sneer off their scaly face.

At the sight of Balric's mouth opening again, Kes stopped listening. He really hated the fae. Ever since they were younglings, he had never liked him. Anytime he spoke at council meetings, Kes would do everything he could to distract him. This time he chose to constantly yawn, as loud as he could. It was a struggle to keep himself from cracking up.

He nearly missed the words the final council member, Georden, said. "If they are nothing but pets, then surely you plan on bringing them to the Lunar Ball in two nights time for the rest of the court to enjoy?"

Kes felt his blood begin to boil. He would rip the hands off of any being who dared touch his nymph. Anin was *his*.

However, the court itself presented a delicate issue. If he were to intervene on behalf of a Day fae, it would make Anin a larger target. If that were even possible. It would also create an untold number of issues for him. If he left her unattended for even a moment, some Night fae would do what he could not. It would be better if, for now, they all believed he was only having a bit of fun parading around a Day fae on a leash.

Now that he could get behind.

"They are both under my protection, for the time being," Ciaran said in a way that left no room for interpretation. "No harm shall come to them. No trickery or deals will be made, but they will be displayed in a distinctly Night Court fashion to appease everyone. Me, mostly." Ciaran let out a devilish laugh filled with dark promises.

Kes mostly trusted Ciaran with his life; however, he did not trust him with Anin's safety. It took all his years of training to keep the look of shock off his face. He realized if he needed to, there was no one he would not fight to keep her safe, not even his cousin. The last time they fought, it was over Kes's anger at him for disappearing. He had only ever picked that one fight with him, and he would do it again if it came down to Anin's safety. He had not even completed the blood oath yet.

How much worse would this get after they shared blood?

Twenty-One
Seamus

Seamus had lost everything. His mother and younger brother died several winters ago from the illness that plagued the village. Nearly every family lost someone that winter. All except the Walsh women. They even went to visit each and every one of the sick and never had a cough to show for it. His suspicions were all but confirmed by the Shepherd. He had arrived in their village two summers prior and had begun preaching about the one true God.

The Shepherd listened to Seamus' concerns about the Walsh women and took them very seriously. He told the Shepherd about all the so-called "healing" they had done over the years, and how they would pick and choose who they were willing to heal. He explained how never once had his family benefited from the witches' choices, even though he had nearly married Etain. The Shepherd explained how witches were the instruments of the Devil and how they were only choosing to save the wicked. Seamus' family was obviously righteous; the God of Light was testing him with his own mission to bring the Walsh women into the light.

The Shepherd told him about the Beings of Light—winged beings of pureness with white feathers that glowed golden. They lived in a place always awash in the Light of God. If he could bring a woman as sinister as a Walsh to the Light, he would be worthy of joining the beings of this land.

Seamus recalled when he was younger, he had been a bit skeptical of such a place. He even began to doubt his venom towards the Walsh women, once the winter had gone. All members of the town had banded together to celebrate their lost loved ones. The Walsh women handmade rings of dried flowers, one for each of the people lost that winter. The rings were sent down the river as a beacon their souls could follow to their final rest. He could not imagine an evil being would ever do such a kind act.

The Shepherd did not agree. He told Seamus a wolf in sheep's clothing is still a wolf. The Shepherd advised him to stay vigilant, because their evil ways would show again. He considered the Shepherd to be of the highest authority and was heavily influenced by his wisdom. He continued on with his life, growing from a gangly young man into a strong, handsome man. He had most of the unattached women in the village vying for his affection.

All but one. Etain showed no signs of seeing Seamus for the righteous man he had become or how he could be her salvation from evil.

Last summer, when Seamus' father fell from his horse, Etain arrived as soon as she heard. Seamus was torn between letting God do his will, or allowing Etain to heal him. He chose Etain, and he wondered every day since that if he had just left it in God's hands, perhaps his father would still be alive. Etain claimed he had something go "afoul" in his inner workings, for it was neither a simple broken bone nor a strong hit to the head. When she heard the specifics of how his father had fallen off his horse, she surmised that it had likely been the cause of his fall to begin with.

With the death of his father, he lost every person he had ever loved. He leaned heavily on his friend, the Shepherd. He shared his deepest desires with him—to have Etain. Even though he blamed her for the loss of his family, and even though he wanted to take from her as she had from him. The Shepherd explained it was not wickedness that led Seamus down these dark thoughts. It was out of the desire to purify Etain from the grasp of the Devil himself. He suggested Seamus begin calling on Etain and preaching the joys of worshiping the one true God for her.

Try as Seamus might, she would not entertain his words and began to actively avoid him. She had even begun denying him entrance to her home and, therefore, access to her. Seamus' lust for Etain was at an all time high. He raged to the Shepherd about the willful woman and her reluctant ways.

The Shepherd suggested taking it further. If Etain would not willingly go to Seamus and the one true God, then he would need to force her. The Shepherd told stories about witches from other towns who continued to worship the old gods and goddesses. They had been purged with flame at the stake to save their villages from evil. These stories began to alienate Etain from the rest of the village as their suspicions grew exponentially towards her. The Shepherd thought her loneliness may be the push she needed to see the light and give into Seamus.

Nonetheless, all was for naught, as she grew even more set in her independent ways.

The Shepherd helped Seamus devise a plan on the night of the fall blood moon, for they knew she would venture into the woods. He told Seamus of a way he could physically purge the wickedness from the woman. Seamus was more than eager to comply, for this aligned perfectly with his own desires. The Shepherd warned him to be quick about it. Capture her, then bring her back to his home and restrain her.

If only Seamus had heeded the wise words of the Shepherd, he likely would not be in a cage suspended several stories off the ground in the bowels of hell. He was surrounded by demons and the hellish sounds they made. Day in and day out, he was witness to all manner of evil creatures coming to inflict their pain on the other demons. He began preaching about the one true God and the land of heavenly light, if only to keep from messing himself anymore than he already had.

There was a creature that appeared to be of pure light in a cage near him, suspended the same way he had been when he first arrived. He thought perhaps she was one of the creatures of pureness the Shepherd spoke of. When he called out to ask if she was one, she looked at him with disgust and annoyance. She told him to give her just one moment of peace from his lunacy, as if he were the craziest thing in this hellhole.

She was evil in the way Etain was. Using their beauty and womanly wiles to enthrall men to do their devilish acts. No, Seamus knew he was righteous; the Shepherd had told him as much. He now knew what he must do. Etain was lost to him in her wickedness, and he would leave her to it. As soon as he gained the opportunity, he would escape this hell and find the Land of Light. He would then gain his God's favor and help destroy the wickedness surrounding him, even if that included Etain.

As if testing his resolve for his new mission in life, the Devil from the woods once again appeared in front of him. He used his wings to stay level with the cage Seamus resided in and said, "I see my mere presence does not incite screaming from you anymore, vile human. Let us see if we can rectify that."

Seamus' cage began to lower, and the righteous resolve he had just felt slowly began to dissipate in the face of true terror.

Twenty-Two
Ciaran

H e needed *violence* to release the anger he had concealed at the council meeting. He decided to pay a visit to the dungeons. Ciaran knew immediately what had truly angered Etain earlier—the memory of her being at the mercy of a man who intended to take what he pleased. He wished he could remove the memory from his little witch. He did not normally involve himself with the violence of the human race. He and Kes had, on occasion, excitedly witnessed all manner of depravity committed by humans. Men against men, women against women, men against women, and sometimes even women against men. It had all been entertainment for them.

He never felt connected in any way to humans, though now he was unquestionably connected to his. He could not possibly care any less for the rest of them, and he desired to make the man he still had hanging in a cage pay for his crimes against his witch. He wanted to break his body everywhere Etain's had been broken. Then he wanted to become the Devil the man had been raving about and give him something to truly fear.

Ciaran was mildly disappointed that the man had lost some of his fear of him. Perhaps he would not pass out so soon this time. He began lowering the cage and took note of any other eyes that may be watching them—spies for other members of the court.

Once the cage finished its slow descent to the ground, he slowly opened it and made the man walk out. It was unnecessary, of course; he could have easily snapped his fingers and had the man already restrained on his table in his personal torture room. It had been a few weeks since he last needed to show a being the true meaning of pain and fear.

The last time he visited his playroom, one of the high fae in his court thought to sow dissent within Ciaran's ranks. After months of what Ciaran liked to call "*exploration*," the high fae had finally admitted to being in league with the Day Court. A hooded figure had promised him a place of higher status once the Day Court took over the Night Court.

Foolish boggart. His ancestor had raised his family's rank from lesser fae to one of the high fae of the Night Court, for of all things, loyalty to Ciaran's own father centuries ago. Apparently, loyalty was not a family trait.

The cage finally came to a halt on the ground. Ciaran made it move as slowly as possible to build anticipation for both himself and the man in the cage. By the time it touched down on the ground, the man was back to the palpable fear that was visibly wracking his body.

"What say you, man? Will you be brave enough to step out of the cage on your own, or will I have to forcibly remove you?" Ciaran would give credit where credit was due; the man was brave enough to glare at Ciaran while stepping out of the cage. Brave, yet foolish.

The second the man stepped from the cage, Ciaran was upon him. He grabbed him around his neck and lifted the large man as if he were nothing but a child, porting them to his playroom. Ciaran crowded the man's face with his elongated teeth in his extra wide mouth. He wanted to remind the man he was not dealing with an ordinary being.

"I will make you feel all the pain you made my tiny witch feel. You are a disgusting specimen of your realm. Not even my kind take without consent. What a lowly creature must you be, stooping to such behavior." Ciaran growled at the man who wet himself again.

Great. Spluttering would come next.

"I...I...am righteous! I was trying to...to...save Etain..."

The man was tripping over his words in an attempt to justify his actions. Ciaran interrupted him to roar into his face.

"You will not say her name ever again! If you need to refer to her, you will call her "Master's witch," "Master's human," or "Master's Pet." You will pay in pain for anything else; Etain is mine."

The man had enough courage to look indignant, before he nodded his head in understanding.

"Good—now that's settled, allow me to get you acquainted with your new lodgings."

Ciaran released the man and could see him eyeing some of the tools Ciaran used during his *explorations*—wheels turning, planning to make his escape. Ciaran enjoyed this part almost as much as the pain he would cause shortly. There was nothing quite like crushing hope just after it bloomed for the first time in one of his "guests."

"Go ahead human, make your attempt. I see you plotting. Do not disappoint me with..."

The man lunged towards the wall of larger weapons. Ciaran sat back and watched as the man attempted to pull one of the battle axes off the wall. He quickly realized he did not have the strength for such a weapon.

Ciaran casually strolled up to the wall, and with one hand, pulled the ax down before passing it to him. Smirking, he goaded the man. "Here, I will help you. I am sure you are used to being one of the strongest of your kind, but you forget human, no one here is of your kind. We are all far stronger, faster, and more powerful than you could ever hope to be."

The man attempted to take the ax Ciaran handed him, but when Ciaran let go of the weapon, the ax head thunk to the floor. Ciaran roared with laughter, and the man's anger flared as he turned bright red and tried once more to pick up the ax. Cutting his losses, he rushed to the other side of the room, where small, sharp blades were laid out.

"Yes, I do believe these blades are likely more anatomically correct for you." Ciaran mused, and the hidden meaning was not lost on the man, for his red face began to turn a delightful shade of purple.

"Well, get on with it! Let's see your grand plan unfold." The man charged Ciaran, who continued to lounge against the wall the ax had been hanging on, his arms crossed and wings casually tucked behind his back. The toothy grin Ciaran had been wearing grew into one of nightmares. The corners of his mouth stretched nearly to his pointed ears, showing off a mouth with far too many teeth.

Ciaran lazily grabbed the man's wrist of the hand holding the dagger, and in a blink, turned the man so his back was to Ciaran's front. The dagger was a hair's breadth from the man's eye. If he blinked, he would slice his own eyelid.

"Do you understand now, puny human? You are no match for my kind, and definitely no match for the Prince of Darkness. Your strength may have gotten you everything you wanted in the past, but your brute force is nothing but a gentle breeze to me." Ciaran watched as the man struggled to keep his eye open. Sighing, he released the man. "Now hop up on the table and lay down like a good boy."

Oh, how the man burned inside with such rage, which made Ciaran exceedingly happy. It was plainly visible how much he hated Ciaran. If only the man knew how much more he would hate him in a few moments.

The man took his time complying, yet he did comply. As soon as he was flat on the table, Ciaran snapped the restraints into place, tighter than was required. The man began to splutter again as he realized he was not afforded any movement beyond that of his eyes, fingers, and toes.

"I am righteous. The Shepherd told me...he...he said I would earn my place in the land of the Light of God!" The man was half hysterical now.

"Your Shepherd lied to you. There is no such singular God. There are many gods and goddesses. I myself am a descendant of the goddess Mórrigan, and I know many others personally. Let's hope, for your sake, they do not decide to smite you for your blasphemy." Ciaran laughed maniacally. "Now, where to begin? Did you know you broke my tiny witch's nose?"

Lightning fast, Ciaran launched his fist into the human's nose, smashing it flat. The wails were music to his ears, until the man began to choke on his own blood. "Well, we cannot have you drowning to death after one hit. Where's the fun in that?" Ciaran healed just enough of the man's nose to keep the blood from suffocating him; he did nothing for the disfigured shape.

"Perhaps you would like to tell me what is so grand about this 'Land of Light' that you would be willing to harm my witch?" Ciaran asked the man while he decided what injury to inflict next.

The man's voice had taken on a distinctly nasally tone as he said, "The Land of Light is always awash with the pure light of God. There are beings of gold who are perfect in appearance, as well as pureness, and have wings of soft, downy feathers. I thought perhaps the creature who had been hanging next to me was one of them, though it seems she is as evil as Eta..." The man tried to take her name back.

Too late.

"What did I tell you, human, about using her name? You kicked her ribs in, I think that will be the next place we 'explore.'" Ciaran took flight, listening to the pleas of the man begging for his forgiveness, before he gave a swift kick to each side of the man's ribs, basking in his screams. Feeling inspired, he snapped his arm for the fun of it.

He contemplated his next move and what the man had said about the Land of Light and its inhabitants. It sounded a lot like the Day Court, and he would not put it past them to meddle in the human world. Ciaran had a feeling they were the ones behind the "People of the Light." He could not figure out just yet what their end game was.

"What does this Shepard look like, human?"

The man was becoming incoherent, and Ciaran wanted his questions answered, so he healed him just enough to take the edge of pain away. Ciaran snapped his clawed hands in front of the man's face and asked him again, "Answer me human! What does this Shephard look like? And do not make me ask again!"

The man's whimpers began to lessen, and he rasped out, "I do not know. I have never seen his face. He wears a dark cloak with the hood always pulled up, hiding his face. I have only ever seen his hands. They are golden and glow in the sunlight." He said this last part with no small amount of reverence.

Ciaran was sure this Shepherd was of the Day Court now. They all have an annoying sunny glow about them, while the beings of the Night Court seemed to carry darkness everywhere they went. He was about to begin interrogating the man, he may have information he does not even realize is important. He was immediately distracted when the spell he placed on his room alerted him to movement. His witch was awake.

"Well, it seems our *explorations* have come to an end—for now. *My* Etain beckons." Ciaran took great joy in knowing the man would be alone, strapped to this table where no one could hear him screaming.

The man began to struggle against his impossibly tight bonds while Ciaran gave him one last menacing grin and ported to his bedchambers.

Twenty-Three

ETAIN

This time when she woke, she remembered where she was and gently sat up. She had the feeling of not being asleep for long. She scanned the room for any sign of Ciaran; it looked as though he was still out. She released a breath, feeling relieved to have some much-needed alone time. It was difficult to go from always being alone to never being alone. While also being overwhelmed by massive personalities. Etain sighed and stretched as she got out of bed.

Etain had the urge to snoop through Ciaran's bedchambers. She told herself it was because she wanted to know more about him. However, if she were honest, she was simply nosy. She wondered what kind of things a fae prince had lying around. She began looking in all the drawers and cabinets to see what they held. It was mostly a disturbing amount of weapons, all black clothing, and a ridiculous amount of jumbled papers and books shoved in the most unreasonable places. It seems her prince's spell did not account for quality control. This was the most unorganized cacophony of a mess she had ever seen. Something told her the brownies of the palace would be highly offended.

Etain had always been a tidy person. She believed everything had its proper place. She sighed and remembered Ciaran's desk and how it looked like he had been working, then rushed off suddenly and left everything as it was. She was beginning to think his desk always looked that way.

As she inspected each nook and cranny, she removed the smashed and crumpled papers as well as random books she found. She stacked the books on a small table next to a wingback chair and started to worry the stack was growing too tall. She smoothed out all of the papers and piled them on the bed. Once she finished her thorough investigation, she sighed and shook her head at the tower of books. It had become too tall for her to stack any more, so she started a new pile on the floor next to the table. She had just begun attempting to bring order to the mountain of crumpled papers, when she felt that pulling sensation in her chest and knew Ciaran was behind her.

"You know, it's considered rude to rifle through another's possessions, little witch," his deep, smoky voice said softly into her ear. She had been expecting him to sneak up on her, which he seemed to enjoy doing often. Even though she had been anticipating it, she was still startled, and goose flesh rippled down her arms. She did not think she would ever get used to the way he moved, no matter how long she resided with him in his tower.

"I was curious," she said on a hitched breath, as Ciaran lightly dragged his knuckles up her arm. She turned her face to meet his gaze.

"Curiosity can get you into trouble, little witch." He moved the tip of a single claw under her jaw and gently directed her chin up. He brought his face down close enough to hers that all Etain would have to do was lean forward, and their mouths would meet.

She hesitated. She could not understand what this need was for him that only grew stronger and stronger with every minute they spent together. That place in her chest where she felt the pull towards him began to sing anytime they were this close together. They barely knew each other, yet it was as if her soul recognized his on the deepest level.

Ciaran must have felt her hesitation. He dropped his hand, stood up straight, and began to scan the mountain of papers. She was having a hard time figuring out if he was upset with her for snooping or not. His silence made it difficult to read him. He found a few he appeared to need and stuffed them into his pocket. He then made his way to the towers of books Etain had created. She was getting nervous the longer he stayed silent. She only meant to help him. Her nerves made her begin to wring her hands together in the way she always did when she grew nervous.

He perused the titles of the books and stopped when he got to a particular one. He shifted the books on top of the one he wanted to the other pile and picked up the book he had been looking at. "Huh. I have been looking all over for this book. Perhaps I should have you snoop in more places." He looked at her with amusement in his eyes. Etain let out the breath she had been holding and dropped her hands in relief.

"My prince, I fear your spell cannot account for organization. It seems things get shoved out of sight. You should see the small arsenal you have spread across the room." She enjoyed the way his eyes lit up when she called him "my prince." It was her turn to smirk at him.

Ciaran's slow spreading smile held only joy and none of the usual wicked intent, which sent a blush creeping up Etain's chest and face. She found herself cursing her fair skin again. It always gave too much away and made it impossible for her to beat Ciaran at his own game.

"*Your* prince? Have you claimed me then, little witch?" he said as he wrapped his arms around her.

Etain felt flustered, as she always did when they made contact. In all her years, she had never felt as off-kilter as she did around Ciaran. His attention always felt so intense.

"I, well, that is... I don't..."

Ciaran just laughed and nuzzled her neck, inhaling deeply.

Etain let out a gasp. She had never been touched in such a way, though she found herself enjoying it immensely. That heat she always felt around him began to spread throughout her body and pooled in her core. She was desperately trying to suppress a moan. She thought she might die of embarrassment if she let it out.

"Do not fret, my little witch," he said while taking a few steps away.

Etain did not understand how he always seemed to know when she was starting to feel overwhelmed and would give her space at the right time.

"I want to take you somewhere I like to go sometimes." He snapped his fingers, and a heavy cloak appeared in his hand. "You will need this. I believe it might be a touch cold for you."

Etain picked up the heavy, dark green velvet-lined cloak, and then looked down at her bare feet. His gaze followed hers.

"Have you been shoeless this whole time?"

She nodded, and he looked at her sheepishly. "Forgive me, little witch, and her icicle toes." He snapped his fingers again, and fur lined leggings and warm boots appeared.

Icicle toes, ha!

Etain made him turn around and promise not to peek as she pulled the leggings all the way up. He found her request amusing, chuckling as he gave in to her request. This did not seem like the best time to mention that he had failed to supply all of her undergarments. Heat creeped up her neck again as she thought about how bare she had been this whole time. She really needed to get control of her flush; she felt it warming her cheeks again.

"Okay, I am ready," she said after getting all of the warm clothing on. He turned with his golden eyes closed tight and one of his famous smirks splitting his face.

"Are you sure you are decent, little witch? I would hate to offend any of your sensibilities." His smirk, which turned into a sensual smile, had Etain's heart picking up; he snapped his eyes open. "Or perhaps I would thoroughly enjoy offending your sensibilities."

Before Etain had a chance to respond, he had her snatched into his arms and ported them away.

They went to what looked like the highest point in the palace.

"Oh, this is quite the view!" Etain exclaimed as she looked around to see a wide, open panorama all around her. She had never been up this high in all her life, and it felt like being in the clouds. She could see every inch of the city below, which had several tall buildings and cobblestone roads. She had never seen architecture like that before. She found herself walking all along the perimeter to inspect the town and palace below her.

Everything was made of black stone or marble and speckled with the illusion of stars. The way they sparkled in the light from the large moon hanging low in the sky was absolutely breathtaking.

"Ciaran, is this your tower?" she asked him without taking her eyes away from the strange land spread out before her.

Ciaran smirked at her from where he leaned against the parapet, content to watch her take in his city. "Yes, we are standing a few stories above the bedchamber."

She looked out at the city again. "The palace is much larger than I expected. What is your city called?" She had only seen his bedchambers, his study, and the view from his windows. It never occurred to her that the fae realm would be this sprawling.

Ciaran laughed at her curiosity and the wide eyed expression she was surely wearing.

"Nightfell. It is the capital of the Night Court. There are many cities and towns spread throughout my lands."

She had only lived in one town her whole life, until she came to the Fae Realm. While the land was beautiful, it was also overwhelming. This was a lot more ground than she anticipated having to cover when he inevitably tired of her.

"Where do the witches reside?" she asked, hoping he would at least give her the general direction.

"East, the witches are in the Borderlands, where the two courts meet, why do you wish to know?" he asked her.

"I think I should know how to find my kind," she said. It was true, she should know how to get to her kind if she needed to. "How far East?" He looked at her for a moment, suspicion on his face.

"It depends on how you travel. Porting would take seconds, flying would take a couple hours, and by foot would take a few nights. Planning to runaway, little witch?"

"No, I am only curious and trying to orient myself. Always know where you are and where you are going, Etain, as my mother often reminded me," she said, mimicking her mother as best as she could. It was getting harder to remember her voice. She stared off, looking at everything yet seeing nothing as her mind drifted.

"Wise words. That way," he said, pointing to what she assumed was the East. "Walk that direction for four nights, and you will find yourself in the Borderlands. However, I do not recommend traversing it alone; there are many wicked creatures between here and there."

"Oh. Well, wicked creatures aside, your land is very beautiful," she said, trying not to let the disappointment seep into her voice. She was hoping it would be a little easier to reach the witches when the time came.

"While I am glad you are enjoying the view, this is not our final destination. This is merely where we will take off."

Etain must have looked confused, she was not sure what he meant by "take off."

"I could port us there, however, we still have a few hours till crescent night, and my wings are in need of a good stretch." He watched Etain's panic build with anticipation, and the adrenaline began coursing through her.

"You want to fly us there? While what...*carrying* me?" She gave him the wide-eyed panicked look of prey that was about to be caught while he strolled over to her.

"Yes—hang on tight, little witch."

Before she could begin to tell him all the reasons this was a horrible idea, he scooped her up in his arms and shot them directly into the sky. She fought the urge to be sick and thought her stomach was about to come right out of her mouth. She locked her arms around his neck as tightly as she could and buried her face into the crook of his neck. She felt a rumbling through his chest and knew he was laughing at her.

"Little witch, I promise I will not drop you. Now do not be afraid and look."

She took a deep breath and peeled her face away from him. She gasped. They were in the clouds, illuminated by the moon and stars. She was positive that this was the most beautiful view she had ever seen.

"I have a feeling I will be constantly updating my number one most beautiful sight often with you as my guide," she said, though she was still terrified and kept her arms wrapped tightly around Ciaran's neck. The beauty spread out around her was worth the fear.

"I have a feeling I, too, will be constantly updating my number one most beautiful sight. With you in all of my views, little witch," he said softly.

Etain's cheeks flushed, and she bit the inside of her lips trying to hide her smile. Sometimes her prince said things that made her simultaneously molten while also making her incredibly flustered. She was never quite sure how she should respond when he said things like that. It was unsettling, and yet she could not find it in herself to be mad about it.

It was difficult to hear over the sound of the wind. Therefore, they were silent for most of the trip; there was a quiet comfort between the two of them. It was as if the physical touch was enough of an adjustment for both of them, and they were taking the time to relax into each other's touch. After a while, his thumbs began to rub back and forth on the arm and leg his hands gripped. It was hypnotic, and she found herself nearly drifting off to sleep. She leaned her head into his chest and relaxed her grip around his neck while they flew across the cloud strewn sky.

"We are almost there, little witch," Ciaran said as he began the slow descent.

She could hear them before she could see them; when they broke the cloud coverage, she saw what looked like the end of the world. Water plummeted over the edge for as far as she could see, creating hundreds of waterfalls. The water looked like flowing ink as it rushed towards the many drops.

Etain noticed they were closing in on a ledge that jutted far out over the fall and was higher than the water, keeping it mostly dry. Ciaran touched down on it and slowly released her. He let her catch her balance before grabbing her hand and pulling her to the ledge.

"Come sit with me, little witch. I need to talk to you about something."

His words made her feel a heavy pit of dread in her stomach, though she let him lead her to the edge and help her sit.

"Why does that sound like something I will not enjoy talking about?" Etain asked Ciaran as he sat and situated his wings in such a way to protect them from the constant mist of water.

"I do not know how much you will like it. However, I know I am not looking forward to it." He then fell silent for so long, looking out at the vast nothingness in front of them. Etain grew nervous in the silence.

"I like to come to this ledge and sit because there is nothing here. No Night Court to rule, no Day Court to thwart, no games to play, and no one watching my every move." He sighed heavily before he turned to meet her gaze. "In two nights, I will need to present you to my court during the Lunar Ball. Rumors have already begun to fly about the human woman I have kept in my room since the hunt two nights ago."

Etain could not believe it had only been two nights since the blood moon. It was difficult for her to track time here with the constant darkness.

"As you can imagine, my court is used to treating humans a certain way. They seem to think you are quite literally my pet and I have been keeping you locked in my room doing unspeakable things to you. I let them continue thinking this to keep any of them from paying any further attention to you."

If his words were not clear enough, his eyes appeared to glow brighter and carried a wicked gleam to them. "We both know I have been quite the gentleman. I do not understand the reason behind my actions. Etain, I mean it when I say I am a very wicked Prince. I have never once in my nearly seven hundred years ever cared for the well-being of another—not even Kes. I tolerate his company at best, but I do not care what happens to him. But you... I, for the first time in my entire existence, I care if something happens to someone else. I cannot be sure why."

Etain did not think Ciaran knew his own heart. She saw him with his cousin and could see the way they both tried not to care for one another, though it was obvious they were close.

Etain had to look away from the intense gaze Ciaran was giving her. He was looking at her in a way that made it clear he needed her to say something.

"I did not do... well, at least I do not think I did anything. I...I am not sure what to say." Etain's nerves began to fray, and she felt hot and cold all at the same time. She began to mess with her hands again and suddenly wondered if a ledge was the best place for a conversation such as this. She wondered if Ciaran thought she was responsible for his feelings. Maybe he thought she had done some kind of witchcraft on him.

Ciaran wrapped his wing tighter around Etain. She never noticed his wings had little claws on the top tips, like bat wings. "Worry not, little witch. I am quite certain it can only be one of two things, and neither is your doing. I am not certain which one it could be just yet."

She gave him a questioning look.

"I will not worry you with the possibilities until I know for sure."

Etain opened her mouth to let him know she did not appreciate him keeping information from her, particularly when it concerned her, too.

"Please do not argue with me. On this, I will not budge. I swear to you—as soon as I am certain, I will tell you everything."

Etain closed her mouth and began to chew the inside of her cheek. She did this often when she was trying to contain her anger.

"I will need to... treat you a certain way in front of my court. They will expect a certain level of depravity from their prince, and I must maintain appearances, if only to keep them from becoming too curious about you." He looked almost pained when she glared at him.

Etain's nerves began to overtake her anger, and her voice went breathy with fear. "Will you hurt me?"

Ciaran's eyes went wide, and he stepped out in the air to stand between her legs. He placed both hands on either side of her, crowding her space. "I would never hurt you, little witch," he said with such vehemence that she would have believed him even if she had not known the fae cannot lie. The corner of his mouth quirked up into that smirk with which she found herself falling in love.

Love?

"That is, of course, unless you ask me to." He began running the tip of his nose up the side of her neck until his mouth reached her ear and whispered, "And you will ask me to, Etain."

Her heart was being frantically as her core went molten.

He lifted his head to look her in the eyes, "I will not hurt you, however, I do not think you will like me much afterwards. Even if your body does. I will frighten and enthrall you at the same time, and I will enjoy every minute of it." He brushed his lips softly against hers.

She found it hard to worry about the Lunar Ball and what she might be forced to endure. She craved his touch more than anything. She knew she should not, but there seemed to be nothing she could do about it. Her prince had already begun working his way into her heart.

Etain let out a breathy moan. "Kiss me, my prince."

Ciaran needed no further invitation. He claimed Etain's mouth, demanding entrance at once with his tongue and nipping her bottom lip with his elongated incisors.

Etain tried to hang on as her mouth was thoroughly invaded. She had never kissed anyone before, and this was not the sweet kiss she thought her first kiss would be. Instead, it was savage and stoked the fire burning within her to near bursting. Ciaran stole her breath and drowned her sense of anything but him.

It was a conquering. It was perfect.

Twenty-Four
Anin

Anin could not have been asleep for very long. She still felt her aching muscles, and her power was only partially replenished. Her head ached, and it reminded her of the one morning after a Beltane celebration many years ago. She woke in an unfamiliar bed surrounded by unfamiliar fae. She knew she had thoroughly enjoyed herself, and others, but she paid the price the entire day after.

She huffed in annoyance at whatever had woken her and threw the covers over her head. She felt the eyes upon her and knew it could only be one being. A male who thought far too highly of himself and apparently had no issues sneaking into her room. She could not wait to have her full power back and be able to put up wards to keep him from barging in on her.

"Go away, Kes. I have not had nearly enough sleep to deal with your cocksure-self."

She heard a chuckle come from the corner of the room where a wingback chair sat, accompanied by a small table and lamp. Before she crawled into bed earlier, she thought it would be the perfect spot for reading. Now it was ruined. She would forever think of it as the chair from which Kes disrupted her sleep and harassed her. A travesty, truly.

"Thinking of my cock already, are you, nymph?"

She suppressed a groan. She should have seen that coming. No male had ever gotten under her skin so thoroughly before, but she was not about to let him know he bothered her. "Only you could gather such nonsense from a rather obvious scorn. The sun would rise in the night court before I have need to think of your cock. Although, I do suppose if the carpet matches the drapes, it may have its uses...as a duster. Now, fly away, little birdy. I am busy." She grinned to herself from under the covers, rather proud of that jab.

She was surprised when he had no quick response, and only silence replied. She mentally patted herself on the back for winning this round. She was too tired to check to make sure he had left and began drifting off back to sleep.

Suddenly, the covers were ripped off her and thrown to the floor. She felt the weight of him on her with his dark, downy, feathered wings spread wide, caging her in. Her heart rate picked up, and she wanted to scoff at herself for *enjoying* the way he felt on top of her and for the way the sight of his wings excited her. Part of her was terrified, but a larger part was exhilarated, waiting to see what he would do.

"A duster indeed. I have no doubts I would thoroughly enjoy any 'dusting' you did with it. Perhaps your sweet little cunt needs to be dusted. Shall I check?" He started to make his way down her body and grabbed both of her legs. She had to hold in the moan that tried to slip through her lips at the feel of his rough hands dragging up the inside of her thighs.

Heat bloomed across her skin and pooled in her core. She had been entirely unprepared for him to be that bold. She should not be surprised by his brazen behavior; it was who he was. She had only caught glimpses of who she was convinced was the true Kes. Every other time, he was always putting on a production. If she were not trying to convince herself she wanted absolutely nothing to do with him, she might admit to finding him funny. She would never tell him that, of course.

"Get off me—you heathen!" she screeched while she tried to dislodge him. She was flustered. His hands against her sensitive skin sent a quake throughout her body and made her core clench in anticipation. There was no hiding her body's reaction to him, and she knew she had just given away how much he had gotten to her. Judging by the way his fingers dug into her flesh as he made to part her legs and the way he looked down at her, he knew.

She was not the only one affected. She could see the proof of that bulging from within his pants. He stared down at her as he slowly parted her legs. Her breathing became frantic, and she began to panic.

If they crossed that line, there would be no going back for either of them. She was not supposed to give in to him so quickly. She lashed out with her magic. Out of the tiniest of crevices, she directed her vines to grow and wrap around the big headed bird's limbs.

He was supposed to walk through fire to prove himself to her, damn it!

Twenty-Five

Kes

She was the most exquisite creature he had ever seen. She was flushed a beautiful shade of green and her chest heaved with her breath. The smell of her arousal had his fingers digging roughly into her flesh he was bound to leave a mark.

Good.

He only wished his mark would last for an eternity, not the few moments it took her power to heal herself. His dick had never been so hard. Gods, if he was not careful, he would finish inside his pants like some kind of youngling fool.

He had never seen her without her wings wrapped around her in some fashion. The vines wrapped around her upper body had shifted in sleep. The pale green cleavage Anin kept hidden had slipped out. He had just a peek at the upper edge of a dark green nipple before he realized his limbs were being secured.

He was suddenly wrenched back and slammed against the opposite wall. He knew he could easily break free from the vines that bound him, but he wanted to see what his nymph would do. Besides, he has never been one to turn down restraints in the bedroom.

He grinned smugly at her and took no small pleasure in the fire he saw burning behind her eyes. "Darling, if you wanted me tied up, all you had to do was say so."

She glared at him, then gave him a saccharine smile, as Kes felt the vines around his body begin to tighten.

"Now that you have me at your mercy, my darling nymph, what do you plan to do with me? I do hope it's something deliciously dirty." He gave her his best wickedly sensual smile and watched as her chest began to rise and fall faster, giving him a beautiful view of her half exposed breasts.

She huffed out of bed and marched up to where he hung against the wall. She stared at him for a moment before she cocked her head to one side. He had begun to notice she did this every time her smart mouth came out to play.

"What to do with a strung up bird?" She asked in a sing-song voice. She let her gaze burn a trail as she inspected every inch of him. "Well, my darling rooster," she said, running her fingers in patterns along his chest.

He had no idea a soft caress could incite such a reaction in his body. Her fingers dipped lower and lower until she skimmed the top of his trousers. She knew exactly what she was doing when her hand brushed across his still straining cock. He sucked in air between his teeth.

"Unfortunately, I am in no need of any kind of dusting. I am, however," she said as she continued to swirl her hands everywhere but where he desperately wanted, "in need..." she moaned as she gazed into his red eyes with her black ones.

"Of taking the trash out," she said before breaking out into laughter. He was momentarily dumbstruck by the sound of it.

Like tinkling bells. He was going to do everything he could to hear that sound over and over again.

She had a vine start slithering towards the door as the vines that held him began to move him towards it. He let her think she was in control for a few moments longer before he broke free of her vines with little effort.

Kes was entirely too satisfied to watch her face light up with shock. She began to quickly back away from him. There was nowhere she could hide in any realm from him.

"The fact you are able to get your vines to grow in the Night Court at all is impressive, darling nymph."

For every step he took towards her, she took one back until her back pressed into the wall behind her. He closed the distance between them and caged her in with his arms against the wall. He brought his mouth right up next to her ear. "I think you may have forgotten who you are dealing with, silly nymph."

He inhaled her scent of pine and flowers before he dragged a hand up her arm as slowly as she had done to his chest. This close he could hear her breathing turn into something more like panting. He dragged his hand up to her neck and grasped it. She let out a startled gasp. He did not apply much pressure, but he liked the way he could feel her pulse throbbing faster and faster. Apparently, she liked having his hand around her throat.

He used his thumb to push her head up so their eyes could meet, and for several moments they stared into each other's depths. He pulled his other hand off the wall and tucked a lank of her golden hair behind her ear. He liked her hair down like this. It was a wild mess of golden and green waves he was itching to run his hands through. He shoved his hand that was still hovering around her ear towards the back of her head and gripped her hair, yanking it so her neck was stretched up to look at him. He released her throat and bent down to grasp her around the waist. He pulled her body up along his to wrap his arm fully around her. He let his mouth hover over hers, and he could feel her back arch to press her body more firmly into his. He brought his mouth even closer before diverting it back towards her ear.

"Next time, I will have no choice but to remind you of exactly who you are dealing with. I'll start by bending you over my lap and getting a good look at what's always hiding under those wings. Then I will enjoy seeing what lovely shades of green your ass turns after my hand connects with it."

She scowled up at him as if she were offended, yet he felt the tremor that wracked her body as he spoke. "You would not dare! The blood oath will prevent you from hurting me." Her voice was raspy, and she tried to look unaffected.

"Who said anything about hurting you? You will beg me for it, my darling nymph—I have no doubts." His red eyes never left her black ones as he said this. He was rewarded with her face flushing a beautiful moss green and her mouth opening and closing several times while she tried to come up with something to say.

Before she could speak, he released her to the ground and took a step back. "Now, now, Anin—I did come here with pure intentions. The council has decided the court should get the chance to meet you and Etain at the Lunar Ball in two nights time. I am sure you can imagine the wickedness the members of the court will bless you with. I will do my best to keep you from most of it, but if I do not allow them some fun, they will become petulant. That would mean I would have to shed blood, and then there would be entirely too much intrigue around you for my liking."

The way the flush drained from her skin, leaving her a sickly faint yellowish color made his chest tighten. She began to walk back towards her bed. All of the heat had drained from her.

He reached out and snatched her hand, pulling her back toward him. This time, he was gentle with her. He cupped his hands around her face, gently bringing her eyes back up to meet his. She looked more tired than she had when he had woken her.

"Do not fret, my darling nymph. If anyone dares touch you, I will remind them why they all fear me. In the most painful way possible. I am the only one to touch you," he declared as he dropped his hands back to his sides.

"And what if I do not want you touching me?" she asked.

"We both know that would be a lie," he said.

They stood there staring at each other. He let her see he meant every word he said. She gave him a slight nod, then began walking back to her bed as he exited the room.

"Sleep well, Anin," he said before shutting the door.

He stood just outside her door for a few moments. He knew he was fucked, he just had no idea he was that fucked. He decided right then and there, he would choose her. Over and over again.

He would always choose *her*.

Twenty-Six

ETAIN

Ciaran teleported them back to his bedchambers, and they landed on his bed with her under him.

Breaking the kiss, he pressed his forehead against hers. "Little witch, if we keep going on like this, I am not sure I will be able to stop." He sighed out his body's frustrations.

Etain was not ready for that just yet, and he seemed to understand.

Standing up, he offered Etain a hand. "It's getting late, little witch. Go ahead and get ready for bed. I will have bedclothes waiting for you again. We have two nights to prepare for your introduction to the Night Court. I have a few things to take care of. I'll return as soon as I can. Sleep well, Etain—we have an early start tomorrow, just after first night. You have a lot to learn in an incredibly short period of time." He ran a hand through his shifting hair as if he were nervous.

He looked at her for a moment, appearing uncertain. He jerked his body forward, and kissed her on the forehead. The action was anything but graceful, as if it were completely foreign to him. She was beginning to understand affection was not something he was entirely comfortable with—if at all. Before she could respond, he was gone.

That was certainly an exit.

Had the conversation they had at the falls changed something for him? She felt entirely overwhelmed. Everything was happening so fast. Her life was hurtling forward faster than a shooting star, and she was struggling to keep up.

She sank to the floor, her knees no longer able to hold her up, and she felt the bone-deep exhaustion of being constantly on edge. She let herself take a moment to mourn the loss of her old life. She had been lonely in her empty two room home, and her village made Etain worry for her future. She woke up every day and knew what to expect. The repetition was comforting.

She had been in the care of her prince for only two full days, or nights, as they said here. Etain felt like she had already lived a hundred years. She knew without a doubt there was no way she could ever return to her home in the Human Realm. She was still worried about how long Ciaran would keep her around, although she was certain she could never walk away from him. Every time Ciaran was near, she felt intoxicated and began to lose all sense of herself, one touch at a time.

Her feelings for him baffled her, both in how strong they were and in how they came on instantly. She may be inexperienced; however, she was not a girl known for falling for any bit of affection. She rejected Seamus multiple times, and he had been unrelenting in his pursuit of her for years. Yet here she was fawning all over a winged blue giant who, by his own accord, was wicked and cruel.

In just two nights, she had fallen for Ciaran, and it made absolutely no sense. At least, based on what he told her at the falls, he appeared to be experiencing the same. She could explain it no other way; her soul called to his, and his called to hers. Their souls chose each other at first sight, while Ciaran and Etain struggled to accept what their souls already knew.

She wished she could talk about this with her mother. She would have one sentence to explain everything. "Fate gets what fate wants," was a favorite of hers. It immediately calmed her when Anin said it at the table.

She truly did miss her mother, now more than ever. She always knew what to say or when to say nothing at all. She did not want to influence Etain's decisions, though sometimes her mother had wisdom worth imparting. As she would say, "There's no sense in us both going down the wrong path when neither one of us had any business being on it in the first place."

Etain wondered what her mother would have to say about her current predicament. She had the feeling her mother knew she would end up in the Fae Realm at some point, yet Etain had to wonder if she knew more than she let on. She wished she had her satchel as well; it held her family's grimoire. She could hunt through it, looking for old prophecies and information about this realm and the role her ancestors played in it. It made her sad to think of it lost forever in the woods of the Human Realm. It was irreplaceable, and she had lost it. She knew for sure her mother would have something to say about that.

She remembered then that Ciaran said he would be back and decided a good soak was in order. The obsidian tub was calling her name. She poured in lavender bath oil and threw some dried flower petals in for good measure. She then slid into the nearly unbearable heat. It hurt so good. She had not realized how cold she was or how tense her muscles had been. She let her mind drift and not focus on anything in particular, giving herself a much needed break from reality. The only thing that could make this any better was if she had a good book to get lost in. Maybe she could find one in Ciaran's massive book collection.

Etain startled; she had started to drift off to sleep. She took that and the cooling water as signs it was time to get out. When she entered the bedchambers, there was a long black, slightly sheer nightdress waiting for her. Slipping it on, she pulled back the covers and crawled in. She tried to wait for Ciaran, anticipating his return for more than one reason. However, sleep pulled her under within a few minutes.

Hours later, she felt herself seeking the warmth in the sheets. She felt something drape over her, the weight comforting, before sleep pulled her back under.

Twenty-Seven
Ciaran

Ciaran could not have left his bedchambers faster. Etain made it nearly impossible to pull away from her. Instinctually, Ciaran knew he needed to earn his little witch's trust before he claimed her body. He *would* claim her; they both knew it. This thing between them was out of their control, intent on making sure they were entwined with each other in all ways possible. It would have been easy to take her, yet he knew she would have regretted moving forward while she still had questions. Ciaran growled low as he paced his study.

What would she think of him after a night with his court? He never cared what anyone thought of him before. He knew these feelings were either the mate bond or the prophecy from the Many Faced Goddess, either of which cursed him a second time. It did say a human would be the key to coming into his full power. Subjectively, he knew only one would make him care what his little witch thought of him; he was just not ready to admit that yet.

He moved at his lightning speed to get to his desk. He had never paid attention to the way he moved until Etain kept mentioning it. Reaching into his desk, he pulled out the spelled parchment and summoned Kes and Anin. They needed to finish negotiating the blood oath contract. Ciaran had a few new ideas to add to Anin's part of the deal.

My study, now. Bring the nymph.

Ciaran had to wait a few minutes longer than he liked before they appeared.

It looked like Kes had let his nymph clean up. Anin's hair was back to being perfectly placed, and she looked a bit more rested. It looked as though his cousin was taking better care of her. If the way he tensed when she was discussed during the council meeting was any indicator, he would be willing to bet his cousin was in a similar situation to himself. Ciaran smirked at Kes to show he knew exactly what was going on. Kes rubbed his hand through the feathers on his head, ruffling them slightly, and shrugged.

Ciaran did find it odd that on the same night, both he and Kes found a female of "interest." He was not one to believe in coincidences, and he assumed this was more meddling on behalf of the Many Faced Goddess. He needed to figure out how to break the curse and confirm that Etain was the human she foretold. He was also growing more concerned about the Day Courts meddling. That would need to wait until after he was able to form a plan to ensure Etain's safety around his court.

Ciaran indicated that everyone should have a seat. "In two nights, Etain and Anin will be subjected to the court during the Lunar Ball. Typically, I would be excited to see what wicked things the court came up with to harass a human and a Day fae. However, I find myself...caring... for Etain's well-being. And you, Kes, will be bound by a blood oath. Though I do wonder if the blood oath is even necessary."

Kes glared at him, which only made Ciaran laugh. He finally had something to ruffle his cousin's feathers with.

Anin opened her mouth, no doubt to argue the necessity of the blood oath, when Ciaran held up his hand. "Fear not, nymph. I fully intend for Kes to follow through on the blood oath. It's why I summoned you both." Ciaran was amused when his cousin and the nymph wore the same expression. He was willing to bet their war of wills would be highly entertaining to observe.

"I have thought about my requirements and demands for you," he said to Anin, "in exchange for Kes taking the blood oath and providing you with your list of demands."

The two looked at each other.

Anin smirked at Kes. "Did you hear that, you overinflated pile of feathers? You have to fulfill my demands."

Kes got out of his seat and went to stand behind Anin so he could lean over the chair, boxing her in with his arms before he dipped his mouth and whispered something in her ear.

Ciaran could not hear him, even with his fae hearing, yet whatever he said had Anin's face turning a bright green.

Kes stood and walked back to his chair with a smug expression on his face. The two stared at each other for a few moments. Anin was trying her best to look at Kes like she hated everything about him. She failed miserably. Highly entertaining indeed.

"As I was saying, you will also tell me everything you know about what the queen and king have been doing to make their power grow. I will require you to identify any known spies and point out any you see in the Night Court."

Anin nodded her head slightly, seeming to have expected this. She likely thought that would be the end of his demands.

Ciaran knew he was taking advantage of the nymph by asking for more, but he truly didn't care. "On top of that..."

Anin took a deep breath and sat up straight in her chair, clenching her jaw tight.

Kes gave him a sharp look that told him, "Watch it."

Ciaran gave his cousin a knowing smile, which made Kes look away. He seemed highly interested in a spot on the table. Kes was definitely having a harder time than Ciaran accepting what fate had thrown at them.

"You will help Etain learn of her family's past and help her learn to use her magic. Finally, you will give Etain a swift lesson on our realm to help prepare her for what will surely be shocking to her in two nights. You may not be from this court, but you know our ways. I'm sure you grew up listening to horror stories about us," he said giving the nymph a malicious smile.

Anin looked at Ciaran as if she were seeing him for the first time. She was quiet for a moment, likely thinking over his words. "I will tell you what I know of any specific plots against the Night Court and anything directly pertaining to your court. This includes my thoughts on their recent power growth. I will inform you of any spies for the queen and king, as well as their inner circle, that I know of. I will gladly help Etain in any way I can. I find it admirable you demanded help for a human witch as part of a blood oath." She held Ciaran's gaze.

He noticed the minor changes, making his requests far more specific, yet it sounded like it gave him everything he wanted. He nodded his agreement without acknowledging her... compliment? No one had ever called him admirable, and he was not sure what to do with that.

"Kes, make the arrangements for the blood oath. It would be best if it were completed before the Lunar Ball. Also, make sure Anin is here by first night tomorrow to begin working with Etain."

Kes knew Ciaran had dismissed them. He got up, strolled over to Anin, and grabbed the nymph's hand before they disappeared.

Once Ciaran was alone, he went to the stack of books he had pulled earlier. The longer he spent in Etain's company, the more convinced he became this was a mate bond. Perhaps it is what the Many Faced Goddess had been seeing in her prophecy. He found it interesting that he, the prince of the Night Court, would find himself a human mate.

If that's what this is.

Not just any human, but one descending from a powerful line of witches who had been part of this realm for generations. Abandoning his research on mate bonds, he began looking for anything on witches, specifically Walsh witches.

It did not take long for him to find an entry from when his great-grandfather was a young fae. He described a powerful witch with the darkest red hair. It turned out he was quite the miscreant and liked to steal witches for his own evil desires. The head witch did not take kindly to that at all.

She cursed him, and any future lines, with access to only half of their true power. His grandfather went on to castigate the witch and her kind for stealing his power in his writings, yet he never said how to break the curse.

Ciaran knew every curse had some way to break it—a way to maintain balance. Typically, there is some exaggerated lesson to learn, or sometimes a ridiculous phrase that must be said in a specific way. He found it all rather tiresome. Ciaran checked more of his ancestors' journals, looking for any pieces to the puzzle this curse had become. He did stumble across another entry several years later from his great-grandfather where he mentioned the witch who had cursed him, and subsequently Ciaran himself, had been a Walsh.

Ciaran stilled; Etain's ancestors caused this problem. He felt his blood start to boil. He could punish her for her ancestors, just as her ancestors have done to him. Ciaran let his anger build. Here he was paying a price for his ancestors' actions while the descendant of the one who cursed him lay sleeping peacefully in *his* bed. Ciaran's jaw cracked from the clenching of his teeth.

Letting his rage carry him, he ported to his darkened bedroom and glared down at the witch in his bed. As he stared at her, his rage began to subside. It irritated him; he was no longer in control of himself when it came to his witch. There was no choice. He knew he would always choose her, and that bothered him to no end. Yet, he was not able to be mad about it. How exhausting it was caring for this little human witch.

Ciaran dressed for bed and then climbed under the covers next to her. Just as he was beginning to drift off, he felt her roll towards him, seeking his heat. He nearly hissed at the shock of her ice cold feet against his legs. He could not understand how all female's feet seemed to *always* be cold. Sighing, he draped his wing over her to help keep her warm through the night.

The last thing Ciaran thought was how it would not be that bad to warm his little witch every night. Even if she had icicles for feet.

Twenty-Eight

ETAIN

Etain was up early with Anin in Ciaran's study just as the moon was starting to rise again. It was difficult for her to understand the passing of time here. The moon rose in the sky twice a night. Their version of daytime they called "first night." It was the first pass the moon made across the sky, incredibly large and just as bright as any sun. On the second pass it made, a crescent moon rose much higher in the sky and reminded her of nights in the Human Realm.

The problem was the tracking of time, because no matter which moon rose, it did not do so gradually. It shot straight up into the sky and would shoot straight down, only to immediately shoot back up again. It did not work its way from one end of the sky to the other, as it did in the Human Realm, and it always rose and set to the west.

"How do you track the passing of time here?" Etain asked Anin.

Anin looked at her as if she were mad. "We do not. We sleep when we wish, and most events are marked to begin with the rising of the sun or moon, depending on which court you are in. We are not as structured as you humans." She gave a slight shrug as breakfast appeared on the round table where they sat.

Things suddenly appearing was another nuance of the Night Court, which Etain was having a hard time getting used to. "I'm not sure I will get used to having food this plentiful. Is it like this for all beings of the realm, or is it only because we are in the palace?" Etain thought she would begin to wear on Anin as she kept blurting out a never-ending stream of questions. However, she was patient with her and happy to answer them all.

"I would say it is like this for most of the realm. Perhaps the only place that may experience some hardships would be the Borderlands between the Day and Night Courts. There is occasional fighting over which Court controls the in-between lands. However, it belongs to the witches and not to either court. There are several covens in the middle of the Borderlands, running from north to south. They have remained neutral and helped maintain the balance for as long as history has been recorded. Unfortunately, the Day Court has been luring more and more witches away to join them. I am not convinced the choice was made of their own free will.

"The politics of this realm are long and convoluted; it would take many of your human years to fully understand them. The most important thing to know is neither realm is good or bad. We fae live for a tremendously long time, and long lives lead to much mischief. Lesson number one is not to blindly trust anyone's words. We have had a very long time to learn the art of weaving words to trick and ensnare unsuspecting beings."

She already knew the fae were master manipulators. Her mother made sure Etain knew fae were not to be trusted. She knew to be careful when striking a deal with a fae and to avoid doing so whenever possible. Before Etain could ask another question, Anin began telling her about the horrors of the Night Court and what she should expect at the Lunar Ball.

Etain was not surprised to hear about the cruelty and bloodlust, though she began to lose her appetite. What she was unprepared for was sexual depravity. Etain was still inexperienced, more from a lack of men to choose from than by choice. She had her first kiss the previous night, and now she needed to prepare to see overtly public displays of the darker side of sexual activities. Apparently, the Night Court is rather fond of mixing pleasure with pain.

Etain felt a flush creep up her face when Anin told her about how "pets" wore collars like animals and were led around by leads attached to them. She remembered Ciaran saying something about the members of his court needing to think she was his pet, and how he would need to treat her as such. She was still confused as to why he would need to debase her in such a way. Why could he not introduce her as a guest of his court?

She must have asked this aloud or the question was plainly written on her face, for Anin explained, "If you are claimed as a pet or even a slave, the rest of the court cannot physically touch you unless you belong to someone of a lesser rank. Since we will be presented as the pets of the two strongest fae of the Night Court, none shall be permitted to touch us. If you were a guest, it would leave you open to be any Night fae's *amusement*."

Etain should not have been shocked to hear "property" was regarded with more respect depending on who owned it. It was not much different in the Human Realm. It never sat well with

Etain how many beings placed objects higher than something living.

"Our humiliation is to be our salvation?" she asked.

Anin gave her a nod with a tight smile. "It will be important that we keep our power hidden. If any of Ciaran's council members or the high court get wind of how powerful you are, or that you are a Walsh witch who returned to the realm, it may inspire some to go against the prince in their quest to gain ultimate power and try to usurp the crown."

Etain gasped, "Would that be possible? I thought only Kes was equal in power to Ciaran."

"He is, and it would be highly unlikely anyone could actually usurp either of them, even if they consumed your power. Though it would be rather unenjoyable for you, Etain."

Etain could feel her hair start to dance around her as she grew increasingly panicked. She did not even know what her powers truly were, let alone how to control them. She could not repeat her performance from the other night if she tried. She had no idea how she did any of that. It just happened. She feared the consequences of letting her emotions get the better of her and what her uncontrolled power would do. Which was a strong possibility since everything was new to her and bound to be incredibly overwhelming and uncomfortable.

"I am sure Kes will bind my magic and power to appease the court. It is almost unheard of to allow a member of the opposite court to keep their life, let alone live outside of a cage. Perhaps it would be wise to have Ciaran do the same to you since your power is untrained and uncontrolled. Ciaran asked me to help you learn to control your power. I must admit, I do not even know where to begin. Ideally, we would find another witch to help you, because it's your own kind who knows how to train your type of magic and power. Sadly, they all live in the Borderlands, and it is unlikely one or two nights of training would make much difference." Anin gave Etain an apologetic look; she could tell the nymph wanted to help.

"Is that how you learned? From other wood nymphs?" Etain was curious about everything.

"My mother and I had different types of power, though she did teach me how to use my magic. A couple of witches taught me a few things I could do with my power. However, my knowledge is paltry at best. It is rather frustrating to have this deep well of power and not be able to come close to using it to its full capacity. For example, I should know how to port, yet there was never anyone around me that knew how." Etain thought the solution to that was easy enough.

"Why not ask Kes? He knows how to do it."

Anin cringed slightly at the suggestion. "I *did* think about it. Ultimately, I think the cost would be too high."

Etain had no idea what she was talking about. The way Kes watched everything she did with a fierce hunger, as Ciaran did with her, said otherwise.

"I think you would be surprised. It does not hurt to ask. If the cost is too much, I will make Ciaran teach you, and then Kes will be mad he is not the one to do it. He will likely put on quite the show with a tantrum," Etain said to Anin.

Anin did such a perfect impersonation of him that they broke out into a fit of laughter at Kes' expense. By the time they began to get a hold of themselves, they both had tears streaming down their faces. She took several deep breaths to calm herself—a few giggles sneaked out.

"Do you know many witches? I would love to meet one. I have never known another witch besides my mother." She was beyond desperate for any information Anin could give to her.

"I actually know many. I may even know some of your relatives. I had to go into hiding when I was still rather young after my mother died. I spent most of my years with the witches in the Borderlands. Perhaps after the Lunar Ball, we can visit the coven I grew up in. I am positive we could find a witch there to help you learn your magic and power."

Etain had not realized how alone she had felt since her mother's death until she heard there were other Walsh witches on this side of the veil. She had family here! Etain did not even try to hold back the smile she gave Anin and let her joy shine through.

Twenty-Nine
Anin

Anin did not want to crush Etain's palpable happiness. There had once been many Walsh witches residing in the coven she spent most of her later youngling years in. Now, she only knew of one still there. Something strange has been happening across the covens of the realm. Witches were disappearing in the middle of the night, leaving notes claiming they had left to join the Day Court. Many of them were Etain's relatives. She had a sinking suspicion Etain was one of the two last Walsh witches to exist.

They were notoriously powerful, however, Etain had the capacity to be the most powerful to exist. Her well was shockingly deep. She might even be the most powerful being in the realm. That all meant nothing if she did not learn how to harness her power and use her magic. The best thing she could do for her new friend was to take her home to the Silver Moon Coven. She knew at least one witch there who would be happy to teach her.

Anin considered the witches her family more than her own kind. Her court was the reason she had to grow up in the Borderlands, hiding from the high fae of the Day Court when she should have been learning how to harness her own power. Had she known a bit more than trivial tricks, she may have been able to successfully flee this realm and avoid *him*.

She knew Kes was her mate, as frustrating as it was. She did not have time for a mate and certainly not for one so obnoxious. Maybe the bond forming between them would help keep her alive once the truth came out. She was not looking forward to the night Ciaran started asking questions she implied she knew the answers to. She just hoped when the time came, her sparse knowledge and theories would be enough.

No one knew where the power came from, yet everyone could feel it. It pulsated from the Day Court and grew regularly. She understood why Ciaran was concerned and wanted to know everything he could about it. There was something about the power that felt oppressive, even wrong. She could not understand how the land could give a power that disrupted the natural balance of the realm. She knew she was missing something, it was just there on the periphery of her mind. Every time she tried to grasp it, the thought would slip away.

She had been tasked by the Many Faced Goddess to uncover what was really happening to the witches. She could tell the disappearances were causing the goddess a lot of heartache. She said all witches were her daughters, and normally she was able to find them anywhere, in any realm. However, something was blocking the missing witches from her sight.

At the time, Anin fought the goddess and even tried to convince her it was a bad idea. The Day Court was hunting her, and she would never be able to search for information across the border. The goddess refused to relent on her request, and that was the end of it. Now she was beginning to think the goddess knew what would come to pass and placed her on this path.

What were the odds of her not only being caught by her mate but also gaining the protection she needed from the Day Court? Then befriending a long lost Walsh witch of incredible power who had also been caught by her mate? All on the same night? This had the meddling of the goddess written all over it and she likely knew exactly how this would all play out. She only told beings exactly what they needed to know, when they needed to know it, and nothing more.

She had to figure out a way to make the disappearances important to Ciaran. She suspected there was a connection between the missing witches and the power growth of the Day Court. Perhaps that would be enough to at least get him to look into it. Anin had a sneaking suspicion the Day Court was looking for a Walsh witch of Etain's depth of power specifically, but she was uncertain to what end. That would likely be enough to garner the prince's attention.

There was no question in her mind that Etain was the Prince of Darkness' mate, however, she did not feel it was her place to tell her. She doubted Etain even knew about mates. No, she would leave that to Ciaran to explain. She was not even sure if Ciaran and Kes knew what either female was to them. Males could be incredibly dense, after all.

Thirty
Ciaran

Ciaran was up before Etain and was pleased to find her draped all over him while she slept. A little too pleased. He got up before she woke and saw his situation.

After he ported Etain to his study, he stopped by the kitchens to order breakfast delivered for the females. It always brought a devilish smile to his face to show up in different parts of the palace unannounced. His presence always caused no small disruption to the fae, sending them tripping over themselves in fear and attempting to look busy. With the exception of the brownies, they feared nothing.

He had been mulling over the discovery he made the night before and knew there had to be a connection between Etain and the Many Faced Goddess' prophecy. He also knew his prisoner's tales of the Shepherd and the Beings of Light were connected to the Day Court's power growth. He just could not see how they all intertwined.

He was almost certain Etain had to be his mate, yet something still made him question if the pull between them was some trick by that goddess bitch. He would not put it past her to make him care for a descendant of the witch to blame for all his problems.

Before Etain, there was nothing he desired more than to destroy any of the Day Court who thought to disrupt the delicate balance of the realm. He never wanted anything—or anyone—besides continuing his wickedness for centuries to come. He still desired this, yet he also desired his witch. The way her skin flushed easily at the smallest touch or subtle innuendos only intensified the feeling. The most troubling was this overwhelming compulsion to bring her happiness.

Happiness, of all things!

He had only ever desired his own happiness before he went out on that fateful hunt. This was the main reason he thought this must be a trick. It had to be the work of the goddess. He could never imagine choosing someone else's happiness over his own.

There was no way Ciaran could possibly care for another in such a way. A true mate bond would likely be with someone as wicked as he. Etain was not wicked in the slightest. She was innocent, good, and worst of all, kind. What sick fate would match him with someone like that? He was sure to cause her pain and suffering, which made his stomach sour just thinking of it. If his court knew he was experiencing such feelings for a woman, they would all think him weak. Which would put Etain in a constant state of danger. It irritated him further how quickly his concern for her wellbeing came to the forefront of his mind.

Ciaran felt his aggression growing over his lack of control when it came to his witch. He needed to work that anger out. He also needed more information to connect the Day Court's meddling in the Human Realm to his little witch. If he could find that connection, it would likely lead him to the source of their sudden increase in power.

It looked like a visit to his human prisoner was in order. Ciaran felt vicious delight bloom inside him and began to manically cackle while porting to his private section of the dungeon. He may have picked up a few tips on making an entrance from his cousin over the years.

He made himself invisible to the human still strapped to the table while his laughter echoed and he scraped his claws across the stone walls. The human flinched and groaned as Ciaran's glee increased. He made his way to the table and peered over at the disgusting human. As soon as his face was mere inches from his, he became visible. He cackled all over again at the look on the human's face. A shrill scream came from the prisoner.

"Miss me?"

"P-please...let me go," the man groaned out. "I promise to not speak of her again."

"Well, of course you will not. Unfortunately—or fortunately, depending on how you look at it—I cannot let you go. You see, I have a desire to hear all there is to know about this Shephard and the "Beings of Light" you speak of. Then, once you have answered all of my questions, I will release you from this room." Ciaran did not find it necessary to tell him he would release him into the waiting arms of Findara. He would hate to ruin the surprise.

The man's eyes lit up at the prospect of freedom. "Y-yes of c-course. I will gladly share the word of light. What is it you wish to know?" he said, stumbling over his words.

"The Word of Light." Ciaran could not help the booming laugh that bubbled out of him and echoed around the stone room. "My dear silly human, this is the Night Court. What need do I have for Light? No, I wish to know more interesting details, such as when did the Shepherd arrive in your realm?"

The man appeared confused by his question. Had he still not realized he was not in his realm any longer? "When was he born? I-I do not know."

Ciaran was getting agitated; he went over to the small knives arranged along the far wall. The man saw what he was going for and began to try to break free from his bonds. "No, p-please! I will answer your questions!"

"I have no doubts you will, human. A little incentive never hurts anyone—well, I suppose this brand of incentive may hurt you. Some things cannot be helped!" Ciaran took the small, sharp blade and used it to cut the man's tunic.

He began screaming immediately. "My gods man, if you scream over your shirt being ruined, I cannot wait to hear the sounds you will make when I ruin your skin. Now stop being ignorant. You are no longer in the Human Realm, and I am sure your Shepherd hails from my realm—the Fae Realm. I know you have heard stories of the creatures from the other side of the veil. I heard Etain scold you for your stupidity in the woods. Now, when did he arrive?"

The look on the man's face was rather humorous. It never occurred to the man to believe the old stories, yet he readily believed whatever his Shepherd told him. Etain had it right, this man was a fool.

Ciaran lowered the blade to the man's chest; he would brand the man a fool by carving it across his flesh. Every time the man looked down, he would never forget what his foolishness had cost him. He wondered briefly if Etain would enjoy seeing her attacker bleeding and branded. Perhaps he would also dismember him so he could never attempt to hurt her in such a way again.

Over the course of several hours, he finished carving the man's chest and was confident he had gathered as much information about the Shepherd and the "Beings of Light" the man had to offer. The Shepherd arrived in their village several years ago, and it seemed his main concern was locating witches and bringing them "into the light," as the man called it. Ciaran thought it obvious the Shepherd was taking witches into the Day Court. Try as they might, the Shepherd and the man could never get Etain to "come to the light." Oddly, he said no other woman was ever labeled a witch in his town. However, he heard of several from some of the towns closest to them.

Perhaps they need the witches to be compliant, and that is why they attempt to make them zealots. Or perhaps since Etain had never crossed the veil and tapped into her power, the Shepherd thought her a simple human hedge witch. Either way, it looked as though the Day Court was collecting witches and possibly searching for something, or someone in particular. It was no stretch for Ciaran to guess Etain was the witch they were seeking, for he had never met another with as much raw power as she had. What a coincidence she wound up in his care, whatever the bond between them is, making him desire to protect her at all costs.

Ciaran did not believe in coincidences. He also knew he was still missing pieces of the puzzle. Just then his stomach rumbled; torture always made him rather hungry. The night after the Lunar Ball would be the right time to talk to the nymph and see what she could tell him about the Day Court and its habit of collecting witches.

He left the man still strapped to his table, groaning. Blood streamed from the word "fool" on his chest that Ciaran had carved in scrolling script; he considered it art.

Thirty-One

Kes

Kes received a message from Ciaran on his spelled parchment to meet them in his study for dinner. He had been out gathering all the things required for the blood oath: a dagger made of obsidian, the herbs to burn, different herbs to mix into the blood, a spelled parchment which would bind their agreement, and a chalice to mix their blood and herbs.

The palace and the surrounding city were alive with preparations for the following night's Lunar Ball. He knew he was being watched, and the items he was collecting were noted. It would not take long for word to spread that he was preparing to make a blood oath. If there was something this court loved nearly as much as being wicked, it was gossip. By the time of the celebration tomorrow night, the court will have concocted some kind of ridiculous story about the type of oath and with whom he was making it. Entering with Anin would likely start a whole new theory.

It had been a long time since Kes had seen a blood oath performed, and he had never performed one himself. He had done everything in his power to never be beholden to another, yet here he was about to be beholden to a nymph from the Day

Court. He knew tomorrow night, at the Lunar Ball, most of the court would be able to piece together who he had made one with. They would still not know the specifics, but they would be more interested in Anin than he would like. He had no doubts in the coming nights he would have to make some kind of show of violence to let the court know what would happen if they dared touch a hair on her head.

While feeling rather put out by being tied to another, especially by a serious oath. He found himself wanting to keep Anin safe from harm anyway. The idea of any other creature being tied to her in any way made his blood boil. He would take great joy from peeling the skin slowly off any other being who tried. The prospect both thrilled and angered him. Something about being tied to her in any way felt right, while the Night fae side of him rebelled at having any such feelings towards a Day fae. He found himself wanting, and that never went well in the Night Court. Wanting anything gave others something to exploit to their advantage. Still, he wanted her. Even if he could not understand why, it did not stop him from always being pulled towards her. He could not seem to make heads or tails of these feelings. They were too new to him, and he could not say he was exactly *thrilled* about them.

He was the last to arrive in the study. As he strode to his seat, in between Anin and Ciaran, he stopped behind Anin's chair, brought his mouth to her delicately pointed ear and said, "Hello, my darling nymph—did you miss me?"

She huffed and swatted at him, which only made him laugh. He enjoyed nothing more than getting under her skin. They both appeared to be waging a mental and physical war against each other. He knew she was struggling with the same pull as he was. It felt as though the more he fought it, the more he wanted her.

When he took his seat, he looked over at Anin and caught her gaze. They both stared into each other's eyes for a few moments before Kes gave her one of his heated smirks. He was rewarded with an eye roll and a flush of bright green across her cheeks. Anin tried to act unphased by him, yet he knew she was just as affected as he was.

"Did you have any trouble procuring all of the items necessary for the blood oath?" Ciaran inquired.

Kes listed off the items he gathered, where he got them, and then filled him in on the many eyes watching him with calculating curiosity. He shared a look with his cousin, both of them unwilling to admit the fear that coursed through them. Neither one of them wanted to share either female with anyone else, and definitely not with their court. Kes knew it was necessary, particularly if they were here to stay. They would teach their court they were off limits, and anyone who pushed the limits would be used as an example.

"Would it be possible to witness this blood oath, or is this something done in private?" Etain asked.

"All of us will be there to witness it, although it is typically something done in private. Since most of the oath on Anin's part is about information she's agreed to give to me, I need to be there to make sure the terms we agreed upon are followed through," Ciaran told her. His cousin always had trust issues and rarely left anything to chance.

Kes had not yet informed his cousin of the bargain he had made with Anin for five truths from her. He knew his cousin saw the matching black inky rings around their fingers but had not inquired about them. Kes planned to hold onto those five questions. They were only to be used when he knew he could not get the answer from her any other way. He also had a feeling using any of the five would be a violation in Anin's eyes.

"Anin told me some rather colorful stories to prepare me for what to expect tomorrow night during the Lunar Ball. Truly, will we be required to wear a collar and a lead as if we are some kind of animal?" Etain asked with no small amount of disgust lacing her voice.

"Yes, little witch, and I do so look forward to seeing you tugged along behind me and kneeling at my feet. You will also be wearing something you might find uncomfortably revealing. Worry not—I will personally remove the hands of anyone who dares to touch you." Ciaran looked rather pleased at the image that came to his mind.

He could not be sure what Ciaran was more excited about. Seeing his witch at his feet or removing the hands of any being who attempted to touch her in any way. Kes had to agree.

"Anin, my darling nymph, you know I must bind both your magic and power before the ball or we will risk the wrath of the court. They will already be plotting once they figure out you are the one I took the blood oath with. Do not worry, darling, you will be entirely at my mercy, and I cannot say the prospect does not excite me." He leaned towards her and whispered so only she could hear, "In more ways than one. Hmmm, I wonder how wet you would get if I bent you over my knee and showed the whole court those shades of green I am dying to see." He inhaled her scent and could smell the arousal coming from her. "Such a dirty, dirty nymph." He was rewarded with her eyes unwillingly filling with heat as she unconsciously bit her bottom lip.

Just then, Etain cleared her throat and gave them each a knowing smirk. Anin grumbled something under her breath about "*stupid males*" and adjusted herself in her seat. He laughed at her knowingly.

Thirty-Two

ETAIN

Etain yawned after getting her fill of the enormous and mouth watering feast set before her. She could not help herself; every time they sat down for a meal, there were always new and delicious things to try. She caught Ciaran watching her eat multiple times, and she could not be sure if he was amused at her love of fae food, or if it was something else. The look in his eyes made her think it was something else. She yawned again, feeling relaxed and satiated. Ciaran took that as his cue to escort her back to his bedchambers.

She thanked Anin for helping her tonight and for answering all of her many questions. Etain was certain they were building what would likely be a strong friendship. It had been a long time since she had a friend. She was excited and wished she could spend just a few more hours getting to know the nymph, though she was exhausted. She knew they would see each other again tomorrow at first night.

After wishing Anin and Kes a good-night, Ciaran ported them back to his bedchambers. He had yet to mention anything about binding her magic, not even after Kes had brought it up to Anin. She walked over to the huge set of windows and looked out at the darkened land while she fidgeted with her fingers.

"Ciaran, I fear what will happen when I no doubt get overwhelmed tomorrow at the Lunar Ball. What if my magic goes crazy again in front of your whole court?"

Ciaran grabbed her hands in one of his and pulled her towards him. He then lifted her chin so she was looking into his golden eyes. "While it would bring quite a bit of trouble, and I find trouble rather enjoyable, I do worry about your safety. It would be wiser to not reveal the enormity of your power until after you have a grasp on it and we have a better understanding of what exactly your power can do. It would make others think twice about coming after you if they knew you could destroy them with a blink." He grinned down at her. "I am loath to do it, yet I suppose if it would make you feel more confident, I can bind your powers before the festival, like Kes will do to Anin."

She thought about it for a couple of minutes. On one hand, it would be taking her greatest weapon away, on the other hand, weapons in the hands of the untrained can be incredibly dangerous to the ones wielding it. Etain nodded and told Ciaran as much.

"Tomorrow will push you well outside of your comfort zone, little witch. I believe your human sensibilities will be telling you to feel indignant. I ask only that you try to be open to the ways of the Night Court. Embrace your darkest nature and let yourself go."

He leaned down, put his mouth next to her ear, and softly whispered, "Let yourself enjoy the feeling..." Then he gently nipped her ear and made his way down her neck. She gasped and felt herself arching into him. He reached down with both hands, gripping each one of her ass cheeks, lifting her easily to access her mouth; her legs wrapped around his waist.

The kiss was much gentler, though no less breath-stealing, than their first kiss. Etain wrapped her arms around his neck and groaned into his mouth as she felt him harden against her core. He began walking towards the bathing chamber and placed her gently next to the obsidian tub. He pulled away from her to drag his thumb across her lips. She felt emboldened and sucked his thumb into her mouth. Ciaran hissed; his eyes turned into molten gold.

Ciaran filled the tub with steaming hot water and added intoxicating smelling oils. He then stood behind her and began to explore her body with his touch. She looked up and found him looking directly at her through the mirror-like obsidian walls.

"Tell me, little witch—has anyone ever touched you like this before? Undressed you like this?" Right as he said "this," Etain felt her dress slide down her body. All she could do was stare as Ciaran brought his large hands up to grasp her breasts and then gave them a gentle squeeze.

"It does not feel fair that here I am bared and yet, you are still fully clothed," she said breathlessly. She may have never been touched in such a way, however, it was not because she did not want to be. Ciaran had her body ignited in heat.

He smirked at her, then unwrapped his shirt and let his trousers fall to the ground. "Is that better, little witch?"

She turned and began to let her fingers trail over his muscular chest. He had many black, inky markings swirling around him, down to his abdomen and around to his back. His arms were covered in them as well. He was a work of art. She knew each one of them was some kind of spell or magic marking his body.

Ciaran turned the water flow off in the tub, guided Etain in, and then stepped in behind her. He sat down and had her sit in front of him with her back to his front. He slowly trailed his fingers up her arms and down her chest, gently caressing her nipples.

She whimpered, and Ciaran let out a low growl. "If you only knew what those little sounds you are making do to me, little witch. Now, tell me, have you ever touched yourself while you were laying alone at night in your bed?"

Etain could only nod. She was no stranger to her own hand. It had even been encouraged while she was growing up. Her mother always told her she should know her own body, and there was no shame in the knowing.

"Show me." Ciaran grabbed her hand and gently trailed her own fingers down her body under the water and towards her center.

She felt like there was a current of energy flowing through her, and she noticed in a far off way how the lights began to flicker. She was too caught up in the moment to consider being embarrassed.

With Ciaran's hand on top of hers, she found her sensitive bud and began to slowly circle it. He brought his other hand around to her breasts and began to squeeze them with a bit more force.

She gasped and pushed her chest into his hand while beginning to speed up and apply more pressure to herself. Ciaran pulled and twisted her nipples in turn, while his hand on her hand began to drift even lower.

The hand that had been bringing pleasure, and simultaneously the edge of pain, to her breasts began to slide up to her neck. He gripped her neck firmly and lifted her gaze to the mirrored obsidian ceiling. "Look, Etain—see how beautiful you look as you fall apart on our hands."

Just as the words left his mouth, a finger from the hand that had been on top of hers entered her. She bucked, sending water sloshing over the sides of the tub. Ciaran began to slide that finger in and out, and then slowly curled that finger until it hit a spot which made her entire core go molten. She cried out and sent another wave of water over the side of the tub.

"That's it, little witch, ride my hand." He pulled his finger out, and just as she let out a frustrated growl, he chuckled and entered her again, but this time with two fingers. After she adjusted to the new full feeling, he began to enter her harder and harder with his fingers, while her hand sped up; his other hand kept a solid grip on her neck. She could not look away from the image she saw of them on the ceiling, slightly obscured by the dark surface.

The water in the tub was churning like a sea during a storm, mirroring the storm brewing inside her. The feeling kept climbing higher and higher.

"Gods, you are incredible. Are you going to come for me, little witch? Let me feel you clench around my fingers."

With those words, Etain came crashing over the edge and cried out Ciaran's name. He slowed his fingers and let her ride out her pleasure.

When she finally came down, he wrapped his arms around her. They laid like that in the tub until the water started to grow cold. He picked her up and dried her off, then carried her to bed. She never felt this languid in her entire life. The fear of the Lunar Ball long forgotten as she drifted off to sleep in Ciaran's arms.

Thirty-Three

Ciaran

Ciaran awoke just before first night and could not help roaming his hands over his little witch's body. She had been magnificent last night in the bath. He had never seen her look more beautiful than when she fell apart on his hand. Thinking about it was making him grow hard, but before he could get any wild ideas, his little witch opened her eyes and smiled sleepily at him.

He could have sworn time stopped for a moment, and a little buzz of something rattled around in his chest. He knew he would burn the realm down for this woman, and he was not sure he cared anymore if it was the work of the Many Faced Goddess. He did not think he could go back to his life before his little witch arrived. It was like he had been living without truly seeing color, and then she came and painted his world with vibrancy.

He wished they could stay locked up in his bedchambers all day and continue what they had started last night. He wanted to become intimately acquainted with every inch of her body.

"Good morning, my prince," she said in a voice still heavy with sleep.

"It's almost first night, little witch, and as much as I would prefer to spend the day being educated on this delicious body, we unfortunately have much to do before the Lunar Ball this night." He kissed her gently on the forehead as a flush overtook her cheeks at his words.

When she turned to roll out of bed, he grabbed her and pulled her back into him as she let out a peel of laughter; it was a sound he would do anything to hear over and over again. He wrapped his arms around her and kissed her deeply. He could get used to waking up like this every night for eternity.

He broke the kiss, then pressed his nose to hers. "You are horribly distracting, little witch. Now quit loitering and get ready to meet Kes and Anin."

She just laughed as she got out of bed. She realized she was naked and tried to pull the sheet around herself. However, Ciaran was nothing if not wicked, and he held on tight to it.

"Really? You brute!" she said to him, with no real venom behind her words. He grinned at her and enjoyed the view. She turned and walked towards the bathing room, her hips swaying with each step; she knew he was watching.

While Etain was using the facilities, He dressed himself and found a random dagger in his trouser pocket. She had not been overexaggerating when she said there was a small arsenal shoved randomly around his chambers. Perhaps he should rework the spell to account for organization after all. He figured his little witch was here to stay; there was no way he was letting her go. He did not think she wished to leave either, and she would likely have demands on the way their chambers were arranged.

He paused, was he really becoming domesticated? He found he did not care as long as it was with her. Perhaps it would be good practice for her to create the spell to her liking, once she had some time to learn her magic and power. He was intrigued to see what she would be capable of doing with that vault of power he could feel residing within her. If she were the key to breaking the curse after all, they would be an unstoppable force.

She emerged dressed in a simple dark green gown, which appeared to be her color of choice, and he was dressed in his traditional black. When they were ready for the day, he ported them to his study where Kes and Anin were waiting. They had already arranged everything on the table in preparation for the blood oath. It looked as though the final thing was to write the agreement on the spelled parchment, and then they could begin. The whole thing would take a few minutes. He went ahead and requested breakfast be delivered in an hour.

"Good morning!" his little witch said cheerily to Anin and Kes. He was growing rather fond of her silly little human sayings.

Kes and Anin smiled and looked unsure of how they were supposed to respond.

"Shall we get this out of the way?" Ciaran asked the room, prompting everyone to take their seats.

"Since you have never seen a blood oath performed, I thought you might like it if I explained the ceremony as it happens."

She looked up into his eyes and smiled. "I would like that very much, prince."

He explained that burning the herbs was necessary to allow their magic to merge. The smell of them began to permeate the room and make everything feel just a bit hazy. He did not need to be this close to explain the steps of the blood oath, though he thought he might have a little fun with his witch. He placed his hand casually on her knee under the table as Kes and Anin in turn wrote out the specific agreements of the blood oath.

He leaned in close and whispered in her ear about the need to write the oath on parchment with a binding spell made specifically for a blood oath. He also told her how the words needed to be excessively specific, or the oath could be too broad and get one or both parties in trouble later.

"We would not want that, would we, little witch?" he asked as he slowly drifted his hand up her thigh.

Etain's eyes shot to his and widened, yet she kept her face neutral. This spurred him on to see how far he could go until he got a reaction out of her. He grazed his lips down to her neck and gently nipped at her while he explained the dagger used was based on the power level of the fae entering the blood oath. Since they were both of unusually high power, the oath required a blade of obsidian since it was the strongest known conduit of power. If they used a blade of weaker strength, one or both of them could easily break the oath.

Her breathing was starting to become faster, and that glorious flush was beginning to deepen to a near crimson. He continued to slowly creep his hand further up her thigh as they watched the two slice their palms, one after the other, with the obsidian blade. Then, they entwined the fingers of their cut hands and squeezed them together above the small goblet, creating a stream of blood that slowly filled the vessel.

Ciaran did not miss how the two locked eyes the whole time their hands were entwined. There was definitely tension building in the room that seemed to be affecting everyone.

He slowly brushed her dark, blood-red hair off her shoulder and continued nipping down to the crook of her neck. In between nips, he explained how a second set of herbs are added to the blood to mix their blood and powers together in the chalice. They both watched as first Anin, and then Kes, drank from the goblet.

"The blood oath is nearly complete. Now they will place their still bleeding hands on the parchment to seal the oath. Nothing will be able to break it once they both lay their hands upon it, until the terms of the oath are complete," he said against her neck, making more gooseflesh rise across her. His hand was so close to her center, and he could feel her moving ever so slightly as if seeking him out to relieve the need he could see burning behind her eyes.

As soon as Kes and Anin lifted their bloody hands, Ciaran pulled his hand away and sat up from Etain. He gave her one of his wickedest grins and was pleased to hear the frustrated noises she was trying to stifle.

She shifted in her seat, looking for relief, which made him chuckle under his breath. Etain glared at him, only making his grin grow wider.

He clapped his hands together once, breaking the tension in the room, and declared, "And that is how a blood oath is done, little witch. Did you find it as tantalizing as I did?"

If looks could kill, then the one she gave him would have him already dead on the floor. He just found his new favorite game.

ETAIN

Etain's skin was on fire. She felt like she was burning from the inside out with need. Ciaran played her body like a stringed instrument, with her strings tuned too tightly. They had returned to his bedchambers to rest before preparing for the Lunar Ball. Now they were alone; she was flustered and unable to center her thoughts. Her nerves were already frazzled in anticipation of the night to come, and now her body was equally on edge. He was shameless. A big blue bat of a shameless male.

He told her he had a surprise for her he had almost forgotten about entirely. She was ecstatic and nearly cried when he presented her satchel. She had thought it was gone forever in the woods near her home in the Human Realm. She had thrown her arms around his waist in unfettered joy and thanked him numerous times for his forethought in bringing her bag along with her.

She opened it and pulled out her family's grimoire. She told him it was the single most important possession she owned. It held the history of her family and connected her to her ancestors. She had not realized how deeply she had been mourning its loss.

Ciaran watched her with a soft expression as she reverently stroked the book that meant everything to her.

"You know, little witch, you should never have to be without the things that are most important to you. I can spell your book to be able to retrieve it from anywhere, in any realm, and at any time."

She looked up in amazement. "Magic can do that?" she asked with no small amount of amazement.

"Magic or power can do anything. Sometimes there is a price to pay if you use either in such a way to disrupt the balance, but this is a simple trick I can teach you in mere moments."

He opened the drawer closest to them and found another dagger that had been shoved into a random spot. "Here—I will show you how to do it on this dagger, and then you can do it on your book."

He told her to imagine the book as if it were a part of her, which was easy enough since she already imagined it was. Then, he said all she needed to do was imagine a tether from the book to her and use her power to will that invisible tether into reality. She closed her eyes to picture it better. She saw in her mind's eye the shimmering strand connecting herself to the grimoire, and she felt her power snap it into place.

Her eyes flew open, and she looked up at him with wonder. "I think I did it! How do I know if it worked?"

He reached down and grabbed the book, placing it in a cabinet, and told her to feel that thread and pull. Etain did, and she pulled hard—too hard. Before she even realized what was happening, the book collided with her chest, causing the air to suddenly leave her lungs. It was no small book, after all.

Ciaran threw his head back and roared with laughter. She glared at him, though she found it hard to be mad when she just used her power for the first time of her own free will.

"Perhaps next time, little witch, try a gentler hand," he said with the last bits of his laughter shining in his eyes.

She got up and placed the book on the bed, then walked several paces away and tried again. She was amazed to see it disappear and, this time, reappear gently in her hands. It was almost as if the book traveled through the invisible thread. "Thank you, Ciaran. You have no idea what this means to me." She closed the distance between them and lifted as high as she could on her tiptoes to reach his shoulders with her hands. He understood what she wanted and leaned forward to meet her mouth in a soft kiss.

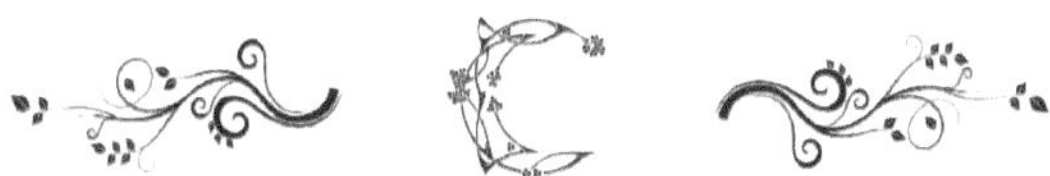

Etain shifted in the overstuffed wingback she had been sitting in, her body still uncomfortable with need. She was looking back in her family's grimoire for any information regarding the earliest Walsh witches. Particularly, anything they may have written that could help with her magic or power, and understanding this realm.

Every time she shifted, she felt his eyes on her as he looked up from his book. He sat across from her, and every time she looked at him, he wore a rather smug grin. He was entirely too proud of himself, and the effect he could easily have on her. She rolled her eyes at him and willed herself to focus on her research.

"Is something bothering you, my little witch?"

She could feel her traitorous body heat her face crimson. "No, I am merely anxious to find what I am searching for."

He gave her a knowing smirk she could feel, since she refused to look at him. "Hmmm, I'm sure. You definitely seem to be searching for something."

She did not dare look up from her book. She had read this page several times and still had not actually taken in the words. Frustrated in more ways than one, she flipped to the very front of the book. She decided to read the whole thing from beginning to end.

Hours passed as she immersed herself in her family's history. She immersed herself in her research. She could almost ignore the heat that was still burning in her belly. She nearly jumped out of her skin when he placed a plate of bread, fruits, and cheeses on the small table next to her. He always moved too quickly and quietly; she was sure it would always unsettle her.

"So jumpy, little witch," he said as he placed either hand on the arms of her chair. He leaned into her space, running his nose up the column of her neck.

She swallowed a groan.

"You smell delectable, little witch. Have you found anything to fulfill your needs yet?" he asked, and the meaning was not lost on her. He knew the effect he had on her and looked to be taking immense pleasure in getting her body more and more unsettled.

She tried her best to seem unaffected by him as she slowly turned the page and kept reading. "Not yet, though I am sure..."

She trailed off and sat up a little straighter as she reread the page to make sure she was reading what she thought she was reading. For once, she was distracted enough to forget her body and the male that was still entirely too close.

"You found something, did you?" he asked.

It took her a few moments to pull her eyes away from the page and look up at him. "I think so. Here—look," she said excitedly, shifting to allow him to read the page as well.

He stiffened slightly as they both read an entry made by one of her earliest ancestors. She was recounting the events that led her to curse the Night Court king of her time. Apparently, he had been stealing witches as they slept in their beds. He did unspeakable things to them. If he returned them, it was several weeks later, and they were mere shells of the women they had been.

"Ciaran, was this your relative? He sounds like he was a real...gem," she said, her voice filled with disgust.

He was quiet for a moment, and Etain began to wonder what was going through his head. "He was my great-grandfather. I told you, little witch, I am a very wicked male, and I come from a long line of very wicked males."

He moved his head back to the side of her neck and breathed her in again before placing his mouth next to her ear and saying, "Although, it seems my wickedness does not apply to you. Well, at least not in a way you do not seem to enjoy." He nipped a trail down her neck until she shivered and gooseflesh erupted on her skin.

She thought she would surely combust at any moment. She was left reeling when he pulled away suddenly and declared it was time for them to prepare for the Lunar Ball. He pulled the massive book from her lap and ushered her off to the bathing chamber. Etain was nearly drunk with the effect he had on her body and barely remembered entering the obsidian room. She did not think her face could heat any further; though, one glance at the tub and her body proved her wrong. She would not be taking a bath, that was for sure.

She strode over to the nook with the heated waterfall in the corner and stepped into it. When she emerged, she felt slightly more relaxed and smelled of jasmine and lavender. After she dried off, she noticed a sheer black gossamer gown hanging against the wall. It looked like it had been adorned with the millions of stars that decorated the night sky. It was absolutely lovely.

There was a beautiful black leather top, cropped to her midriff, and matching black leather bottoms, barely covering her unmentionables. She had never worn such scandalous undergarments. She was uncertain of the leather and thought it would be especially uncomfortable. She was proved wrong as soon as she put them on, the leather was incredibly soft and fit her perfectly.

When she pulled the dress down from its hanging spot, she was first confused about how to put it on. After some fidgeting, she realized it wrapped around her body, and straps held it together at her waist. That's when she noticed how incredibly sheer it was. You could easily make out her undergarments through the shimmering material.

Embarrassment began to color her cheeks when she thought about everyone seeing more of her than was proper. Then, she glanced at herself in the dark, reflective surface of the walls and thought she looked rather magical. Perhaps she should let go of her human sensibilities. If the Fae were comfortable with their bodies, surely she could be as well.

Thirty-Five
Ciaran

Ciaran immediately opened Etain's family grimoire the moment she disappeared behind the bathing chamber door. He continued reading from where he had left off. The list of misdeeds his great-grandfather had committed was not unknown to him. He had just been reading his great-grandfather's own account, where he was practically bragging about the splendid ways he tortured the many witches he stole.

As he read the account from Etain's great-grandmother, he learned she had to flee the Fae Realm and hide in the human world, because his great-grandfather had been enraged and would not stop hunting the witch that cursed him. It was not until the witch was with child that she fled, fearing more for her child than herself. He kept reading, confident that if there was anyone who would have made a record of the curse itself, it would be the witch who placed it to begin with. Sure enough, as he made his way down the following page, there it was.

"In order for the curse to be broken, a descendant of my body must fall in mutual love with the descendant of his body. As soon as the two are bound and ascend the throne, the curse on that descendant's line will be broken, and full power will be restored.

It must be true and honest love, for this love will greatly balance the wicked ways of the Night Court and bring with it a new era of harmony."

Ciaran groaned. Of course, the witch would make it an impossible task, one that could not be cheated in the slightest. As he thought about it, he wondered if it was truly as impossible as he first thought. If he had learned of this information before meeting Etain, he would have found it impossible, just as his great-grandfather had. He would have gone on his own rampage, destroying any witch he came across, unless they could find another way to break the curse.

He supposed it was a good thing he had not found that journal entry from his great-grandfather sooner. How interesting he found it now, considering he had searched every library in the palace and many others across the Night Court. Yet he never once stumbled across it, only to find it easily the other night.

The way the witch spoke of the curse made it seem like every descendant of his great-grandfather was cursed to half their power. Not just the one in line for the throne, like he assumed this whole time. This would mean Kes was cursed as well. Part of breaking the curse is to ascend the throne. He wondered if this knowledge would make Kes want to betray him and make a move for the throne to break his own curse. Perhaps he will keep this knowledge to himself for the time being. Once he and Etain ascended their thrones, he would then divulge the information to Kes.

Ciaran heard Etain moving around in the bathing chamber and figured his time for snooping was coming to an end. He put the book down in the chair She had been sitting in. He tried to make it look as if he placed it there when she first got up and then quickly dressed for the ball. It was a quick change, for the only thing he wore were black leather pants and his boots, leaving his chest bare. He completed his look with his black obsidian crown, which he only wore when dealing with the court.

He heard Etain making her way to the door and quickly took up his place in the chair he had been reading in all afternoon—or at least trying to read. Every time she shifted in her seat, seeking relief from the need he had been building in her all day, he would catch the scent of her arousal in the air. It would take restraint that Ciaran had never possessed before to maintain his air of cool nonchalance. He did not think she had any idea of the effect she had on him.

He was purposely bringing her need higher and higher all day in hopes she would have a greater chance of embracing the depraved debauchery of the Night Court. If he brought her higher and higher the rest of the night, he had no doubt he would be inside Etain's eager body in his bed this very night.

The door opened, and Ciaran was momentarily dumbstruck. He was the one who picked out Etain's wardrobe for the Lunar Ball, and now he was about ready to murder anyone who dared to glance her way. She looked like a goddess of night.

She had not looked up to see him yet, as she inspected her wet strands of hair, which looked near-black. She had missed the way he suddenly stood and practically lurched towards her.

"Ciaran—it's going to take hours for my hair to dry. I do not suppose you have some way to speed it along? I do fear the dripping is making my gown..." She trailed off as she looked up and found him gawking at her. She then took in his own attire, letting out a soft sound as her mouth fell open.

"I have never seen you wear a crown before. It does make you look rather regal." She said as if that was the only reason for her reaction.

Ciaran gave her his most devilish, toothy smile as he sauntered up to her. He reached out his hand, holding it just above her hair. In moments, her hair was dry and shiny, with a gentle wave cascading down her back.

"Yes, my little witch. I do indeed have a way to speed it along," he said softly next to her ear before stepping away. "I will teach you this simple trick later. You are a vision of night." He was rewarded with the flush he loved so much, which rose from her chest to her cheeks. Leaning down, he brushed his lips across hers and said, "I can smell your arousal, little witch, and I intend to bring you to the edge of desperate need. I plan to make you beg for me when we retire to our chambers after the ball."

Her eyes widened and her pupils blew wide. Her breathing increased in such a way that it made her chest heave with her breath in their leather confines. Ciaran enjoyed the view immensely.

They stared into each other's eyes for a few moments before Ciaran made sure she still wanted him to bind her power for the night's festivities. As soon as she confirmed, he began to focus his power around her, creating knot after knot, until she was cut off from the well of power within her. He frowned slightly at her bereft-sounding gasp as she blinked rapidly. He had never been cut off completely from his power, though he knew the frustration of not being able to access its full extent. He heard being cut off completely felt like losing something as vital as a limb.

He cupped her face and lifted her so she was looking into his eyes again. "At any time, all you must do is tell me you wish for the binding to be gone, and I will remove it. You are in complete control of when your power returns."

She gave him a watery smile and simply nodded. He ran his hands down her body until they reached her hips, and he roughly pulled her flush to himself. "I am going to greatly enjoy plucking the eyes from any being who dares to let their eyes linger on you for more than a moment. If anyone is foolish enough to dare touch what's mine, they will be stripped of their foolish hands. That's what you are, you know? Mine."

Etain gasped, and he was pleased to see the heat back in her eyes. It appeared she enjoyed how possessive he was of her. "And are you mine, then prince?" she asked him with a voice full of desire.

"There is no question about that, little witch. I have been yours since the moment I first saw you in the woods."

Her face softened a bit from the heated expression she had been trying to mask all day to one of adoration. Ciaran could not be sure which one he loved more. He leaned down and gently touched his lips to hers in a soft kiss he hoped conveyed his feelings for her.

He wasn't used to being this vulnerable. He pulled away and went to run his fingers through his hair, as he was prone to do when feeling uncertain. He forgot he was wearing his crown and nearly knocked it off his head, which made her giggle. He couldn't decide what sounds he loved more from her—sounds of happiness or need. Good gods, he also wasn't sure when he had become such a besotted fool. He decided if it was only when it came to her, he could accept it.

He pointed at the knee-high leather boots with a slight heel and told her he had not forgotten her shoes this time. He explained to her he would be dropping her off with Kes and Anin in his study. Kes would be escorting both of them to the festival, so Ciaran could make sure his court heard his threat of dismemberment clearly before she entered.

He reached into his pocket and pulled out the final piece to her ensemble—a thin black obsidian collar that matched his crown and that only he could remove. The lead was built into the stone and had a barely-visible silver shimmer that was spelled so only he and Etain could touch it. He would not risk anyone else thinking they could drag her around by the neck. Not even Kes or Anin.

As soon as the stone touched her neck, it sealed itself around her. Ciaran draped the lead in such a way it looked like an intricate necklace. She looked slightly uncertain and softly touched the stone around her neck. When she looked up into his eyes and saw the hungry way Ciaran stared at both the collar and her, she relaxed.

"Now hurry and get your shoes on before I rip the gown from you and throw you on the bed—then we'll never make it to the ball at all."

Etain's eyes lit up, and a sultry smile emerged before she turned and slowly bent to step into her boots. Ciaran was sure she was beginning to understand she held all the power between them. Even when she had no access to her own, she still owned all of his.

Thirty-Six
SEAMUS

Seamus could not be sure how long he had been strapped to the table. He had long ago lost his battle with the urge to relieve himself, and he could no longer feel his appendages. He never felt thirst like this, and his stomach was cramping from hunger. There was nothing he wanted more than to be free from this demon cursed place. He cursed Etain, not for the first time, and he knew it would not be the last time either. Seamus had come to the conclusion this entire situation was her fault. If she had agreed to join him on his journey of ascension to the Beings of Light as his wife, none of this would have happened to him.

All she had to do was truly listen to what Seamus told her about the preaching's of the Shepherd. He knew her views and beliefs would change if she just listened to him the way any good woman should listen to their betrothed, but no—she had to be stubborn. Her selfish ways had led him to follow her in the woods that night and call upon desperate measures to make her pure. She caused that; Seamus had only been doing what he could to save her.

The blue demon of a beast was the most vile thing Seamus had ever seen. He would love nothing more than to squeeze the life from his evil form. If his life mission had been to join the Beings of Light, this creature would be the exact opposite. He assumed he was being tested to see if he was truly worthy of ascension. He was desperate to get out of these bonds and prove himself. Shifting as much as he could, he sucked in a sharp hiss of breath.

He had nearly forgotten the demon had carved the word "FOOL" into his chest. He was indeed a fool for ever thinking Etain could be saved, especially if this was the type of creature she worshiped. The demon protected Etain in exchange for her loyalty and body, no doubt. She quickly gave that monstrosity her body, he just knew it to be true, yet she had denied *him* repeatedly. She was nothing but a demon whore.

Seamus had never felt such rage and indignation. If he ever had the chance again to take it out on Etain, he would. It was her fault he was strapped to this table, and she had not intervened on his behalf. He never did anything except try to bring her into the Light to save her. How did she thank him? By dodging him in public and shutting doors in his face in private.

It was not his fault he had to turn the townsfolk against her over the past several years. She forced him when she continued to insist on her independence. He wanted her to be completely dependent on *him*. He could take better care of her and make her welcome the Light. She was an *ungrateful* whore as well.

Seamus was in the middle of another mental tirade when he heard the shifting of the wind announcing someone's arrival. He tried not to flinch at the idea of spending any more time with the demon. He did not think he would ever forget the look on the demon's face as he carved into Seamus' chest. It would haunt him for the rest of his days, and he hated the demon even more for having that kind of power over him. He readied himself as best he could. However, he knew there was no preparation for the demon's version of fun.

"Seamus." He knew that voice. Seamus felt something wet slide down one cheek. He had come for him, just like Seamus had been praying for.

"Shepherd." Seamus' voice was dry and raspy with disuse.

"Hello, Seamus—a shepherd never leaves one of his flock behind." He was quiet for a moment, and Seamus felt immense love for the man who had become like a father to him.

"Seamus, you have found yourself in a position to prove to the Beings of Light you are fit to ascend to the Kingdom of Light. All you must do is complete your test. A mission that has been prepared for you by the God of Light himself. Do you accept your test?"

Seamus felt a warmth of pride in his chest. He would do whatever they asked of him; he was ready. "Of course, Shepherd—whatever the Light demands, I will give," he said confidently.

The Shepherd began to outline a plan that made Seamus smile for the first time in days; he did not even care his lips cracked. The God of Light and he were on the same path. This would give him the two things he wanted most: off this table and revenge on Etain. He could not have been given a more perfect mission.

"Wonderful, Seamus. I knew we could count on you. I will remove your bonds in a moment. However, the gift of healing I am about to place on you will keep you immobile for the next couple hours. It will only heal; it will not remove your scars. You need to be reminded of why we must work hard to bring all into the Light."

"I will wear them with purpose, Shepherd," Seamus said with conviction.

"As soon as you can move your body, throw this orb at your feet, and it will take you right to where you need to be. Here is a map of your route out of the palace once you have completed your mission. There will be a horse and wagon waiting for you. Follow the map left in the wagon, and I shall meet you along the way." The Shepherd waved his golden hand along Seamus' body. Seamus felt everything go stiff, and he started to panic.

"Relax, Seamus. I am giving you the gift of healing Light. It will heal you fully and swiftly—you need to be at your strongest for your mission."

At the mention of the mission, Seamus forced himself to calm down and relax. He had already been strapped down tight, so it was not much of a change. He told himself he could adjust to this, knowing soon he would be healed and able to move his body. It was a miracle, and Seamus was in complete awe of the Shepherd.

"Remember, you must go immediately when you are able to move your body. Everything is timed specifically around your healing. There will be others on their own missions, and you will not know them. You are not to speak to any of them if you should meet." Seamus felt the straps around his body disappear. "Oh, and Seamus? Try not to get caught. We will not come for you again." As suddenly as he had appeared, the Shepherd disappeared.

Seamus relaxed back into himself and smiled in his mind. He began to think of the way he would exact his vengeance on the demon whore once they were alone. He had many glorious ideas. Her life would become filled with pain the second he had her. He was coming for the witch, and she would beg his forgiveness. Seamus would make sure she begged.

Thirty-Seven

Kes

Kes and Anin arrived in Ciaran's study last, but it could not be helped. Anin came out dressed in nothing but a wide black leather band that wound around her body, barely covering her. He thought he might get his wish for violence after all as he drank his fill. She made flowers bloom on the vines that always wrapped around her, and she left her hair down. The wild golden curls cascaded down her back and were streaked with tiny strands of sparkling bright green. She looked every bit of the Day Court she was.

He could not stop finding reasons to touch her and then turn that touch into a caress which made her gasp in pleasure. That was until she remembered herself and used her vines to push him away while he howled with laughter. It did not keep his hands away from her for long, hence the reason they were late. He was not remotely sorry for it.

Before they left his chambers, Anin tucked her wings around her to create a sheer, shimmering gown. Every day she tucked her wings in different ways to give her a never ending wardrobe. Kes approached Anin and reached out softly to tuck one of the nymph's wild curls behind her ear. He was constantly in awe of her beauty. Her wildness was captivating, and her eyes were like the deepest abyss. Kes would love nothing more than to explore every bit of that abyss. He briefly thought about not going to the ball at all, but then he did not want to deal with the backlash from his cousin.

"Do you wish for me to bind your power now, my darling nymph, or wait until the very last moment?"

Anin sighed, and she looked like she was preparing herself for death.

"I wish to not have my power bound at all, but I suppose if I must, I would rather wait till the very last minute." She shuddered at the thought of not having access to either her power or magic. Unlike Etain, Anin had used her power her whole life. She did not even realize she was using it half the time. It would be like having to learn to walk immediately after losing a leg.

He frowned. He had never considered how cruel it actually was to bind someone's powers. He supposed he would rather like the fact it was cruel, if it was anyone but Anin.

Kes stepped behind Anin and lightly dragged his fingers down the intricate folds of her wings. He said in a voice heavy with lust, "Do you think you will be able to keep me away when your little vines cannot help you, nymph?"

She sucked in a gasp. "I guess we will just have to wait and see, darling."

He groaned when his spelled parchment materialized in front of them—a message from Ciaran to hurry up. Kes hung his head against Anin's shoulder for a moment, willing his body to cool off.

"Oh! I almost forgot." A simple black obsidian circlet appeared in his hand.

Anin furrowed her brows at the sight.

"Technically, I am considered a prince as well, because we share the same great-grandfather and my power's strength matches Ciaran's. He happens to have a better claim by blood." He reached up and pulled the circle down upon his forehead.

He hated wearing the stupid thing, it made his feathers stick out ridiculously, which he assumed was happening if Anin's smirk was anything to go off of. Then, he pulled out of his pocket a slim black obsidian collar with a nearly invisible lead attached to it. Etain would be wearing the same one. Ciaran and Kes had chosen them specifically for the spell, which allowed only Kes to touch Anin's lead and only Ciaran to touch Etain's. Of course, both females could touch their own as well.

Anin looked at him wearily. Not only was she going to have her magic bound, but she was also to be collared like the pet she was meant to be. Kes saw the look of surprise when the collar locked into place and she could barely feel it. He slowly took the lead and draped it in a way around her neck and shoulders that made it look like an ornate piece of jewelry. He took every opportunity he had to softly drag his fingers across her skin, loving every gasp she tried to conceal.

"Time to go, my darling nymph." Kes grabbed her hand, and as he kissed her knuckles, they ported to Ciaran's study.

Surprisingly, Ciaran did not seem too bothered by their tardiness. Typically he would have broken half the objects in the room, hurling them at Kes while berating him for wasting his time. Nothing about the past few nights has been typical. It seemed he was as put out by the Lunar Ball as Kes was. Instead, his cousin just grinned at him with his arms crossed.

"Took you long enough. Did you get lost?"

"You know how these things go, cousin. Sometimes you just end up with a view you simply must explore.. Every inch of," he said, allowing a slow grin to form and never taking his eyes off Anin.

Ciaran barked out a laugh as Anin rolled her eyes. Not many were immune to his charms, he could not think of one female who did not fall over themselves to get into his bed before. However, the way she acted like such a haughty high fae when he laid it on her made him desire her submission even more. Preferably from her knees. She was a challenge he gladly accepted.

"Wait for the signal, then appear standing directly behind my throne," Ciaran reminded him. Then he looked at the two females and said, "I do not think I need to tell you how important it is you do exactly as you are told. My court is volatile and unpredictable. None will think twice about killing you, even if it costs them their own lives. Many of them do not care about anything, including staying alive. All they want is to cause devastating pain and depraved debauchery."

They both drained of color.

Ciaran leaned in close and whispered softly to Etain. He spoke too low for Kes to hear it all, but it must have been something reassuring; she relaxed marginally. He stepped away glancing at Kes, the two nodded at each other confirming their plan—a silent agreement to help watch over both females. Then, he was gone.

Several minutes passed. Etain and Anin whispered to each other with nervous energy.

"Anin?" Kes summoned.

She turned her head towards him, and her face became unreadable. He grabbed her hand and kissed it again, something he was finding he enjoyed doing. Partly due to the look of surprise she wore each time, but mostly he enjoyed the feel of her skin beneath his lips.

"Are you ready, darling? It's time."

She sighed deeply, and then nodded to him. He envisioned his knots all around her until he heard her gasp in shocked pain. She stumbled ever so slightly, and he grabbed her elbows to steady her.

"Are you okay?" he questioned.

Anin took several deep breaths before she stood straight again. She clenched her jaw a little bit, then put back on the mask of indifference she wore so well.

"Fine," she said sharply. He did not blame her, he would never let anyone bind his power.

Just as he was getting ready to lean in and see what shades of green he could get her face to flush, the scroll appeared. It was time to go make a spectacle—his favorite. He grabbed each of their hands, and in the space of a breath, they were all standing in the massive ballroom directly behind Ciaran's throne.

Showtime.

Thirty-Eight

ETAIN

Etain was immediately overwhelmed. The room was vast and filled with all kinds of beings, from the beautiful to the terrifying. All eyes were on her. She was having a hard time focusing on what Ciaran was saying, only catching the tail end of it. It sounded like he was giving everyone ample warning of the promise he made to her. She really hoped she did not have to witness any hands or eyes being removed, but she was grateful for it. She did not wish to be touched by anyone, and she only trusted the three beings standing with her.

Etain drifted closer to Ciaran without even noticing it. It was as if their bodies were opposite ends of a magnet and could not help but find each other. He must have felt her drawing near him, because he held his hand out to her from where he lounged on his throne. He had one leg thrown over the armrest opposite her, giving off a general air of boredom. She placed her hand in his, and he gave her a gentle squeeze to reassure her. Then he pulled her around in front of him and directed her to sit on the cushion at his feet.

Etain bristled, taking her seat, remembering they all had a part to play in keeping her and Anin safe. On the step below

Ciaran's throne and off to the right was a chair—not quite a throne, but still too grand to be just a chair. Etain watched as Kes led Anin towards it by the shimmering strand attached to her neck. The room turned its attention to them with the movement.

Immediately, you could hear the animosity in the heated conversations that had begun to erupt throughout the room. Apparently they had not noticed Anin until that moment, and the idea of having a Day Court member in their midst was highly unsatisfactory. It was likely made worse by Ciaran informing them neither his nor Kes's pets were to be touched.

Kes gave the whole room a menacing glare. The disruption had died down enough, so he took his seat and directed Anin to a cushion similar to Etain's at his feet. Everyone seemed to fear him, and no one in the room was willing to cross him. Now that the room had quieted again, Ciaran stood and clapped his hands together a couple of times to gather the attention of all the beings in the massive ballroom.

"Now, now, my delightfully wicked court," he said as he began to gently caress his fingers over the top of Etain's head. "Let us do what we do best and celebrate the Moon in all her glory by making this the most dissolute and horrifying Lunar Ball yet!"

This sparked hundreds of cries and shouts of celebration around the room.

"Let the fun begin!"

Immediately, hauntingly aggressive music began to play. Etain had never heard anything like it. It made you want to dance as much as it made you feel like you were in some kind of trance. All the revelers parted to create a dance floor, which quickly filled with the most diverse group of beings Etain had ever seen. There was a beautiful female who looked entirely human, except she looked perpetually wet, yet she never left a puddle.

The dance floor became a sea of moving bodies. She had never seen dancing like this before. They would transition from harsh, jerking movements into fluid, flowing ones. Every being had paired up, and the whole floor moved together as one. The dance was violent and sensual at the same time. Bodies were as close as they could be, and on certain beats, all the dancers would let out a shout while they stomped their feet, making that single beat deafening. She could watch them dance all night. They were incredibly mesmerizing, and she watched their steps and tried to learn the dance from where she sat.

She wondered if she were allowed to speak to Ciaran, or if she was expected to sit here in silence. She was about to discreetly ask him, but she noticed a line forming at the bottom of the stairs to the dais. She assumed they were the beings who wished to greet Kes and Ciaran, and likely gawk at her and Anin.

She was mostly ignored by the never-ending throng of creatures approaching Ciaran, many of whom took his warning to heart. There were a few whose gazes began to linger longer than Ciaran liked, even if they were only out of curiosity, causing him to growl a warning and ask if they enjoyed having their eyes attached. There were also a few who gave her a disgusted sneer before firmly ignoring her. Etain didn't mind being ignored. It gave her the chance to observe the creatures uninterrupted. She hoped Anin was faring just as well.

Left to herself, Etain turned her attention back to the ball. The room was absolutely magnificent. It, too, was made entirely out of black obsidian that was given a mirrored finish. The walls and incredibly high ceiling had millions of tiny, shimmering silver specks set into them. It made it look as if they were encased by the night sky. The effect was dizzying, making the room feel both too big and too small at the same time.

Everywhere she looked, there were shimmering silver candelabras with stacks of white candles burning, even though their wax never seemed to melt. The ceiling was decorated with several silver chandeliers with a giant white ball of light floating in the center. She supposed that was meant to represent the moon. The entire perimeter of the room boasted many lounge areas with chairs, couches, cushions, and round plush platforms that appeared to be large beds. Some gave the illusion of privacy with sheer curtains draped around them, while others were lit with an unseen light from above to draw your eye.

Long tables of food were scattered everywhere, along with fountains overflowing with wine. Etain would have loved a glass of it to settle her nerves, and perhaps a chance to peruse the tables laden with food. She had not been able to eat much earlier, with her nerves making her stomach flip. Before her stomach could begin to make its demands heard, Etain moved her eyes away from the tables and watched the dancers once again.

She had been making notes in her head of questions she wished to ask Ciaran later, when they could speak again, and had not really been paying attention to the conversations that were happening right next to her. The group of what Etain had guessed were pixies, little winged creatures with mouths of razor sharp teeth and claws on their hands sharpened to points, were moving on. While the next fae were making their way up the stairs to Ciaran.

The two creatures were wildly different. The male was an ugly, short, green being with incredibly large ears and sharply clever eyes. He was accompanied by a beautiful female whose hair was the palest silver silk. It truly looked like moonbeams. Her skin had a shimmering opalescent hue and was slightly transparent. She looked regal in her tight, black silk gown, which clung to every perfect inch and curve of her body, flaring slightly at the end. It had a long slit up one leg that ended above her hip, showing off her beautiful skin. She could almost pass for a human if it were not for her liquid silver eyes and a neck that had to be nearly double the length of a human. She also had the standard features Etain was beginning to notice in all fae – elongated fingers and pointed ears.

Etain sat up a little straighter and decided she hated this female when she noticed the way she was looking at Ciaran. Something inside her screamed that Ciaran was hers, and she would kill this female fae for daring to look at him in such a bold way. She was even close to growling at the female if she did not stop her perusal of her prince.

As if sensing her rising agitation, Ciaran began to softly caress her head and play with her hair, his touch calming her nearly at once. Doubt began to creep in when the male began to speak.

"Prince, I'm sure you remember my beautifully vicious daughter, Leona. I believe at the last Lunar Ball you got to know each other rather well, if memory serves me right. I was told you both put on such a show that there have been murmurs of a possible repeat this festival."

Ciaran's hand stilled for just a split second. She was sure she was the only one who noticed. She did not know if it was anger or excitement. Etain thought there was no way any male would not want that beautiful fae. She felt her heart begin to crack. Ciaran told her he belonged to her; perhaps she misunderstood what that meant.

The female came nearer and stood close to Ciaran, placing a hand on the leg he still draped over the armrest on the opposite side from Etain. "My Prince, I would be delighted to give the court another sho..."

Etain sneered, and a growl wrenched out of her from somewhere deep inside. How dare this female touch her prince? She was the one who wanted to remove hands now.

Leona jerked her hand away from Ciaran's leg only to raise it and send it flying faster than Etain could track towards her face. The fae screeched her disdain for the human who dared challenge her.

Etain flinched, preparing to take the hit. However, Leona's clawed hand never came down on her. Instead, it lay dripping and shimmering with pale, opalescent blood on the ground in front of them. It felt like the whole room held its breath before a glass shattering scream came from Leona.

"If you valued your hand, you should not have raised it against my pet after my explicit warning of what would happen if anyone dared touch her. Shut your mouth before I shut it for you," Ciaran said. She had never heard him sound this vicious.

Leona pulled her mouth shut, ending her deafening cries.

Etain was surprised Leona had even heard Ciaran's menacingly quiet words. With her cries quieted, Leona glared at Etain with murderous rage.

"I suggest you learn from losing your hand, Leona, and not lose your eyes as well."

Her eyes widened in shock, and she looked away.

Ciaran turned his eyes on the green man and scowled at him for a moment. "Royad, remove your daughter from my sight at once, and if you ever dare to openly push me again, it will be the last thing you do. I told you my thoughts on your daughter already, and now you have caused her to be humiliated in front of the entire court." Ciaran rolled his eyes when the green man began to mumble indignantly about the loss of his daughter's hand, and Leona began to whimper again.

"Oh, quit your whining," said Ciaran. "You both only further embarrass yourselves. It will grow back, and you both look weak for complaining about it. Now, get out of my sight and do not forget my warning, Royad. This is the last time I will give you one."

The rest of the line, who had been waiting to speak with Ciaran, took one look at the hand on the ground and dispersed. Etain heard Ciaran release a deep breath.

"They will be back. However, they will give me time to cool down and relax." He held his hand out to her and sat up a bit more on his throne.

The second Etain placed her hand in his, he had her pulled up and turned to sit in his lap, her back to his front, before the gasp could leave her mouth. "So let's let them think I am using you to relax myself and give you a chance to ask all those questions I see burning behind your eyes."

Etain adjusted herself and sat sideways on his lap to make it easier for her to caress his face, ears, and neck. "I do have many questions about the members of your court, yet I seem to have forgotten all of them at the present," she said breathily.

Ciaran's hands openly roamed her body for anyone to see. The fire that had been simmering inside of her began to gain more momentum at the thought of everyone witnessing him claim her body. A loud moan ripped from her body as Ciaran's hands dipped into the fold of her dress and caressed her inner thigh. She was going to come undone by his touch alone.

Ciaran chuckled darkly into her ear before nipping it. "Careful, my little witch. If we do not stop now, I fear I will not be able to help myself. We will give this court a view, which will result in many eyes being plucked." Yet he did not pull his hand away; he left it there, so close and yet so far from the place she wanted it most. He pulled her even closer to him to allow them to whisper conspiratorially.

"Now, what of these questions?"

Etain took a moment to gain her breath back before she began asking him about the different types of fae gathered for the night. Ciaran freely answered all of her questions, sometimes attempting to hide his laughter at some of her more colorful observations. They continued like this for hours, all while Ciaran left his hand on Etain's inner thigh. The only movement was his thumb making slow circles. She was certain the spot would be forever branded by those tormenting strokes. She wished time would go by faster, then they could retire to Ciaran's chambers and she could finally get relief from the incessant ache burning inside her.

Just as the thought entered her head, Etain spied groups breaking off to the little lounge areas around the room. She noticed several of them were going for those plush platforms awash in light, while others went for the ones giving a slight illusion of privacy. She was watching them intently, and Ciaran must have been following her gaze.

"Ah, little witch, it is that time of the night where you will get a true glimpse of the court's depravity." His hand between the folds of her sheer gown began to squeeze her slightly while still maintaining the torturous strokes. He placed his other hand low on her abdomen and began a slow and equally tortuous trail up her body. "Keep your eyes on the platform, little witch," he said in a low, smoky voice into her ear.

Etain watched as one female and two males, all high fae of some kind, climbed onto one of the platform beds. All three began to caress each other, and both males began kissing and nipping at the female's throat. Etain could not believe beings were this bold. In the Human Realm, it was nearly unheard of to see couples even kiss in public. The female let out a loud groan as the males' hands began touching her in much the same way Etain's prince was touching her.

The fire inside her was becoming even more of an inferno, when suddenly it began to dissipate. She remembered what the green goblin, Royad, had said about Ciaran and his beautiful daughter giving "quite the show" at the last Lunar Ball. She knew it was ridiculous to be jealous, yet she could not help the way she felt betrayed. Ciaran had joined that fae on one of those platforms and let the whole court watch them. She felt like such a fool. Of course, Ciaran would not belong to only her, not in the way she would belong to only him.

"What's bothering you, little witch?" he asked, in between kissing and nipping along the length of her neck and shoulder. She did not want to tell him, because she knew she was being ridiculous. She would need to get over the fact that, while she had never had the opportunity to experience another, Ciaran had likely experienced several. Probably more than several. "Is it what that imbecile Royad said about me and his daughter?"

She did not know how he was almost always able to guess her thoughts. "I know I'm being absolutely absurd to think you would be only mine," Etain said, trying not to let her emotions slip into her words.

"I am only yours and have never been another's," Ciaran said. Etain was confused and turned to look into his eyes. "I am several hundred years old, little witch, and I have never belonged to another. Have I used another's body before? Yes—but that was all it was. I do not remember any of them, because they meant nothing to me."

Etain was having a hard time caring how that was a terrible way to treat other living beings. He did say he was a very wicked male, but she was still having a hard time understanding what he meant.

"I never cared who they were or even listened to what they said. Typically, I was too drunk on wine and didn't even see them. I did not care if all of the realm saw them on display." He brought his hand to cup her face, and she subconsciously leaned into it. "You, my little witch, I want to hear every word you ever speak. You, I have every single moment with burned into my memory. I will not share you with anyone. I do not even want to share the sight of you. If anyone dared to look at you while you are in a state that is only for me to see, I would end their lives. Etain—I would set the realm on fire for you. I care not for anything else the way I care for you."

Etain blinked back the tears that had gathered in her eyes. "Ciaran..." Before she could finish whatever it was she was going to say, Ciaran cut her off.

"You see, Etain, there has never been anyone before you." He pulled her face to his, and their lips barely touched each other. "There will never be anyone after you." His lips crashed into hers. She felt the promise of his words and the promise of his kiss as he worshiped her mouth with his. When he pulled away, he took Etain's breath with him. They gazed into each other's eyes for a few moments before he pulled her back into the position she had been in before, with her back to his front. He leaned in to brush his lips against her ear. "Now, little witch—enjoy the show."

When Etain looked back to the platform, things had progressed quite a bit in the short time she had looked away. All three beings were completely naked. When Etain realized what they were doing to the female, she let out a gasp of surprise. She was bent over on all fours with one male in front of her and one behind her.

Both of Ciaran's hands had crept further up her body. One wrapped around her throat to keep her gaze on the platform with the three fae, while the other was gently brushing against her core over her leather undergarment. She let out a frustrated groan.

"Shhh...my needy little witch. Do you wish I would take you right now, the way they are taking her?"

Etain was burning up inside. She could barely think of an answer as the idea of Ciaran doing just that made her moan and grind herself against him, which made him laugh darkly and low in his chest. "Do you wish my cock was stretching your throat at the same time my cock drove into you from behind?"

Etain did not know if such a thing was possible. However, she did know she wanted it. "Y-yes." She panted. He was bringing her too high. She thought she might cry because of how badly she needed him.

He cupped her sex with his hand and applied pressure while moving his hand back and forth. It was like being close to water after a drought, yet still being too far away to quench your thirst. She began grinding herself into his hand and lap, feeling how affected he was behind her.

"Such a needy little witch, aren't you?" he asked, and her only response was a whimper. "Do you need some relief?"

She let out sounds that were supposed to be a yes, but he knew what her answer was. He pushed his hand inside her leather undergarments, yet he still did not touch her where she needed him most.

"Tell me what you need, little witch."

She groaned and tried to move herself to where she wanted his fingers to be. "P-please, Ciaran.." She tried to form a sentence. However, her brain did not seem to be working properly. She had no idea how he had such a strong effect on her body.

"Hmmm...please what? Etain, I want to hear you ask for it. What do you want?"

She could hear the masculine pride in his voice, but she could not be bothered to care. "T-touch m-me, Ciaran... p-please." Her voice was growing louder.

"Shhhh...little witch. Do not draw attention our way, or I will have to stop and pluck out several eyes."

She knew it was wicked, and she should be disgusted, though she could not help the moan escaping her at the thought of him covered in many different colors of blood, because they dared look at what was his—*her*. Perhaps she was more wicked than she knew.

"Ciaran..." she begged with a breathy moan.

"Is this where you want me?" he asked as one of his fingers found her most sensitive spot and began to circle it. She thought she pleaded with him a few more times before he finally let his finger land exactly where she needed him. She nearly cried in relief as he applied pressure using slow, deliberate movements.

"Do you see what they are doing now, little witch?"

She had completely forgotten the performance on the platform. When she opened her eyes to watch them again, she was shocked to see the female was taking them both from behind now. Etain did not even know that was possible. As she watched, Ciaran picked up speed until Etain and the female both tipped over the edge. Ciaran placed his hand over Etain's mouth to keep her cries from escaping.

"Such a good little witch," he said as he pulled his hand away and went back to tormenting her with the strokes of his thumb.

Thirty-Nine

Kes

He never had much patience for these events. It was a big part of why he had no wish to be king. He was content to be adjacent to the throne, having nearly as much power with much less pressure. His patience was quickly dissolving as he witnessed creature after creature hurl insults at Anin. In the beginning, she sat high and let their vitriol slide off her. Not even an hour later, her shoulders began to droop inward. Sometimes she would physically flinch, and it took every ounce of his willpower to stay in his seat and not rip out the offender's tongue.

He was thrilled when the throng of beings left them alone, and Anin took a deep breath and straightened her back. Kes placed a hand on her shoulder, one that would look as though he were dominating the nymph, but he could secretly caress the back of her shoulder with his thumb in comfort.

This was the first Lunar Ball Kes and Ciaran were not already fall-down drunk at this point. Normally by now, they would have murdered several court members for any number of insults. At this point, they would be making their way through each of the lounge areas around the room, never remembering any faces. Many of them were already filled, and several shows were being put on. He had the nearly uncontrollable desire to drag Anin over to the most visible platform and make his claim publicly, proving she belonged to him. Then, right after, kill anyone who dared to watch.

He kept his gaze roaming across the room; there was a tension in the air that kept him on edge. He could have sworn he saw someone shifting in the shadows. Immediately, Kes grew suspicious. If it was not the Day Court trying their hand at espionage, then it was someone from his own court either trying to climb higher in rank or simply to cause mayhem. Possibly all three.

Kes knew he should go investigate but was loath to leave his nymph alone. He would not be able to keep her safe if he were not next to her, and he did not want to drag her through the mass of Night Court bodies where anything could happen, even if he were right next to her. He sighed and snapped his fingers, and a spelled cage appeared. Anin raised an eyebrow at him, reminding him of their agreement. If he forced her into a cage ever again, it would nullify their agreement. He did not want to give up his five questions.

"I'm hoping you will choose to go in there for your own safety."

"I see nothing to be concerned about." Anin looked around for any hint of foul play. She studied him, and then her eyes went wide. "You plan to leave me here—alone," she said incredulously.

She did not ask. She knew that's what was happening. Her mask of indifference slipped off her face long enough for him to see how terrified the idea made her. She would be alone without the use of her power; she would be completely defenseless. Kes knew Ciaran did not want anything to happen to Anin since she had not yet provided the information he sought, or maybe even more so because it would upset his witch. However, he also knew his cousin would not risk leaving Etain unguarded for the sake of his nymph.

"Do you see that shadowed alcove over there?" he asked her. Maybe she would be more agreeable if she could understand his concerns.

"Yes, what about it?" she asked, staring into the shadows.

"Watch closely," he said, knowing at any moment the unusual movement would appear again.

"What was that?" she asked, surprised.

"That is exactly what I want to know. Normally, I would not think anything about it," he said, looking around for any other unusual activity in a room full of unusual beings.

"Well, why do you now?" she asked. He could hear the annoyance in her voice, and it made him show off his pointed teeth in a grin. One she immediately rolled her eyes at.

"What if it is one of your little friends from the Day Court?" her eyes widened. His nymph had not thought she might be in danger from more than the Night Court tonight. "Imagine what a spectacle that would be! I do enjoy putting on a good show. Nothing would make the night better than the slow and painful death of a Day fae." He leaned down to place his mouth right next to her ear so that when he spoke, his lips brushed the sensitive skin. "Well, maybe not nothing."

"I am a Day fae," she proclaimed after clearing her throat.

"Yes, but you are my Day fae. That is different." He loved watching how his words made her both annoyed and excited. Which he thought would likely make her even more annoyed.

"Yours? I am not something to be owned, Kes," she said with her attempt at a snobby high fae voice, making him smile bigger.

"And yet, you are still *my* darling nymph," he said, staring into her onyx eyes as he dragged his knuckles softly down the column of her neck all the way down to the black strap barely concealing her breasts. He was pleased when she involuntarily shivered. There was a brief moment, and if he had not been paying attention to every minor move she made, he would have missed her leaning into his touch. Of course, she instantly pulled away and scoffed at him.

"You could be right, however," she said with a sigh.

"About owning you? Of course I am." He laughed at the sound of disgust she made. "About the shadows? I hope it is nothing more than younglings trying to get an eyeful," he said. Younglings would be the easiest to deal with and would be the most likely culprits.

"You are insufferable," she said, bringing back her haughty voice he loved.

"No my darling, I am spectacular," he proclaimed as he stood with a flourish before bending down and offering his hand like a true prince charming.

"There is truly no other option, is there?" she asked, eyeing the cage.

"If there were, the cage would not be here." She sighed in resignation before taking his hand and allowing him to pull her to her feet. She stepped into the black birdcage he created to be the perfect size just for her

"Although I must say, I do love the way you look in a cage." She clenched her jaw and glared at him as he sealed the door, disguising the opening. He brought his face slightly down, directly in line with hers, before he growled, "When I return, I will show you just how mine you are."

"Kes?" she asked when he turned to walk away, causing him to turn around and take the few steps back to the cage.

"Yes, darling?" He was truly curious to hear what she was about to say.

"Be... Just hurry back." He was certain she was about to tell him to be careful. A devious smile stretched across his face.

"Forgive me, *my darling* nymph. I would much rather we were back in my chambers to see how you manage to get away from me without your little vines to protect you." He grinned at the heat that ignited behind her eyes, both in the desire for his body and the desire to slap him across the face. He laughed and then gave her a wink before he made his way up the dais.

Kes quickly approached Ciaran and leaned down to quietly fill him in. He saw Etain's eyes shoot over to where Anin was in her cage with a look of concern. He did not linger with them; he was eager to be done with the shadowy figure and get back to his nymph.

After pretending to graze at one of the tables and grab a drink from the fountain of wine, he made his way casually over to the shadows, trying not to be too obvious. He expected it to be nothing more than a few of the younglings lurking in the shadows, hoping to spy without being caught.

He should have been more cautious before stepping into the unknown.. In his haste, he did not feel for any spells that may have been placed and walked right into one, triggering it immediately. They came at him incredibly fast and from every direction. It was impossible to dodge them or call on his magic and blow them away. More obsidian blades flew at him and embedded themselves in his flesh than he could count.

He crumpled to the floor, blood pouring freely from him. The blades were still protruding from his body, making it impossible for him to heal. He started to pull a few out, only for the blood to gush from those wounds.

He tried to get his hands underneath his body to push himself up. If he could get just beyond the shadows, his cousin would come. It was no use; he could barely move. Any movement he was able to make caused him to slip in the pool of blood rapidly growing beneath him.

When he began to cough up blood, he knew the end was near. He was more distraught over who would keep his nymph safe after he was gone than he was over his impending death. He tried to drag himself out of the shadows one last time, but it was no use. He was far too weak and too far gone. He tried; he really had.

He took one last breath, choking on his own blood. A lone tear tracked down his face, knowing he would never see her again. He had only just found her, and all they had together were the last couple nights. He was not mad about the time; anytime with her he was thankful for. As his eyes closed for the last time, he pictured her face just before he turned to walk away. Neither of them knew it would be the last time.

Time—he wished he had more time with her.

Forty

Anin

Several minutes had passed since she watched Kes disappear into the shadows, and he had yet to reemerge. She stared at the black velvet drapes of the darkened alcove and willed him to reappear.

Come on, Kes.

She glanced around the room, looking for any signs of foul play. She noticed the goblin, whose daughter paid for her mistake with her hand, standing in the corner speaking to a tall, thin fae male. His rage was palpable as he spoke animatedly to the other fae while never taking his gaze off Etain. The second she turned her attention to the other male, she visibly recoiled, finding his eyes locked on her. The oily smile he gave her sent chills down her spine.

Something is wrong. Something is very wrong.

The pull in her chest that made her naturally gravitate towards him was growing fainter, as if he were very far away from her. Her panic sent her thoughts scattering. She needed to do something. Shaking the bars of the cage and knowing it would do nothing, she raged at her inability to do anything.

Ciaran.

"Something is not right!" she yelled up the dais. The prince was not paying attention to anything but Etain, however, the witch heard her. She locked eyes with Etain and shouted again, "Something is wrong with Kes. I can feel it!" Etain quickly looked up at Ciaran and spoke urgently to him. As she spoke, his brow furrowed, and he looked down to where Anin stood, clutching the bars of her cage—panic clear upon her face.

After saying something to Etain, he stood and held the thin, glinting string attached to her collar before they both walked down the few steps to where her cage stood. She clutched at her chest; not only was the pull growing weaker, but it was becoming a deep ache within her. She begged the gods to please not let him die. She promised them she would try to trust him again if they did this one thing for her.

"This better be important, nymph, you have upset Etain," Ciaran growled out. Under any other circumstances, she would have rolled her eyes at him the same way Etain had. As it was, in that moment all she cared about was helping her mate.

"Something is wrong. I watched Kes step into the shadows over there," she said, pointing to where she last laid eyes on Kes. "He never came back out, and there appears to be a shadow growing wider on the floor from the shadows. I do not think it is a shadow at all." A sob ripped its way out of her, and she quickly covered her mouth. She could not break down, not yet.

"Hmm..." Ciaran studied the direction she pointed before narrowing his eyes. He inhaled deeply, scenting the air of the ballroom. His eyes widened and then shot to hers. He did not say anything as he picked up Etain, placed her in her own cage, and ported away before Anin could blink twice.

Etain held her gaze for several moments, offering what comfort she could from a look alone. Anin nodded in appreciation before returning her attention to that ever growing shadow on the floor. She knew exactly what that shadow was—blood—Kes's black blood.

Beings began to turn towards the shadowed alcove, likely scenting the blood in the air. There was no mistaking that pungent copper smell, and there was no pretending the dark pool was a shadow any longer. It was a small miracle no one came to harass either female with their escorts missing.

The room began to take on a wild energy. Many beings began to engage in even more depraved forms of carnal activity, the scent of blood sending them into a frenzy. The scent of blood became more overwhelming as more blood was spilled throughout the room.

If Anin had not already been feeling sick with worry for Kes, she would have been then. She could not decide if she found their behavior amusing or disturbing. A crowd had begun to form, making it impossible for her to monitor the growing puddle of blood.

Another sob escaped her, and she felt fear so potent she nearly suffocated under the weight of it. She held her body frozen, afraid if she moved, she would collapse. She was distracted trying to catch any glimpse of Kes, she did not notice a door had appeared on the back of the cage and opened. Nor did she notice the robed being who snuck up behind her and hit her hard on the back of the head, knocking her out instantly.

Forty-One
Seamus

Seamus stood in the shadows for several minutes, waiting for a chance to make his move. He watched as the demon who tortured him the past few days held Etain as if she were a delicate flower. They kept their heads close together as they shared words with each other. Seamus was sick with disgust. How dare she allow the demon that caused him such pain to hold her.

He planned to make her pay for not only getting him into this mess, but also for allowing him to suffer at the hands of one she obviously had power over. If she thought Seamus would ever want to touch her in the way a husband touches his wife after she allowed that demon to soil her, she would be sadly mistaken. He would cause her pain and suffering, just as he felt at the hands of her demon lover. Then he would deliver her to the Shepherd to fulfill his mission.

Seamus smiled as all attention began to shift to a far corner of the room. He watched the demon delicately place Etain into a cage and then disappear, likely to investigate. The Shepherd orchestrated this chance for him to sneak up on Etain without her being any wiser. He pulled his hood tighter to further obscure himself as he made his way around the edge of the room to come behind the dais, sticking to the shadows the whole way. Once he was there, he slowly climbed the back of it, staying low to keep hidden in case anyone turned to look back at the throne. He got closer to the cage, and there was no door. He began to panic, wondering how he was supposed to get her out. Suddenly, a door appeared directly in front of him and silently opened.

He watched her for a moment; she was starting to get agitated. Following her gaze, she spied another individual on the same mission as Seamus. A large robed figure was sneaking up behind the cage of the creature he had thought was a Being of Light when he first arrived. If Seamus was not fast, she was going to make a lot of noise trying to warn her friend.

She took a deep breath and prepared to yell at the creature in the other cage. He hit her as hard as he could over the back of the head with the silver candlestick he pilfered along the way. She dropped like a sack of potatoes.

Seamus wasted no time and slung her unconscious body over his shoulder, then snuck back into the shadows. He pulled out the map the Shepherd left for him as he raced down empty hallways and stairwells, never running into another soul. Seamus knew that was the Shepherd's doing as well. After running for several minutes, he began to tire, thanks to the added weight of the whore on his shoulder. Finally, he saw the door that would take him outside the palace.

He had just a little further to go until he came upon a wagon attached to a horse. He did not hesitate to use the rope that had been left in the back of the wagon to firmly hog tie Etain in case she woke before they got away. Just as the Shepherd had claimed there would be, another map was waiting for him on the driver's seat. He opened it, then set off in the direction indicated. However, he would not go straight there. Instead, he would look for a quiet spot to pull over and wait for Etain to wake so he could watch the pain fill her eyes as she suffered. He did not think the Shepherd would mind; he would likely understand and tell Seamus it was the least he was due. Seamus smiled wide when he thought about how the Shepherd would likely commend him for teaching Etain the error of her ways.

Seamus had been driving for hours, and he could no longer hear the bustling of the palace or the city behind him. He slowed the horse to a trot and kept his eyes out for a good spot to rest and wait for Etain to wake. Finally, he came upon a small glade and pulled the wagon off to the side of the overgrown trail he had been traveling. It had obviously been forgotten, making him even more confident in his plans.

He got down from the wagon and went around to the back of it to slide Etain out. He untied her enough to be able to toss her over his shoulder once more and began to make his way into the glade. Finding the perfect spot for her in between a few trees, he dropped her none too gently to the forest floor. She was still unconscious. He took the time to tie each limb to one of the trees surrounding them, pulling tight; her limbs slightly lifted off the forest floor. When he was perfectly happy with her binds, he found a comfortable seat against a nearby tree and waited.

CIARAN

Ciaran was not prepared for the sight that greeted him when he appeared in the shadows. His cousin was filled with an unimaginable number of obsidian blades and was on the brink of death. He was not certain he would be able to save him in time. He placed his hand on Kes's body in the first spot he could find free from blades. Ciaran needed to heal him faster than the little remaining blood Kes had left could leave his body as he pulled each blade free.

"This is highly inconvenient, Kes."

With each blade he pulled from his cousin, his anger grew. The scent of a powerful spell still lingered. He did not know too many Night fae with that kind of power. He knew it had to be the Day Court. They had finally pushed him to the edge. He was so close to having his full power that he could feel it. As soon as he did, someone would pay for this.

After what felt like hours, Ciaran was beginning to fade. He had successfully pulled all of the blades out of his cousin, saving him from complete death. Even with nearly all of Ciaran's power depleted, he was not sure it would be enough. Ciaran picked his limp body up off the floor and flung him over his shoulder.

"Good gods, what do you eat?" Talking to him helped take his mind off of the nagging feeling in the back of his mind that something was terribly wrong, and not just his cousin's near murder.

He quickly ported his cousin to his chambers and dropped him on his bed. Even as close to the veil of death as Kes was, Ciaran heard him mumble Anin's name.

"I will bring your nymph to you. Rest now and heal. As soon as my power restores, I will speed it up again for you." Ciaran was eager to return to his witch. He was furious at the unknown assailants who had pulled him away from Etain and caused him to deplete his power to such an extreme. He was not sure he would be able to stay standing for much longer. He hoped he had enough power to collect the females, drop Anin off to tend to Kes, and get him and Etain back to his bedchambers.

He knew he would have no choice in the sleep that was coming quickly for him. He would sleep for at least a night; luckily, he could do it with his little witch curled up next to him. Not the night he had envisioned for them, though he would be sure to make it up to her as soon as he woke.

Porting directly to his throne, a cold panic began to take over his body. The cage he left her in was empty. He began to frantically look around. Not seeing her anywhere, he searched through the bond, which had been getting stronger and stronger over the past few nights. She felt far away, as if she was no longer anywhere in the palace. He let out a rage-filled roar that shook the room and extinguished many candles. There was one particular fae that was known for being adept at breaking spells, and Ciaran had every intention of making him pay for his treason. He turned his gaze to Anin, perhaps she had seen something. Only to find she was also missing. He saw the black begin to creep into the sides of his vision and knew he needed to port immediately.

Ciaran barely had enough time to port to his bedchambers and send the last dregs of his power down the bond with Etain in hopes he could unbind her magic from such a distance. He was not sure if it had worked, or if it was even possible, although there was nothing else he could do.

Just before the darkness took him, he threw open the window and roared Etain's name into the night sky—a promise and a threat all in one. The last thing he remembered was his attempt to stumble towards his bed and not quite making it.

Forty-Three

ETAIN

Etain woke slowly, her head feeling like it had been split in two. Groaning, she started to blink her eyes open. She could see trees above her and surmised she was lying on the forest floor. Her head was scrambled. She was having a hard time remembering where she had been. Slowly, the Lunar Ball started to come back to her.

She had been sitting on Ciaran's lap, learning about all the different types of fae from his court...among other things. Even as slowly as her brain appeared to be working, she felt the heat creep into her cheeks while thinking about what they had done on his throne.

How did she end up on the forest floor? Had everything been a dream? Could it have been a cruel trick played on her by some fae the night of the blood moon? The thought of none of it being real hit Etain with such sadness, she let out a little cry of despair. That would be the cruelest trick anyone could have played on her. She felt tears begin to fill her eyes.

"Ah. You are awake." The voice sounded like Seamus, but slightly off—a bit too nasally.

Etain gasped when she remembered how Seamus had pinned her down and forced himself on top of her. Etain tried to move her arms and sit up, but realized she could not move, not even an inch. She rolled her head to look down her arm with bleary eyes and saw she was stuck on something. When she looked to the other side, she realized she was not actually stuck on something, she was tightly tied to trees.

"Seamus, help me get untied." Her voice came out raspy and low. The more she became awake, the more panic began to set in. She looked down and noticed she was wearing the black dress she thought she had been dreaming about. If it was not a dream, where was Ciaran, and how had she gotten here? She tried to think back to the last thing she remembered. They were at the ball and something happened. Etain tried to remember. She remembered being in the cage, and then...she gasped.

Anin!

Etain saw a cloaked figure sneak up behind Anin's cage and raise something to knock her over the head. She guessed something similar happened to her, too, since the back of her head was throbbing in tune to her heartbeat. She heard Seamus approach, and her fear crept even higher. She was loath to admit it, but Seamus terrified her.

"Why would I help a demon whore like you, Etain? When you did nothing to help me!" Seamus crouched down to get in her face. As he yelled, spittle flew out of his mouth, and his face began to turn beet red.

She noticed his nose was rather flat now, where it used to be rounded. He looked unkempt with his usually clean shaven face covered in a few days old beard. It was clear he had not showered in what smelled like months, yet could only have been nights. Etain clenched her eyes shut and tried to focus on what he said. She had no idea what he was talking about.

Help him with what?

"Help you? Help you when?" Her voice was starting to wake up. She wanted to shout at him and ask him why he thought he would be deserving of her help in general, after he tried to violate her. Though, considering she was tied up and he was not, she thought better of it. Seamus looked down at her with such disgust that she had to hold back a flinch.

"The entire time you were gallivanting with your demon lover, I was strapped to a table in his dungeon! You could have asked him to release me. We could have gone home, and forgotten this whole thing. You still had a chance at being my wife and ascending to the Kingdom of Light with me. Now..." he sneered, "now that you have made yourself the demon's whore and left me to rot. I will never tie myself to you."

Etain felt herself mildly relax with his words. At least she did not have to worry about him trying to finish what he started that first fateful night in the woods. She was still fearful of him, remembering the pain he made her body feel.

"Seamus, I did not know...," she started, before she was interrupted by his cruel laughter.

He smacked her across the face and glared at her.

"Everything that has happened to me is your fault, Etain! You had to be stubborn instead of doing as you were told! Not only did your lover break my bones in a way he said was vengeance for you, he also did this!" Seamus ripped his shirt open, showing his scarred skin. Carved across his chest with even spaces between letters was the word "FOOL." It was in all capital letters and beautiful calligraphy, which almost made an even bigger mockery out of it.

Etain made a mental note to commend Ciaran on his penmanship. She was beginning to think anything she said would only further infuriate Seamus, so she decided to stay quiet. He told her of how he escaped the room of torture and how easily he had snatched her right out from under Ciaran. Then he listed off all the ways in which he planned to hurt her before he delivered whatever was left of her to the Shepherd.

She was in such a state of emotional duress, the fact the Shepherd was in this realm did not even register. He obviously had his hands in something. She felt herself growing hotter as her panic took over completely.

"You know what I am going to start with, Etain? I thought it would be nice to let the world know exactly what you are for the rest of your life." He pulled out a small blade he had likely stolen from a plate during the festival. It looked painfully dull.

"H-O-R-E. I'm going to carve the letters across your chest just as that demon did to me!"

Etain was completely frozen with fear, or she would have at least yelled, "That's not how you spell 'whore, you fool," although she could not force her mouth to move.

As Seamus began to carve the letter H, the pain was horrendous. He had to use tremendous force to break the skin, bruising her while he carved her. That heat she thought she felt earlier, was not what she thought it was after all.

She started to feel her power build. She felt herself pulling more and more from some deep, dark place within her without knowing how she was even doing it. She desperately needed it to go somewhere else and release it from her body. She was becoming overwhelmed by it, and could not understand how she had access to it. Had she somehow broken the bind Ciaran had placed on her?

Seamus had just finished the H and was moving on to the next letter when she felt like she was near to bursting with power. She knew she needed to let it out; she just did not know how. Soon, she knew, she would not have a say in it at all.

Seamus looked up from his handiwork, made a startled sound, and crab crawled away from her. "Demon!"

At first, Etain thought he meant Ciaran had arrived. Then she realized he was looking directly at her. He steeled himself and leaned closer, while his eyes were still blown in panic. Etain had finally reached her tipping point and felt her power ripping out of her as she screamed. Her body bowed off the ground with the force of the power purging from her. It felt like her body was being pulled inside out.

Seamus had no time to run. Everything within a few feet of Etain exploded, sending splinters and gore flying everywhere. When she had fully released all the power she had spiraled into her body, she sagged hard against the dirt floor. She was mildly aware she was covered in blood and full of splinters when unconsciousness took her again.

Forty-Four

Anin

Anin felt her body jostle from side to side, and her head felt like it had been split open. She could not remember where she was or what she had been doing. The only thing she could hear was a high pitch ringing in her ears.

Why was she not healing?

Her power was not working, which meant she was not healing at her normal rate. She may as well be a human without it. She had a fuzzy memory of having her power and magic bound... for something. She had been in the Night Court. There was a party. No, that was not quite right. A ball? Yes, that was right, and Kes bound her before it. How did she get from the ball to wherever she was now, and where was Kes?

She nearly jerked her body, which would have given away her alertness, when her final memory of the ball came back to her. The last thing she remembered was feeling Kes's imminent death through the bond.

Tears pricked her eyes, and she thought he was likely dead. She felt desperately for that pull in her chest. She remembered how it had been terribly weak the last time she felt it. She had sobbed alone in that cage, thinking that bond was disappearing forever.

Tentatively, she felt for the bond, afraid of not finding it there. When she felt it still there, she allowed one tear to escape her. It was stronger, which meant he was stronger. Relief coursed through her, and her breathing became easier.

He's alive.

Anin thanked the goddess, then slowly tried to open her eyes. There was enormous pressure inside her head. It pushed on her eyes, making it difficult to focus. As her vision cleared, she could see the crescent moon overhead. At least she was still in the Night Court. Slowly, she surveyed her surroundings, noticing she was caged in on three sides by wood. That, combined with the movement, meant she must be in the back of a wagon.

What was she doing in a wagon?

She felt like her brain was moving at snail's speed. Things that should be obvious felt like puzzles to her. It was ridiculous how long it took her to realize her hands and legs were bound. She squeezed her eyes shut and forced her mind to clear. She needed to be able to think.

They had finally gotten to her, and were likely responsible for Kes's near death. She needed to be alert and get away before they crossed the border into the Day Court. If she crossed that line, she would never see Kes again. Never see anyone again, for that matter. To the Day fae, her life was considered a betrayal to the natural balance of the court. More importantly, her existence threatened the Day fae way of life. She represented a new possibility, one that would turn everything upside down.

It was interesting to see how fate wove itself to intervene all at once. The attempted murder by her court put her directly into the arms of the one who would become her truest family. She wondered if she would have ever met Kes if the Day fae had not chosen that exact moment to come for her. The timing of events was impeccable. Anin was beginning to think a certain goddess had intervened to make sure fate came together. A goddess who had a connection to both Etain and herself. Anin would need to thank her the next time she saw her.

She began making little movements so she could position herself to see who was responsible for her current predicament. Some Day fae looking to elevate their status more than likely. She used the bumps in the road to make her movements look like she was being jostled. It took a long time and more bumps than she found comfortable to get her first glimpse of her captor. She was frustrated when she discovered they were hiding under the hood of a cloak.

Coward.

Her field of vision was extremely limited, and she once again used the natural movements of the wagon to adjust her position. She was hoping to find one end open so she could roll herself out of it. She could free herself from her binds once she was away from the cloaked figure. Unfortunately, there was no open space for her to sneak through.

Her only other option was to wait until they stopped. While the driver was preoccupied with securing the horse, she could creep away into the darkened woods. She would need her hands free to be able to untie her legs. She was not going anywhere unless she got these ropes off of her. She attempted to see if she could reach any of the rope with her sharp nails. It was awkward and painful the way she had to twist her wrist on one hand to have the nail of her smallest finger reach the rope. She hoped her weakest nail was strong as well as sharp enough to cut through the thick rope. She moved her nail back and forth over it, her motions matching the rocking of the wagon.

She had no idea how long she had been in the back of this wagon, but based on how sore her body was, she had to have been laying in one spot for a decent amount of time. While her pinky kept up its pace, she checked the bond again, relieved to find it still there. Ciaran must have done something to save him. The fact he had not already tracked her down spoke to how severely wounded he was. She wondered if Ciaran had already caught the beings who carried out the attack. If he had, she hoped he made them pay. Repeatedly.

She might be a wood nymph, and nymphs are typically nonaggressive beings, but that's not all Anin was. She was beginning to settle into a calm rage. If she had her power, she would have already released it in its raw form and ripped the driver apart. She tried not to let the frustration get to her. If she were to let her emotions get the best of her, it would weaken her and slow her progress. She needed to remain calm and remind herself that she is more than the sum of her power, and she could do this. Just as she thought the words to herself, she felt the first section of rope split.

Forty-Five

KES

His body felt like it had been entirely regrown. Since he was still alive, that was not too far off from the truth. Looking around the room, he was surprised not to see Anin or Ciaran. From the way he was lying on the bed, it felt like he had been tossed and left there, as if someone had been in a hurry. Surely Ciaran would have left Anin with him.

"Anin!" Kes tried to yell, but it came out sounding more like a croak. He waited a few moments, listening to the sounds of his chambers. Silence had never been louder. His heart started to beat faster. There would only be two reasons Anin would not be there with him. Either she was in the study with Etain and Ciaran, or she was gone. He tried to move his arm, but could do no more than twitch it. He was stuck there, waiting for her to come back while he waited for his body to heal enough. He knew deep down if Anin were in the palace, her scent would be fresh instead of faded.

His setup had obviously been a cog in a much larger plan. He wondered who had her—someone from his own court, or had the Day Court finally caught up with her? It was embarrassing how quickly he had been removed from the equation. His attempt to be quick had not only nearly gotten him killed but was also, ultimately, the reason his nymph was not there beside him. He only had himself to blame.

Ciaran must have reached him in time. He likely spent his entire well of power trying to save his sorry feathered ass. His body would have forced him to sleep off his burnout, and gods, he hoped he woke soon. While his body screamed in pain from every single place a blade had entered him, it was more painful to be stuck and unable to move with only his mind as company.

There are only so many beings in the entire realm who could set a trap that powerful. He would find every single one who had a hand in setting him up, placing Anin in terrible danger. He promised himself he would kill them all slowly and imaginatively. Maybe then his anger would fade.

He felt for that spot that pulled to her and found it still there. He breathed a little easier knowing, at least in that moment, Anin was alive. He spent the next several hours drifting in and out of sleep. When awake, he spent his time thinking through every possible suspect that could have been involved.

Sleep held restless dreams. In them, he would watch as his blood poured from several stab wounds pooling on the ground. He would try to stay conscious and keep pulling out the blades while healing each stab wound. Every time he pulled one out, three more would take their place. He would slow and finally give into the darkness. All he could do was kneel and continue to gush blood. Each time, at the end, Anin would be there, sobbing in a corner. Unknown beings would bring her out and kill her in front of him before he finally succumbed to his wounds. Over and over, he had this dream.

Some versions were more gruesome than others. Sometimes the hidden beings would make Anin be the one stabbing him crying the entire time. When he was on the brink of death, she would stab herself through the heart with the same blade she used on him. The worst ones were where his blood seeped out of every pore, causing him to slip as he tried to reach her before her time ran out. He never got to her in time, unable to do anything but slide around in his own blood until she was beheaded and he finally died.

The hours ticked by, yet Kes had barely regained his ability to move his fingers. He really needed Ciaran to come and speed this along. He knew no matter what Ciaran said, the second he was able to move, he was activating that tracking spell and going directly to Anin. He would not leave her on her own for longer than he had to. He made a blood oath to keep her protected, and not even one full night later, he failed. The only thing he could do was lay there, staring up at the ceiling of his bedchamber, waiting and thinking. He begged any god or goddess listening to help heal him faster and for Ciaran to wake up.

Forty-Six
CIARAN

iaran woke with a massive, deep breath, like he had forgotten to breathe while asleep. His eyes shot open, and he sat up, rubbing the sleep from them. He needed to find Etain. He was kicking himself at that moment for not installing a tracking spell on her for times specifically like this. He recalled Kes saying he had placed one on Anin. Since both females were missing, it's likely they were grabbed by the same being. It was time to go see what state his cousin was in. Kes had still been very close to death when he left him. Ciaran teleported into Kes's bedroom, hoping not to find him cold and empty of life.

"It's about time you woke up from your princess nap," Kes hissed at him. "I've been lying here for hours, unable to move much of my body while wide awake. I know something has happened to Anin or she would be here. Now tell me what you know while you heal me, then I will find her and make whoever took her pay for thinking they could take what's mine!" Kes raged.

Ciaran decided to let the "princess nap" comment slide. At least he had been knocked out the whole time. Kes would have woken and had no knowledge of anything from the moment he was stabbed nearly to death until now, conscious but unable to do anything.

"Well, if you had not walked right into a trap, we would not be here at all—would we?" Ciaran placed his hands on Kes and began to heal him. "You almost did not make it, cousin. It took nearly every drop of my power to get you to the point where you *maybe* might not die. I had enough power left to port you to your chambers, toss you on your bed, and go back to retrieve Etain and Anin. However, when I returned, both cages were empty, and neither was anywhere to be seen. Not a single soul had been watching them. The smell of your blood sent half the room into bloodlust, and the other half was busy watching the first half. Either way, I didn't have time to interrogate anyone before I passed out."

Kes's jaw dropped open, not out of shock over the behavior of the Night Court, it was likely because someone was asking for a war.

"This reeks of the kind of shit the Day Court would pull. They set everything up perfectly and tried to kill me in the process. They knew I would go to investigate anything suspicious, and taking me out would leave you on your own. What I do not understand is why take Anin and Etain? Anin is just a wood nymph, while she has a surprisingly deep well she does not seem to know what to do with it. And as far as I know, we are the only ones that know Etain is a powerful witch."

Ciaran thought about it all for a moment while he continued healing Kes. Just a few more moments, and Kes would be good enough for them to move.

"Do you remember the other human I found on the night of the hunt? The mad one?" Kes nodded. "Well, he might not have been the type of madman we originally thought. He told of this being called 'The Shepherd' who had been hunting down witches. The Shepherd told humans about 'the Beings of Light,' the 'God of Light,' and how they all lived in the 'Kingdom of Light.' The man was entirely unwavering in his convictions and would gladly do anything this Shepherd asked of him. He said he never saw the Shepherd, and had only seen glimpses of his hands, which glowed golden. All of this sounded like the fucking Day Court to me."

He finished healing Kes as well as he could, though he needed most of his energy reserves to face whoever or whatever had taken Etain. He took a step back and helped his cousin sit up.

"The way I see it," Kes said, "we can either go to the dungeons and see if we can quickly get anything out of the madman, or I can set off this tracking spell and hope the two are together. I know which option I vote for."

Ciaran thought about it for a moment. "Let's divide and conquer. You get a map out and zero in on Anin's location, and I will go quickly to see if the man knows anything else about who may want Etain. They could have simply taken her because she is mine, however, it does not hurt to be thorough."

Ciaran wasted no time porting to his fun room and was shocked to find it completely empty. He wanted nothing more than to rage and smash everything, until he thought about Etain and how she needed him. Instead, he began closely inspecting every inch of the room to see if he could find any evidence to prove who let his prisoner go.

The only thing he could find was a spot on the ground where glass was shattered, likely containing a spell at some point. Too much time had passed, and he was unable to get a clean scent of what kind of spell it could have been. The only thing he could smell for sure was that there *had* been a Day Court being in this room. Although, he could not be certain if that was who helped the human escape, or if it was perhaps one of his previous prisoners. Considering the door was still sealed shut, giving the illusion of there not being one, he assumed the shattered glass had likely contained a porting spell. That also meant whoever had helped the man had been able to port in and heal him in some capacity. Ciaran doubted the human would have been able to crawl even a few feet on his own in the state he left him in.

Seeing no reason to linger any longer, he ported to Kes to find him marking a spot on the map. Kes looked up and could tell from Ciaran's face that something was wrong. "Did he have any new insight?" Kes asked.

"It seems not one, but two humans are missing from my care."

Kes's downy brows furrowed, and he seemed to be at a loss for words. "Well, that is unfortunate, but we can worry about him later. I have located Anin's general location. It seems she is moving along one of the old, forgotten roads on a direct path to the Day Court. I cannot let Anin cross the boundary. I will never get her back if she does. I have to go. Now."

Ciaran thought the chances were high that whoever had taken one must have taken both. Maybe they had enlisted the help of the man he had in his dungeon. He told Kes as much, and the two gathered as many weapons as they could carry. Then they changed into clothing that offered a bit more protection than what they had worn to the ball a full night ago. Kes was still covered in blood, yet he did not spare a moment longer to clean himself off. It took no time at all for them to be ready, and they promptly ported to Anin's last known location.

They were standing on an overgrown road surrounded by dark woods and could make out the sound of a wagon ahead of them. Kes slinked off into the woods, while Ciaran did the same on the other side of the road. They stayed hidden in the trees as they made their way towards the sound of wheels rolling on uneven ground and kept pace with it. Ciaran could only see two beings: a large, hooded figure driving the wagon and Anin tied up in the back. He could see her working her hands together. The rope that bound her wrists was nearly frayed enough for her to break free.

Ciaran stopped and waited for the wagon to get ahead. Then he crossed to the other side of the woods and sprinted silently to where Kes was still keeping pace with the wagon.

"It's hard to see from this side. However, your nymph nearly has her hands free. I suspect she will be making her move soon. We should be ready to step in. I want the driver alive. He may know where Etain is."

Ciaran could not mask his disappointment at not finding the two females together. He had no idea how he was going to find Etain. The pull he always felt towards her would take him forever to find her in the Fae Realm. He tried not to panic and readied himself to deal with the foe in front of them. He no longer questioned what kind of bond he shared with her. There was no doubt in his mind she was his fated mate, and he would never fail to protect her again.

"We will find her, Ciaran." Kes put his hand on Ciaran's shoulder in a rare moment of affection.

Ciaran nodded, and the two took off after the wagon again, just in time to see Anin sit up and begin working on the rope binding her feet together. The hooded figure at the front of the wagon noticed she was close to freeing herself and began to slow the horse. Just as the wagon was coming to a stop, Anin leapt from the back and sprinted for the trees.

Forty-Seven
Anin

Anin did not look where she was running, nor did she care. She just *ran*. The hooded figure was quickly approaching, and she was desperate for her wings. Her hands were sweaty, making it impossible to untie the rope coiled around her. It pinned her wings down, preventing her from taking flight. She pulled and pulled at the knots and gave a frustrated scream through her teeth. The hooded figure reached out to grab her. If he got his hands on her, that would be it.

She would have screamed, but a collision with a rock-hard body stole her breath. Strong arms snaked around her as she looked up into the face of the one being she wanted to see most. She let out a sob of relief. A large part of her thought she would never see him again. Whatever happened now, she knew she would be safe. Kes immediately unbound her magic and power, making her feel whole again as he pushed her behind him.

"You seem to have been caught stealing from my cousin and my court," Ciaran said. It was a surprise to see him there, leaving Etain on her own.

"She does not belong to your court or your cousin. She is a subject of the Day Court and belongs to it and its queen," the cloaked figure said.

"Oh, you foolish Day fae. Show your face and let's see who has been so bold," Ciaran demanded. The being paused for a moment and then began to chuckle as he lowered his hood. She gasped.

"You! Of all the beings I could have expected, you were not among them!" she exclaimed, shocked. The Day Court must *really* want her dead.

"Ciaran, could you imagine being a king and sent out as an errand boy?" Kes asked, laughing darkly.

"No, how humiliating," Ciaran said, tisking his disapproval at the golden king.

Suddenly, off in the distance, there was a great explosion of raw power shooting up into the sky. It made a deafening boom. Ciaran immediately took flight, heading towards the location of the blast, leaving her and Kes to deal with the king.

"I will give you one chance to leave empty handed. This courtesy is only given because of your status. If you were anyone else, you would be dead already," Kes said, having never taken his attention away from the king.

"You think you can defeat a king? No, here is your chance to leave with your life. The nymph will be returning with me to the Day Court," Reminold said confidently before shedding his cloak and revealing his large white downy wings and his glowing golden body.

"So it's going to be a fight, then? How exciting!" Kes exclaimed. He truly sounded excited.

"You feathered fool," the king scoffed.

"I could say the same," Kes said as a maniacal grin cut across his face.

Using her power, she rid herself of the rope around her body. She was caught up in disbelief and had nearly forgotten it was there. She groaned as she stretched her crumpled wings. The sound seemed to awaken the violence always simmering just below Kes's surface.

Wind began to pick up and gather around Kes, while the ground began to rumble beneath them. Kes brought the wind into a tight ball before he flattened it into a disk and shot it at the king. She had never seen any display of his magic before. She had not even known his element was air.

The ground shot up in front of the king and slowed the blade of wind down enough that he easily avoided it. Anin had to flutter her wings, or she would have been knocked to the ground by the waves of rippling earth he sent their way. Before she could get her legs back under her, spikes of earth rose and tried to impale Kes.

Kes growled out his frustration as he built a huge cyclone around him. The tunnel of wind began pulling everything towards it, including her. She shot her vines out to the nearest tree and held on, hoping they would hold as she was lifted off her feet. His cyclone, now filled with the earth the king had just displaced, raced toward the king as he flung the whole thing at him.

The king had buried himself in earth up to his waist to avoid the pull of the wind, which made him slower to move. He tried to force the earth to drag the wind to a stop. However, all he succeeded in doing was slowing it down. The twisting earth hit the king and sent him sprawling into the trees, creating a path of destruction pointing to where he landed.

"*Shit*," Kes swore under his breath as the earth began to turn liquid beneath him, sucking him down. He flapped his wings and began to slowly lift himself out. The king, parting the earth in front of him, raged as he made his way out of the woods.

She knew she needed to join the fight before it went on too long. Vines began to whip out from the woods he walked through, weaving themselves around him, trying to at least slow his progress. Once again, she found herself angry she never had the opportunity to learn how to use her power. Maybe if she had, she could have been a better help.

The two volleyed back and forth while she did the best she could to trip him or distract him with her vines. A few times, he shot at her with giant masses of earth. Kes was quick to slice them in half, so they parted around her each time.

She could tell Kes was beginning to tire. He had nearly died not so long ago. It was impressive that he had been able to go full steam for this long already. The king noticed and sent walls of earth from all sides towards Kes, closing in on him quickly. Kes took off in flight, but he would not make it before he was crushed. She was desperate to create a distraction. She uncoiled the vine that wound around her arm at all times and lashed out to whip the king across his face.

Roaring in pain and outrage, he grabbed the vine and yanked her towards him. She stumbled, somehow managing to keep out of his reach. He lunged for her again, his desperation making him sloppy. Anin twirled gracefully out of the way while Kes avoided the walls of earth.

Anin saw the king's attack coming too late. He lunged toward her and attempted to snatch the thin strand that shimmered around her as she twirled. She had completely forgotten about the collar still around her neck and the lead attached. The king reached out to grab it, a look of triumph on his face. She tried to pull the shimmering strand back, but it fluttered perfectly into his open hand.

The second his hand wrapped around the lead, he pulled on it, instantly dropping like a stone to the ground. Anin stared at his unmoving body in shock.

"Please tell me you did not have the collar spelled to *kill*! He's just under a spell, right?" she asked Kes with panic in her voice. His shrug did nothing to calm her nerves.

If Ciaran did not manage to come into his full power soon, the Night Court would not stand a chance against the queen of the Day Court.

"Well, shit." Kes swore. "He should not have touched what's mine. I cannot say I am all that upset by his death. I am only disappointed it was not by my hand." He began to laugh maniacally. "What are the odds something so delicate would take out the King of the Day Court? How embarrassing." He began to laugh harder while tears gathered in the corners of his eyes.

He picked up the string and collapsed to the ground, pretending to die. "Look at me; I am the King of the Day Court, and I have been killed by a sparkling little string." He clutched at his stomach as he laughed hysterically. Anin could not help joining him; his laughter was contagious. He was right—what were the odds a forgotten piece of what was basically a glorified bit of jewelry would be the unmaking of a king.

Anin sobered quickly when she thought about the wrath that tiny bit of jewelry was going to bring down on them. The Day Queen would demand her retribution. Anin sent a prayer out to her goddess. She had to trust the goddess had a plan that was already set in motion, making sure everything came to pass the way fate intended. That did not mean Anin was not terrified. The events of this night likely meant her truths were going to be revealed, no matter how hard she tried to run from them.

She looked over to her mate and wondered if he had figured out yet what the bond between them was, or did he still think it was just the blood oath? Either way, she was not going to be the one to spell it out for him, because she kind of enjoyed the looks of confusion that would flit across his face when he was particularly kind or thoughtful towards her. Though those moments were usually followed by an overly sensual display of wickedness. It was as if he needed to show her he was in control; she smiled at the thought. There was no controlling a mate bond.

Kes picked himself off the ground and was dusting himself off while still laughing. She walked up to him and wrapped her arms around his waist. He paused, caught off guard by her sudden display of affection, and his laughter cut off abruptly. Gently, he raised his arms to wrap around her. The walls they each carefully constructed around themselves cracked, leaving fissures behind. Creating small spaces for the other to take root in. He held her as close as he could and nuzzled his face into her neck, breathing her in deeply.

No matter what the future brought, she knew she was no longer alone. He would always come for her, just as she would for him.

Forty-Eight

ETAIN

E tain startled awake, and everything came crashing back. She looked around the now much larger clearing and saw the debris from the trees that exploded under her power. Seamus was also spread everywhere.

She did that. She killed a man with her uncontrolled power. He was an awful man and deserved to be held accountable for his actions, yet did he deserve death? Such a gruesome one at that? Etain felt rung out, as if her body had been running for days. She looked around at the devastation her power brought; it was sobering.

Suddenly, she was acutely aware of how Seamus was...all over everything. She felt hot, as well as sticky, and looked down to see she was covered in gore, with several large splinters sticking out of her. Luckily, the splinters looked fairly shallow. She wondered if her power had somehow slowed them down to be more bruising instead of bloody. Considering how warm Seamus's blood was still on her body, she must have only been out for a couple minutes. She began to freak out at the thought of Seamus's blood.

She just killed a man, or more accurately, her power killed him—a power she could not control. She killed a man, and now he drenched her, the evidence of her crime. She felt the overwhelming urge to not be anywhere near that clearing any longer. She stumbled away before promptly heaving the contents of her stomach. Once she stopped retching, she took off, running into the woods as fast as the obstacles of the forest and her decimated body would allow.

She desperately hoped she could find a stream or lake to rinse off in. However, she was not sure if she should trust a body of water in this realm. She heard stories about creatures that pulled unsuspecting people into the depths of their dark waters to drown their prey. She did not think she wanted to risk such a death. She needed to find her way back to the capital. However, she had no idea which way it was. She would not have a sense of direction until the moon set and rose again, though she had no way of knowing how long that would be. She supposed she could find a clearing to see the moon, wait for it to set, and then reset. If she was going in the wrong direction and the moon was still hours away, at least she would not be any further away. She felt antsy at the idea of sitting still in these woods for any number of predators to hunt her, even though her body was screaming at her to rest. She decided at least to slow down and walk. Hopefully, she would make less noise to not draw any more attention to herself.

She walked for what felt like an hour when she came across a beautiful, crystal clear lake surrounded by trees. Above the little lake, there was the perfect break in the canopy of trees, which allowed the moon to light up the water, making it look like it glowed and was filled with moonbeams. She stood there, marveled at its beauty, and was completely lost in appreciation that she almost did not see the creature rise out of the water.

She could not be certain what they were, because they appeared to shift form constantly until settling on a handsome human man. Etain screamed as he approached her; he screamed back and clutched at his throat. The shapeshifter opened its mouth to speak, though she was already running into the woods. She was not going to let them drag her down to the bottom of that lake, even if it would be a lovely place to die.

She was lucky her scream caught the being off guard, and she was able to get away. It never occurred to her that she might be terrifying to the creatures of the woods, dressed in black and blood with bits of wood stuck to her, as she screamed like a banshee.

She slowed to a walk not long after she ran from the lake, because her body was going to make the decision to rest for her soon if she did not slow her pace. She found many beautiful views all over the forest. For a while, she walked next to a giant, dark rock wall that shot straight up, far further than she could see. It was covered in millions of tiny, glowing flowers. She found if she said anything, they would mimic her voice and light up, creating a chain reaction. It sounded like an echo down the wall, with a wave of multicolored lights. If she had not cursed a branch she tripped over, she would have never witnessed the amazing blooms.

Hours must have passed, and still the moon had not set. She was starting to think she would not know when it did set because of the heavy canopy of trees. She was losing her mind out there; she even thought she heard someone calling for her. She felt a sinking in her stomach. Wild ideas began to torment her. What if Seamus was not really dead, and he was coming after her? Or what if whoever Seamus was supposed to meet was chasing after her to get revenge for killing him?

It almost sounded like the voice was getting closer, and she bolted through the woods again. As her body came close to passing out, she came across a funny shaped little hut. It looked decrepit, and Etain was not sure if anyone was home. Honestly, she was not even sure she wanted anyone to be home. The top of the hut looked remarkably like a mushroom cap covered in moss. So much so, she thought perhaps it truly was a mushroom cap. The walls were made of crooked wooden boards, some of which cracked as if the structure had been frequently dropped. There were no windows or chimneys; there was only a single door in the front.

Etain was getting up the nerve to cross the clearing to knock on the door, when it blew open. A woman walked out. She could not see her face very well from where she was, yet she had the strangest feeling she knew this woman. She had not even realized she begun walking towards her until she heard the woman say, "I have been waiting for you, my child."

Etain froze mid step. This could all be a terrible trick; after all, she was in the Fae Realm. Her heart told her she could trust this woman, even if her own mind was uncertain. Etain grew close enough to finally see the woman's face and gasped in shock. This was no woman—at least not one woman. The woman's face was constantly shifting between many different faces; she never saw a single one twice. Every time her face shifted, she could swear it was a different woman staring back at her. She dropped to her knees, for the being standing in the doorway of the silly little hut was the Many Faced Goddess.

"Oh, do not be silly, child—come in and have some tea. We have much to discuss."

Etain entered the mushroom hut and was surprised by the size of the home.

The goddess must have read the look on her face because she chuckled. "Do not believe everything you see, my dear. This realm is full of surprises."

The room she was standing in reminded her of the main room of her two-room home back in the Human Realm, only with more of everything. It was larger and filled with even more dried herbs and many jars filled with a wild assortment of...things. There were books and scrolls shoved into every nook and cranny, and hundreds of candles were strewn and stacked everywhere. Between the candles and the overly large hearth with the blazing fire, the room was brightly illuminated.

The goddess indicated a chair she should sit in at her table by the hearth. Etain sat while the goddess retrieved a kettle from the hearth and poured them each a cup of strong herbal tea. She took a sip and felt strength already returning to her body, and she began to relax. The goddess' face began to slow down its incessant shifting and morph into something vaguely familiar to her.

"I have a gift for you, child. This face has been screaming from the background since you came into my presence."

Etain was stunned. Her hand flew to her mouth, as tears began to slide down her face. "Mother."

K es grabbed hold of the dead king's hand and dragged him across the ground towards the wagon, uncaring if the body was damaged along the way. Once he stood beside the wagon, he reached down to pick up Reminold's body and unceremoniously dumped him into the back of the wagon. He could tell Anin was worried about what the Day Court King's death in the Night Court would mean for them all. Truth be told, he was feeling rather unsettled about it himself.

That was a problem for another night, for now they had to figure out what to do with the body, and he desperately needed to bathe. The dried blood was beginning to itch, and now that Anin was safe, he started to take issue with the way his feathers were matting together.

"We need to send the body back to the Day Court border. There is no point attempting to hide it. The queen is aware her mate is dead," he said, keeping his tone light.

Anin nodded her agreement, walked up to the horse pulling the wagon, and touched its head for a few moments. Before he could ask what she was doing, the horse began to move. He watched in amazement as the horse, wagon, and dead king made their way towards the Day Court border at a leisurely pace.

"Wood nymph magic," Anin said with a smirk. "We can talk to the animals. I simply asked him to continue his journey without a driver, and luckily, he was rather agreeable. They are not always." She shrugged as if it were no big deal, and to her it likely was not.

He wondered what other impressive things her magic did that he had yet to see. He had only seen her use her magic. She never used her power unless it was something her body naturally did, like healing. He knew there were secrets she was keeping, no nymph contained a fraction of the power she did.

"I desperately need a bath. Let's get back to the palace. After we freshen up, we can try to locate Ciaran and see if he's had any luck hunting down Etain," Kes said as he scratched away a bit of dried blood on his neck.

"What do you mean 'hunting down Etain?' What happened to Etain?" she asked, her voice going shrill at the very end.

Kes had forgotten she would not know Etain was taken as well. He kicked himself for not being more delicate delivering the information. While the two had only become friends a few nights ago, it was clear they were already quite fond of each other.

"Ah, yes, it seems you were not the only one taken the night of the ball. We hoped to find the two of you together, but it appears the Day Court had several beings involved. Which makes sense now that I am able to think clearly. It would have taken multiple hands to pull off the events leading up to your kidnapping. I am positive the dearly departed king is who I had to thank for the trap that nearly killed me." Kes would never be satisfied with the king's death, no matter how funny it was. He deserved a bloody, painful end like the one Kes had been quickly approaching.

Kes told Anin about the trap he foolishly walked directly into and how Ciaran had barely kept him from death's open arms. While healing had been painful, there had been no greater pain than not being able to get to her. It had been agony not knowing what happened to her, but knowing something had. He knew when he could not hear or smell her in his chambers. Anin's face softened, and the sight made his chest feel the fluttering of wings flapping inside it.

He was really starting to itch and mentioned returning to the palace again. She either did not hear him or could not hear him, she looked so deep in thought. He was contemplating the merits of not asking and porting them to his chambers. As he was trying to gauge how mad she would be, her eyes flew wide and locked on him.

"We cannot go back just yet. I need to get to the Silver Moon Coven," she said randomly.

"Where?" he asked, wondering where this conversation was going and why visiting a coven could be more important than his need to get clean.

"It's where I grew up. I must warn the witches," she said adamantly.

"Why do you need to warn the witches?" He was confused and itchy, and the combination made him irritable.

"I grew up in the Borderlands between the Day and Night courts at the Silver Moon Coven. For the past several decades, many of the most powerful witches from the coven have left to join the Day Court. Never to be seen again."

Kes's downy brows lifted in surprise.

"There had been nothing in particular that made me think something was amiss. No screaming or signs of a struggle. Only a note was left on their beds, and all of their belongings were left behind. Like they just got up and walked out," she said.

"Why would they leave their belongings if they were moving to the Day Court?" Kes asked. He had always thought witches were neutral. It made no sense any of them would join one court over the other.

"Well, that's the thing. These witches would never leave in the middle of the night to go to the Day Court, of all places. Further, they would never leave their family grimoires behind. Witches worship the moon and gain significant power from it. Hence, they are more likely to join the Night Court, if they are even inclined to pick a side. They have no desire to be involved in any politics, which is why they stick to the Borderlands and remain neutral. They would never upset the balance the realm relies on willingly."

Kes was not surprised to hear any of this. The witches kept to themselves. They would not let it be known outside of their community they were somehow being lured away. He was still not sure what she was desperate to warn them about, which took precedent over his grooming. "What is it you need to warn them about? Are you positive we cannot go bathe first? Maybe take a little nap? Why is this more important than finding Etain?" he asked.

She looked guilty at the mention of her friend's name. She looked at him like she could not believe he did not get it and threw her hands up, shouting, "Isn't it obvious? The Day Court has gained a massive boost in power no one has been able to figure out. Yet we now know they are abducting witches. I think the witches are somehow being drained of their power so the Day Court can use it as they see fit. Witches are in trouble. They need to be warned immediately to go into full lockdown, and maybe even go into hiding. The most unsettling of all is that many of the missing witches are Walsh witches."

That grabbed Kes's attention. He thought about it for a moment. If that was how the Day Court was gaining power, it would benefit the Night Court if they could not get their claws into any more witches. It also meant the urgency to find Etain was paramount.

"Okay, here is what we will do. I will port us to your coven and leave you with them to help prepare in whatever way they need. I will patrol the border in case whoever has taken Etain makes a break for it. The Day Court cannot have her. I have a feeling she will be our Queen, and her well of power would give the Day Court a disastrous amount of power."

Anin nodded. Kes grabbed her hand, brought it to his lips to kiss it, and then ported them to the Silver Moon Coven. He thought he saw her smile at his kiss.

Fifty

ETAIN

Etain never thought she would see her mother's face again. She was staring and knew that while it was her mother, it was also not her mother. "How? How is this possible?" she asked the goddess.

"To know that, you must first know who I am, where I came from, and where you came from as well, my dear. It is a long story—please try not to interrupt. Your prince is on his way, and we do not have much time."

Etain glanced at the door and smiled at the prospect of seeing Ciaran soon. However, she needed answers. She hoped he did not show up before she got them.

"I was not always the Many Faced Goddess. That is the name that was given to me not all that long ago, compared to my never ending immortal life. Fae live thousands of years, yet they still age and eventually die, if they are not killed first. In the realm I come from, and even in places in your world, I was known as Hecate. My realm contains beings of true immortality. Once we are created, there is no death for us, therefore, you can imagine how one would want to explore all the realms and find as many adventures as possible. Eventually I grew bored with my travels…"

Etain could not help it; she was bursting with her question. "There are other realms?"

"Yes, there are many realms that all center around your world. Some, like the Fae Realm, only connect in one location. Others have multiple connections all over your world. Your human world is incredibly vast, child. Did you not know?"

Her jaw dropped, and she could only shake her head. It never occurred to her the human world would be anything larger than the land where she grew up.

"Well, perhaps you should get comfortable with the idea that there is much you do not know, and much you will never know. Now, can I get on with the story?"

Etain looked sheepish and nodded while she sipped her tea.

"Wonderful—where was I? Oh, yes, I was growing bored, and after you have lived so very long and have seen all there is to see, what is one to do to continue to enjoy life? Many of my kind go into a form of stasis every other century. When they awaken, there are likely new things, inventions, and places to explore. I have never wanted to enter stasis and have always prided myself on never needing it, even though I was reaching a point where I was considering it.

"Mankind was only starting to become more than grunting animals. They were forming tribes and beginning to lay the foundation for your very culture. I stepped out of the veil of my world with my dear friend, Mórrigan. She wanted to show me the ceremony the humans were performing that night in her name. Ah, I see you recognized the name. Your prince is long descended from her. She's a bit scattered like that, leaving off-spring all over the realms. Anyway, the ceremony was barbaric and bloody at best.

"I found myself enchanted by a human man for the first time in my long existence. He was tall and had long, dark hair that was always wild when down. He had a chiseled face that wore a beard well. I am not usually a fan of beards, however, he kept his neat and tidy. Compared to the men around him, he was leagues above them. I would watch him when his tribe would battle another. There was something thrilling about the way his body moved. His dark eyes were cunning, and his mind was sharp. It was no wonder he became the leader of his people.

"I kept coming back to watch him, until one night I took my physical form and let him see me. He fell to his knees, knowing he was in the presence of a goddess. It was a fun game we played for a little while. He would always look for me. Sometimes I would let him see me, and sometimes I was more interested in what he would do if I did not show. It was as if he knew I was there anyway, because he would talk to me in his silly, simple little language.

"One night we finally came together under the full moon, and it was as if he waged war on my body. His body moved much the same way it did when he was in battle. It was primal and raw. I think he must have known he would never see me after that night, and thus he did not stop once all night. It was magical in its own way, because that man created a life within me.

"I was no longer interested in the man, for now I had something brand new to me—a child. I knew I could not be like my friends, who left their children with other beings to be raised. The idea of watching something come from me and then become its own being entirely sounded thrilling and gave me a renewed purpose. I stepped through the next veil I could find and walked right into the Fae Realm. I was shocked to find a realm I had not explored and immediately fell in love with having access to the moon day in and day out. I decided this would become my home, where I would raise my child, then help raise their children, and so forth.

"In the thousands of years I have been here, I have only left the realm a handful of times. It has always been because I could feel the need of one of my descendants calling me in such desperation that I could never refuse. Your mother calling to me from her deathbed was the last time I left this realm. She was nearing the end, and all she could beg of me over and over was to please guide her daughter, who would be left alone in a world becoming increasingly volatile. Her last wish was for you to be safe. I spoke through her to you that day, giving you a prophecy of your own." Etain choked back a sob, remembering the last conversation she had with her mother, which guided her to the Fae Realm.

"My love for all my children is absolute, and in their deaths they are returned to me to rest and join their ancestors. It is my pleasure to sacrifice my own face to give them each an intermittent moment of life again. In this way, they live on forever. You see, my child, your mother is not really gone. She will live eternally within me—loved, protected, and waiting for the day you can join her.

"Although, I do think your soul may come with a guest. Oh, how he would hate that!" The goddess threw her head back and cackled while still displaying her mother's face.

Etain was not sure what she was talking about. She was sure her confusion was plain as day on her face, because the goddess explained herself without Etain needing to ask.

"The prince is your fated mate. I have been doing everything I could to make sure fate worked out the way it was supposed to for you. You must have felt a deep, instant connection to him?"

Once again, Etain's mouth was wide open with shock. "I have indeed, although I thought I was under some spell. I did not know there was such a thing as fated mates. What does it mean?"

"It means your lives and souls are forever tied together. Fate destined it long before you were ever born, it was put into motion when Ciaran came to life in this realm. It means, my dear sweet child, that you will be the Queen of the Night Court. You will face great challenges to get them to accept you, but your mate will always have your best interests at heart. Together, you and your friends will bring a balance to the realm it has never seen."

There was a loud commotion outside Hecate's hut, and Etain could hear Ciaran screaming something that sounded like, "You stupid bitch of a goddess. I know you have her!"

Etain looked at the goddess and cringed at Ciaran's words.

"Oh, do not worry. I find his antics amusing. He loves you more than anything, Etain. He has desperately needed something to love and to love him back. His life has not been easy."

Ciaran pounded on the door and screamed some more colorful names at the goddess.

Etain stood and was torn between running to the door and into her mate's arms or staying with the goddess, who, for now, wore her mother's face. "I should probably go before he hurts your home, or more likely, himself." She paused for a moment, unsure if she should, and then quickly came around to the other side of the table to hug her many greats grandmother and her own mother all at the same time. "Thank you for letting me see her again, and thank you immensely for sharing with me. I do hope to see you again."

The goddess squeezed her back in a rather maternal show of affection. Finally releasing her, Etain began her walk to the door.

"Etain, there is one last bit of information I must give you, though in the very near future, you will want to do differently. Your place is at the Night Court. Do not leave it. The witches will need you, and you will need them. Open your doors to them, or I fear they will not survive."

Etain had her hand on the doorknob, and she paused to look back at the face of her mother one last time. "I promise you, I will." Etain opened the door and stepped out.

Fifty-One

CIARAN

Ciaran knew he had to be nearing the location of the raw power blast he had seen through the canopy of trees several moments ago. He continued to circle the area from above, looking for any treeless gaps. He was about to scream his frustrations when he spotted it—a gap in the trees. As he neared, he noticed something odd lying on top of parts of the canopy. He quickly realized they were large shards of wood, as if several trees had exploded and their pieces went up and out.

He slowly descended into the clearing, knowing she was not there at first glance. The ground looked like a war zone. It was covered in debris and gore. For a split second, he panicked and thought perhaps she had detonated herself with her power. Then he picked up the scent and recognized it as the human man who had escaped his dungeon. He hoped to find out who helped him escape, yet he could not say he was not thoroughly pleased with the way he met his end.

He noticed the epicenter of the explosion easily, because everything fanned out from that one spot, which rather resembled his little witch. He carefully picked his way to the center, not wanting to disturb anything or make it harder on himself to track her movements. Studying the ground, he saw where she shuffled or crawled away; he was not sure which. He followed her footsteps to the edge of the woods and saw where she had apparently not been as thrilled as him with her personal brand of justice, clearly unable to stomach it.

He looked out and marked the path she took easily. She likely sounded like a boulder crashing through the otherwise quiet woods. It had been a long time since he had visited the forest. Even now, it was in search of his mate and not to admire the beauty he came to love as a child. He and Kes would often run off for nights at a time to the woods before they made it to their tenth year. He would return full of excited energy and stories about all the magical and beautiful things they found. His mother always gave an amused smile, while his father would berate him for being too soft and loving. He would tell him the Night Court has no place for such sentiments.

He remembered the last time he and Kes went on one of their forest adventures. However, not because of the time spent with his cousin. His father finally had enough. He took Ciaran right back out into those woods to see all the wondrous things he just finished telling his mother and father about, only to have his father force him to destroy all the beauty in cruel ways. He never went back to the woods. Not because he did not still enjoy it; it was his way of protecting the beauty from himself.

Now, as he followed the path of destruction Etain made running through the woods, he found a sudden change in her trail. She slowed down, and for a moment, he had a hard time picking her trail back up. Once he did, it led him to a crystal clear lake filled with moonlight. He knew this to be the home of the water shapeshifter Nagada, and thought perhaps they saw her.

He walked to the water's edge and calmly ran his fingers along the top of the water. It was like knocking on the door of a being who lived underwater. He only waited a moment before the water began rippling. He took a couple steps back to avoid getting splashed.

Nagada's physical form shifted several times before settling on a lovely fae female with dark violet skin and a long sheet of silver hair that rippled as she moved her head.

"Oh, hello—prince. What a surprising honor to be called upon by you." Quieter, and slightly under her breath, she said, "And what a busy night it's been."

Ciaran thought perhaps she spoke of Etain. "Hello, Nagada. It has been a long time, my friend. I am looking for someone, and it seems she has likely come by here. She is a human woman with long, dark red hair and dressed in a gown like the night sky?"

"Ha! I thought she was a banshee the way she screamed at me! I came out of the water to ask her if she was lost. I even made myself into a handsome human male, and you know how much I hate taking a male form. However, as I opened my mouth to speak to her, she screamed right in my face! Do you know she was already terrifying enough as it was? She was completely covered in red blood. I could not even tell you the color of her skin. There were *chunks* of remains on her, my prince. Chunks!"

Ciaran could not stop the rumbling laughter that crept its way up his chest and out of his mouth. The idea of his little witch frightening anyone was incredibly funny to him. "Okay, what happened after she screamed at you?"

"Well, I screamed back, naturally. I was already on edge, and she caught me entirely off guard." The shifter shivered as if the memory of his mate would later give her nightmares. "She ran off that way like she was afraid of me doing something unspeakable!" Nagada pointed in the direction Etain went.

He thanked his friend and said he would be sure to bring her back to meet her under better circumstances. He nearly laughed again when Nagada cringed at the thought. He followed the direction the shapeshifter pointed, and soon enough, he picked back up on her trail. He followed it for a bit longer until he noticed he was next to the wall of glowing mocking blooms; they were once a favorite of his. Ciaran and Kes would shout all kinds of obscenities and laugh so hard they wound up rolling on the forest floor as the flowers repeated everything they said. He smiled at the memory, and picked up his pace, eager to have her back in his arms.

Eventually, he came to a clearing and stopped dead in his tracks. He knew that mushroom hut well. It had a habit of showing up wherever and whenever it pleased, exactly like the goddess that resided in it. He growled in anger. Who knew what garbage that bitch was filling Etain's head with. She spoke in riddles and never made anything easier for him. If anything, she did the opposite.

He began to yell at the goddess to release his mate! If she did not listen to him soon, he was going to bust down the door, using whatever it took. He grew impatient with his pacing and shouting. He decided he would bang on the door as well to make the goddess understand he was serious! He backed up several paces from the lone door, preparing to give it a blast of his power, when it casually opened and Etain stepped out.

She looked up at him and smiled as she walked toward him. His breath caught as he stared at her; she had never looked more stunning. She was covered in dried human blood, her hair was matted with gore, and she had two tracks of clean skin running under her eyes where tears washed away the grime. His feet began moving without his knowledge, and he met her halfway. They wrapped their arms around each other in a fierce embrace.

"Hello, little witch—did you enjoy tormenting the wood folk?" he asked with an abundance of mirth, recalling the look on Nagada's chosen face. He was doing his best to ignore the exceedingly strong urge to take her to their bedchambers, never let her leave again, and kill anyone who dared even glance her way.

"Me? Tormenting them? I assure you, it was very much the other way around. Why, I just barely escaped some creature who posed as a human man to no doubt drag me down under his waters and eat me!"

Ciaran threw his head back and roared with laughter.

Her face was full of confusion, which was slowly morphing into annoyance. She tried to pull away from their embrace. He told her about his conversation with Nagada and held her tighter as she began to laugh. Ciaran felt sure the look on Etain's face would be one he would often recall fondly.

"Well, I suppose I never considered what I looked like. Honestly Ciaran, I was afraid I would never find my way back to you." She looked up into his eyes, and he could see the fear that had been plaguing her.

"I will always come for you, little witch, however, it seems my attempt to be your prince charming and come to your rescue was unnecessary. I should have known you would save yourself. You are a strong woman, Etain, and yet I will always wish to protect you. I failed horribly at the festival, and I will spend the rest of my life making it up to you, if you will have me?"

She smiled softly up at him. "Take me home, Ciaran."

Fifty-Two

Anin

They had to port just outside the gates to the Silver Moon Coven due to the heavy wards all around it. They were immediately greeted by several witches. All of them appeared to relax once they saw Anin, even if they were unsure of Kes. She smiled brightly as two curly blonde heads pushed through the throng of witches. Lyra and Panella were the closest things to real sisters she had. It had taken her a while to warm up to anyone after having to run to the Borderlands after her mother died. The two witches had been persistent and eventually broke her barriers down.

"Where have you been?" Panella cried as she nearly knocked her to the ground with the impact of her hug.

"Oh sister, do not ever worry us like that again!" Lyra exclaimed as she jumped on top of her two sisters.

"I know, I know, I should not have left like that," Anin said sheepishly. She could audibly hear Kes's feathers bristling. She broke away from them, saying, "Kes, these are my sisters; Panella and Lyra." He visibly relaxed when she introduced them as family.

"And, um, this is my... Kes." She felt her face flush immediately. She did not know what to call him, and she almost said he was her mate. Her sisters would never let her live it down, and if Kes's smug face was anything to go off of, neither would he.

"It's nice to meet you both," he said, grinning at her. She was surprised he did not make some ridiculous gesture as he addressed her sisters. He was never one to pass up a show, and yet he did. He must be far more tired than he was letting on.

He placed his hand on her lower back and then leaned in to whisper into her ear, the act making her knees feel wobbly. "As soon as I see you safe behind those walls, I will start my patrol. I will be back shortly, try not to take too long. I really am desperate to bathe."

She never met a male more concerned with his hygiene than potential danger. She nodded and followed her sisters into the coven. As the gates were closing, she saw him stretch out his massive black, downy wings and shoot into the sky.

It was almost strange seeing the half-and-half sky after even just a few days gone. Since they were in the Borderlands, the sky showed exactly where one court ended and the other court began. They had the perfect amount of sun and moon at all times. Anin took a moment and put her face toward the sun. Being a member of the Day Court, the sun always recharged her in a way no other thing could. She felt physically stronger, and her power felt like it went even deeper. The longer she spent in the night court, the weaker she would grow. The thought worried her, because her mate was of the Night Court. She doubted he would want to leave it, and she wasn't sure she could spend the rest of her days without the sun.

She sighed and considered this a problem for another day—first things first. She needed to meet with the head witch and tell her what she suspected. Her sisters looped their arms through hers, and she knew the teasing was about to begin.

"*So*, are we not going to talk about 'your Kes'?" Lyra asked, saying "your Kes" in a sing-song voice.

"No." She sighed, knowing there was no point in trying to move the subject away from him.

"*Your* Kes does have quite an impressive wingspan," Panella said, her innuendo clear.

"Oh, look at how she blushes!" Lyra exclaimed. The two roared with laughter at her expense, and she just rolled her eyes at them. It was several minutes before they were able to speak again.

"While we are always happy to see you, dear sister, something tells me the reason you are here is rather dire if the condition of 'your Kes' was inferred correctly," Panella said. She was slightly taller than Lyra and the two were blood sisters. They both shared the same rich brown skin, golden blonde curly hair, and near-black eyes. They said the only thing that made people question if Anin truly was their sister, was her light green skin. Anin did not care if they looked alike or completely different, she loved them just the same.

"Unfortunately, you are as astute as ever, Panella. I must speak to the head witch urgently. Please tell me she's in?"

They nodded in confirmation, and the three set off towards her chambers. As they walked, the two witches peppered Anin with questions about Kes. Neither of them asked how they came to meet, somehow knowing it would be a long story, and one that could not be rushed. Anin had not felt this light since the last time she had been around her sisters. She had missed them terribly.

Once they arrived at the head witch's chambers, Anin knocked on the door. A few moments later, it opened on its own. The three sisters stepped into the receiving room and helped themselves to the refreshments that were always waiting for guests who came to visit the head witch. Anin had just finished her glass of herbal water when Galetia, the head witch, entered the room.

"Anin! What a wonderful surprise to see you! I had feared I would not see you again when you suddenly left without leaving any word."

Her sisters made sounds of agreement.

"Have you returned to us permanently? We have all greatly missed you." Galetia was a kind, old witch, and like most witches, she looked human. The only thing giving her away as "other" was the branch-like antlers sprouting from her gray streaked, dark red hair, marking her as having some bit of Day Court in her blood along the way. Galetia had gladly taken her in after her mother had died and she had fled the Day Court. She had become a mother in kind to Anin over their many years together.

"Regrettably, I have much to tell you, and none of it is good," she said solemnly.

"Well now, that is not entirely true, is it? You have met your fated mate after all," Panella said, unable to hide her sly grin. Anin nearly groaned, knowing the head witch was going to want to know everything.

"Really? Oh, how exciting! Who is it?" Galetia asked. She sighed again. She seemed to be doing a lot of that since she returned.

"Kes, Prince of the Night Court," she said, immediately regretting her choice of words. Why did she have to say he was a prince?

"Oh, he's a prince now, is he?" Lyra asked sarcastically.

"Yes," she said, glaring at her sister. "Did you all miss the part about him being a Night fae?" she asked, finally voicing her concern.

"Fate knows what it wants, and makes no mistakes, Anin," the head witch declared, wise as always. However, Anin felt fate may have gotten it wrong this time. She did not want to discuss her current feathered *situation*. Besides, she really needed to get to the real reason she was here.

"I guess, anyway, enough about Kes. I think I might know what is happening to the missing witches, or at least why they are being taken," she said, knowing this would grab their attention.

"Tell me *everything*," Galetia demanded, sobering instantly. She told them all about what she believed the Day Court was doing.

"I do not think you are safe here if they are able to get around the wards," she said. This was her biggest concern. She did not feel like her family was safe.

"Perhaps not," the head witch said, still deep in thought over Anin's possible discovery.

"There is something else—concerning," Anin said cautiously. Unsure how to deliver this news.

"What?" her sisters asked in unison, like they often did.

"The Day King took me from the Night Court..." They immediately interrupted her, angry that she had not already told them and wanting to check her over to make sure she was unscathed. "Yes, I am fine. However, the king? Not so much. He is, um...he's dead," she finally forced herself to blurt out. There was a long moment where no one said anything.

"Good. If he were not already, I would have hunted him down myself," Lyra said, and Anin knew she meant it. Kes, in many ways, reminded her of Lyra. They are both quick with a laugh, however, both could be deadly serious when it comes to the ones they... Did he love her?

"Of course, I am happy to hear he has paid for his crimes against you. I only worry what this means for all of the witches standing between the Day and Night Courts if this turns into a war," Galetia said, worry clear in her voice.

"I have the same concern. The Queen is already unpredictable, I cannot imagine how much more chaotic she will become with grief," she said, feeling guilty for placing them in this situation. She ran off on her own to protect them and still managed to place them in harm's way.

"We will need to spread the word to all of the other covens," Panella said. Witches were amazing at thinking of the community over the individual.

"Yes, everyone must prepare. I was not the only one taken. It seems fate has been busy because Ciaran has also found his mate," she told them.

"No? Truly? That is most unusual. They are not so common, are they?" Galetia asked, surprised.

"No, it becomes even more unusual when you take into account who his mate is. She is a human witch." This caused another long silence before all of them erupted with laughter.

"I am sorry, that is just too funny," Panella said.

"What must be going on in their minds! I bet it is a mass of confusion," Lyra said through her laughter.

"It is rather funny watching the expressions on Kes's face when he does something out of character because of the bond. I have not told him. It is far too fun watching him figure it out," she said, grinning at the witches.

It was a lot to lay at their feet. Honestly, she could not believe it had been a few short days or nights, depending on what court you were in, since this whole nightmare had begun. Then again, if it had not been for this nightmare, Anin was not sure she would have ever met Kes. She amended her thought to mostly nightmare, because Kes could be a real nightmare sometimes. Then she ultimately decided she was originally correct, this whole thing was a nightmare.

"I cannot hold back on this anymore, Galetia—she is a Walsh," she said. Anin had been so excited to finally share this information with her.

"Truly? I thought I was the last one, with the rest of my kin disappearing to the Day Court." She smiled at the way the head witch's eyes sparkled with emotion . "You will, of course, bring her here. I am sure she is in desperate need of training. I will personally see to her education," Galetia declared.

"I have no doubt she will be more than elated by your offer," she said, knowing it to be true.

"Did you happen to see if she had a large leather-bound grimoire with her?" Galetia asked, hopeful.

"I have not, however, that does not mean she does not have it here with her," she said, hoping it was true.

Galetia explained that several generations ago, the head witch of this same coven was a Walsh witch. She placed a curse on the ruling bloodline of the Night Court. As soon as she became with child, she fled to the Human Realm to keep her child protected from the cursed King. When she and her sister concocted the plan, it was decided the sister going into hiding would have greater need of the grimoire, and she took it with her to the Human Realm. Anin knew if Galetia was able to hold and read it, it would connect her to her ancestors and give her an even deeper sense of her power.

There was a knock at the door. A youngling witch opened it and informed Anin her "bird beast" was hollering for her outside the gate, and that his screech was starting to hurt her ears.

Anin laughed as she stood. She hugged Galetia and promised to bring Etain as soon as she was back safe and sound. Her sisters stood to walk her to the front gate. She patted the youngling on the head and thanked her for coming to get her. She promised she would be sure to let Kes know his screeching needed improvement. The youngling smiled conspiratorially up at Anin.

Anin's sisters looped arms with her again, as was their custom when walking anywhere together, but this time they held on even tighter. None of them knew when they would see each other next, or if they would all be able to survive what was coming. As they got closer to the gate, they could hear Kes bellowing. Her sisters began to applaud the young witch and her perfect description of the noise their new brother was making. Anin smiled, and something loosened in her chest at her sisters' acceptance of her mate. She hugged them both fiercely.

"I'm truly sorry for leaving in the night without any word."

Her sisters pursed their lips, and Anin knew how much it had upset them. She had not said anything to them or left word, because she knew they would try to come with her.

"Do not *ever* do that to us again, Anin. Neither of us had ever been devastated like that in our lives. Sometime you must tell us where you ran off to, and why you did not think you could trust us," Lyra said as Kes let out a particularly horrid bellow, which had all three of them flinching.

Anin promised she would explain when she came back with Etain.

"You must also tell us how you came to meet the bird beast bellowing away out there," Panella said with a grin.

"Well, the two are connected."

Her sisters shared a look with each other. She hated it when they spoke to each other like that, it was the only time she did not feel like their sister.

"I have missed you both horribly," Anin said as she hugged Lyra. "And, I love you both," she said as she hugged Panella. She made them promise if it ever got too dangerous at the coven, they would flee to the Night Court and come to the palace. She knew Etain would protect her fellow witches, no matter the cost.

The gate opened, and she nearly laughed at the sight her mate made. He was scratching himself like a beast with fleas. He had been preening his feathers until he noticed the gate opening and immediately stopped. It looked like the little witch had made another exemplary description when she referred to him as a "bird beast."

The second he laid eyes on her, he adopted his typical air of arrogance and a cocksure smile graced his dirty face. When she reached him, she grabbed his hand, turned back to her sisters, and waved one last time before Kes ported them back to his chambers.

Fifty-Three

ETAIN

Etain was completely drained. She let Ciaran lead her into the bathing chamber and undress her. There was nothing heated about it, they were both desperate to be clean, warm, and in bed. He guided her under the delightfully warm, falling water. She let him scrub her hair and scalp using a couple of the bottles in the little alcove next to them. Neither of them said anything, content to be with each other in comfortable silence.

She let him rid her of all traces of Seamus and her trek through the woods. He traced the "H" Seamus carved into her skin with anger flaring in his eyes. When she released her explosion of power, it healed the injury, yet it did not remove the reminder.

She grabbed his hand and said, "It's okay. He's gone, and it's behind us now."

"I can remove it completely, little witch. You should not have to be reminded of your torment every day," he said as he tucked a wet strand of hair behind her ear and brought his forehead to hers.

Part of her felt she should keep it, however, the bigger part of her agreed with him. She gave him a slight nod, and he placed his hand over the mark. Within moments, she felt a warmth tingle under his hand before he pulled his hand away; the mark no longer marred her body. She sighed in relief and tipped up on her toes to give him a soft kiss, hoping it would convey her gratitude in a way words never could.

They stared into each other's eyes for a moment longer while he cupped the side of her face and gently caressed her cheek. Then he kissed the top of her head and moved himself under the water. She watched as he quickly and efficiently cleaned himself. He then used his magic to dry them both before they quickly dressed in their night clothes. She was in another gauzy black shirt dress, and he was in a pair of the softest fabric pants. Etain thought she might have to steal them at some point.

They both crawled under the blankets on the bed. She was mesmerized by the way he shuffled and tucked his wings in such a way as not to crush them. It did not even seem like he needed to think about it; it was second nature to him. She found herself wondering what it would be like to have wings. She realized there was a great deal she did not know about her mate, and she supposed they would have time to get to know each other over the years to come.

Once he was situated, she found herself scooting over towards his side to rest her head on his shoulder and place her hand over his heart. They lay there in silence for a few more moments before he spoke.

"I feared I lost you, little witch, when I only just found you. It was the single most terrifying moment of my life."

"Was it because we are mates?"

He thought about her question for a moment as he slowly ran his fingers up and down her arm.

"Yes, however, it is not that simple. You are the other half of my soul, which I never knew I was missing. To lose you now would be to suffer a half-death. If you were lost to me, I would be lost to me, too."

She felt her eyes begin to water with emotion, and she knew exactly what he meant, because she felt it, too. "Ciaran, I am only a human, and my life is much shorter than yours. I do not wish to be the reason you suffer for the rest of your nights." It was something she had been thinking about ever since Hecate told her Ciaran was her fated mate. She had another sixty years if she was lucky, and that was nothing to a fae.

"My love, you are no longer in the Human Realm. Here, your life span is connected to your well of power. The more power you have, the longer your life will be, and you have more power than I do at the moment. I can feel it. As soon as we ascend the thrones, we will also inherit the power of the Night Court, and our lives will be even longer. We can, of course, still be killed, making it of the utmost importance that you learn how to use your power to protect yourself as soon as possible."

She was stunned at how easily he talked about her taking the throne beside him. She had yet to wrap her head around it. She knew it was her future, yet there was still a lot to process.

"I must admit, I am having a difficult time coming to terms with the idea of being queen. Though I think the beings of the Night Court will have an even more difficult time with it."

"Leave them to me. I think at first they will be openly hostile, but that is their way with anything. Mostly, they will be pleased to have me come fully into my power. It's been generations since we have had a *true* king and queen on the throne."

"Your parents were not the king and queen?"

"In title only. A true king and queen of the court would not only inherit more power, they would in turn replenish the power of the court as a whole, making us all stronger. I'm assuming this is why the Day Court has been able to pull off things like they did the night of the Lunar Ball."

"I do not understand. Why were they king and queen in name only? How does one become a true king and queen of the Night Court?"

He was quiet for a moment, then he lightheartedly chuckled. "The only other person who knew of this was Kes, because he and I come from the same line. A few nights ago, I found an entry in my great-grandfather's journal where he told of a curse placed on him. He was the last true king of the Night Court, and his entire line had also been cursed, binding half his power away in retribution for the mistreatment of witches he tormented. This kept him and future generations from accessing the power of the land. Perhaps because the land found our power lacking, it therefore found us unworthy. I am still not sure of the exact reason, though this feels right.

"Then, the other day, you and I found that entry in your family grimoire about a curse placed upon the ruling line of the Night Court. It was your ancestor who cursed my family, and it is our bond that will break it. As soon as we complete the mating ceremony, the curse will be broken. Then we should be able to ascend the throne as the first true king and queen in generations. We will also be the first mated pair, as far as I know."

She was shocked and a little perturbed Ciaran kept this from her, although she supposed everything unfolded the way it needed to. She was already incredibly overwhelmed. If he had put the pressure of breaking his family's curse on her shoulders from the beginning, she was not sure how she would have responded. She was too tired to continue talking about curses and future plans.

"Hecate."

"What?" he asked, confused by the sudden shift in conversation.

"The Many Faced Goddess. Her name is Hecate. She is not from this realm, and she is the creator of the original witch. The many faces you see her wear are all the witches who have come before. Someday, she will wear my face as well."

He growled deep in his chest, clearly taking issue with anyone besides him having any part of her.

"We all return to her for our final rest. She did find it greatly amusing you would be joining me, since you would be annoyed and content knowing your soul would rest within her, to stay with me."

Before he could begin whatever tirade he was opening his mouth to start, Etain cut in. "She wore my mother's face while I visited with her. She said my mother had been screaming to come to the front as soon as she had been in my presence. She was my mother, and yet she was not. She was Hecate first and always, as was my mother, too. I could see my mother in her expressions, which she wore so easily. It was such a gift, Ciaran. I have desperately missed my mother, and I never thought to see her again." She could feel the tears starting to lazily roll down her face once more.

He must have felt them, because he squeezed her tightly and kissed the top of her head. "I do not know what it is like to love a parent. I thought I loved mine when I was very young, and quickly realized I had mistaken their approval for love. I do not know if I knew what love was until the mate bond forced it upon me. It is terrible and wonderful all at the same time. It is a weakness, as well as a strength. I am not sure I will ever be worthy of it, because I am terrible and wicked. It is for you and you alone that I can be good and kind."

"What happened to your parents?"

"Nothing exciting or nefarious. Fae live incredibly long, and ruling fae even longer. They wait to have children until they are thousands of years old to enjoy a life without them first, yet eventually they must create an heir. My parents never inherited the power of the court, and my father's power was reduced, meaning their lives were half the expected length. One night they began to age, and a couple hundred years later they were gone."

"Oh, Ciaran. I am sorry you were robbed of time with them."

"Do not be, little witch. I know I am not. They were not only horrible parents; they were also truly poor rulers. It has taken me a long time to get this court into something less bloody. Believe it or not, at one point, our numbers were dwindling considerably by our own hands. The lesser fae were terrified to join in celebrations since they were often tormented and killed. I understand our nature is to be wicked, but we cannot be allowed to be our own demise."

She thought on his words for a few moments. "Perhaps something has begun to fester in the power of your court due to the curse? Perhaps an unseen side effect? Curses are volatile like that. My mother always told me to be wary if I ever had to place a curse, because there was always a price to pay. Perhaps that was the unseen price."

"I have never thought about it. The court has always been this way as long as I have been alive, therefore, I have no idea if it has ever been different. It is worth looking into, my clever little witch."

The two continued talking for a while longer about nothing in particular—books they read and stories from their youth. She felt content and full of love and affection between her time with Ciaran and her time earlier with Hecate. She knew the future was going to be difficult, though she could face anything with him by her side.

Also, knowing she would be with her mother again after the end of her very long life with her mate, left her feeling more at peace than she thought possible. Her heart was light as she drifted off to sleep in the arms of her mate.

Fifty-Four

Kes

Kes immediately shed his clothing as he walked to his bathing chamber, not embarrassed in the slightest to walk nude through his quarters in front of Anin. If anything, it made his ego swell knowing she was looking at him. Even if she tried to act like she did not want to be looking at him. He turned to look over his shoulder before disappearing into his private chambers. "Like what you see, my darling nymph?"

Her only response was to scoff, roll her eyes, and then cross her arms over her chest in an attempt to seem unaffected. This just made him laugh and raise a downy eyebrow at her. "You are welcome to join me, Anin. I'm sure I would thoroughly enjoy watching the particular way water would run down your...vines." His grin grew positively devious as he watched her skin flush.

He was feeling rather full of himself until her entire demeanor changed. She began sauntering towards him, wearing a sultry expression he had yet to see on her.

He swallowed hard and suddenly wished he was still wearing his pants to hide how she was affecting him. She came within arms reach and slowly scanned him from head to toe before finally settling on his face. She cocked her head to the side and gave him a too-sweet smile.

"Now my *darling feather duster*, you must understand something about me. I am not swayed by a mere body. No matter how..." she waved her hand up and down his body, "defined they are. That is not to say I am incapable of enjoying another's body and have done so many times. That is the same to me as when my leg itches—I scratch it or when I am hungry, I eat."

Kes was trying his best to not explode with rage and immediately hunt down any other being who had touched her. Before Kes had an opportunity to start collecting names, she continued.

"Bodily need is not the same as when the mind craves another. So you see Kes, if you want me and not just my...vines, you must first win my mind, and the rest will follow."

Kes became nervous; he was not sure he had ever felt that before regarding any other female. He found he did want that—every facet of her, and not only her body.

Anin stepped into his space and lifted up on her toes, leaving her mouth a bare breath away. "When you take your shot, make sure your aim is true. There will be no second chance." With that, she swiftly turned and walked off towards her bedchambers.

He could not decide if he was incredibly turned on or terrified. Perhaps he was both. He made his way to the bathing chamber with a little less swagger than he had a few moments ago. He could have cried proverbial tears of joy the moment he entered the room. There was absolutely nothing Kes despised more than being covered in filth. It was all he had been able to think of from the moment Anin was safe. The whole time he had been flying the Borderlands, it took all his willpower to stay focused on searching for Etain. Every so often, he would find himself drifting into a daydream of being just where he was now.

Wasting no time, he strode towards the falling water that took up the entirety of one wall. It was difficult to clean feathered wings, particularly ones the size of his. He spread his wings wide and stood under the warm blast, allowing the heat and pressure from the water to remove the caked-on blood and relax his body. He would never let anyone know he was still healing from his near death. He could still feel where each individual blade had pierced his skin. It was only a dull ache now, and he knew he would be back to normal after a night of deep rest. He ruffled his feathers and slightly flapped his wings while shaking his head to make sure to get every nook and cranny clean.

He did not typically preen his feathers, but he was extremely filthy and many were damaged. He needed to do a full inspection and pluck the damaged ones. Brand new ones would emerge as soon as they were pulled. Once the water rinsed clean, he stepped out and started looking through his feathers.

It took ages, and Kes was getting frustrated when he could not see whole sections on the back of his wings. He knew he was going to need help, and Anin was right out in the lounge of his quarters. He heard her emerge a while ago and had been enchanted listening to her movements and sighs while he did the repetitive task of pruning his feathers. It was oddly soothing.

Decision made, he put pants on to join Anin in the lounge. She was straddling a chair meant for winged beings to sit in and read, cocking her eyebrow at him when he entered.

"My, are you not quite the indulgent one? You were in there for a rather long time."

Kes sighed. He never enjoyed asking for help, and she was not making it easy for him. It was not her fault; he usually enjoyed her ball-busting. How was she to know he was struggling with the necessity of requesting assistance?

"Well, I had many of my feathers damaged in the attack. It affects my flying, and they can get uncomfortable if left alone."

"Oh, I did not know that." All sarcasm was gone from her voice. "Feathers seem to be a bit of a hassle."

Kes laughed, "You are not wrong." He took a deep breath and rubbed the back of his neck. "Look, I cannot really see the ones on the back of my wings..."

"I can help you. Here, come sit and tell me what to do." She did not even hesitate and even smiled as she stood and indicated for him to take the seat she had just vacated. He felt like an idiot as he just stood there staring at her. "Well, come on. Walk your bird-beast self on over here."

"Bird-beast, huh?" He began walking, the banter between them easing his nerves a bit more.

"Oh yes, the youngling witch who came to inform me you were there waiting to retrieve me, declared that your name, and I think it rather fitting. She also had much to say about your screeching."

Kes wanted to feel indignant, but he could only find the humor at his own expense and began laughing as he took the seat. "Perhaps I should look into some vocal training, then I can sing like birds. It is truly unfortunate it was not a feature I was gifted."

Anin threw her head back, laughing behind him. Kes turned a bit in his chair to keep from missing the sight.

"Okay, okay." She turned him back around as her laughter ebbed away. "Now, tell me what am I looking for...oh, I think I see." Her hands slowly caressed through his feathers stopping on a particularly sore spot.

"If you see any broken or sparse feathers, pluck them out. New ones will sprout immediately."

"Pluck them? Like a chicken?"

Kes groaned. He regretted this already, but then her hands grazed through his feathers once more, and he wanted to groan for a totally different reason.

"Kes, I am only teasing. Truly though? Pull them? I do not wish to hurt you. Why are there so many?"

"I promise it will not hurt, if anything it will be a relief. The damaged feathers are the remnants of where the blades entered my body."

Anin's hands stalled, and she gasped. She gently touched each spot on his back and wings where Kes could still feel the lingering pain.

"Oh, Kes...," she said quietly. She then took a deep breath and began plucking the feathers.

Kes laughed when she nearly shrieked at the speed at which a new feather came in to fill the spot left behind. They went on like that in silence until the task was done a long while later.

Kes was sure Anin thought he did not see her take one of his feathers and tuck it away in a fold of her wings, but he had. He would never say anything about it, because something warmed in him at the idea of her wanting to have a piece of him with her at all times. Kes was beginning to wonder if their bond was not more than what the blood oath had created. If he were honest with himself, he had felt a bond there before the blood oath. Kes was beginning to think Anin was his mate, even if it was crazy to think of being mated to a member of the Day Court. He had no idea how that would work.

He was not sure he cared. He wanted her, and he would do whatever it took to make sure she was his. She was keeping secrets from him, he had known this from the beginning. He wanted to give her the time she needed to trust him enough to tell him whatever it was she feared revealing.

Dread grew in his gut. He needed to push her for information soon if he were to keep her safe. He had failed once, and he did not want to ever fail her again. He did not think he would survive it.

Fifty-Five
Ciaran

Ciaran woke up with one hand clutched at where his little witch's thigh had been thrown over his hips and held her waist with the other. She was having a dream that had her moving against him in such a way that it was taking every ounce of his self-control to keep from flipping her over and taking her right then and there. His hips thrust on their own accord when her leg ground against his desperately hard and straining cock. He groaned out in pain or pleasure, he was not sure. He gripped her a little tighter to wake her.

"Little witch, if you keep this up, I am going to lose all self-control and take you right now, hard and fast."

She gasped, and her eyes flew open. Her pupils were blown, and she was panting. He could feel her dampness through his pants. She tried to pull away, seeming embarrassed.

"No. You are in need. I can feel it." He inhaled deeply and growled out, "I can smell it."

Her cheeks flushed that beautiful scarlet he loved.

"What kind of mate would I be if I left you in such a state?" he asked as he rolled her onto her back and kissed her deeply. He pulled away to say against her lips, "Not a very good one."

He began to kiss and nibble down her neck as he said, "And..
.we...cannot...have...that." Once he reached her sleeping gown,
he grabbed it at the neck with both hands and split the material
all the way down, exposing her to him. He took a few moments
to admire the beauty of her fair skin glowing in the moonlight,
while her breasts heaved with her heavy breath.

"Ciaran...please..."

"Please what, little witch? Please, *this*?" he asked as he licked
the valley between her breasts before moving to one and sucking
her peak into his mouth. He bit down just hard enough to elicit
a hiss from her before he laved over the sting with his tongue
to sooth it. He made his way to the other side to make sure her
other breast did not feel left out.

She was squirming underneath him, her body searching for
a deeper sensation.

"Is that what you wanted, Etain? Are you satisfied now?"

"N-no—I mean, yes, I l-liked it. Ciaran please...more. I need
more."

"As my mate wishes." He worked his way down her stomach,
then picked up one of her legs. He kissed and licked her from her
ankle all the way up to her inner thigh, then left the leg on his
shoulder while he did the same on the other leg. "How about
now, little witch? Are you satisfied now?" he asked her again
with one of his too-wide wicked grins.

"Ciaran! Please!"

"Please what, my love? You must be specific." He then leaned
in and licked her core from one end to the other. He had to
hold her hips down to keep her from flying off the mattress. Her

hair was starting to float around her, and the lights, which had previously been off, were beginning to flicker.

"Oh, gods—yes!" she tried to scream, but her voice was too thick with desire.

"Mmmm, I suppose it's a good thing that I happen to be ravenous, and you have offered a feast in front of me." He blew gently over her wet slit, and she cried out in frustration, which only made him rumble with laughter. He stopped teasing her and buried his face between her folds. He paid very close attention to what he was doing when he heard her say things like, "oh gods" and "yes," and his personal favorite, "Ciaran."

She began to grow bolder as he sucked on her little bud of pleasure and entered her with two fingers, hearing her gasp at the sudden fullness and then groan out her pleasure. She grabbed his hair and ground against his face. Her arousal was dripping down his chin, and he could feel her beginning to clench tightly around his fingers. He knew she was close. He curled his fingers, finding that spot inside of her, while simultaneously sucking her in hard. She detonated—in more ways than one.

Glass shattered around them, lights flared, and the banked fire in the fireplace roared to life while her body gripped his fingers and flooded his face. He was in complete awe over how wild and free she was at that moment. As she started to come down, her eyes fluttered open and locked with his. She smiled shyly at him, a need still burning within her eyes.

"Please, Ciaran. I need to feel you inside me. Please." That was all he needed to hear. He let one of her legs drop from his shoulder, bringing the other one with him while he worked his way back up her body. He kissed her deeply again.

"Do you like the way you taste on my mouth, little witch?"

Her only response was to grab his face and kiss him hard again, while he removed his pants and lined himself up with her entrance. "This may feel uncomfortable for a moment, though I promise to be gentle with you."

"I do not want you to be gentle. You will not break me, Ciaran, and I think I might enjoy you trying to," she said urgently, while she gripped his hips, trying to bring him closer to where she needed him.

"If you keep saying things like that, I may not make it long enough to give it my best try." He locked eyes with her as he entered her just an inch before smiling wickedly down at her. He pushed almost all the way in on one hard thrust, then covered her mouth with his to swallow her gasp. He was trying to give her a moment to adjust to him; however, she started moving, and he hissed. He grabbed her hands and held them above her head with his free hand while he pulled the leg in his other hand up higher.

"Ciaran, please... I need you to move."

"Hang on tight, little witch," he said before pulling out almost entirely. She whimpered at the sudden loss of him. Before she could complain, he began a fast, hard pace, rolling his hips to hit that spot inside her each time. He loved the little gasps and noises that would slip out of her mouth at the top of his thrusts. They only served to spur him on harder.

He released her hands and grabbed her other leg while lifting up on his knees. He then gripped her hips, allowing him to give her a whole new sensation. Her eyes closed, and she gripped the sheets as her upper back lifted off the bed. Again, he could feel her body clenching him, but this time it was around his cock, and he had to think about council meetings to make sure he did not finish just yet.

"Look at me, Etain. I want you to see who is bringing you to the brink of ecstasy. Feel how well your body takes every bit of me. I want you to see whose cock you are falling apart on."

She opened her eyes, and they stared deeply into each other's souls. As she came again, she cried out Ciaran's name, and their eyes never strayed. He had not noticed at first, it was not until he began thrusting up and not down into her, he realized she was beginning to levitate. He spread his wings and rose with her.

The sight of his wings seemed to drive her wild. She began meeting his thrusts again while they floated several feet above the bed. He shifted their position, and she was riding him until they reached the ceiling. She put her hands up to brace against it and rode him with abandon. She was lost to sensation, and he did not think he could hold on much longer.

"Once more, Etain. Come with me this time." As if on cue, he felt her starting to peak again. This time, he went over the edge with her when she crested, roaring his release. He hoped the entire Court heard him claim his mate for the first time. As she started to settle down, she began to laugh.

"What could possibly be so funny, little witch?"

"We are on the ceiling," she said with more laughter.

"Why yes, we are—entirely your doing. I just went along for the ride, and what a ride it was." Her eyes flared with heat, and this time it was he who was laughing. "Come mate, let's get some rest so we may wake up and do it all again."

She smiled and nodded as she yawned, and he led them back down to their bed. They found each other again, multiple times, throughout the night before the early hours of first night began to find them. He was positive he would never, in a million years, get enough of his mate. However, he was sure going to try to get his fill before they met their physical end. He knew there would never truly be an end for them.

Fifty-Six
ETAIN

They were late meeting Anin and Kes in the study—excessively late. The hours leading up to first night had been filled with exploratory touch and pleasure, the likes of which Etain could only have imagined. He gave her the space and encouragement to explore her desires, and she could not wait to delve into them further. Her face must have been starting to flush, because when he looked at her, his face morphed into one of equal parts smugness and heat.

"If you keep thinking about whatever it is you are, my little witch, I will have no choice and take you right back up to our bedchambers. Then we will never have our mating ceremony or ascend our thrones. Honestly, taking you back to our bedchambers sounds like a better idea to me. Fuck the Night Court." The heat in his eyes told her he was entirely serious. While part of her wanted nothing more than to do just as he said, the other part remembered what Hecate said about the role she would need to play in the future. That future depended on them ascending to their thrones.

"You know we cannot. You will have to prove to me later how poor of a decision I made by showing me all of the things we could have been doing."

He laughed and promised her he would do just that. They stood in each other's space, staring between them, when Kes cleared his throat. She remembered their friends were in the room, and they were here to help them prepare for the coming ceremonies. She grabbed Ciaran's hand and gave it a little squeeze before turning to face Kes and Anin.

"Sorry, we are late. We should have let you know we were running behind."

Anin's smile grew wider as she looked between them. It was as if she could read every sordid detail about what the two had been doing and why they were late. Kes, ever the clueless one, started to complain in his haughty way. Anin shoved her elbow into his ribs, and Kes's diatribe ended before it even really began.

"Oh! It's not a problem at all. We are both happy to see you back and unharmed. You are positively glowing! You must be so happy!" She emphasized the "so" confirming what Etain already suspected; she knew exactly why she was glowing. Etain tried to hold her smile back with her teeth.

Anin walked up to her and embraced her, whispering conspiratorially in her ear, "You have much to spill later." She pulled away, winking at Etain, both of them giggling.

Kes and Ciaran looked between the two females, then at each other, shrugging as if to say, "I have no idea," which only made Anin and Etain laugh harder. Linking arms, the two walked towards the table, which thankfully still held breakfast, because she was starving. She regarded her friend out of the corner of her eye, checking her over to make sure she was okay.

"I'm fine, and you?" Anin said, catching her perusal.

"I am fine, as well. I think we have much to share with each other."

"We certainly do," said Kes as he took his seat next to Anin. Ciaran and Etain were the only ones eating. Kes and Anin ate earlier while they waited for the other two to arrive. It was decided Kes and Anin would share first, while Etain and Ciaran replenished their energy. While the two told their tale, she found herself almost in tears over Kes's near death. He must have seen the emotion in her eyes, because he assured her he was right as rain. Anin was quick to say there was nothing "right" about him, which lightened the mood dramatically.

When they began to share the fight with the Day Court King, Ciaran was seething. He interrupted with threats of death; Anin and Kes shared a look. Anin told of how, as she whirled and dodged the king, the thin strand from her collar started to unwind around her. Ciaran interrupted again, however, this time with laughter.

"No," he said in between deep belly laughs. "Please tell me he grabbed the lead? Oh gods, I do not know if I will survive the laughter if that actually happens. It's what happened, isn't it?"

Kes and Anin nodded in unison, and he roared with laughter. She never heard him laugh that hard, and judging by the look on Kes's face, he had not for a long time, if ever. Kes bellowed with laughter with his cousin, while Anin and Etain looked at each other and shared a smile with a head shake. Only their mates would find the death of a king hilarious.

She paused for a moment, looking between the two, wondering if they were mates. She assumed they were after learning what fated mates were. She guessed she would find out definitively at some point, whenever they were ready to share the news. She realized they did not know about Ciaran and Etain being mates either.

Ciaran started to tell their story, and she could not keep it in any longer.

"We are mates," she said, interrupting him.

Neither Anin nor Kes looked surprised in the slightest. Anin even said she had thought as much since the first time she saw them together. Ciaran smiled softly at her. Obviously, her interruption had not bothered him; if anything, he loved hearing her claim him. Etain told them about her visit with Hecate, the Many Faced Goddess, and what she learned from her. The comment about the witches needing to seek solace in the Night Court under Etain's protection had Anin sitting up straighter.

She could see the worry written on her friend's face. They could all feel a heaviness looming over them. Since they did not know what was coming, the best they could do was prepare themselves for whatever the future might bring. For Etain, that meant learning magic and how to control her power. The last thing she ever wanted to do was blow someone up again. She could not be certain that the next time it would not be one of her friends, or even worse, her mate.

"I desperately need to learn to control my power and how to access my magic. I fear I might harm someone by accident, and I need to be able to protect myself. Ciaran cannot be by my side at all times, and neither should he need to be. Please tell me one of you knows someone who can teach me," she pleaded.

"Actually, I wanted to tell you—the high witch of the coven I grew up in has personally offered to help you not only learn your power, but master it. While that is wonderful, I think you will be most thrilled to know she is also a Walsh witch." Anin gave her an excited smile.

"She's my family?" Etain breathed out.

"She is. I have been incredibly excited to tell you, and I am sorry I did not tell you sooner. I wanted to tell her first. She is overjoyed to meet and train you. It's been years since she had any kin, and she has always wanted to meet the Walsh's from beyond the veil."

"Me, too," Etain said in awe. "When can we go?" she asked the room.

"Kes and I have a council meeting approaching. As soon as we finish here, we can take you both to the Silver Moon Coven. When you are ready to be picked up, send me a message on a spelled scroll."

Etain's smile was enormous, and she thought her cheeks might never recover.

"The only thing we must do before we leave is plan when the mating ceremony and the ascension should happen. I had already been of the opinion sooner rather than later. However, now with the death of the Day King, and the likely drama the Queen will bring our way, I would rather it be as soon as possible."

While she was still overwhelmed at the prospect of being queen, she did understand the need for Ciaran and the court to be at full power. She would need to ask him later what would happen after the mating ceremony. She was concerned that there would be new things she would have to cope with. Since coming to this realm, it has been one surprise after another. It would be rather helpful if she could have a heads-up this time. She did not fear solidifying the mating bond with him, quite the opposite—she could not imagine not doing it. They were linked forever, yet she could feel a final thread that would take the bond even deeper. She assumed that was what the mating ceremony would do.

"Tomorrow, the crescent night will be a burning moon. To witches, this is a blessing for unions. The burning signifies a new beginning, since fire clears the old and allows the new to grow," Anin said. "I know it is very soon, though—it seems like a good omen to me."

Ciaran agreed, and Etain could not help but agree as well. The date was set. Tomorrow at crescent night, they will have their mating ceremony and become the King and Queen of the Night Court.

They ported to the front gates of the Silver Moon Coven. Before they could blink, the gates were opening, and Anin's sisters were there to greet them. This time without the gawking mob of witches Kes had spoken of the night before.

"I sent a message to my sisters just before we left to allow them to be a touch more prepared for us," Anin said with a wink. She turned and ran toward her sisters, doing her best to tackle them. The three looked determined for someone to wind up on the ground. They wrestled around like the farm boys used to do in Havenston when they were avoiding their chores.

Etain laughed as Anin used her wings to keep her sisters from being able to pull her down. They shouted over the lack of fairness before all of them broke out into laughter.

Ciaran appeared completely perplexed by the behavior of the three seemingly savage sisters.

"I swear she always cheats!" the taller of the two witches bemoaned in a teasing way.

She felt a pang of jealousy; she never had a sibling. She also never had many friends when she was little, and by the time she left Havenston, she had not even one friend to count. The easy way Anin interacted with the two witches spoke of a history built out of love and experience. She found herself longing for what Anin had.

Ciaran seemed to sense her sadness and gently pulled her into his arms, wrapping his wings around them. He then took her face in his hands and looked into her eyes.

"Are you okay? If you are not ready for this, I will happily take you back to the palace. Just say the words."

"No, it's okay. I'm fine. I was thinking about how lonely my childhood was, and how I wish I had what Anin has with her sisters."

His thumb caressed her cheek, and his eyes softened not in pity, but in understanding. While Ciaran had Kes growing up, the way of the Night Court kept them from becoming truly close. "I hope one day I can fill that void for you, little witch."

She reached up on her tiptoes, and Ciaran met her halfway, their lips meeting in a gentle kiss. After confirming she was ready to face the group again, Ciaran unfolded his wings.

"Sorry, I needed a little privacy with my mate," he smirked, alluding to having a small tryst, rather than giving away her need for a moment to collect herself. Her heart warmed at his thoughtfulness. Who knew the Prince of Darkness could be sweetly attentive to her while being truly brutal to others. Etain knew it was callous of her, yet she rather loved he gave that side of himself to only her. She gave his hand a squeeze in thanks and told him she would send a message on her spelled scroll. She used her magic to connect a thread to the one Ciaran procured for her earlier to be able to call upon it anywhere.

She warily joined Anin and the two blonde witches, yet was quickly relieved to be pulled right into the group, linking arms with one of the females she did not know. Her name, as it turned out, was Panella, and the other was Lyra. They were Anin's adoptive sisters, as she learned as they entered the coven.

Etain stopped in her tracks and marveled at the place. The building was a palace in its own right, yet logically, it should not stand. On the bottom was a simple hut, much like the one she left back in Havenston. Then stacked upon it was a hulking stone creation of arches, towers, and corbels. She even saw a stairway, that came directly from a window and abruptly ended several steps up to nothing. There were spires that twisted and moved to one side, only to twist back up again, far into the clouds. None of this was visible from outside the gates, making the sight even more surprising.

She could not decide if it was beautiful or a monstrosity, though it was definitely something you could not help taking in. The longer she looked, the more baffled her mind became. She was sure she was going to catch flies if she did not shut her mouth soon. Panella still had her arm looped through Etain's, and it was her laughter that snapped her out of her amazement.

"I always forget how to newcomers, this place must look impossible. Lyra and I were born here, so this is what we compare to everything else. You must understand how boring we think the palaces and manors of the courts are."

Etain could not contain her laughter. She could see how this was true if this was Panella's standard. "I never knew it was possible for a structure to be this wild and free. While at first I must admit it is unsettling, I become intrigued the more I look."

"Well, unfortunately, we do not have time for a tour today," Anin said. "We must get you to the head witch, Galetia, for your lessons. I fear you have much to catch up on, and I have a sinking suspicion time is not on our side."

She felt it as well. She felt the need to prepare for something, for what, she was not sure. She nodded her agreement, and the four of them entered the little hut. They took many twists and turns before climbing up a set of stairs. They reached a short hallway with a single door at the end of it.

Etain was suddenly nervous. She never met another member of her family besides her mother. She was illogically afraid Galetia would not like her. She thought she might take one look at Etain, deny her, and send her on her way. She knew this was highly unlikely. However, she was desperate to feel connected to her family again. Therefore, she could not help thinking the very worst.

Anin knocked on the single door, and within moments it swung open. The three sisters entered without being greeted, like she was sure they had done many times before. She watched as they made themselves comfortable on chairs and lounges around the receiving room. Anin got up, poured Etain a glass of something, and brought it over to her.

"You look like you could use something to settle your nerves. Do not worry, it's only herbal water, and I find it always settles me. Come sit with me. Galetia will be here when she is able."

Etain gratefully accepted the drink and followed Anin to one of the lounges. As she sipped her drink, she did find her mind began to ease and her muscles relaxed. Whatever was in this water, she would need to learn how to recreate it.

"I would have known you as a Walsh witch at first sight!" said a woman with her hands clasped together in front of her heart. Her hair was nearly the same color as Etain's, only streaked with gray, and there were antlers protruding from her head. They appeared to be made of tree bark and were somehow rather feminine. The effect was magical. She both looked human and fae, and her deep green eyes held unfathomable wisdom. The woman strode towards Etain, who had not realized she was standing, and grasped her hands.

"Hello, my dear—it is wonderful to be with kin again. My name is Galetia, and I am overjoyed to meet you." Still grasping Etain's hands, she looked towards the three sisters to send them on their way.

All three kissed the head witch on her cheek in farewell, and to her amazement, all three did the same to her. She was going to have to get used to having a community that openly accepted her.

"I'm positive this is all a bit much. We witches are nothing if not ostentatious. Please come sit down and let us get to know a bit about each other. Then we can decide where to begin, shall we?"

She sat back down in the seat she had been occupying, and Galetia took the seat Anin vacated just a moment ago.

"Thank you for meeting with me and offering to teach me how to control my power. I must confess, it does frighten me a bit. I fear hurting someone if my emotions get too out of control." Etain felt she might as well be honest and put the worst out for her to know. If Galetia wanted to refuse her, it would be better for her heart if it were sooner rather than later.

"Well then, it sounds like we know exactly where to start. My dear Etain, please do not fear your power. We have all had to learn to control and wield it. It is not something we are born knowing, and it takes everyone, witches and fae alike, trial and error to figure it out. Try not to be so hard on yourself. This is all brand new to you, and no one expects you to be a master in the short time you have been in this realm."

She let out the breath she did not realize she had been holding and smiled at Galetia. "Control would be wonderful and would give me peace of mind. I feel the power inside me is like a raging storm, and I do not have the slightest idea how to calm it."

Galetia thought that over for a moment or two, then grabbed Etain's hands again. "I want you to close your eyes and find that raging storm inside you. I want you to visualize the way it feels."

She could feel her hair tossing around her. She heard something shatter.

"Do not concern yourself with anything else. Now that you have your power visualized, I want you to see if there is anything your power is trying to accomplish with all of its wild energy. Can you see anything?"

Etain studied the image of her power. There were many colors: red, orange, green, violet, and blue. Within the cyclone of colors was a black, smokey mass. It was calm, and yet it felt deadly. Yet at the same time, she did not fear it. It called to her in the same way Ciaran did. She told Galetia all of this.

"The color black has many meanings for witches. It can mean a violent power or even death. Because it is calm and loving, it is obviously for your protection. It is likely a power resurrected in you from your long-ago grandmother, who fled this land to protect her unborn child. She was the last known Walsh witch to be blessed with sight, and she, too, had a black center to her power. See if you can touch the colorful whirlwind. And when you do, think of things that often calm you."

She thought back to a time when she and her mother had been snowed in for six days before the storm finally relented. They had laughed nearly the whole time, discussing how dreadful certain neighbors' homes must be at the moment. Trapped inside their small homes with some of the most deliberately heinous individuals, it had to be complete torture. Yet they could not find it within themselves to feel sorry for them. They often spent their time pondering the creatures they had read about in their grimoire and whether they were real or not. They discussed ways to improve certain remedies while trying new herbal tea combinations. Most were enjoyable, a few however, were not.

They had been prepared since they had been taught from generation to generation to read the weather. Unfortunately, most of the town thought they were completely mad. They spent the better part of the prior week stocking their home with firewood and a plethora of ingredients they used often. They baked many extra loaves of bread to deliver to the elderly as soon as the storm cleared. They had made what must have been a hundred candles and had fully restocked all of their herbal remedies by the time the snow stopped falling. It was one of Etain's fondest memories of time spent with her mother. Havenston had heeded their warnings from then on, and her mother felt exceedingly proud of that.

Feeling the way the memory had calmed her, she told Galetia she was reaching out to the violently swirling mass of color.

"Wonderful! Now take that feeling and gently push it into the swirling mass. It should begin to slow."

She took the calm and slowly fed it into the chaos. After a few moments, she made a small sound of surprise as the colors began to slow. She had not realized her skepticism until she saw and felt the difference instantly within her power.

"What do you see now, Etain?"

"The colors are slowing and are now merely orbiting the black mass. It looks far more peaceful, as if it is ready and waiting for something."

"Do you think you are able to touch an individual color and see what emotion it brings?"

Etain reached out for the red one; she felt confident in her sexuality and within her body, like she could seduce anyone if she wished for it. She only wanted to seduce one male, and she knew he would thoroughly enjoy her practicing this side of her magic.

She then reached out for the orange one and felt the urge to create. This one allowed her to see the threads of power all around her, which she could wield to create any spell or illusion as soon as she learned how. She was particularly excited about this one, because creating new remedies and recipes had been one of her favorite things to do in the Human Realm.

Green was the smallest of the colors, and it gave her a feeling that sent her heart racing. It felt like a future possibility for her and Ciaran, if they ever wished to take it. She smiled softly and gave it a gentle caress to nurture it. She knew they would need an heir, and she was pleased to feel the warm way it seemed to study her. Someday this magic would get to see the world.

The next one, violet, created a sense that *something* was coming. It felt urgent, and as she touched it, she felt fear. It was not for herself; it was for someone close to her. She could not get a feel for who it was, so she immediately feared for Ciaran. Needing to keep a hold on her calm feeling, she decided to move on to the final color orbiting the black—blue.

This one calmed her even further, and she felt strength as never before, both physically and magically. She felt she contained the power to protect all those around her, if only she knew how to use it. Of all of her gifts, this one felt the strongest.

She knew without question that if she trained this particular power, she could not only defend herself, but she could defend the defenseless as well. She felt called in a way to do just that; it was empowering.

After she began to get a feel for all of her powers, Galetia asked her if they were still circling the black mass in the middle.

"Yes, but casually. I feel as if I simply will them to stop, they will."

"Try it. See what happens."

She knew she could demand they stop, though she had always been one to mind her manners, she decided to simply ask if they would be willing to stop. She knew at once this was the correct decision. They felt almost sentient, as if they were becoming a team within her.

"Okay—I asked them to please come to a stop, and they have. What should I do now?"

"You are doing wonderfully, Etain. Absolutely marvelous. Now, if you can reach through and touch the black as if you were greeting an old friend."

She slowly reached her hand out in her vision and gently caressed the black mass. It rippled in appreciation, and she did it again. This time the black began to wrap around her arm gently. She did feel like it was an old friend, or like a piece of herself that had been kept hidden from her. She felt the black swirl all the way up her arm before it settled into some shape on her back.

It was then she heard a gasp come from the head witch—one of shock and awe. She felt it was only right to tell her powers to continue circling if they wished. Since the black was gone, they looked content to float around peacefully. She did ask them to please not become the raging storm they had been before, unless they felt it was life or death. Somehow, she got the feeling they agreed. She felt it was safe to open her eyes and come back to the receiving room she had been sitting in this entire time.

She fluttered her eyes open, feeling an inner peace—a wholeness. The only thing she felt was missing was the final connection of the mate bond. She looked up and was surprised to find tears in Galetia's eyes as she regarded her in a near reverent way.

"What is it? Did I do it correctly?"

"Oh, my sweet dear. You did beautifully. You not only tamed your wild powers, somehow you became one with them in a matter of moments. Look down at your arm. You now wear the black smokey magic under your skin. If you look at the crook of your right elbow, you will see an eye just below it. This is to signify that you are gifted with Sight. Did you feel the power settle anywhere else on your body?"

"My back. I felt it settle into some pattern I could not discern. Can we take a look?"

The head witch was certain they should, and she was excited to see what beauty her magic had blessed her with. She wondered if this was how Ciaran got his black swirls all over his torso. She undid the top of her deep green gown and revealed her back to Galetia.

"Oh, my dear, you must see this. It is truly amazing." She created a mirrored surface from thin air that wrapped around Etain so she could see.

It was as if smoke formed in the shape of wings. There were no defining edges, though you could clearly make out what they were. She thought they were beautiful adornments, and she sent gratitude to the power she recognized as the black effervescent entity.

"Etain, I apologize. I forgot you are brand new to this and assumed you knew what this meant."

At her puzzled face, the head witch continued. "This mark is the rarest of them all. We have not seen a witch with this mark in ages, and I am not sure I could even find any written text on it here. You would have to go to the Coven of Remembrance, for they are tasked with keeping all the histories of our kind. I do know enough to tell you that if you can master this magic, you will produce wings of black smoke. You will be able to fly wherever you wish, just as your mate's wings can for himself."

She was stunned for several moments, unable to form words. Collecting herself, she was finally able to verbalize her thoughts and ask, "And what of this Sight you mentioned?"

"Some think it's a gift, and others a curse, because you will see things that will come to pass, or even might come to pass. It will be up to you to interpret the meaning of what you feel. Trust your gut and not your heart when it comes to these visions—do not ignore them. It will sometimes be joyful, sometimes sorrowful, and sometimes there will be warnings. Regrettably, I do not know much about this gift. I think it would be best for you to visit the Coven of Remembrance at your earliest convenience."

Etain tried to take in what she said, however, she was finding it difficult to come to terms with. Galetia clearly tried to hide her dread to keep from scaring her. The feeling the magic was giving her was one of commitment. A commitment to help keep the Night Court and all of the witches of the Borderlands safe;

she intuitively trusted it. She felt energized and exhausted at the same time, yet also settled. And mostly, she felt powerful.

Galetia told her the work they did with her power over the last several hours should have taken multiple sessions to conquer. She thought they had reached a great place to stop for the day, and she agreed as her exhaustion started to seep in.

"Out of all your colors, what do you wish to focus on next time? Perhaps you would also like to learn a little witch magic?" the head witch asked her.

"Oh, yes! I would love to learn anything you can teach me," Etain said eagerly before considering the colors of her power. "I think the blue. It was one of strength and protection. It seems wise to learn to defend before learning to attack. All the more, I have found I do not have a stomach for bloodshed."

Galetia laughed and told her it was probably for the best, considering her mate had enough of a penchant for bloodshed for multiple beings. She laughed in agreement.

"Etain, I know you are tired, and if you wish me to wait until next time, I will, however, I have a question I would very much like to ask you."

She felt like she owed this witch much more than an answer to a question, because she had given her peace in only one session. "Of course, you may ask me anything."

"When your many great-grandmother had to flee this realm, she and her sister decided it would be best if she herself were to take the family grimoire since it would be the only connection to who you all truly were. I was wondering..."

Before she could finish asking, Etain called upon the book, which lay resting in her lap. "Yes, I do indeed have it. Thanks to

Ciaran's forethought to grab my bag. He taught me the handy trick of tethering objects to yourself. Would you like to keep it for a while and see what the human witches were up to all these years?" she passed the book to Galetia. The woman held it with the utmost reverence, as if she were having a hard time coming to terms with the book finally being in her hands.

"Thank you, my sweet, sweet Etain. You have no idea what this means to me. If you ever need it, please do not hesitate to call it to you. Would you mind terribly if I linked it to myself as well?"

"Of course not. It is just as much yours as it is mine. We are the Walsh witches, and this is our grimoire." Etain sent a message to Anin saying they were finished, and if she could please come and escort her out of the maze that was this coven.

While she waited for Anin, Galetia told her stories of her youth. Her father had been a wood nymph, that was how she got her beautiful antlers. They bloomed in her youth with brightly colored flowers along the base of them, which prompted all the other young witches to wear crowns of flowers to mimic their beauty. She could not wait for her next session with Galetia; she had already learned much in the few short hours she spent with her.

Anin came strolling in a little while later. Etain embraced Galetia tightly and tried to convey her gratitude for all she did for her today. She promised she would be back after the mating ceremony and her ascension to the throne. "Oh! You should come! The whole coven should come! You are my only known family member—well, besides Hecate. Unfortunately, I do not know how to contact her; she seems to show up exactly where she needs to be. Perhaps she will surprise us."

The head witch looked uncertain, and Anin voiced her agreement. She made the point that it was only fair the new queen had her people there to bear witness as well.

She promised she would make Ciaran keep the Night Court in check. It was also her understanding that witches knew how to have a good time and would likely fit right in. Galetia told Etain and Anin she would ask the coven immediately, and it was not likely for witches to pass up a party. She would be honored to attend. She agreed to send a spelled parchment with the details as soon as she had them, then gave the head witch one last hug before she and Anin began their twists and turns toward the gate. As they walked, Etain sent a message to Ciaran to retrieve them, and within a few more steps, he responded they were waiting outside the gate.

Anin's sisters joined them halfway along their journey, and Anin told them of the invitation that had been extended to the entire coven. She had never heard such squeals come from grown females before, and it made her laugh over their excitement. The sisters began talking about possible dresses they could wear and the many different ways they could style their hair.

When they finally made it to the gates, she turned around one last time to take in the ridiculousness of the building. She found she was already quite fond of it—stairs to nowhere and all.

Stepping through the gates, Ciaran was waiting for her, just as he said he would be. She smiled at him, and his face lit up as he smiled back at her. Soon they would complete their mating bond, and he would be hers forever. It was another thing she could not wait for.

FIFTY-SEVEN
CIARAN

As usual, Ciaran and Kes were the last to enter the council chambers. The rest of the council members had been waiting on them for an excessively long time, and Ciaran could feel the animosity pouring from around the table. Ciaran had been running behind all night due to the way he and Etain spent their early hours before, and even well into first night.

He could not find it in him to care one bit—not that he tried—if the deplorable beings who made up his council had to wait a million first nights for him to show. If that meant he got to spend his time coaxing the small sounds and gasps from Etain, he would happily oblige. Everyone of those sounds made the more animalistic side of him want to beat his chest in male satisfaction. Ciaran smiled to himself. If they were angry now, they were about to be in full outrage. He could not wait to ruin any scheming he knew a few of them had been planning, and he really hoped he got to shed some blood at this meeting. He would not mind creating a whole new council. Most of these creatures had been appointed during his father's time, and they were as weak-minded as his father had been. He would take swift and exacting action against anyone who spoke in a threatening manner toward his mate.

"Ah, I see we are all here," he said to the gathered fae.

Kes chuckled softly under his breath when a few faces flushed so deeply with anger they looked like they might explode.

"I have much to discuss..."

Before he could finish his statement, he was interrupted by the ugly green idiot, Royad. "Prince Ciaran, I believe you owe me and my daughter an apology. At the very least an explanation as to why a human pet was placed above my daughter at the Lunar Ball. Along with why you felt it appropriate to take her hand for correcting the human that you should have had better control over. If you cannot control a simple human, how will you ever control this court?"

It was not often he was stunned into silence, yet he could not believe the audacity of Royad. If he wished, he could have killed his daughter, or Royad, at any time he pleased; he did not need a reason. He saw Kes straighten in his seat and glower at the slimy goblin. Ciaran took a moment to inspect the faces of the remainder of his council, noticing who appeared to side with the goblin. He was not surprised to see Balric wearing a smug expression, since he was likely in on this blatant display of treason.

"Yes, prince," Balric said with venom. "I hear you and Kes both lost your pets. Taken right out from under you. The 'all powerful' prince and his cousin could not even keep two females in line. Perhaps we have been duped into believing you were strong enough to ascend the throne. And after the less than ideal

Lunar Ball, I for one am beginning to question your capabilities."

He had been thinking about the night of the ball nonstop. He came to the conclusion that the Day King must have had inside help.

Balric was ambitious and conniving. He also had an entire network of informants. He knew Balric had heavy influence over the political-social elite of the court and also had knowledge of the comings and goings of the beings who worked within the palace walls. Perhaps it was his fault for allowing Balric to get this out of hand. There was no question in his mind, Balric had something to do with Etain and Anin being taken from the palace without a single alarm being raised.

As Ciaran thought about it a little longer, he realized no human would have been able to go unnoticed by the entire palace unless there had been a path cleared for the man in the halls. There was only one being he knew who had the power to get that done, besides Kes and himself. He had yet to comment. He rose slowly from his chair and walked around the table until he stood directly behind Balric. He placed his hands on Balric's shoulders to ensure the fae could not turn to look at him.

"Do you know what I have been thinking about, Balric?"

He shook his head; his earlier bravado quickly dissipated.

"I was thinking about how it could have been possible for a human to carry another human out of the palace. How he could have passed through all the halls he needed to traverse and not once been noticed by a single soul." he felt the male stiffen under his palms. "It would have taken someone rather knowledgeable of the internal mechanisms of the palace. I'll be honest with you—I'm not even sure I am *that* knowledgeable about it currently. Do you know who is, however?" Ciaran let his claws slowly protrude from his fingers, then he clenched Balric tightly, watching his tunic darken with blood at his shoulders. "I promised to remove the hands of anyone who dared touch Etain, as Royad and his daughter are well aware. What do you think I will take for colluding with the Day King to take what was not his?" he yelled.

There was a gasp from someone at the mention of one of their own working with the Day King. Ciaran held his grip firmly on Balric as he tried to escape his clutches. He was not stupid enough to believe he was getting out of this unscathed. Ciaran looked at Royad and noticed the sweat dripping down his temples.

"I tell you what, Balric—you tell me who else in this court was committing treason with the Day King, and I will be merciful to you." He watched as Royad shifted in his seat.

"My prince, is this really necessary? You seem to have your culprit," Royad said as Balric's head turned toward the green goblin.

Ciaran made eye contact with Kes, silently indicating to go secure Royad. Kes got up and stalked over to Royad, then stood behind him. Kes placed his hands on Royad's shoulders and dug his claws in, securing the goblin to his chair.

"Oh really, Royad? You expect me to take the fall alone? For you?" Balric spat at Royad.

This is exactly what he had been hoping for. There was decidedly little loyalty in the Night Court. He thought he should have a council that was at least loyal to him. He was not sure how he had not seen it before—the rot festering in this court. He enjoyed being wicked as much as the rest of his court, yet there was a difference between wickedness and treasonous scheming with the Day Court.

"Ah, Balric, do you mean for me to think Royad was the mastermind behind all of this? Royad, really?" Ciaran laughed as Royad turned a dark shade of green. "I think we can all agree there is not much going on behind that ugly face of his. Honestly, does anyone even know how he got on this council?"

"Your father..." Royad began, and Ciaran cut him off.

"My father was a weak male. He may have been the king, however, it was in name only. None of you can be dense enough to believe he inherited the true power of the court."

It was the closest he had been able to speak of the curse. He looked around at the three other members of the council. None of them were bothered by what was happening. Syndari actually looked as if this was the best council meeting of their life.

"Balric? Do answer the question, or I shall have too much fun making you answer in my fun room," Ciaran said with as much hostility as he felt for the fae.

"N-no. He was not the mastermind, and neither was I. Royad and I did not know we were each a part of it until our paths crossed. The Day King tasked me with clearing the halls on a particular path. He told me he would help me take the throne once you and Kes had been eradicated."

Kes laughed darkly, likely thinking of the attempt on his life that night.

"Ah, you fully admit to treason not only against me, but also treason against the Night Court itself? To let the Day King wander the halls of this palace, where we keep many of our most valuable secrets, was negligible at best, and treasonous at worst." Ciaran pulled the male up from his chair and walked him towards the head of the table. "Are there any other names you would like to give in exchange for more mercy?" he took great satisfaction in the way Balric shook under his hands.

"I do not know, my prince. I would guess there were several more, however, none that I can confirm."

Before Balric could continue, Ciaran placed his hands on either side of his head and whispered in his ear, "This is a mercy. I would have loved nothing more than to keep you in my playroom for nights upon nights for daring to put her in harm's way." Ciaran jerked Balric's head to the side and pulled with an unnecessary amount of force. He held his dismembered head in his hands. Not spending a moment longer on Balric, he chucked the head behind his back and approached Kes and Royad.

"How about you, Royad? What was your 'special' task, and what promise did the great Day King give to you?"

The goblin tried to be indignant and vehemently deny the accusations, and Ciaran reminded him that his playroom was empty at the moment.

"Fine! He approached me in the shadows after you maimed my daughter in front of the whole court. He saw how pathetic it was to treat a human with more respect than my daughter. He told me if I made sure the females' cages were open in the back when you both were away from the dais, he would then ensure my daughter became queen. I had no idea what he spoke of at the time, yet he assured me I would know as soon as the time came… and I did. As soon as you left to investigate Kes, I spelled the cages open and left the ballroom to check on my daughter."

Ciaran laughed a full bodied laugh. He knew it had been Royad who opened the cages. No other goblin would have been stupid enough. "Well, I can promise you this, Royad—your daughter will never be queen, and the Day King will never help her get there." Ciaran knew Royad was willing to sacrifice himself if it meant getting his daughter on the throne. Through this whole exchange, Royad maintained a sense of smugness. He believed the Day King would still hold to his end of the promise, since fae cannot lie. Royad's brow creased at his confidence.

"Do you want to know why?" He gave the goblin his most wicked grin which stretched too wide across his face. It showed too many teeth and allowed his sharp incisors to be on full display. He placed his hands on the table and leaned as far into Royad's space as he could. The goblin swallowed hard and waited for Ciaran to reveal what he knew.

"Because he's dead." He had never seen a goblin go such a pale shade of green before. He motioned to Kes to make Royad stand.

"Cousin, would you care to do the honors?" he asked. Kes's red eyes seemed to glow brighter for a moment before he gripped the side of the goblin's head and ripped it from his body. He would have the heads displayed on spikes in the most common hall of the palace, as a message he was hunting for those involved. Ciaran and Kes both took their seats again, ignoring the dark blood soaking them. Looking at the rest of his council, he was pleased to see they smiled in devilish delight.

"Well, we seem to be two members short," said Ciaran. The fae around the table laughed. "I already have someone in mind for one of the seats, and I think I shall leave the appointment of the second seat to her."

The room fell quiet.

"Do I dare ask who this 'her' might be?" Georden asked as he leaned forward in his seat.

"My mate."

This information sent the room into a confused uproar.

"Etain, the human I presented as my pet, is actually the most powerful witch to be born in any of our lifetimes. She also happens to be my mate. We will be having the mating ceremony, as well as the ascension to the throne as the true King and Queen of the Night Court, tomorrow at crescent night."

The three council members were talking over one another, each trying to be heard. Kes and Ciaran sat back and let them digest what he had just said.

"My prince, I am truly pleased you will finally be ascending the throne, however, a witch as a mate? There must be some kind of mistake. Surely you must be bewitched."

Ciaran had to work to keep himself under control, though he did not begrudge Fiandra the question. Even he considered it a possibility in the beginning.

"I understand how it must look, and I wish I could tell you everything, however, I am quite literally unable to speak the words to anyone except my mate. If any of you take issue with who and what my mate happens to be, speak now and vacate your seat." He made eye contact with the remaining three, letting each know he would be uncompromising when it came to his little witch. No one stood or spoke.

"Good—now that's covered, prepare yourselves. There will be change coming, and you will either get on board or you will be removed in any manner I see fit. If I catch even the hint of a whisper of anything threatening towards my mate, your death will not be swift, and your head will adorn the hall as well."

Ciaran and Kes exited the council chamber with a snap of their fingers, leaving the three remaining members in stunned silence. Ciaran was determined to have a council that did what it was meant to—help him run the court.

He was even more intrigued to learn all he could about the ancient fae and how they ran the Night Court many generations ago, both in leadership and culturally. He knew none of the libraries in the palace held the information he sought, long since been censored to reflect a court his ancestors deemed appropriate. He felt an intense desire to go to the archives, as if fate were telling him what he sought could be found there. As he considered his next step, he did not notice he had stopped walking and was staring off in thought.

"Cousin? Are you well?" Kes asked with one of his downy brows lifted—half in concern, half in jest.

"Of course. I'm not sure if I have ever been better, if I'm being honest. I was just thinking about something—have you ever wondered if the way of our current court has always been the way things were done?"

Kes's brows furrowed as he considered Ciaran's question. "I would not say I have ever wondered if things had been different, per se, yet I have often wondered why things are the way they are. The way we kill each other off without just cause and for simple fun feels counterproductive to strengthening our court. I am also not sure the whole 'high fae' and 'lesser fae' titles are necessarily a great thing either. It's as if telling our creator they made a mistake, and that does not sound very wise."

Ciaran had not even considered the lesser fae, and he was mildly annoyed with himself. Even if he had not thought about it, he knew his mate would take issue with the way lesser fae are treated.

"I think we should go to the archives. I do not think anyone has been down there in several generations. Hopefully, it has not been purged of the information we seek. What do you say, cousin? Shall we rummage through the dusty chambers in search of answers while we wait to retrieve Etain and Anin?"

Kes agreed, though not before letting Ciaran know he was not thrilled to be getting all dusty and how hard it was to clean dust from his feathers. Ciaran rolled his eyes, and the two ported to the one place in the palace neither of them had ever been. It was tricky to do such a thing. They knew the general location. However, they could not guarantee landing in a desirable spot. The last time they ported without knowing their desired location was when they were younglings. They had been trying to get into the kitchen and put an herb in the stew for the evening, which was bound to send everyone who ate it running to relieve themselves and spend the rest of the night with stomach cramps. They thought it would be hilariously cruel. Alas, when they landed in the kitchen, they fell into the pile of rubbish. Instead of enacting their prank, they spent the remainder of the night scrubbing the stench off their bodies.

Luckily, this time they both managed to arrive in decent locations, only stirring up thick piles of dust that had been undisturbed for centuries. They both called light orbs to themselves, illuminating the pitch-black room. Locating a fireplace, Ciaran snapped his fingers, and a roaring fire immediately occupied it. Between the fire and their orbs, the archives were decently lit and easy to see.

Kes looked around at the stacks of scrolls and books piled high on every shelf and surface. There was no obvious rhyme or reason to their organization. "Well, this looks like it will be... fun," he said dryly.

Ciaran was not sure where to start, and decided they should attempt to decipher if there was any organization in the archives at all. "How about you start on that end, I will start on this end, and we will see if the fae of the past at least put like with like? I doubt we will find what we are looking for tonight, and I might send the brownies down here to see if they can do anything to improve the state of this place. If they can, it would at least make the next time we are down here more productive."

"And cleaner," Kes agreed. He even attempted to get Ciaran to send the little clean freaks immediately. Ciaran waved him off in the opposite direction, making it clear they would begin their investigation now.

Ciaran was not sure how long they had been down in the windowless cavern of a room. Neither of them found anything of importance until he found a door nestled between two hulking shelves. It had been hidden behind a tapestry that caught his attention because it depicted a scene he had never seen before. He would not have even noticed it if there had not been a shift of air from behind the tapestry. He pushed it aside, revealing the door. Then he pushed the door open and was greeted with a spiraling downward staircase. He called Kes over, and the two of them made their way down the stairway, illuminated only by their orbs. Neither of them thought twice about descending the stairs to an unknown part of the palace.

Once they reached the bottom, they were both stunned by the sight. There were piles of artwork, treasures, more books, and scrolls that looked to be far better organized than those in the room above them. Before they could make their way further into the chamber, Ciaran received the message he had been waiting on from Etain. The two males tried to port out of the room to the gates of the coven, yet neither of them were able to do so. There must have been wards all around this room blocking certain types of power and magic, which only grew Ciaran's curiosity further.

They quickly made their way back up the stairs, shut the door, and covered it up with the tapestry before porting to the gates of the coven. Ciaran could not stop thinking about the contents of the mystery room he stumbled upon. He never heard any mention of such a place, nor had he ever read about it in any of his ancestors' journals. All thoughts of the room vanished as Etain appeared and ran to his waiting embrace.

"Did you enjoy your time, little witch?" Ciaran asked Etain, even though he could see the excitement in every step she took, and in the way her face was lit up in wonder.

"Oh, Ciaran, it was wonderful! I have loads to tell you! Why are you covered in dust? Oh, I invited the whole coven to our ceremony."

Ciaran's eyes went wide, and then he threw his head back in laughter. He would enjoy watching his court attempt to navigate such dramatic changes so quickly.

"Of course you did, my little witch. It will be good for you to have your people there to witness not only our mating ceremony, but our ascension as well. I'm sure it will feel like a monumental occasion for them, too."

Etain looked up at him quizzically.

"There has never been a witch to take the throne of any court, my love. You will be the first."

Etain's eyes grew wide.

"As for the dust, well, you are not the only one with 'loads' to tell."

"Well then, I suppose you better take me home. I also find myself rather hungry," she said in a sultry voice Ciaran had yet to hear from her, "...in more ways than one."

Ciaran wondered what exactly she had learned from the head witch. He needed no further enticement, as he ported them to his bedchambers and quickly began undressing his little witch. She ran from him, giggling, and he caught her easily. He knew he would do anything to make sure Etain kept that lighthearted laughter and playful nature as they fell into bed.

"You really are quite dusty," Etain said as she ran her hands through his hair. Those were the last coherent words out of her mouth as their bodies began to move together.

Ciaran's male ego grew as Etain made a variety of different sounds of pleasure. He decided at that moment that he would know all the sounds she could make before they left this realm for the afterlife.

Fifty-Eight

Kes

Kes knew from the beginning that Anin was keeping secrets. He had been content to let her keep them, but with the death of the Day King, he now felt he needed to know everything. What had the Day Court wanted with Anin? Why was the Day Court trying to kill her? He did not know how he was supposed to protect his nymph when he had no idea what danger was coming for her.

She obviously feared something or someone enough that she fled to the Human Realm. Once Kes had captured her and the blood oath was agreed upon, the only thing she truly requested was the strongest protection available.

The question still remained: from whom exactly in the Day Court did she need protection? With everything that happened, there had been no time to question Anin for the information she held about the Day Court. After discovering what the Day Court was doing with the witches it had taken, Ciaran's questions were answered. His main priority was to keep Etain safe. The best way for him to do that was to ascend the throne and fully come into his power.

Kes, on the other hand, was afraid of failing to protect Anin again if she did not let him in just a little bit. He could not understand why she still did not trust him. He thought he had repeatedly proven to have her best interests at heart. He had even taken a blood oath for her, and if that did not convince her, he had no idea what would.

He supposed he could use his question. Although, knowing her the way he did now, he did not think that would go over too well. She did not like being backed into a corner or forced to do anything. The only time he had seen her let her guard down was with her adoptive sisters. He considered trying to talk to them, to see if they could give him any insight. On second thought, he was pretty sure they would never reveal information Anin did not freely give.

He knew she had to be more than simply a wood nymph. Her power was too vast to be just a lesser fae. It felt nearly as powerful and as deep as Kes's. What about her lineage gave her that kind of power? Who was more powerful than her that she needed to be protected from? Why did she have no real grasp on how to use the power within her? She was fluent in her wood nymph magic, yet incredibly behind on her power. His feathers kept ruffling, giving away his agitation.

"Kes, my darling fluff ball, you are extra fluffy these days. I must say you do look rather enticing—to make an extra plush mattress out of." Anin smirked from where she sat in one of her favorite chairs in the lounge of his quarters.

It was really *their* quarters now, he supposed. He knew she enjoyed bantering with him and normally he did as well, but the dread he was feeling kept him from being able to volley with her. Sensing his forlorn mood, her smirk slowly slipped away. Something in Kes's chest sank at the sight of her joy dissipating. He despised being the cause of it.

"Well, out with it. You are absolutely dreadful right now," she said as she crossed her arms. She sat a little straighter and grew tense as if she knew a discussion was coming—one she would not want to have.

He knew he needed to tread carefully or she would close off from him entirely. If there was one thing Kes was not, it was being tactful. He knew he was about to mess this up, but her safety was too important not to try. He could deal with her hating him, hopefully just for a little while, as long as she stayed safe and free from harm.

He strode over to the seat opposite her and leaned forward to allow his wings to drape along the sides and clasped his hands in his lap. "Anin, I am trying to respect your right to keep secrets, but I am also trying to protect you. I am at a loss for how I can do that competently if I do not know what I'm protecting you from."

Anin stiffened at his words, and Kes sighed, knowing he had already messed this up.

"You say you are trying to respect my right to keep my secrets, yet you use my safety as a way to manipulate me into telling you what I am not yet ready to share. Kes, I do not think knowing my secrets would give you any advantage to keeping true to your blood oath."

Kes's feathers bristled again. "Anin, you must know by now it is not simply the blood oath that bonds us. I have this gut feeling that I am vastly unprepared for what is to come."

"And what is it that bonds us, Kes? Your gut seems to be a you problem," she said with a growing edge to her voice.

"I do not know what it is. All I know is I hold your safety above everything else."

Anin softened slightly at his words and sighed. "Oh, my darling feather duster, you can be infuriating and lovely all at the same time. I want to trust in you. Truly, I do. I am just not there yet."

While Kes knew this was true, it still stung to hear the words come directly from her mouth. "Oh, my darling nymph, you can be so cruel and yet wildly thrilling. You must understand, trust is important if I am to do my job adeptly. Do you at least trust I value your safety over everything?"

Anin was quiet for a moment before she gave him a sad smile. It told him everything he needed to know. She did not trust he placed her above all else. Kes felt incredibly forlorn; he felt something in the bond between them strain.

She must have, too, because she suddenly rubbed at her chest and looked concerned. "With the exception of my sisters and Galetia, everyone has abandoned or betrayed me. My mother died when I had barely grown out of my youngling stage, leaving me entirely alone. I never knew my father. My own court abandoned me and chased me away. I had to flee to the Borderlands. It was lucky I showed up at the gates of the Silver Moon Coven. Galetia took one look at my sorry state and took me in immediately. They could not help me cultivate my power since witches seem to have a completely different kind of magic from most fae. I grew up with my sisters and learned what I could alongside them, though the day finally came when there was nothing left for the witches to teach me. The head witch called upon a fae she thought trustworthy to come and give me lessons.

"The nymph showed up to our coven a few days later and taught me everything she could that a nymph should know. She felt the depth of my power and likely figured out who I was, so she went running to tell the high fae who she had found and where I had been hiding. I would imagine she was hoping it would give her higher status. The lesser fae are treated even worse in the Day Court, compared to here. We received word they were coming to kill me, apparently no longer content to have me out of sight. Hastily, I ran the night of the blood moon, determined to live the remainder of my life in the Human Realm. I needed to protect the witches I had come to view as family, free from my court's torment.

"I knew my sisters would fight to the death for me, and I could not bear to be the reason they died. I do not think my court can reach me here Kes, not after how poorly it went for the Day King."

Kes was grateful for the information she had freely given, though none of that told him anything he really needed to know. If anything it only gave more credence to the questions he already had. He was loath to do it, but he would use one of her five questions if he must. He would keep the question vague enough, giving her the chance to cleverly word her response in a way not to tell him too much, but he would at least learn something.

"Anin." He said her name with such sincere regret, she shrank as far back as she could in her chair, preparing herself for something she knew she would not like. "I hate to do this, but I am calling on one of the five questions you have sworn to answer."

Anin had turned her head to look off to some far corner of the room, but at his words, she whipped her head back around and glared at him. She was so angry, she was turning a deeper shade of green, and her nostrils were flared with her heavy breathing.

Kes had known this was not going to go well, but he decided there was no turning back. He took a deep breath and swallowed hard while considering his next words wisely. "Why does the Day Court want you dead?"

He felt this was the safest option and it was technically a question about the Day Court. She didn't have to reveal anything too momentous, but perhaps if Kes knew why, he could be better equipped to handle whatever it was he could feel coming. Anin seemed to realize what he had done, and her anger dissipated mildly.

"Because, you nosey bastard, I am not just a wood nymph even though my physical traits take after my mother. My father was...powerful. According to my mother, she had little to no choice in their affair. My court sees me as a threat to their power and wishes to eliminate me before I am able to cause them any trouble," she said snidely.

"Why would you cause them any trouble? You had not given them any reason to think you would while you lived in the Borderlands, right?" Kes was regretting his choice of question.

Her answer had only created further questions for him. It made no sense to spend that much energy and time on a fae if she hadn't stepped foot back in the Day Court.

"Are you using your personal question, *Kes*?" she asked in an overly sweet voice as she renewed her glare at him, clenching her jaw tightly.

He did not want to push her too hard, and he hoped she would answer this question freely. "No, I am not. I am just trying to help you, Anin."

"You sure were not trying to help me when you tricked me into a bad deal and then left me in the cage anyway. I even begged. That was only a few nights ago, Kes. You cannot expect to earn my trust back so quickly." She held his gaze as the silence stretched between them. There was nothing he could say to that. Everything she said was true.

Anin stood and looked down on him. "Well then, that's enough questions for you. I have plenty to do to prepare for the ceremony tomorrow night." She stormed away from him and entered her bedchamber, slamming the door behind her.

Anin was mad. She was *really* mad, and Kes did not feel like he was any better off than he had been prior to their conversation. If anything he was worse. He dropped his head in his hands and rubbed his temples. Maybe if her sisters would not tell him anything, they would at least help him keep a watchful eye during the ceremony and the celebration to follow. It was the best he could hope for at this point.

Maybe at first night Anin would be feeling slightly more forgiving, and they could at least go back to their verbal sparring. Kes could hope, but he had a feeling Anin was not the type of fae to quickly release a grudge. Knowing her, she would take great joy in making him suffer for the foreseeable future. He smiled when he thought about how wicked she could truly be sometimes. For some reason, she reserved all of it entirely for him. It pleased him to no end that she gave that part of her to him alone. There was nothing he desired more than Anin when she was being particularly snarky towards him.

His smile dropped as he got up from the chair and made his way down the hall towards his bedchambers. He paused at Anin's door and listened for a moment—all was quiet. He knocked on her door and was not surprised when she did not answer. "Sleep well, Anin."

The response he received was something crashing against the door and shattering. He was definitely in trouble. He could not deny her anger and attitude built a heat inside of him that had been burning into an inferno. He rubbed his chest while he made his way to his bedchambers, still feeling as if something had torn inside him, almost like a fraying of something important. He began to think he knew what that pull in his chest was, but he had no idea what this new sensation could be. He knew it could not be anything good, as he rubbed at that spot in his chest again. No, it definitely was not good.

Fifty-Nine

ETAIN

Later that night, after Ciaran had bathed, he redressed in something less dusty. Etain could not stop smiling. She had not had a day this perfect in a long time. He had already told her he and Kes had gone to the archives earlier, and how that had been the cause of his dusty appearance. Apparently, no one had been down there in a significantly long time. He suggested a flight to their spot at the falls to enjoy the beauty from above the Night Court; they could tell each other all about their days.

He ported them to the same spot high above the palace, and she took a few moments to really admire the view of the city below. Tomorrow at crescent night, she would become one of its rulers, and that felt surreal.

It was also unsettling. She was terrified the fae would never accept her, and she could not stop the anxious thoughts running through her head as she braided her hair back. Last time her hair had been down, it had blown all over the place. This time, she followed Ciaran's lead and braided it just as he did. The city was lit up with all types of light, from glowing orbs to lanterns of fire. It made the city feel alive with all the activity of its dwellers.

"What's it like in the city?" she asked. She wanted to go, yet she had not had the time to ask him to take her.

"It's filled with restaurants and businesses. Many of the fae in the city live in what we call apartments. Each floor is someone's home. It allows more beings to live comfortably in the city. There are places to go and dance all night, if you wish, and others where you can watch all manner of live performances. After our ceremony, we will go into the city often so they can get to know their queen, and we can have some fun."

She could not even picture most of what he spoke of, however, she was excited to find out. After the chaos of the Lunar Ball, they truly could use some fun.

"Shall we, little witch?" he asked as he spread his wings and made to pick her up.

She nodded and wrapped her arms tightly around his neck, preparing for the gut-wrenching feeling she experienced the last time they took off. As he took to the sky, she did not get the same feeling of having her stomach in her throat. Instead, she felt freer than she had ever felt before. Adrenaline flowed through her, and she let go of his neck. She spread her arms wide while she threw her head back and bellowed with abandon. He smiled at her wild display with a look of amazement in his eyes.

She told him everything she learned about her power earlier that night. She told him of the multitude of colors she saw and how each one made her feel. Then, she finally told him about the black markings on her arm he asked about earlier when he had her naked beneath him. At the time, she had been unable to formulate a thought, much less explain the intricacy of her magic. She simply told him she would tell him later.

He was intrigued by the eye marking just under the crease of her elbow, and she told him how it marked her as a seer. She had yet to have any visions and she was not sure how she would react to one. Would she lose all connection to her surroundings while a vision took over her mind and body? Or would it be something more in the background? She was equally nervous and excited to find out. She hoped her first one would be in private, or at least with the few trusted beings she had in her circle.

That was also something new. She never had enough people she trusted to even have "a circle." She was also beginning to understand she was a part of their circle, too. It was nearly over-whelming to have made such connections in such a short period of time. It would still take her some time to adjust to leaning on those around her when she was in need of help or guidance. As soon as they got to their spot at the falls, she would show him her back and the mark that apparently meant she could sprout wings. She did not think he noticed her back earlier during their earlier tryst.

It was a clear, crescent night free of clouds. They were able to see far more villages below them this time, she could see far-off cities, which had their own palaces. She had not realized there were other cities. She asked Ciaran about them and if there were other rulers of the Night Court.

He explained that every city had a palace for the king and queen to stay in when they visited from the capital city. Mostly, the palaces were used to house the fae nobles from all over the court. Most high fae resided in Nightfell, the capital city of the Night Court. He pointed out the lit-up city in the distance and told her that one was called Lunarmist, the city of the moon and falls. It was the city closest to the falls, which Ciaran loved dearly.

Etain suddenly felt like she was highly unprepared to be queen. It never occurred to her to learn about the Night Court as a whole. She had not thought other cities existed. She had not even remembered the name of the city she had been living in these past few nights. She was beginning to realize how vast this court truly was, and she had much more to learn than she originally believed. She was incredibly overwhelmed.

He must have sensed her panic, because they were suddenly on their rock. He had her turn to face him, with his hands softly rubbing up and down her arms. "What is it, little witch? What has you so troubled?"

"I know very little of your realm, court, its beings, and its traditions. I fear I am entirely unqualified to be queen."

Ciaran gave her worries just a brief thought before responding. "I would argue that you are uniquely qualified to be queen. You did not grow up in the Fae Realm, and you also did not grow up with your powers. This gives you a point of view no being in this realm could ever have. This is not a weakness, this is an advantage. Where I might completely overlook something I have become blind to, you will likely not. This is why I am appointing you as a member of the Council. It's a place the queen should have in general, and I am also leaving a chair open for you to appoint the next council member. I wish for our rule to be one of prosperity and wicked enjoyment.

"The lay of the land, the creatures who reside here—all of that can be learned easily. As far as our traditions go, many of them are vile. The Night Court is for the wicked, which does not necessarily mean evil. You have me thinking about what the Night Court was like many generations ago, and if the curse on the ruling line had begun to poison the realm, or at least this court. I am beginning to believe whatever is rotting our land has been around longer than the curse on my family line. I wonder if we are destined to make great changes for the court, and possibly the realm. You, the strongest witch born in generations, and me, the one to break the curse—it feels like we are fated for something big."

She was stunned by his words. He not only made her feel worthy; he also made her feel capable. She wrapped her arms around him and leaned her whole body into his. She hoped the gratitude she felt at that moment would pour into him.

"Thank you for that, Ciaran. You have greatly eased my doubts." She considered everything he said and realized she felt it, too. She had been feeling a dread of something to come, which had been overshadowing the feeling that together they were fated for something realm altering. "I feel it, too."

They stood embracing on the side of their rock that jutted out far over the falls, and found a moment of peace. Eventually, her mind began to grow loud again with questions, and he began to laugh.

"Little witch, I can almost see the questions running laps around your head. What is it you wish to know?"

She smiled up at him. "Well, for one, is fae power like witch power? Do you see different abilities wrapped in different colors?"

"No. Many things are mostly the same for every magical being. It's the type of power that's different. While witches see their power represented by colors, fae have something like elemental power. Every fae has a specific connection to an element of our realm. Kes is connected to the air. He can effortlessly manipulate the air to speed his flight along, or twist it into a great cyclone and take out much of the battlefield. He can also take the air away from any being. Since he, too, has a deep well of power, he can create spell after spell for hours on end before fully exhausting himself."

"Magic and power are not the same?"

"No—whatever type of magic you have is a skill you are born having, with the exception of blood magic. That has been obtained, however, it's been out of use for a very long time. The cost of using it threw our realm's balance off, and had something to do with the last war between the courts. I do not know much. It has been generations since someone has used it, and there is not a lot of information about the last war between the courts that survived the purge." Etain never heard about either blood magic or the purge. He shook his head at her questioning look.

"The purge is an entirely different story. I will tell you another time." Etain was about to object, however, he continued on as if the purge had not even been mentioned. He appeared frustrated by the topic. "Naturally, you can become tired physically, though there is no end to the amount of your magic you can use. Power is something not all fae have, and the amount of power differs greatly. Your well of power has an end, and once you hit the bottom of your well, you fall into a sort of comatose sleep. Nothing can wake you, and you have no say in the matter. This is why most fae do not like to reach near enough to the bottom of their well, because it leaves them vulnerable. It's what happened to me after I used my power to heal Kes. It took nearly every drop of it, and by the time I ported him to his bed and found you gone, I was unable to come after you immediately. This was likely the precise plan of the Day King."

"It seems rather strange that the Day King *and* Seamus had been able to sneak around the palace undetected. Well, perhaps it would be easy enough for a king, yet Seamus was just a simple-minded human man. How was he able to get around and simply carry me away?"

"We have traitors in the palace. I have never trusted anyone beyond Kes, and I still find it difficult to fully trust him, even though he has consistently proven he is worthy of it. Backstabbing and plotting against each other is common practice in this court—well, realm. However, plotting in favor of the Day Court against the Night Court ruler is treason. Two of those responsible have already been dealt with, yet I fear there are more to be discovered." Ciaran's mouth twisted into a cruel smile as he said, "This is the exact reason their heads have been mounted in warning in the main hall. I will find the rest of the beings involved with the Day Court, and remind others what I am capable of when crossed."

Her face scrunched up in disgust. She had no desire to pass through that hall and see his gruesome display, although she did see the point of it. If a random fae was thinking about going against the crown and then saw the results of such actions, they would perhaps think twice. Then again, he once told her some members of the court crave only wickedness and have no care even for their own lives. It was possible they would find working with the Day Court weak and not wicked at all, which she thought was likely.

"Well, I will leave the severed head art installment to you, my prince."

He laughed at Etain's colorful way of describing his warning, or his brand of gruesome art, as she liked to think of it.

"Ciaran, I have not told you everything about the black smokey magic. Not only did it give me the sign of a Seer, it also..." She began to loosen the straps around her bodice.

"Allow me, my little witch. You know undressing you is like unwrapping a gift. Please do not rob me of the pleasure."

She let his hands take over. "Okay, no funny business, though. I have something I need to show you on my back." She tried to give him her most serious face.

"Oh, of course not," he said with a wink, which made her chuckle. Once he had the laces undone, he pulled the bodice open and pretended like he was inspecting her breasts for some magical marking "Hmmm, nothing here."

She rolled her eyes and turned around as she pulled the bodice down her body. She slid her hand under her hair and pulled it off to one shoulder. "This is what I wanted to show you. I have been marked with the apparent ability to produce some form of smoky wings and fly." She felt him drift his fingers softly along the abstract shape of the wings on her back, sending a trail of heat along her naked skin.

"I do not know how to make them appear, therefore, I am not sure..." She was having a hard time finishing her thoughts as he moved his hands to brush along her sides, then across her stomach, before moving up to grasp her breasts in either hand.

He began to knead her flesh as his mouth descended on the side of her neck, then began gently kissing it. After the first moan to slip past her lips, he alternated between pinching and pulling on her nipples, which brought her just to the brink of pain before switching back. The kissing became sucking and biting, which led to even more moans from her.

At some point, he slipped her leggings down to her knees and freed himself from his own pants. "Do you trust me, little witch?" he whispered in her ear as he trailed his hand down towards her core. She gasped as his fingers brushed over that spot, which sent her flying higher.

"Yes," she hissed out as pleasure began to fully take over her body.

He walked them to the very edge of the rock cliff, then used his other hand to firmly grasp the hair on the back of her head at its roots. He pulled her head back as he began to work her faster with his other hand.

He used his foot to spread her feet apart a bit more before lifting her to meet his cock with her core, using only the hand that was still rubbing the sensitive spot. "Let yourself be wild and free. Trust me, I have you," he said as he entered her in one swift motion. Then he used his grip on her hair to push her upper body forward and down, dangling her off the side of the cliff.

The only thing keeping her from falling was the hand between her legs and the hand gripped in her hair. She knew she should be afraid, yet she was not. The only thing she could feel was the way Ciaran was pounding into her. He continued to pleasure her from the front, and there was a slight sting in the back of her head where her hair pulled. The view was breathtaking, and the pleasure mixed with the adrenaline took her to a higher level of pleasure she never thought possible.

She felt her walls begin to pulse as her pleasure began to reach a crescendo. He increased his pace, and she felt his wings beat the air around them just as she noticed they were moving even higher. He was flying as his cock continued to claim her. He pulled her head up to his chest, only to move his hand from her hair to wrap around her throat. "Are you going to come for me, little witch?" He asked as he climbed higher and higher into the sky, right alongside her pleasure.

Just as she felt herself reach the crest, Ciaran took them plummeting towards the obsidian waters far below. The combination of pleasure bursting from her and the adrenaline of the free fall had her screaming out her release. She thought she might black out from the overwhelming mingling of feelings. Just before they hit the water, he roared his pleasure as he released inside her. Then he snapped his wings out, and they coasted just above the water. He began to slowly fly them back up to their rock.

She had to hold on to Ciaran for several moments after they landed to make sure her legs would hold her. She gave him a wicked smile when she said, "That, my prince, was incredible. I had no idea such a thing could be done. I think this is my favorite spot now as well."

He threw his head back as he laughed. He helped her retie the laces of her bodice, then ported them back to their bedchambers. Neither of them had much energy for anything else, they changed for bed and climbed under the covers to find each other's embrace before falling asleep. They did not have time to stress over the coming ceremony and celebration the following night.

SIXTY

CIARAN

"What?" Ciaran asked. Kes had been speaking, though he had not heard a word of it.

That morning, he woke before Etain and decided to arouse her by kissing his way down her body. She slowly stirred and smiled down at him, still half dazed from sleep. He could tell her body had fully awoken well before her mind did, as he brought her pleasure with his mouth—twice. He was still feeling particularly smug over the way Etain easily responded to his touch. The sounds he could get her to make made him feel like a god.

Kes rolled his eyes, clearly annoyed with how distracted he was. It was hard to keep his mind off his mate, with their ceremony happening in a few short hours. He wondered what it would feel like to have the mate bond completed.

He heard stories that some mates could communicate with each other over long distances through the bond. He even heard they could share power back and forth in a way that made each of their wells drain slower. If he were honest, he was mostly intrigued to find out what new ways the bond would give him to elicit his favorite sounds from Etain.

He thought it was funny that all his life he had been focused on breaking the curse and making the Night Court strong enough to defend against the ever growing power of the Day Court. However, he never once thought about what his power would be like after he and Etain ascended their thrones. It would happen immediately following their mating ceremony, yet he found himself focused solely on the completion of their mating bond.

"Ciaran, we need to be prepared for anything this crescent night. I fear for Anin's life, and she will not give me any answers to help me keep her safe," Kes let out in a frustrated huff.

"Why not use one of your five questions?"

Kes looked surprised that he even knew about them. Of course, he did. Kes and Anin wore the markings on their fingers, and he knew what that specific marking meant. His father used it—among other things—on him when he was just a youngling. It resulted in his father having immense power over him, knowing his one weakness—Kes. From that moment on, Ciaran built a wall between himself and his cousin. Certainly, that seemed to be weakening more and more over the centuries his father had been gone.

"I did. I used one, and now she is completely ignoring and avoiding me at all costs. How am I supposed to protect her? She is absolutely infuriating. The best I could come up with was enlisting her sisters to help keep an eye on her, at the very least, if they will not tell me what I need to be ready for."

He thought about everything they learned about Anin. It really was not much, and what they did know was mostly irrelevant to the situation Kes found her in.

"I do not think you have ever been shunned by a female, dear cousin," he said with a chuckle, hoping to ease some of his cousin's anxiety. It worked mildly, and Kes barked out a sarcastic laugh.

"No, I suppose I have not. She is difficult, mouthy, and quick to fight back. Normally, I enjoy all of that to no end. However, when it comes to her safety, I find myself unable to compromise. What am I to do, cousin?" Kes, ever the dramatic fae, threw himself on the couch with a huff. "Oh! Do *not* even get me started on the ways she teases me. I have not been this hard all the time since we were young fae!"

Ciaran laughed at his cousin and, not for the first time, wondered if perhaps Anin was his mate. He needed to tell Kes about the rest of the curse he found out about through Etain's grimoire, and he felt it was only fair to share before he took the throne. "Kes, while I am sorry to hear you are feeling a little...backed up, I do need to tell you something that directly affects you."

Kes sat up straight and gave his cousin a questioning look. He tried to figure out the best way to tell him that unless he ascended a throne in the realm, he was to be cursed forever.

"Whatever it is, Ciaran, you can tell me," Kes said it in such a way that Ciaran believed him and decided to come straight out with it.

"Kes, you are cursed just as I am. It was not just the heir in direct line for the throne. It was any descendant of our great-grandfather. Unless you ascend the throne, you will be cursed for the rest of your life, and any younglings you help bring into the world will also be cursed."

Kes was quiet for a moment, and Ciaran was beginning to think he was about to rage, when instead, he threw his head back and laughed a full belly laugh. "Oh, cousin. Thank you for that. I needed a good laugh. You should know by now that I have no desire to sit on the throne. It is enough responsibility for me to be on your council, I would never want to be the head of a court. Thank you for telling me, although I think you are more concerned than anyone. I have never missed power, which I did not even know I was supposed to have. While I would not mind more, the price is too steep. I am happy for you to have the curse end in your line. Since I am the only other living descendant of our wretched great-grandfather, there is no one else to warn."

"What of any offspring you have?" he asked.

"Ha! Do you think I am fit for younglings? I would be surprised if the opportunity ever arose. I suppose if it ever did, I could tell them about the curse or choose to never let them know. Then, like me, they would not know what they were missing."

"I think you would be fit for younglings with your mate," he said to see what Kes's reaction would be.

"Yes, well, I do not think I will ever have one of those," Kes said as he rubbed the spot where Ciaran knew the mate bond resided. Although Kes's looked like it pained him, as if something was wrong with the bond that he was now certain his cousin shared with Anin. He saw the extent of his cousin's turmoil when he let his mask of happy indifference fall for a moment.

"Mate's are fated, cousin. And fate has a way of getting what it wants."

Kes nodded, yet looked as if he did not truly believe it.

Sixty-One
ETAIN

Etain was sitting in a chamber called the "Queen's Suite." The room was bustling with so many beings, making her dizzy with all of the activity. Anin sat quietly next to her, seemingly distracted. She kept rubbing at the place on her chest where Etain knew a mate bond could be. Etain thought Anin and Kes were mates for a while, yet she had not wanted to ask, feeling it might be rude to inquire about something that personal.

"Are you well, Anin?" She thought that was a safe enough question to ask.

"What? Oh, yes—thank you. I must have eaten something that disagreed with me."

Etain was sure that was not the problem. However, she was not going to pry into her friend's business. If Anin wanted Etain to know, she would tell her.

"Well, you must be incredibly excited to see your sisters soon?" Etain asked to change the subject for Anin. The effect was immediate. Her face lit up at the mention of her sisters. She began to tell Etain exactly how she thought things were going at the Coven. This was the first time most of them had ever been to the Night Court, let alone to the capital for a mating ceremony and coronation. In fact, there were a good number of them who had never left the coven. Anin described pure chaos of the best kind. Excited younglings running through the halls, dirtying their finest dresses. Elders halfheartedly yelling at them to settle down. Then, the rest of them put even Kes to shame with the amount of preening they were surely doing.

"Are you sad to be missing it?" Etain could see Anin struggling to find the right answer. "It's okay if you are. They are your family after all."

"I am sad on one hand, yet not on the other. I get to watch the spectacle up close and personal." As the words left her mouth, another being came bustling in with the most outrageous poof of a black gown either of them had ever seen.

Etain leaned in closer to Anin. "Am I supposed to wear that?"

They both broke out in laughter again at the outlandishly gaudy creation. The fae holding the gown indicated for Etain to come and stand in front of her so they could begin to dress her. She did her very best to seem pleased, although she was sure her forced smile gave her away. She let them continue to prepare her, and by the time she was done, her hair was tightly braided around her head in a way she did not think suited her. She did like the way they lined her eyes with black kohl; it made the warmth of her eyes seem even brighter. However, the red stain they placed on her lips felt like too much with everything else. It all felt like too much.

Finally, she was alone in the room with Anin, and she looked at her friend with a horrified expression. How was she supposed to face a room full of beings looking like... Well, she was not sure what to call her look, but it was not flattering in the slightest. She had a sinking suspicion they did it on purpose. The beings of the Night Court were not yet ready to accept a witch as their new queen.

Anin rose from the chair and walked around Etain, studying every angle of her. She felt the material of the gown and even lifted it a bit to see what was underneath that made it that big. Then she looked at Etain's hair and felt it to see what it was that helped hold the braids. Finally, she came back around to look Etain in the face, and Etain was preparing to hear exactly how horrible Anin thought she looked.

"I can work with this," said Anin.

Etain blinked in surprise.

"It will not be perfect, however, it will be much better than this disaster. Do you think they did this on purpose? There is no way this is the style of the Night Court."

"I do think it was likely a bit of a rebellion. I imagine it would be hard for them to accept a witch as their queen, and I will win them over in time. Likely, lots of time."

Both of them laughed at that.

"Please, Anin, do whatever you can with this. Anything is better than…" She waved up and down at herself.

Over the next several moments, Anin ripped out a bunch of the fabric under the main gown, which made it absurdly large, then began to tuck the dress around Etain in much the same way she did her wings. When she was done, the gown transformed from an explosion of black fabric to a sleek, elegant gown. Anin made it interesting with all the folds and tucks she gave it. Anin removed the sleeves to show off Etain's markings. She said she wanted to remind the Night Court of Etain's power, should they have forgotten. Etain felt beautiful in this version of the gown.

Next, Anin had her sit and took down all of her braids, immediately giving relief to her scalp. The braids gave her hair a wonderful type of curl, and Anin pinned it expertly around her head to lay across one shoulder. The effect made it look effortless, and the texture the previous braids gave added an etherealness to the style. For a final touch, she pulled some tendrils to fall loosely around Etain's face.

Etain could have kissed Anin; she felt immensely better. She felt like the queen she was to become. The only thing Anin was not going to touch was the garish red stain on her lips, fearing she would only smear it and make it worse. Etain decided she could live with red lips since everything else looked beyond better. Anin made her look every bit the Night Court Queen she was to become.

"I believe the Coven is to arrive at any moment. I wish to greet them with a friendly face and help them find their seats," Anin said as she inspected Etain one last time.

Etain hugged her friend and thanked her again for making her feel beautiful before she was left alone in this unfamiliar room to wait. She was too full of nervous energy to simply sit and wait. Etain decided to look around the room and was almost saddened to not find a bunch of nonsense hidden behind every drawer and cabinet. The room was mostly empty. She was about to give up and sit back down to wait when she found a hidden part of the bedside table. It was a little square that looked like she could push it in. As soon as she did, she heard a click, and a hidden compartment opened underneath the drawers.

Inside was a single book—a simple, soft leather-bound book with strips of leather holding it closed. At first, she thought it was black. However, when she looked closer, it was really the deepest red. Intrigued, she opened the book and found it to be a journal, likely from a previous queen. Unsure of how much time she had before someone came to get her, she quickly bound it to her. She could see the thin, shimmering strand connecting her to the book and placed it back in its hiding spot.

She just sat back down on the settee when Ciaran ported into the room. She was not sure of the customs of this realm. In the Human Realm, it was bad luck to see the bride before the wedding. Then again, she supposed she was no bride. She was a mate and a soon-to-be queen.

She had not forgotten the way he had woken her earlier. Nor had she forgotten the way he pinned her hands down with shadowy magic to keep her from touching him. It drove her wild and made the feelings inside her even more intense. She smiled her most mischievous smile as an idea came to her.

Ciaran was watching her and could tell she was up to something. Before he could say anything, she closed her eyes and pictured the colors of her power. She touched the red one and let it flow through her. When she opened her eyes, she stood and approached Ciaran in a graceful, provocative way. She smiled as his eyes grew wide. He was not willing to interrupt whatever she had planned for him.

Etain led Ciaran to a chair that allowed him to sit and lean back comfortably with his wings. When he tried to grab her, she tutted at him. She grasped some of the mass of fabric that had been torn from her gown and began to tie his hands to the chair. Then she tied a piece around his eyes.

"You know I can easily break these bonds, don't you, little witch?" he asked in amusement.

"Of course you can, but you will not," she said confidently.

"Oh? Why is that?"

Etain began to undo his pants and freed his already hardened cock. She softly placed her lips next to one of his ears.

"Because, my prince." She switched to the other ear. "You will not get your surprise if you do." She began to fist her hand around his cock and slide it up and down.

"What might that surpr…" Before he could finish his question, she went down on her knees silently in front of him, then put her mouth around him. He groaned in pleasure. She saw him begin to pull on his bonds, desperate to touch her. She pulled her mouth away from him.

"If you are not going to be a good prince and play by my rules, you will not get the rest of your surprise."

He immediately stilled, and Etain felt like she held all the power over him at that moment. She used her tongue and ran it up the underside of his cock, watching how it jumped a little. She did it again, and Ciaran clenched the arms of the chair his hands were bound to. Finally, she put him back in her mouth and noticed that her red lip stain was leaving little rings around him. She thought she would see how many she could leave before he finished.

He was long and thick, and she pushed him past her throat and swallowed him down to leave a ring as close to his base as she could. She hummed in delight, and Ciaran swore. She heard the arms of the chair crack from the force it was taking for him to control himself. Etain swallowed him down several more times, enjoying the strangled noises that came from him. She felt him begin to thicken further, and she knew he was close.

She swallowed deeply one last time before she felt the thick ribbons of his release slide down her throat and coat her tongue. She slowly pulled herself free from him and swallowed every last drop. There were several red rings left by her lips on him. However, the thickest one was closest to the base, where she left several in nearly the same place. She smiled as she stood and walked to the mirror to check her lip stain. She was pleased to see the red had faded dramatically, giving her just a hint of color.

She walked back to where Ciaran was breathing heavily. His whole body had gone languid. She took pride in the fact that she was the one who made him feel that way. She slowly untied his hands, making sure to remind him that he was still not to move. When she leaned in to untie the fabric from his eyes, she whispered shamelessly in his ear.

"Now, when we seal our mating ceremony, you will taste yourself on me just as I tasted myself on you this morning."

"You wicked little witch," he said heatedly. "Next time you decide you want to taste me, you better let me watch." She made a noncommittal noise as she freed his eyes.

He made to grab her again.

"Ah ah ah! Do not dare mess up Anin's beautiful work. You should have seen the disaster of a dress they put me in before Anin rescued me from embarrassment."

Ciaran did not seem pleased his court tried to undermine their future queen.

"Let it pass this one and only time. If it happens again, I will handle it. They need to know I am powerful in my own right beyond just being the mate to their king."

Ciaran agreed and stood up. When he looked down to put himself away, he laughed at all the red rings around his cock.

Etain grinned up at him. "Did you like your surprise?"

Ciaran laughed again and told her how he was going to show her after the festivities just how much he loved his surprise. Etain felt her cheeks heat in anticipation. Ciaran grinned his wide, wicked grin at her, grabbed her hand, and kissed her knuckles.

"Are you ready? It was almost time when I got here, making it likely past time now." He did not seem bothered in the slightest by making the entire court wait for them.

"I'm ready, my prince."

With that, Ciaran ported them to where Etain was to wait and walk alone down the aisle towards him to signify her willing participation in solidifying the mate bond. He kissed her knuckles one last time before telling her he would see her in just a few moments. He leaned in, placing his lips next to her ear.

"I love you, my little witch." Then he was gone. Etain was left with a fluttering in her chest and a smile so large it hurt her cheeks.

Sixty-Two
Anin

Anin could not wait to see her sisters. She needed to tell someone about Kes and his ridiculous behavior before she burst! She made her way down to the front entrance of the palace, passing a gruesome display of heads mounted on spikes in the main hall. If Kes had not been such a brute, she would have been able to ask him about the heads, but she refused to speak to him.

With their soon-to-be queen a witch, and it well known Anin was under the protection of the crown, she was able to walk through the halls of Nightfell Palace unmolested. She was pretty sure Kes must have said something. Every time she walked by someone, their eyes would grow wide before they ran off, terrified. She was loath to admit she was grateful for whatever it was he did.

She did not have to wait long before the witches arrived. Witches did not actually fly. They spelled objects they could ride and made *them* fly. Most used something easily discarded, like a broom, but some arrived flying in wingback chairs. One witch was even riding a whole couch. She had to laugh to herself;

witches were always over the top. It was one of the things she found endearing about them.

Finally, she spotted her sisters riding in on what looked like their fighting staffs. They were always prepared for a fight. She smiled and ran down the steps to meet them halfway. This time they all tried to remain slightly more dignified by not attempting to take each other down in their usual greeting; they blamed it on the finery they were all wearing. She embraced each of her sisters with gentle hugs to not disturb their gowns. Although they had just flown through the air for miles and were looking slightly windblown.

Linking arms, as was their way, they began to ascend the stairs. Just as she knew they would, they immediately started to tease her about her mate and asked where the dashing bird happened to be. She launched right into the story of what had taken place the night before, getting more and more fired up as she relived the whole conversation. She still could not believe he had used one of his questions on her.

Once she finished telling her sisters all the details, the two shared a look with each other which often meant she was not going to like what they had to say. She groaned loudly and untangled her arms so she could stand and face them.

"Can you truly not take my side in this? I am your sister after all." Anin crossed her arms and was ashamed of the way her foot gave a little stomp.

"It is *because* you are our dear sister we must be honest with you," Lyra said.

"Kes has a good point. He *should* know who is after you and why they want you dead if he is to do his job. Not only as your sworn protector, but also as your mate. Even if he has not realized it yet, it does not mean he is not affected by the bond," Panella said.

At the mention of the bond, Anin rubbed her chest again. It felt like something was torn inside her, and it was rather uncomfortable.

"Sister, does the bond pain you?" Lyra asked.

Anin told them during the fight with Kes, she felt like something inside her had torn or frayed, and it was mildly uncomfortable. Her sisters shared another look that had Anin groaning, *again*.

"What now?" she asked, frustrated that not only were they not on her side, but they were ganging up on her as well.

"It sounds like when you fought, you might have rejected him in some way and strained the bond. You must be careful. Without a mating ceremony, the bond can be permanently severed," Panella said.

She told him she did not trust him, had that been the moment? Anin panicked slightly at the idea of having the mate bond torn and Kes lost to her forever. Then she thought perhaps it would be better that way so it did not destroy him when the Day Court finally got their way and killed her.

"Try not to worry too much sister. It can be repaired, and quite easily." Lyra looked like she was trying to hold something back, and Panella was giving her a look that meant "keep it together." "I must confess something, Anin," Lyra blurted, causing Panella to sigh. "Kes came to the coven on his own earlier today."

"He—what?" Anin asked in shock.

"He came to speak with us," Panella finally conceded. Before she could continue to tell Anin why, she blew up.

"He tried to get you two to answer the questions I would not, did he not?" She seethed as she mumbled about egotistical males under her breath.

"Actually, no, he did not," Lyra said, stunning Anin silent. "He said he knew asking us would be the worst thing he could do, and he knew we would not say anything anyway."

"Well then, why was he there?" Anin asked, confused by Kes's behavior.

"He said he assumed we knew what trouble was coming for you, and what it might look like. He simply asked us to keep an eye out during the ceremony and the festivities that will follow. I do not think he intends anything but your safety when he asks for your secrets, Anin," Panella said, which made Anin question her own behavior. Her pride was making it difficult to see she may have overreacted with Kes. Perhaps she would let him sweat it out this crescent night. She would speak to him when she must, after her sisters left to return to the coven, leaving no more excuses to be made.

"Well, he's still a bird beast."

All three sisters laughed at that.

SIXTY-THREE
ETAIN

Etain's happy flutterings soon turned into ones of nervous energy. She started to work through a list of "what-ifs" in her head. What if she messed up? What if she fell? What if the court made snide remarks and then Ciaran went on a rampage? What if... the possibilities were endless in her head. Her palms were beginning to sweat, and she started to feel a little faint as she stood at the double doors. They would open any minute, and she would begin her walk down the aisle.

Before she could spiral any further, the doors swung open, revealing another cavernous room of the palace she had never been to before. The walls were covered in a dark motif, which resembled the woods she ran through a few nights prior. The painting was realistic and gave the illusion of being in the woods. The ceiling was painted like the night sky, with flecks of reflective silver for stars. Another of the large, glowing white balls hung from the center of the ceiling to represent the moon.

The members of the court and the witches sat along benches that looked like two trees bent just above the roots and then carved into seats. The legs of the benches looked like roots, and where the two trees met in the center, the branches twined together all along the back of the seats, leading down to the ground. The craftsmanship was stunning.

She realized she had just been standing still while everyone watched her take in the room. Her cheeks flushed with embarrassment. Then her eyes found Ciaran's, and the "what-if's" went silent. As if she were under a spell, her feet began to carry her down the aisle towards her mate. She no longer cared about the worries that had been plaguing her a few moments prior, because she was about to be forever connected to her prince in an unbreakable way. She smiled at him as she made her way closer.

She was still several paces from where Ciaran stood at the altar when she began to see a bright white creeping into the edges of her vision. She panicked as the white took over more and more of her sight. She stopped walking and cried out for Ciaran before everything went white.

Etain was aware she was herself, yet she was also not. The white began to disperse into a fog, then cleared just enough that she could see something happening. However, she could not make out faces or hear anything specific. She tried to think if this could be some sort of memory, though she had no recollection of anything like this. It felt more like a dream than a memory, yet she knew she was not dreaming. She saw a room filled with Night Court creatures, although she could not recognize any of them. She knew they had faces, however, although as she looked directly at them, their faces blurred. She saw a large group of beings suddenly appear, with one in particular standing out. She could not figure out if it was male, female, or something entirely different.

The one who stood out was surrounded by a black, oily substance that immediately made her recoil. It was a black of malice, death, anger, and despair. This being, whatever it was, had something rotting from within and wore a shroud of grief. She wanted to feel pity for the being, yet she was certain the creature meant to do serious harm. She saw the black, oily mass around the being reach out and take someone. Then the beings who had suddenly appeared left the room all at once.

She knew somehow it was someone important to her who had been taken. She could not see who; she could only feel the pain their absence created in her. The being left behind flared with rage. As she watched, they let out a great explosion of despair, as half of it seemed to vanish, no longer whole without the one who was taken.

She felt tears dampen her face, and she knew her physical body was crying. She felt the being's pain so acutely that she wondered if she was seeing a vision of herself, and that could only mean Ciaran had been taken from her. Panic engulfed her as the white fog thickened. She tried to brush it away to see the face of the now half-being, but it made no difference. The fog became solid white again, and she began to fall back into her physical body.

SIXTY-FOUR

CIARAN

Ciaran had already begun making his way towards her before she cried out for him. He felt something was not quite right, and he rushed towards her the moment she screamed for him. He watched as her beautiful brown eyes turned completely white and her hair began to float around her. She then lifted herself off the ground, like she often did when her emotions were heightened. Suddenly, her head was thrown back and her chest thrust out as if there was some great force pushing her from behind.

He heard the room gasp a split second before he saw *them*. Her wings exploded out from her back in the form of a black, smokey substance, which immediately began to take the shape of wings. They were not solid, yet they fluttered and propelled her even higher. He flew with her in case her power should leave her as quickly as it came. He began to call Etain's name to try to wake her from whatever trance she was in.

"Prince Ciaran."

He looked down to see the head witch standing right below them in the aisle.

"She is having a vision. Her gift as a seer and her wings are connected to the same color of power. It seems when one flares, the other does as well."

He nodded to the witch, finding it hard to care for any explanation given. His mate had been terrified, and now she was here, yet not. He kept his hands around her waist, ready to catch her should she need it.

Long moments went by, and then he saw the tears begin to run down her face, dragging the dark kohl with them. He tried to call out to her. He was on the verge of shaking her to see if that would wake her from whatever nightmare she was seeing. Until he heard the witch urge him not to force her out of the vision. To pull her from one too soon could cause her to not fully come back from the plane she was on. She would live in a constant state of confusion and would never know if what she saw was a vision or real. It would be detrimental to her life and their life together. As much as it went against everything he felt he must do, he heeded the witch's words and waited impatiently for her to come back to him. Finally, he saw the center of her eyes begin with a pinprick of color, which slowly expanded before returning to the warm brown eyes he adored.

She blinked several times before registering that he was in front of her. "Ciaran. S-something... Something horrible is going to happen," she said shakily.

"What's going to happen, little witch?" he asked as he pulled her closer. He tried to give her comfort and privacy in a room filled with night fae and witches.

"Someone will be taken, and it will rip another in half when it happens. I could not see faces, or even discern any other physical attributes, yet I felt the pain sharply as if it were my own. What if it is you who will be taken, and I am the one torn apart without you?" Her eyes were filled with fear and lingering pain from her vision.

"As soon as we ascend our thrones, we will be too powerful for it to be one of us, my love. Could you see where or when this would happen?"

"No, all I could see were several beings I knew were of this court without actually seeing their faces. Then several beings appeared suddenly, and I knew they did not belong. There was one creature that stood out from the rest. There was something wrong with it. There was a black, inky substance surrounding it, which made me fear going near it. It was that black, inky presence that seemed to swallow the being who was taken."

"Perhaps, once we finish our mating ceremony and become the true king and queen of The Night Court, we can find the head witch. She might be able to help you figure out what it all means."

She nodded, then looked around. "Why are we flying?" Her brows creased in confusion.

"Well, little witch, it seems your wings decided to make an appearance as well. You put on quite the display of power. I have never heard my court so quiet." He tried to bring her smile back to make the situation a little less horrifying for her.

Her eyes opened wide. She turned her head from side to side to catch a glimpse of her wings. "I really do have wings," she said quietly as the smile he hoped for began to creep back out. "I wish I could see them fully."

He ported them from the ceremony and into a room filled with mirrors. He guided them far enough down to allow for a full view of every inch of herself. She let out a little laugh as she moved her wings one at a time.

"It's a wonder they actually carry me. I would never think something like smoke could ever bear the weight of anything solid," she said in awe of her own wings.

"Magic and power do not follow the same rules as the physical world. It often does not make sense, and I would imagine it would make even less sense to one raised in the Human Realm."

"It would appear I am continually learning something new every day." She made a sound of dismay when she noticed the black that ran down her cheeks from her tears. He found the effect to be beautiful and told her as much. She gave him a look that said she clearly did not believe him, though she left the streaks and told him she was ready to return. He ported them back to the altar to finally solidify their mate bond.

Sixty-Five

ETAIN

When they returned to the woodsy room, many of the beings were out of their seats, unsure of what they should be doing. Kes had been standing in front of everyone, attempting to keep the room from breaking out into chaos. The second everyone saw them reappear and take their places at the altar, it took only one harsh look from Ciaran to send everyone scrambling back to their seats.

She knew the mating ceremony was similar to the blood oath Anin and Kes took because there would be a blood component, yet everything else was completely different. The creature presiding over it looked like bleached tree branches artfully twined together to create a tall, willowy being.

He told her they were called "Chroniclers," and they belonged to neither court. They presided over every mating ceremony, coronation, birth, death, and major historical events. Ciaran said he did not know what they did with the information, though one always arrived when needed without being called.

Etain was staring. She knew she was, and she knew it was rude. She had never seen anything this otherworldly, and she had seen a lot of different types of creatures by now. It might be the way it felt completely indifferent, neither warm nor cold. She thought perhaps they had seen far too much to ever become emotionally attached to any other creature. She also wondered if perhaps these beings went between the other realms Hecate mentioned.

The Chronicler spoke directly into their minds with a voice that was neither male nor female. Everyone appeared prepared for this, everyone except Etain, who startled a bit at the intrusion. The being must have sensed her wariness when it seemed to speak only to her.

"Fear not, daughter of Hecate. I cannot read what is in your mind, nor can I place thoughts upon it. This is the way my kind communicates."

She realized they had no mouth, and she nodded her understanding to the being.

The Chronicler led them through several motions that symbolized different aspects of what it is to be mated. They held a large rock together in their hands as a symbol of the strength they would have for one another if the other was lacking. They washed each other's hands in a large emerald bowl to symbolize the way they would care for one another. Then they each cut a locket of hair and gave it to the other to show their willingness to give themselves to each other.

The final part of the ceremony was the exchange of blood. As she had seen Kes and Anin do, Etain and Ciaran sliced their palms with an emerald knife and clasped their cut hands over a chalice. The Chronicler gave them the words to repeat out loud together.

"Blood of my blood, heart of my heart, together we share this life.
My body is yours, my mind is yours, and half of my soul lives
within you.
Our bond will be unbreakable, as will be our love.
In this life and the next, I shall follow you.
To whatever may come and whatever shall pass,
You will always be my constant.
As I will be yours.
With my blood, I make it so.
With my words, I make it true.
With my soul, I am bound to you."

Ciaran lifted the chalice with his free hand to her lips, and she took her drink. Then she did the same for him. Still holding their bleeding hands together, they sealed the ceremony with a kiss.

The second their lips touched, she felt the place in her chest she knew to be the mate bond suddenly begin to burn. It only lasted a breath. Then it felt like the bond, which had always felt stretchy and pliable, became as solid as the rock they had held earlier. She realized she could feel what he felt now, as if he were sending his feelings directly down the bond to her. He was overjoyed, and the love he felt for her was near breathtaking.

The newly mated pair turned to face the crowd as they lifted their joined hands as high as she could reach. Noticing he only had to bend his elbow and raise his forearm, she worked her wings and flew high enough to help his arm reach up just the way hers did. The room broke out into a raucous cheer—even the court members, who clearly did not want Etain to be their queen.

It looked like none were unaffected by witnessing a mating ceremony. Anin told her fated mates were typical enough, that everyone knew of them, yet not common enough that many had never seen a mating ceremony take place.

He wrapped his arm around her waist and pulled her in to kiss her deeply. In the past, she might have been embarrassed to be this bold around so many beings. Now, she found herself uncaring who witnessed their love. He untangled their hands, and she noticed he had already healed their cuts, leaving their marks behind. A mate bond's mark could never be healed away. It turned the same emerald green as the knife had been. She inspected Ciaran's and noticed his was the same, just a little less visible on his blue skin.

"Well, my mate, are you ready to become a queen as well?" he asked.

Her nervous flutters returned to her stomach. Ciaran must have felt her emotions the same way she had felt his because he remarked, "There is nothing to fear, little witch. Remember what I said at the falls?"

She recalled the way he had eased her mind. She repeated the moment in her head over and over until she finally believed herself ready to be queen again.

"I'm ready," she said with a nod.

He smiled proudly at her, then set her down to move on to the coronation. She grabbed his hand and squeezed it. He looked back down at her.

"I love you, too, my prince." She realized it would be the last time she could call him that. He was about to become a king, and she a queen.

Sixty-Six
Ciaran

Ciaran guided Etain to the dais, and they each stood in front of their thrones. He kept their hands entwined between them. He was not completely sure what to expect. It had been generations since a true King and Queen of the Night Court had sat on the thrones. He knew the magic the land of his court held would crown them itself since the curse had been broken. He could tell it had been broken the second his lips met Etain's. The bottom of his well of power crumbled away. He tried to feel its new depth, though it seemed to have no end.

He was surprised when the Chronicler told the room about the curse he had been under, and how Etain was the one to break it. No one besides Kes had ever known about it since it was not something he had been able to speak of before. Only now, he knew why. Kes was also cursed.

The Chronicler went on to explain how Ciaran and Etain were the first true king and queen to take the throne in generations, and how the previous kings and queens had crowned themselves with crowns of their own making. Since they were the true king and queen, the Night Court itself would anoint them with a crown of the land's creation as soon as they sat on their thrones. The land would then imbue them with the specific powers it chose to gift each of them.

The Chronicler indicated they should take their seats. Neither of them released the other's hand as they sat with their hands held firm between them. He began to grow concerned that perhaps he was not the true king after all, since nothing was happening. Then suddenly, from underneath them, moonlight shot up into the sky, and a powerful force twirled around them as if it were inspecting both of them closely. The force settled as if it had come to a conclusion.

Ciaran could feel the force communicating with him, telling him of his new powerful abilities. He could feel the entirety of the Night Court. While overwhelming at first, it slowly seeped into the back of his mind and became more of an awareness.

He saw himself pulling a star from the night sky and throwing it to decimate whatever was in its path. He knew this was something he could use once in his lifetime as a last resort. His final gift was the ability to shadow walk. Not only could he move anywhere in the realm as long as it was from shadow to shadow, but he could also create shadow duplicates of himself.

The final thing the land wanted to convey to him was a plea. The land was rotting away, both in the Night Court and the Day Court. The balance had been thrown off for far too long, and the land was dying. It was a plea to save it, and Ciaran promised the land he would do everything he could to restore balance and end the rot. It was as if the force of the land believed him, and it swirled around his head several times before it, and the moonlight, vanished.

Ciaran looked at Etain, her eyes wide in disbelief. Whatever she had been given obviously surprised her. It was then he noticed two things. First, her wings had retreated, likely from the force of the power that had just poured through them. Second, there was a crown on her head. It looked to be made of starlight and held the full moon in the center and two crescent moons on either side. They appeared to contain actual moonlight, which he realized was also the symbol of the witches.

He leaned over and told her what he saw, then asked what his crown looked like. She studied it for a bit before describing it as a crown of shadows, which flickered like a flame and looked to hold a million stars within it. She was about to explain what she experienced, when he reminded her they were surrounded by beings. Some of them were likely traitors, best if it was a conversation held in private. She nodded in agreement.

The Chronicler then asked everyone to rise. The room was told to bow before the King of the Night Court and Shadows and the Queen of the Night Court—the first Queen of Witches.

He cut a curious gaze at Etain after hearing her new title, and she gave him a tight half smile, which looked to say, "I tried to tell you."

He gave her hand a little squeeze, letting her know everything would be fine.

When he looked back, he saw the witches walking towards them in a single file line. Each one kneeling before Etain and greeting her as "My Queen." They all looked upon her with reverence, as if this had been something long ago foretold.

Ciaran scrutinized his own court. He saw uncertainty about their queen also being the witches' queen, and what that might mean for the future of the Night Court. They also looked like they had witnessed something they would never forget—the power of their land.

Once the long line of witches had finished greeting their queen, he clapped his hands, and the room transformed into a ballroom. It was the same woodland room filled with woodland inspired decor, yet now it held a dance floor, tables piled high with food, fountains of wine, and of course, the lounges off to the side. No Night Court celebration could be complete without them.

The whole room vibrated with excitement, waiting for him to declare the party had started. He turned to thank the Chronicler first, only to find they were already gone. He turned back to the room of revelers and grabbed Etain around the waist to pull her into him.

"Let the celebration begin!"

Music filled the room, and he dipped her so low that he had to bend way down to kiss her in a way that held a promise of the crescent night that was to come.

Sixty-Seven

Anin

A nin had been sincerely moved by the mating ceremony. She could not help looking over at Kes, who was sitting in the front row of seats with an empty space next to him. Anin had chosen to sit with her sisters, who never failed to point out how cruel she was to her mate. It was clear they did not approve. As the ceremony progressed, she found herself wishing she had swallowed her pride and sat with him. She craved his presence.

Once the party had begun, she had not really been trying to avoid him. She just wanted to dance with her sisters and the other witches like she used to do at the coven. She could pretend she was not being hunted by her court, and her life was once again normal.

Periodically, she would make eye contact with him across the room and give him a small smile. He would start to make his way over to her, only to get intercepted by one of the members of his court.

She wanted to ask Etain about her vision, although one look at the mated pair made it clear they were not to be disturbed. They were deep in conversation with the head witch, likely trying to unravel whatever she had seen. Watching her friend have a vision in such a powerful way was frightening and awe-inspiring at the same time. She had a feeling sometime during first night tomorrow they would go to the coven to help further decipher the meaning of it. Whatever it was, it appeared to terrify Etain.

Anin knew she would have to come out with her secrets soon. She was placing this whole court in danger by not letting them know who they were harboring her from. She was not entirely sure why she had not told them already. She could blame the Lunar Ball and her unwilling trip with the Day King for not mentioning it before Kes had come for her. But now she was not sure why she was so hesitant and had adamantly refused to tell Kes when he had asked.

Well, perhaps that was not entirely true. She feared telling him. What if he discarded her after she told him, because she was more trouble than she was worth? It was easier to keep the wall between them than it was to let her guard down and be rejected by him. However, it was not fair to hurt him the way the mate bond informed her she had.

All this ran on constant repeat in her head, distracted only by her sisters and their crazy dance moves. They danced for hours, barely pausing to replenish their wine and fill their bellies. She watched the beings on the dance floor and was surprised to see several members of the Night Court mingling and dancing with many of the witches.

She knew Etain, being both Queen of the Night Court and of the witches, would tie the two together. She was curious to see what that would look like after this night. Many covens worked only with the moon to strengthen their magic—would they be freely welcomed into the land of Night? She looked around to the outliers of the room and thought perhaps change would not come that easily, as she took in their sneers and obvious distrust of the witches. Then again, she had come to know Etain and Ciaran, and they were both formidable forces when it came to achieving a goal. With their alignment through the completed mating bond, she would like to see anyone stand in the way of the future they demanded.

If only the Day Court had such rulers. The Queen was ruthless in her pursuit of more power, or "ultimate power," as Anin heard she called it. Anin was sure the land of the Day Court had abandoned the queen and king. Both had worn crowns of golden metal, nothing like the ethereal crowns of moonlight and shadow Etain and Ciaran received. Perhaps they had worn crowns from the land at one point, or maybe the land had found them lacking and never gave them gifts or crowns to begin with. It would explain the queen's constant desire for more and more power. If the land had not given her power freely, she would find a way to take it, she was relentless in that way.

The hour was growing late, and the witches still needed to fly home. Anin said her goodbyes to her sisters and the rest of the coven. All looked to have enjoyed themselves immensely, and Anin was elated they had been able to attend this momentous event. She knew the other covens would be just as curious to hear every single detail, as they were bound to be jealous.

Right before her sisters flew off on their staffs, they gave her one last talking to about the way she had been treating Kes. She assured them it was heard, and she would go back into the ballroom and find him immediately after their departure.

Seemingly appeased by her answer, the three hugged and reminded each other of their love for one another.

Anin stood under the stars and watched her sisters fly off, waiting for them to pause and turn back to wave. As soon as they did, she waved back and watched until they were too far in the distance. Sighing, she made her way back to the ballroom to find her mate. She hoped it was not too late to repair what she had fractured.

Sixty-Eight

ETAIN

Etain clung to Ciaran for dear life. She was terrified that her vision was about them. She could not stop the memory of the pain she felt from resurfacing over and over. She tried to distract herself with the many members of the Night Court who came to greet them at their thrones, much like they had the crescent night of the Lunar Ball. Only this time, they reluctantly gave her small bows with their heads, and each time Ciaran would give a growl in warning until they gave her the same respect they showed him.

While she knew she should be doing her best to pay attention to who each of the fae were, she could not seem to focus. She saw Galetia in line, several turns away. She was the only being standing before them that she wished to speak with. She was desperate to get her thoughts on the vision. She turned her attention to the dance floor, hoping the dancers were entertaining enough to make the time go by faster.

She was pleased to see many of the witches from the Silver Moon Coven had taken to the dance floor, along with many of the fae from the Night Court. Where the fae all danced in jerky, seductive ways, the witches spun and moved their bodies in naturally fluid motions. It took her a few moments to recognize they were doing a choreographed dance of sorts. Instead of partnering the way the fae did, the witches all danced in lines, each line doing something different before shifting to the next line.

She glanced back to the line of beings waiting to greet them and saw Galetia was now just a few beings away. She turned back to the dance floor to keep herself distracted for a little while longer, and she was shocked at what she saw. Several fae and witches began to try to mesh the two styles of dance together. It was turning into one of the most beautiful dances she had ever seen. She could not help but smile at them. It felt promising for the future of the realm.

Finally, as Galetia was ascending the steps to greet them, Ciaran indicated the next group should wait at the bottom of the steps to give them some privacy while wrapping them in a sound barrier. Etain sat forward on her throne, while still keeping her tight grip on Ciaran, as the head witch joined them.

"Galetia, I am happy you have come and brought the coven with you. I am sorry to take away from any fun you might be having, though I must speak with you about the vision I had earlier," she said, rushing the words out.

Galetia smiled at her and nodded her head. "I, too, wished to speak to you about it. I was sure you would need some assistance processing your vision," the witch said kindly. "Tell me everything, leave nothing out. I want to know how it looked and felt as it came on. What you felt and saw during the vision, and how you felt coming out of it." Galetia reached down and grabbed

Etain's other hand in comfort. It was something she often liked to do when having a serious conversation with another.

She was grateful for the connection. It helped calm her enough to gather herself to be able to tell Galetia every minuscule detail she could remember. From the blinding white light to the foggy scene, she had not been able to see clearly. She nearly cried again as she told the head witch of the pain she felt as she watched the being get swallowed by the black, inky substance. It instantly made Etain recoil. She recalled how she tried to hold on to the vision, even as everything faded, to try and see who had become half the being they had once been. Last, she shared her fear that it was Ciaran who would be taken from her, since the pain she felt had been extremely intense.

Galetia was quiet for a moment as she considered everything Etain said. She suddenly pulled a book to herself from nowhere and turned to a page that had already been marked. She scanned the page, looking for something in particular.

She glanced at Ciaran and noticed he appeared to be off in thought. She could not seem to get a feel for what he was mulling over. Finally, they heard Galetia make a noise as if she had found whatever it was she had been looking for. This caused both of them to focus on her once more.

"After our session, I began to go through all the books the coven had on seers of the past. This particular book looked to have the most information in it, and I began marking pages that could help you understand your gift better when it finally emerged." She squeezed her hand. "I did not think it would manifest this quickly, I must confess." She smiled kindly at Etain.

"You seem to have found something. So what is it?" Ciaran asked with little patience in his voice. He gave the witch an apologetic nod when he noticed her glaring at him over his tone.

"Indeed, I believe I have. I am not sure how much this will help you. If you look here, it says something about the seer looking in on an event that may come to pass. It is possible for the seer to feel the strongest of emotions from her vision. The fact that it says it *may* come to pass makes me believe all visions are not destined to come to fruition. I do not think you have to worry about your mate. We can look further into meaning and symbolism tomorrow. The black, inky substance you described, however, is rather unsettling, and I have never heard of such a thing."

She was still weary of her vision, yet she felt better knowing it was only a possibility.

"During the coronation, the Land spoke to me," Ciaran said, grabbing the attention of both females. "It spoke of a rot in the realm that was beginning to kill the land of both courts. I wonder if there is a connection between the rot and the disturbing black substance Etain described."

She thought back to the way the substance made her feel. She could definitely describe it as rotten.

"The land spoke to me as well. It not only told me I was to be Queen of the Witches, but it also informed me of the rot in the realm. It said the witches needed to be protected. Interestingly enough, it was something similar to what Hecate said to me."

Ciaran nodded while he looked deep in thought.

"What could it all mean?" Galetia wondered out loud. The three began trying to find ways in which her vision, the messages from the land, and Hecate's warning all came together. They had been deep in their discussion for so long, the line of beings waiting to greet the new king and queen dispersed.

She was not dissatisfied with her power to see the possible future, although she did find it rather difficult to discern what it meant. Galetia seemed to think keeping a journal might help over time. She could begin to find consistencies that would help her understand her future visions. The mention of a journal made her remember the hidden journal she found in the Queen's Suit—another mystery to unravel.

Etain sighed and rubbed at her temples; she was beginning to get a headache.

Sixty-Nine

KES

He was encouraged by her little smiles every time their eyes met. However, each time he attempted to make his way over to her, he was intercepted by a member of the court voicing their disgusted opinions about the witches being in attendance. They were always careful to never mention their queen.

The current high fae male in front of him contained two beings in one body. The only distinction between the two was their faces. Two faces on one head, one in the front and one in the... other front? Each time a different one spoke, their head would spin around.

"We cannot possibly allow the witches to roam our lands unmolested," said one face. "That is not the Night fae way!" exclaimed the other.

"Are you both implying your king is not Night fae?" he asked them. He was growing tired of the same conversation repeating with different fae.

"No! Of course not... We meant... Only..." the two faces competed to bluster at the same time.

"You both either think the king is wrong or you are both complete idiots. Or are you like the fools decorating the main hall and in a partnership with the Day Court? Are you both traitors to the crown?" This question usually leads to disbelief and disgust that any self-respecting Night fae would ever work with the Day Court.

"What?" one said nervously. "Of course not," claimed the other. They suddenly looked like they wanted to be anywhere but in front of him.

Interesting.

"That would be quite the self-fulfilling prophecy if you were." Each head spun in turn to look at him in confusion. "It would be rather two-faced, do you not think?" He chuckled to himself as he shoved them out of his way. He would need to keep an eye on them. They were definitely up to something, and he had no doubt there were still traitors among them. He would talk to Ciaran about them tomorrow.

He glanced around the room and noticed the witches had all left, likely because they had a long flight ahead of them. Had Anin spoken to him at all today, he would have told her he would happily port her sisters home if they wished to stay longer. Since he could not see Anin anywhere, he figured she likely walked her sisters out to say her goodbyes. He was just about to go looking for her to make sure she had not been accosted by one of his court, when she walked back into the ballroom.

Kes released the breath he had been holding; he had begun to panic that something had happened to her. The feeling that something was coming had been building exponentially. He knew Anin needed to spill what she had been avoiding soon. He only hoped her sisters had been successful in convincing her.

When he ported to the coven earlier, requesting an audience with her sisters, he had not expected to find them easily agreeable. They even admitted that Anin could often be stubborn and think the worst. It had taken them years to build their bond, but they agreed Kes needed to know to best protect Anin. They also agreed they would not betray their sister by telling her secrets to him. He had hoped the little smiles Anin had given him all night meant they had gotten through to her.

Anin looked to be searching for something, or someone, as she made her way through the beings. Then she spotted him and relaxed. He pointed off to the side of the room a bit out of the way to talk, and she nodded in agreement. As he made his way over, he tried to think of what he was going to say. He was nervous he would put his clawed foot in his mouth again. They reached the spot at the same time. As he got close enough to her, he opened his mouth and hoped for the best.

"I'm sorry," they blurted at the same time, which made them both smile and laugh nervously.

"Kes, I let my pride get in the way. I should have apologized when you knocked on my door and wished me goodnight. The truth is, I fear telling you what exactly I am running from in case you feel the risk is too great and reject me." Anin shifted her gaze away in embarrassment.

Kes was stunned she could even think such a thing. He cautiously reached out his hand to cup her face and was pleased when she leaned into it. "Anin, there is nothing I would not protect you from. There is nothing you could do that would make me not want you. I know I have been a bit slow to realize it, but you're my..."

Suddenly, Etain stood and shouted, "This! This is it! This is what I saw! I can feel it!"

Everyone in the room was buzzing with confusion as a huge flash of golden light appeared. Etain screamed again and fearfully latched onto Ciaran with all her might.

Kes felt Anin step into him, intertwining her hand with his. He squeezed it tight. The golden flash revealed hundreds of Day Court warriors dressed in golden plate mail armor. The being standing menacingly in front of them was the Queen of the Day Court.

"Well, it seems my invitation was lost along the way. Do not despair; I heard of the celebration anyway. It seems congratulations are in order. I see the Night Court finally has a true king and queen to sit upon its thrones. Even if the queen is a witch, of all things," the Day Queen sneered.

"What are you doing here, Tatiana?" Ciaran said, his wide, toothy grin filled with malice. "You know you are not welcome, or you would not have arrived with such a show of force. Speak your peace, and then leave us to our celebrations before you start a war between the two courts."

"You are harboring the murderers of my mate!" The Day Queen could not keep her voice from going shrill at the mention of her mate. She had a wild look in her eyes, and Kes saw how truly unhinged she was. She got a handle on herself before she continued. "The late King of the Day Court was murdered on your land by a member of your court and a fugitive of *mine*."

Kes shifted to hide Anin behind him. There was no doubt who she was talking about. To Ciaran's credit, he did not once look over in their direction, which would have given their slightly hidden spot away.

"Come now, Tatiana; you must know he technically killed himself. If he had not been sneaking away with what was not his to take in the first place, he would still be alive. He was not killed by anyone's hand. He was dumb enough to touch a spelled bit of string, which is no one's fault but his own."

Tatiana barely contained the rage rolling off of her in waves. "If you will not hand over the fugitive, then I will take her myself." Before anyone could even attempt to stop her, she moved in a golden flash directly in front of Kes. "You took my mate from me, and now I will take yours from you."

Kes could not move a muscle. Somehow the Day Queen had use of blood magic, it was the only thing it could be. It had been deemed too dangerous centuries ago, because it disrupted the natural balance of the realm disastrously. His hand unwound from Anin's against his will, and the queen reached and pulled Anin out from behind him. He could not even speak to tell her all the things he had not had the chance to say. The only thing he was able to move were his eyes, and they locked on hers, willing her to look at him. As soon as she did, he tried to convey everything he felt for her and tell her he would not give up until she was back safely in his arms. Anin's eyes filled with tears and she nodded.

"Awe, is this not incredibly touching? This is what you took from me!" the Day Queen screeched in Anin's face before pulling out a long black obsidian blade.

No one around them made any move to intervene. Either she had used blood magic on those close enough, or they simply did not care for what happened to Anin. It was Day Court business to them.

Kes glanced at Ciaran and saw him torn between protecting his mate, who clung to him with a fierceness he had yet to see from her, as if someone were about to rip him away. Kes knew there was no stopping whatever was coming, so he held Anin's gaze for as long as he could. His eyes drank in every bit of her and committed it to memory.

"Hmmm...decisions, decisions. The bird or the nymph?" the Queen sang as she tick-tocked the blade between Kes and Anin. "Who gets to feel my blade?"

Anin tried to stand in front of Kes, clearly trying to protect him from the queen's blade. It was interesting that the queen did not have complete control of Anin. Maybe the Day Queen could not use her blood magic on her for some reason. He tried desperately to plead with the queen for him to take the blade, to spare Anin the pain. Kes was no stranger to the feel of obsidian parting his flesh.

Anin quickly lunged for the blade, unfortunately, not fast enough. The queen grabbed Anin by the hair and pulled her back to her chest holding the knife to her throat. "It looks as though your mate has volunteered. How sweet," she said, staring Kes in the eyes as she dragged the knife down Anin's body before she buried the blade into her stomach.

Anin cried out, while Kes tried with all his might to break the hold the queen had on him, but all he could do was twitch his fingers. He locked eyes with Anin again, this time pleading for her to live.

The queen twisted the blade, which caused Anin to scream so loudly that glass shattered.

"Ah, how I have longed to hear that sound come from your lips, dear sister." The queen and all of her warriors were gone in another flash—Anin with them. The only thing left behind was her gold-green blood that had spilled onto the floor.

Kes sank to his knees as soon as his body was his own again. He felt as if he had been torn in half by having his mate ripped from him in such a way. He released his pain and anguish into a deafening bellow, which could be heard miles from the palace.

He felt for the bond and knew it was still there, only softer now. He tried to push as much of his magic down the it as he could, hoping to help heal her. He knew she had to be more than just a nymph. It never occurred to him the reason the Day Court was after Anin was because she was possibly an heir to the Day Court throne.

No wonder they chased her off the land; the land could have chosen her at any time. He was not sure he could have protected her, even if he had known who she really was. The queen's use of blood magic had deftly kept him from being able to access his own magic or be any kind of obstacle in general.

He felt a fresh wave of anguish at not being able to protect her once again. He sent more power down the bond, if only to tell her she was not alone, and with it he sent the same words over and over, a promise he would keep.

"I will come for you."

THANKS!

Writing a book, publishing said book, and all the steps in between is so much harder than I ever imagined. It has also been one of the most rewarding and amazing things I have ever done in my entire life. The way the characters seem to write themselves and the words seem to pour out of you in an unexpected way is incredibly thrilling. I will never forget the moment I finished the rough draft of *Prince of Darkness*, my very first book. I felt so many overwhelming emotions I cried and in that moment I proved to myself that I am capable. It was very surreal. I couldn't have made it to this point without the help of some incredible people.

First and foremost I want to thank my parents, Dave and Lisa Thoma, for encouraging me and helping me see this through. They have always believed in me which has given me the courage to try new things and be less afraid of failure. Thank you for instilling such confidence in me. A big shout out to my whole family who allowed me to be a hermit while writing but also gave me reasons to leave my house and take much needed breaks. Thank you guys and I love you all so much.

To my sister friend, Jess Bosworth, who has read every single sentence of every single thing I have ever written. Even the projects that went nowhere. Thank you for your input and hype, you kept my inertia going into each chapter. Your friendship and support has been a driving force behind every project I have and will ever work on. Thank you my friend, my sister, I love you.

I will be forever grateful to my fellow author and friend, R J Strong. Without our accountability and motivation for each other I would never have finished this project. Your mentoring has been priceless and I am looking forward to what we will both continue to create. We are unstoppable!

Thank you to my good friends; Jen Loso, Samantha Lehman, Amber Shields, and Allison Castro. All of you have been such an amazing hype squad and I am so grateful to have people like you in my circle. Love you all!

I am so lucky to have two amazing editors as family friends. Kimmie Chonko has always been like a little sister to me and I could not be more proud of the woman she has become. I look forward to watching your business as an editor grow. Michelle Mullen has been like another mother to me for over half of my life even taking me to appointments when I was being treated for cancer. She worked as a White House speechwriters staff for Jimmy Carter. Thank you to both of these wonderful women for helping me bring my dream to fruition, I couldn't have done it without either of you.

A big thank you to my excellent beta readers Jess Bosworth, Karen Moler, and Katie Shumate. They not only gave me the critical feedback I was looking for but also gave me the valida-tion I needed. I couldn't have asked for a better beta team. I'm looking forward to hearing what you all think of the books to come!

Thank you to my cover artist Maria with Miblart. They made my vision come to life and were an absolute joy to work with. Miblart has top notch customer service and I highly recommend them. I can't wait to see what you come up with for the next book!

Shout out to my ARC readers for taking the time out of your busy lives to read *Prince of Darkness* pre-release and for leaving an honest review. ARC readers are invaluable to any author's success so I am truly grateful to each of you. I value your honesty and support, thank you for being a part of my team.

Finally I would like to thank every single author of every single book I have ever read. You have inspired me to not only write but you have also kept my childhood imagination alive. As George R.R. Martin wrote; "A reader lives a thousand lives before he dies. The man who never reads lives only one." Here's to another thousand lives to come and a thousand more worlds to explore.

ABOUT THE AUTHOR

 Growing up in Northern Virginia, Amber has always been an avid reader. From *Boxcar Children* to *Goosebumps* to Epic Fantasies, she's always had her nose in a book. In 2021, she moved from the ever busy DMV area to a small town in Southwest Virginia to be closer to her family out of a desire to be a constant presence in her nieces and nephews lives.

It was this move that gave her the opportunity to take the time to write a book. She started her debut novel *Prince of Darkness* in the fall of 2022 and completed her first draft mid-November 2022. She plans to continue writing many series under the *Realms of Lore*.